Abby Finds Her Calling

Center Point
Large Print

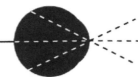

**This Large Print Book carries the
Seal of Approval of N.A.V.H.**

Abby Finds Her Calling

Home at Cedar Creek

— Book One —

NAOMI KING

CENTER POINT LARGE PRINT
THORNDIKE, MAINE

The text of this Large Print edition is unabridged.
In other aspects, this book may
vary from the original edition.
Printed in the United States of America
on permanent paper.
Set in 16-point Times New Roman type.

ISBN: 978-1-61173-413-3

Library of Congress Cataloging-in-Publication Data

King, Naomi, 1953–
Abby finds her calling / Naomi King.
pages ; cm
ISBN 978-1-61173-413-3 (library binding : alk. paper)
1. Large type books. I. Title.
PS3613.A277A64 2012b
813'.54—dc23

2011051168

For Rhonda,
who knows a lot about forgiving,
letting go of the past,
and moving on to a new adventure

Acknowledgments

Thanks once again, Lord, for showing me how, when one door closes, You've already opened another one for me. And thanks for leading me through this story these past months when our move from Missouri to Minnesota brought so many distractions.

Many thanks to my agent, Evan Marshall, and to my editor, Ellen Edwards. I so appreciate your enthusiasm and vision as we enter into this Cedar Creek series together!

Special thanks to Jim Smith of Step Back in Time Tours in Jamesport, Missouri—the largest Old Order Amish settlement west of the Mississippi —for your indispensable insights and assistance as I write this series. Blessings on you, Jim! It's a real pleasure to work with you.

Much love to you, Neal, for keeping me centered and sane while we sold a home, bought and remodeled another one, moved, and meanwhile shared a one-bathroom, one-bedroom apartment where I worked at a tabletop office.

And forgive us our debts, as we forgive our debtors.

—Matthew 6:12

But the wisdom that is from above is first pure, then peaceable, gentle, and easy to be intreated, full of mercy and good fruits, without partiality, and without hypocrisy. And the fruit of righteousness is sown in peace of them that make peace.

—James 3:17–18

— Chapter 1 —

James Graber inhaled the crisp October air and grinned up at the rising sun. It was his wedding day! All his life he'd lived in anticipation of something grand, something beyond the immense satisfaction of his carriage-making trade, and finally, in about an hour, he would achieve that dream when Suzanna Lambright became his wife.

As he gazed across the road, at the lane where horse-drawn carriages were entering in a steady stream, the Lambright place took on a new glow in his eyes. There was the Cedar Creek Mercantile, where Zanna's elder brother, Sam, sold groceries and dry goods and where her sister, Abby, ran her sewing business. Beside it, Treva Lambright, Zanna's mamm, had a glass greenhouse where she raised and sold a variety of vegetables and flowers. Down the long drive stood the tall white farmhouse where Treva lived with Sam's family—his wife, Barbara, and their four children, Matt, Phoebe, Ruth, and Gail. And farther up the lane was the little home Abby had built for herself this past spring. These places, surrounded by sheep sheds, the barn, and acres of rolling green pasture, felt more special to James

9

today, even though he saw them every time he stepped off his own front porch.

And who could believe all these wedding guests? Nearly four hundred family and friends—some from as far away as Pennsylvania, Ohio, and Indiana—were arriving to celebrate with the Grabers and the Lambrights, families who had moved here to Missouri generations ago. The *clip-clop! clip-clop!* of the horses' hooves made his heart sing to their ageless rhythm.

ZAN-na! ZAN-na! James heard in that beat. Silly, the things he thought of when he envisioned her pretty face as she gazed at him in that playful way she had. *Lord, please help me make her happy every single day of our lives!*

James was glad to be marrying on a perfect autumn day, after the harvest was in but before the traditional marriage month, because it meant these folks from back East had a chance to celebrate with them. Here in Missouri, Old Order Amish married anytime during the year, not just in November, when the many weddings meant that folks had to pick and choose which ones they attended. And what a backdrop the countryside provided: the sweet gum and maple trees blazed in their red and orange glory, with a hint of frost to make them sparkle in the sunrise.

James's younger sister, Emma, joined him in front of the house, smoothing her new purple dress. "That's a mighty fine smile you're wearing, brother. I hope to see it gracing your ugly face every day from here on out," she said, her brown eyes sparkling.

James cocked an eyebrow. "And what would you have to make fun of if I were a handsome man, Emma?" he countered with a laugh. "Zanna thinks I'm downright perfect, you know."

"Gut thing, too. Old as you're getting, none of the other girls would have you."

"We'll see what you say about that when *you're* within spitting distance of thirty," James shot back. Then, with a welling up of love for this young woman who kept their household running as well as anyone could now that their parents were aging, he slipped his arm around her. "Denki for keeping Mamm's head from spinning off these last couple weeks, getting ready for this wedding," he murmured. "A lot of the weight falls on your shoulders, taking care of her and Dat."

"They're our parents, James. They've been taking care of *us* all our lives."

"Of course they have, Emmie, but . . ." James sighed, focusing on the window of Zanna's upstairs room in the white farmhouse across the road. He couldn't see inside, of course, but he liked to imagine her there . . . putting on her new blue dress and white apron about now, with Treva and Abby helping her get ready. "Not my place to ask Mamm and Dat to move into the dawdi haus, but I can't help wondering . . . Do you

11

think it'll go all right, when Zanna comes to live with us?" he asked quietly. "Mamm's tongue wags pretty constant and cuts pretty sharp, and we all know how Dat's hearing gets worse, and his brain a little fuzzier, when he doesn't want to listen to all her carrying-on. And neither of them is able to handle anywhere near as much as they used to."

"Zanna's known them all her life, same as everybody hereabouts. It's not like she's walking in blind," Emma replied, resting her head on his shoulder. It was a rare moment of physical affection from this girl who was usually busy at the stove or the sink or the washer, or looking after their parents, while he built custom carriages in his shop beside the house. "Truth be told, brother, Zanna's all grins and giggles when she talks about you. Her eyes light up, and she's been a different girl since you asked for her hand. I'm real happy for the both of you."

James smiled. His sister hadn't been as generous with her praise for other young women he'd courted over the years. Maybe he was making up things to worry about—wondering how Zanna would adjust to the Graber household—which wasn't normally his way. All in all, his times with Zanna had been among the happiest he'd known. He looked forward to a long life with her and many children to bless them.

Even Sam, James's good friend and Zanna's older brother, had remarked what a fine couple they made—and had thanked James for asking to court Zanna rather than keeping his intentions secret, as was the custom. James had felt that the passing last spring of Leroy Lambright, Sam and Zanna's dat and the head of the Lambright household, was an important reason to get Sam's blessing early on, out of respect for Leroy and the family's feelings. Sam had said right out that he thought James would be the steadying influence his youngest sister needed now that their father was gone.

Imagine that—Sam Lambright, a stickler for the proper order of things, thought he, James Graber, could fashion Suzanna into a fine wife and mother. James suspected that might take some doing. Zanna wasn't one who took to being molded into anyone else's ideal. But what a happy challenge it presented. And what a fine-looking woman she'd grown to be. Truth be told, James secretly admired her tendency to think and speak for herself rather than to automatically submit to the men in her life.

"Over the next several weekends you'll spend visiting kin and collecting your wedding presents, we'll all have time to adjust to Zanna's being in the family," his sister continued. "It's the same kind of change every family goes through after a wedding."

"Change has never been Dat's favorite thing. And he hasn't been the same since his stroke."

"And Mamm's gotten crankier, keeping after him. There's that," Emma agreed with a sigh. "But Lord love them, they're getting by as best they can. I'll work on them while you and Zanna make your family calls these coming weeks. They may as well get used to the fact that their last two kids have lives of their own."

And what would they do when Emma married? James wondered. Would she move away like their two elder sisters, Iva and Sharon, had? James breathed in deeply and then exhaled, consciously relaxing the tightness this thought caused in his belly. Inevitably, the day would come when his sweet, capable sister would cleave to her own husband and start a home . . . which would leave him, as the only son, and Zanna, as his wife, to care for his parents. As well they should.

But this was no time for such concerns. His bride was waiting for him. James lightly kissed Emma's temple and then released her. "I'd best go over to help Sam with the last-minute details. See you in a few. Or would you rather I took Dat over to—"

"Get out of here! What with Daniel and Amos, our big, burly brothers-in-law, staying with us last night, I've got lots of help with Dat this morning. And Sharon and Iva are in there helping him dress." Emma shook her white apron at him to send him on his way. "If you dare to poke your face into that Lambright kitchen full of women,

14

you might see how Mamm's doing. Tell her I'll be there directly."

James hurried down his family's gravel lane, pleased to see the pie pumpkins that remained in Emma's garden. He stopped beside his shop to wave at Zeke and Eva Detweiler in one buggy, and the two buggies full of Detweiler children that followed them—including the carriage he'd designed to accommodate young Joel's wheelchair. Then he crossed the road and strode alongside the mercantile, which was closed on this Thursday so the Lambrights could celebrate this special day.

It struck James how many of the tipped-up buggies behind the Lambright barn had come from Graber Custom Carriages—how every family in Cedar Creek depended upon his vehicles and repair work. It was a blessing, indeed, to live among the friends he served and to be entrusted with getting their families where they needed to go. And today it seemed every man, woman, and child for miles around was showing up to wish him and Zanna well. Fellows in their black hats and suits stood chatting in clusters outside the house while their wives gathered in the kitchen to finish preparing the wedding feast.

He gazed again at Zanna's upstairs bedroom window. As he recalled tossing pebbles against it those first Saturday nights he'd courted her, James grinned like a kid. She'd looked so pretty in the moonlight, smiling down at him before she'd let him into the kitchen. She'd seemed tickled that a successful, established fellow she knew so well wanted to win her heart.

Had Zanna come downstairs for the wedding yet? Did she feel as frisky and excited as a new foal, the way he did? In his black vest, trousers, and high-topped shoes, with a radiant white shirt, James was filled with an excitement he'd never known. He greeted Matt's border collies, Panda and Pearl, with exuberant pats on their black and white heads. "Dressed for the wedding, I see," he teased.

In less than an hour, Zanna would be seated with him and their four newehockers. It might be difficult to sit through most of the long wedding service, and Bishop Gingerich's lengthy sermon, before they were at last called to stand before this gathering of family and friends.

James paused when a familiar figure stepped out the Lambrights' front door. Ordinarily folks came and went through the kitchen entry, but something about Abby Lambright's expression announced that she was on no ordinary mission. She glanced across the yard, where their many male guests stood visiting, and then she headed straight for him.

"Gut morning, Abby!" he called out, hoping to dispel her gloomy frown as she pulled her shawl tighter around her shoulders. Abby was a maidel,

16

a few years older than he, and in his entire life he'd never known her to raise her voice or lose her temper.

"James," she replied with a stiff nod. Her eyes looked puffy, but her gaze didn't waver as she stopped a few feet in front of him. "There's something we've got to tell you, James. And since Sam's talking with the bishop, he's asked me to let you know that . . . Well, there's no easy way to say it."

Frowning, he stepped closer. "Did somebody fall sick? Or get hurt carrying all those tables and pews and—"

"I wish it were as simple as that," Abby interrupted. She bit her lip and took a deep breath. "James, Zanna is nowhere to be found. As far as we can tell, she didn't sleep in her bed last night . . . and we have no idea where she might have gone."

— Chapter 2 —

Abby regretted being the bearer of this bad news. James surely must have felt like he'd been kicked in the chest by a spooked horse. As he crushed the brim of his hat in his sturdy hands, Abby ached for this man in ways he couldn't imagine. Never had she felt more embarrassed and sickened and worried.

"What do you mean, Zanna's nowhere to be found?" James demanded. They might have been talking in a cavernous empty room, the way their voices had become hollow with shock.

Abby cleared her throat. "I spent the night in my own house—to leave more room for out-of-town kin here at Sam's—so I'm not sure what all was said and done," she hastened to explain. "But when Phoebe and Ruth heard Zanna slipping downstairs in the wee hours, they thought she was meeting up with *you*."

He swallowed so hard his Adam's apple bobbed above his black bow tie. "But I was home last night, keeping Dat and Mamm settled so they'd be rested for today's festivities."

"I know that, James, and—and I'm so sorry this has happened." She gazed at him with as much compassion as she dared. This was no time to pour out her personal feelings. Her little sister had done something beyond belief, beyond unthinkable. And now their two families and four hundred guests were about to suffer for it. "Matt and Sam drove out looking for her earlier, as soon as we realized she was missing, but they didn't find her."

James crammed his hat on his head and then yanked it off again. *"Missing?"* he said hoarsely. "How does a girl in a house full of folks, with a

18

brother who lets *no one* get away with any shenanigans, go missing on her wedding day?"

"If we knew the answer to that, maybe we'd know where to look. Or what she was thinking, to disappear this way." Abby shrugged, helpless and at a loss for the right words. "Sam and Matt came back without her, knowing we had to decide what all to do by the time the bishop got here."

Abby glanced back at the house. She simply couldn't burden poor James with their other discovery—Zanna's new blue wedding dress snipped to ribbons and left lying on her bedroom floor. If that sight had torn *her* heart in two, what might it do to James, her lifelong friend, who was looking more devastated by the second? "Mamm's fit to be tied—same as your mamm," she said sadly, "while Barbara and the girls are fretting over all the food that's been fixed. And now hundreds of people are arriving, expecting a wedding."

"But we can't have a wedding without a bride. Is that what you're telling me, Abby?" he demanded curtly.

Tears spilled from her eyes. Of course James was more upset than she'd ever seen him, asking her questions no one could answer. What man wouldn't be? But that didn't help either one of them deal with this sticky situation, did it? "That's the way of it, James. I'm so sorry," Abby said as she turned back toward the house. "Truly I am."

The aromas of roasted chicken, creamed celery, and pumpkin pie mocked her as she headed for the kitchen door, hugging herself as if to hold body and soul together. At least the hardest task was over; she'd said what had to be said.

But I can't tell you that Zanna's shredded dress means you can marry someone else . . . or that I've wanted to be that someone since we were scholars together in the one-room school . . . or that I turned away other fellas because they weren't you, James Graber.

Abby grimaced, covering her face as she fought back tears. It wasn't the right time for such thoughts. The day belonged to Zanna and James, even if her sister had chosen not to show up.

Breathing deeply, Abby refocused her thoughts. There was nothing to do but entrust their dilemma to God and wonder if her sister had any inkling of the feelings she'd hurt . . . the lives she'd changed before this day had even gotten started. They had a kitchen full of women in tears, worried about what had happened to Zanna—and what they'd tell their guests. Abby paused on the stoop before she went in.

In the yard the bishop, Vernon Gingerich, listened with his head tilted to one side while Sam spoke with even more frustration than he had when they first discovered Zanna was missing.

". . . should've seen it as a red flag when Suzanna insisted on such a worldly nickname,"

Sam stated. "It wasn't a gut idea for Dat to allow it, but—"

"It seems a common part of rumspringa for young folks to see how they feel with a different name. I myself went by—"

"But, Vernon," Sam interjected, "you surely never ran the roads in a car. We caught Zanna *driving!* Out on a county highway with—"

"I tested my parents at every turn, Sam," came Bishop Gingerich's reply. "But none of this second-guessing solves our problem. All these guests are here, and the feast is prepared. And the bride's in hiding."

The men's conversation came to a halt. Sam raked his fingers through his steel gray hair, exhaling harshly. "Abby?" he called, waving her over. "The bishop wants a word."

Aware that her older brother's clipped tone had sometimes inspired Zanna's resentment, Abby did as she was told. She noted that Sam stood stiffly while Vernon appeared more stooped than usual. The bishop's beard, salt sprinkled with pepper, brushed the top of his black vest as he fixed his gaze on her. His eyesight might not be so sharp anymore, but he saw through to the heart of a matter better than most.

"Gut morning to you, Vernon," Abby said with a sad nod. "Not that it's one of our *better* mornings."

"It's another day our Lord's given us to

21

celebrate, no matter how we choose to glory in it—or to make a mess of things." The old man's expression remained unruffled. "We've gathered here to worship God, so ask the women to join us for the service now, Abby. Then we'll proceed with the meal, as planned."

Abby frowned. "But if the bride doesn't come home—"

"Suzanna has chosen not to be here. She'll have to face the consequences of that decision," the bishop pointed out.

"And we can't send folks away without feeding them and visiting with them, not after so many of them hired drivers and traveled hundreds of miles to get here," Sam insisted. The lines around his eyes were etched more deeply now; their youngest sister would indeed deal with the humiliation and worry she'd caused him these past few hours . . . along with the ongoing speculation of every person in Cedar Creek, since they all did business in his store. "So we'll start the service in ten minutes. It's better if *you* tell Mamm that, rather than me," he said to Abby.

Her eyes widened. Surely Sam wasn't *afraid* to enter a kitchen filled with upset women. Raising three daughters and a son—and becoming the head of the Lambright family after their father's death last spring—had given him the authority to quell arguments and protests with a single purposeful look. But then, Sam had never dealt with the mother of a missing bride, or the sympathetic friends who'd banded together to help Mamm and his wife, Barbara, and James's mamm, Eunice Graber, get through such an unexpected turn of events.

"We'll be over directly, then," Abby replied quietly.

She gripped the doorknob, studying the familiar faces through the glass: some stood near the stove to comfort Mamm and Barbara while others clustered around Eunice, beside the long table laden with serving bowls, platters, and pitchers that they would use for the noon meal. Their eyes were wide, their kapps bobbing as they discussed today's dilemma in voices that came through the Dutch door. It wouldn't be proper to get their attention with a shrill whistle between her fingers, but Abby figured it might require that.

The rapid-fire clatter of horses' hooves made her look up to see James Graber racing down the road in his open buggy. Even from this distance, Abby could tell from his urgent expression and his focus on the surrounding fields that he wouldn't be attending the church service.

And why would he? What groom would sit humiliated on the bench up front, the object of everyone's curiosity and pity, after his bride hadn't shown up? *He's looking for Zanna and, dear Lord, please help him find her . . . Help us all find answers to questions we never dreamed we'd be asking on their wedding day.*

Abby opened the kitchen door and stepped inside the noisy room. Best to inform her mother and Barbara first, and proceed from there. The two of them were pulling covered casseroles from the oven to hand over to their friends. "Mamm! Barbara!" She spoke through the chatter. "The bishop's made a decision."

As the two of them looked up at her, the kitchen suddenly got quiet. All eyes were on Abby, all conversation suspended.

Abby clasped her hands, hoping these women wouldn't challenge what she was about to say. "We're to go over for the preaching."

"Zanna's come home, then?" Barbara straightened to her full height, her expression cautiously optimistic. "So the ceremony will go on as though—"

"And she's not come in here to explain to me first?" Mamm demanded.

Abby sighed. Mamm looked the worse for wear, eager for news of her runaway daughter yet prepared to give Zanna a piece of her mind for the worry she'd caused.

"No, it's not like that," Abby explained with a sigh. "There's still no sign of Zanna. Vernon's decided worship should go on, followed by the meal, rather than wasting everybody's day and all the food we've cooked. We'd better get ourselves seated now, so the hymn singing can start."

"And does James know about this?" someone

24

called from across the crowded kitchen.

"I suspect not!" Bessie Mast exclaimed. "I saw the poor fella racing down the road, no doubt lookin' for her."

"And what of poor Eunice here?" Beulah Mae Nissley asked. "She's never been all that keen on her boy marrying that girl anyway."

"Please! We shouldn't make the others wait." Abby looked sharply at Beulah Mae, their neighbor from down the road. She had made a beautiful wedding cake in her bakery, Mrs. Nissley's Kitchen, but nobody needed the clatter of her sharp tongue when Mamm's composure was unraveling and Eunice looked ready to burst into tears. It wasn't good that the mother of the bride and the groom's mamm—lifelong friends—stood in the same room, yet seemed miles apart. "We'll know more about what to do after we listen to the bishop's wisdom," Abby said.

Thank goodness Phoebe, Barbara's eldest daughter, took her mother by the elbow and the rest of the women fell in step as they started for the barn. Abby stayed to make sure that the ovens were turned off and the perishable food was stored in the fridge. Her other nieces, Ruthie and Gail, draped clean dish towels over the hot casseroles and then filed outside ahead of her with their heads bowed. It felt as if they were going to a funeral, even though their new dresses were the rich colors of fall foliage rather than black.

Abby gazed past Matt's sheep sheds, scanning the green pastures for a female figure, but only the ewes and their lambs grazed there, peacefully unaware of the human turmoil. The trees along Cedar Creek sparkled yellow and orange in the sunrise, the most striking panorama of color they'd displayed in years. Autumn had always been Abby's favorite season, but at this moment she felt bereft . . . troubled by the day's events and by her inability to make them right.

Why had Zanna run off, when she'd appeared so happy to be marrying James Graber? And what would the poor man say to her if he found her?

"Abby! Abby, wait— What's going on?"

James's sister sprinted toward her down Lambright Lane. Emma Graber was a few years younger than Abby, but they'd been best friends through thick and thin. How pretty she looked in her purple dress—and what a shame to have this occasion spoiled, when Emma so seldom wore new clothes. She came to a breathless halt, reaching for Abby's hand. "What's this we hear about Zanna running off?"

"She slipped out in the night, far as we can tell."

"But why would she do that, Abby?" Emma's face looked splotchy beneath her fresh pleated kapp. "She and James have been so excited. They've planned all their visits to the aunts and uncles and—" Her expression sobered as she glanced at the women filing into the barn. "You don't think something . . . *dangerous* has happened, do you?"

Abby sighed as they walked toward the end of the women's line. "We've wondered about that, jah. But finding Zanna's wedding dress cut up on the floor sort of told the tale."

"Oh, Abby! And you made all our dresses so perfect, too!"

Abby gripped Emma's slender hand, which was calloused from doing all the cleaning and yard work her mamm could no longer manage. "And what of James? I felt so bad, having to tell him this news."

"Ach, he was so stunned he could hardly talk! As upset as I've ever seen him, but really worried," Emma replied in a tight voice. "Truth be told, after James raced out of the house, Dat got so rattled that Daniel and Amos said they'd stay home with him so he wouldn't fall and hurt himself—or pitch a fit during church if Zanna showed up after all."

"She's gotten a lot of threads in a nasty tangle, for sure and for certain. I'm sorry your dat's not taking it so well."

Emma smiled ruefully. "I'd better check on Mamm. No doubt she's been stirring the pot over here amongst the women, and she might walk out of the service when she sees that Dat didn't come. If there's any way I can help, Abby, you know I'm here for you."

As though she didn't have enough to do, keeping track of her parents and now her brother, too, Abby mused as Emma slipped between the women in the barn doorway. *Lord, be with us all as we figure out what to do next. And especially be with Zanna, wherever she's gotten herself off to.*

— *Chapter 3* —

Zanna awoke with a jerk. Achy from hugging herself to keep warm in the Masts' big old barn all night, she sat up to listen.

"Zanna? Zanna Lambright!"

James! Right outside, by the sound of it. She burrowed deeper into the straw, and then clapped her hand over her mouth to keep from crying out. A pair of doleful brown eyes gazed at her between the wooden stall slats. The Belgian whickered, as though to ask why she'd been napping there.

If anybody comes to hitch up these horses, the whole world will know where you spent your wedding day.

Tears welled up in her eyes, which were already itchy from crying all night. Mervin Mast wouldn't be doing any fieldwork today—or at least not until he and Bessie came home from the wedding. Would the bishop proceed with the service without the wedding ceremony? Would everyone stay to eat all the food that had been prepared, so it wouldn't go to waste? If James had come looking for her, did that mean the bishop had dismissed the crowd, or just that James, too, was not there for the service?

She shouldn't have dozed off. Shouldn't have ducked into Mervin's barn to get warm, either. How long did she think she could hide?

"Zanna? Zanna, if you're hurt, can you holler at me?"

Her heart thudded. If James thought she was ill or injured, would he and the other men start up a search party? She hadn't intended to cause so much trouble.

"And if you're not hurt . . . can we talk about this?" His voice drifted off on the breeze. James sounded so confused and disappointed, she started to cry.

Why did you pretend things would work out and everyone could be happy?

Zanna mopped her face with the sleeve of the smelly old chore coat she'd taken from a peg. She should have stayed home. She could be wearing her new blue dress and taking her vows to become Mrs. James Graber, so there would be no looking back—

Move along! You've got to keep moving because you certainly aren't thinking straight.

She rose on legs that were stiff from being

tucked underneath her. Shaky from too much crying and nothing to eat since she'd picked at last night's dinner, she peeked out a knothole.

James was driving down the road. If she cut through the woods, past Pete Beachey's place, she could follow the county blacktop to Clearwater. Maybe she should take the Belgian in the next stall instead of walking all that way . . .

The two twenty-dollar bills in your pocket that you took aren't bad enough? You'd steal a horse, too? Not that this Belgian, trained to the plow, would take kindly to a rider.

When James became a speck in the distance, Zanna slipped out the barn door. She *had* to find something to eat. Maybe Bessie had baked bread yesterday, or had some cookies in the jar on her kitchen counter.

And now you're sneaking into houses? Taking food?

"Oh, God," she mumbled wearily—and then caught herself. Would He hear that phrase as a prayer, or think she'd taken His name in vain? "Show me where to go. Give me the right words . . . because I'm not getting anything right doing it on my own, ain't so?"

From where James sat in his buggy on the ridge between the Nissley farm and Mervin Mast's place, he could see for miles in every direction, west toward Bloomingdale and east past Clearwater to the Iowa line. Peaceful old silos and white houses nestled among the gentle hills . . . pastures dotted with cattle and sheep . . . groves of sycamores and maple trees growing along the creeks. James had the feeling he wouldn't spot his intended even if he had brought his binoculars: there were too many places for her to hide.

And why was Zanna hiding? Why had she run off on the most important day of their lives?

He thought back, looking for clues. The golden-haired girl across the road had always had a special sparkle—and just enough spunk to take on a catchy new name when she'd entered her rumspringa at sixteen. The locals—his mother among them—had shaken their heads and speculated about such a girl's future, but James had never doubted Zanna's innate goodness. Soon after Cedar Creek witnessed Jonny and Gideon Ropp's departure from the community—in Jonny's flashy new van—Treva and Leroy had seen that their daughter took her instructions to join the church. The Lambrights didn't want the notoriety of having a girl who left the faith.

Wasn't that about the time James had started wandering over to the mercantile more often, to catch a glimpse of Zanna stocking the shelves? And who could have guessed Leroy Lambright would keel over from an aneurism that burst in his brain? The poor man hadn't even gotten to witness Zanna's baptismal vows the following month.

Is she hiding . . . from me?

James held his head in his hands. Had he pursued her too intently? Asked Sam for her hand too soon? Zanna was just seventeen, but she'd looked so forlorn after her dat's passing that James couldn't help reaching out to her.

And oh, how Zanna had blossomed. Her laughter had teased at something deep within him, promising a life made richer—more adventurous —by her presence, even if she could sometimes be as willful as a Missouri mule, even if her youthful sense of humor sometimes went a little too far . . .

What if she had watched him race away this morning and then gone back home? Maybe she'd been sitting on the pew, grinning . . . making him look like the one who took off.

James clucked to his gelding and headed back toward Cedar Creek. His expression wavered between a hopeful smile and a grimace as he imagined all those guests listening to Bishop Gingerich talk on and on, waiting for the groom to appear.

He entered the Lambright place from the back road, noting the dozens of tipped-up buggies that still filled every available space along the lane and between the barn and the house. He drove past Abby's neat little home, shiny and white in the morning sun. Now *there* was another riddle no man could solve.

Abigail Lambright would make someone a perfect wife, yet she'd not *resigned* herself to becoming a maidel—she'd *declared* herself one. And wasn't it just her way to take on the task of telling him about Zanna this morning? Abby saw what needed to be done and got on with it. No finger-pointing. No hysterics.

If only this crisis with her sister could blow over, and he could marry Zanna after all. Then maybe he'd chat with Abby about how to help guide Zanna into her role as a wife and eventually a mother. Now that he thought over the past few weeks, he realized there had been times when Zanna had acted a little skittish. James had excused her behavior as prewedding jitters and the fact that Zanna and her mamm were often at odds. Maybe Zanna—and he—needed the kind of advice Abby was so good at giving. Where had Abigail Lambright learned so much about love and life, anyway?

As James stepped down from his buggy, a hymn drifted from the open doors of the large barn. He knew the song well: the Old Order wedding ceremony hadn't changed in generations, so there had been no need for a rehearsal. Certainly no talk of writing his own vows, as some of his English friends had done.

Swallowing his humiliation, James slipped in through the back door. He peered around the men in black suits who were packed into the pews.

No one sat up front in the row reserved for the wedding party.

His face prickled with heat. As the hymn ended, James turned to go, even though he had no idea to *where*.

"James Graber! We're glad you've returned, son," Bishop Gingerich hailed him from the front of the gathering. "Did you find your bride?"

James wanted to shrivel up and blow away, except there was no escaping the hundreds of eyes now focused on him. "No. No sign of her any-where."

The bishop folded his hands, smiling with sad compassion. "There will come a day when we'll see the wisdom the Lord is teaching us during this time of trial, James," he declared solemnly. "Until then, we wait and watch. And we'll pray for our sister Suzanna, and for you, James, that you'll each find a peace that passes all understanding. God is with us more than ever in those moments when we feel the most alone."

As Abby bustled between the long tables of wedding guests with her water pitcher, she couldn't help glancing at James, her dear friend, who shook the hands of the many folks who commiserated with him. They were serving the meal in Mamm's big greenhouse, and while the potted mums made a pretty setting, the glass walls and ceiling seemed to magnify all that had gone wrong.

Poor James. Perhaps he would always feel more love for Zanna than she was capable of understanding or returning. Maybe someday he would realize that.

And poor Mamm. She sat among her closest friends, allowing them to cluck over her. The first shift of folks left the tables so others could take their places on the pews they'd moved in from the barn. Barbara and her girls, along with Emma and several of the neighbor women, carried pans of hot chicken and refilled the bowls of creamed celery, mashed potatoes, and so many other favorite dishes Abby had looked forward to feasting on. Not a forkful would go to waste, yet it seemed so *wrong*. This whole occasion felt like such a sham without Zanna there.

And what would she write for the *Budget*? Abby was the local scribe for the nation's Plain newspaper, and she'd reported on Zanna's engagement with such joy a few months ago.

Her great-aunt Mattie reached up for a hug. "I hope your sister turns up real soon, Abigail," she murmured. "It'll be your mamm's undoing if she doesn't."

"Jah, we'll keep you in our prayers," Mattie's sister, Fern, agreed. "We've never seen the likes of this before!"

Abby set down the pitcher to embrace these elderly ladies, who had hired a driver to travel all the way from Indiana for this big day. "We're so glad you came," she replied. "We don't get to see nearly enough of you."

Mattie pursed her thin lips. "Well, I won't be making the trip again—even if they set another wedding date and Suzanna convinces everyone she'll go through with it."

"I don't imagine Sam would be any too keen on footing the bill for that, either," Fern speculated as she scanned the crowd for him.

Abby glanced at her older brother, noting how worn he looked. "Sam was hoping James would be the fella to settle Zanna in some kind of purpose. He's not used to having his plans thrown back in his face."

"Things'll get interesting, for sure and for certain," Mattie agreed.

Fern's smile resembled her sister's. "We'll be waiting for your letter, telling us what all this was really about."

Abby smiled glumly. It wasn't always a joy to be the one who started the family's round-robin letters. Where did she draw the line between keeping her aunts informed and telling tales on her little sister? Even if Zanna had a perfectly good reason for running away . . .

But what reason would any woman have for leaving James Graber in the lurch? For humiliating him this way?

It was an answer only Zanna could give.

— Chapter 4 —

"When any of you scc Zanna," Sam announced as they all sat in the kitchen late that evening, "you're not to let her in this house. Understand? Not until she's answered to me for the way she's disgraced us today."

Mamm's face crumpled, and Abby grabbed her trembling hand. It was after eight. Their out-of-state guests had started for home, and after a long day of commiserating, their neighbors had finally left, as well. They were all exhausted.

"Sam," Abby said, softly chiding her brother, "this is Zanna's home, and—well, we'll see the situation in a better light after a night's rest."

"You think any of us will *sleep?*" Sam glared at Abby from the end of the table. His four children and his wife sat back, as though to stay out of the line of fire. "I plan to keep watch until that young lady apologizes. She'll have plenty to confess before the church, as well."

Barbara cleared her throat gingerly. "I'm thinking she's still not herself after her dat's passing and—"

"He was my dat, too!" Sam smacked the table with his palm, making them all jump. "And right now I wish he were still alive so he could march that girl out to the barn for a gut talking-to."

"Sam!" Barbara said with an apologetic glance at her mother-in-law. "Your parents did their best to raise her."

"And you kids should consider this fair warning," he continued, looking pointedly at his three daughters and Matt, in turn. "Don't think for a minute that I'll make excuses for you if you duck out of such a solemn promise as your aunt Suzanna made to James Graber. It's indecent, the way she treated him today, and I'll have no more of it in my house."

His voice rang in a kitchen that had gone painfully silent. The ticking of the clock marked the minutes until Mamm rose slowly from her chair. She looked about a hundred years old. "Going to bed," she murmured. "I've had about all I can take of this day."

Abby blinked back tears. "Can I make you some chamomile tea, Mamm? Or sit with you until you sleep?"

"I've got a lot to pray on, and I'd best do it alone. But denki, Abby," she added with a sad smile. "You're a gut girl."

Abby's tears welled up again and she could only nod. They had all fretted enough today that such a loving thought should have soothed her soul. Yet in her mother's tenderness Abby heard regret . . . a silent condemnation of the daughter whose behavior had marked them as a family of scandal. It would be weeks before their friends, making their everyday purchases at the mercantile, would stop asking about Zanna. Mamm couldn't avoid such curiosity in her shop, either. Treva's Greenhouse was in its peak fall season, with her selling ornamental gourds, pumpkins, and potted mums of every color. Folks would inquire about the runaway bride out of concern, but their questions would take a toll on the family's emotions.

And what if we get no answers? What if she's gone for good?

Abby stood with a tired sigh. "Guess I'll run some hot water, then," she murmured to her nieces. "You girls grab the scrub brushes and we'll redd up this kitchen for your mamm. The best cure for heartache is hard work, ain't so?"

Abby knocked on the door in Sam's back hallway and then slipped inside the dawdi haus. This addition had been built on when her dat's parents were aging, and Dat and Mamm had moved into it when Sam took over the store a few years ago. These rooms kept everybody close and cared for, on land the Lambrights had owned since her great-grandparents had come here from Lancaster, Pennsylvania, to help start the Cedar Creek community. "Mamm, are you all right?" she whispered as she entered the bedroom.

"I'm better now, jah." Her mother sat in a rocking chair by the window. With only the moon for light and her silvery hair trailing down over her white nightgown, she resembled an angel. "Figured you'd come for a visit, Abby, so I waited up."

"I'm sorry Sam got so testy."

"He's worried about Zanna. He has a tougher time showing it than the rest of us." Mamm patted the edge of the bed, and when Abby sat down, they clasped hands. "Your dat was a tough one, too—on the outside," her mother continued. "But Zanna knew he loved her. I believe she wouldn't have run off had Leroy been here to talk to her."

"Jah, I've thought so, too."

"She might not have gotten engaged to James, either, truth be told."

Abby's eyes widened. Where was *this* line of thought coming from?

The rocker creaked when Mamm leaned closer so her voice wouldn't carry through the walls. "Your dat and I hoped Zanna might wait a while to marry . . . have more running-around time for her rumspringa, after she stopped seeing the Ropp boy."

Abby recalled that difficult time. The whole town had discussed Jonny's dramatic departure from his family and the church in a fancy red van. He'd broken all ties, never came around any-more. "But Zanna took her church instructions."

"Because your dat wanted to be sure she'd become a baptized member."

"And then she latched right onto James when he came calling on her," Abby whispered bitterly. She was too tired to discuss this now, but Mamm would understand feelings shc could share with no one else. "If Zanna wasn't ready to settle down, why did she have to shatter his dreams by agreeing to marry him and then running off?"

Mamm sighed and squeezed her hand. "She's barely seventeen, Abby. Hardly a woman, much less ready to be a wife. I suspect she doesn't know who she is yet, or what she wants to do with her life," her mother explained. "James is a wonderful-gut man and I'm sorry he's never spared you a second glance, Abby. I know you've always cared for him."

Abby swiped at sudden tears. This was foolishness, to dredge up feelings she'd thought she'd put to rest. "Sorry," she whispered hoarsely. "I just have to keep believing God's got different ideas for me—"

"That's why you took up your sewing, using your best talents to start up your own business—right there where you could help Sam run the store," her mamm reassured her. "And it's why your dat built you a little place across the lane, knowing that someday Matt would marry and have his family in this house, where his sheep and the gut pastureland are." Mamm shook her head wistfully. "Sam might rant about how Leroy favored Zanna, but your dat looked ahead to what each of you kids would need . . . how you'd best follow your own paths yet be able to stay here, near the homeplace."

Abby nodded, her sadness stabbing her. *Why did you have to leave us so soon, Dat?* It was a question they'd all asked many times, even while believing his death had taken him home to God. She closed her eyes, praying for stronger faith— and the maturity to get beyond the fact that James Graber hadn't chosen *her*. "Do you want to come stay with me until Zanna shows up?" she asked her mother. "I know how Sam's temper wears on you."

"I'll be fine, Abby. But denki for asking." Mamm thumbed away a tear and then sat straighter, drawing in a resolute breath. "Let's hope your little sister hasn't gotten herself into something she can't get out of. She's never been one to think things through the way you do, Abby. Your dat and I were so proud of how you always made sensible decisions."

"Even though I didn't marry?"

Her mother smiled. "It's not such a bad thing, being a woman with her own business . . . her own life. Goodness knows where I'd be without the greenhouse," she admitted. "I might have buried myself under the covers like a scared cat after Leroy passed, and never found out how strong I can be. And how much I still have to contribute."

Abby considered this as she absorbed her mother's praise and confidence. Where would she be without the love and support of her family?

Mamm was sounding more like herself now, so Abby stood up. "I won't be worth much tomorrow if I don't get some rest. After we clean up the greenhouse, I have curtains to finish for Lois Yutzy. And the care center in Clearwater has ordered more lap robes."

"We'll stay busy and believe the best about Zanna," her mother said with a decisive nod. She squeezed Abby's hand before letting it go. "It's gut you stopped by, ain't so? We're both feeling better for it. Sleep tight, Abigail."

"You, too, Mamm."

The next morning James stood on his front porch and gazed across the road toward the Lambright place. The October dawn nipped at his ears, and fog hovered in Matt's sheep pasture where Cedar Creek cut through it. It was such a peaceful scene at first light, yet he was still too upset to fully appreciate it. The only thing to do was help set the buildings and the yard to rights, even if his wedding day had been a fiasco. Cleaning up after the festivities was a newly married couple's first responsibility.

Had Zanna slipped in last night? What on earth would he say if she was there?

He chuckled mirthlessly and started walking.

43

It would only be fair for *her* to speak first—if Sam left her any words.

And what if she wanted to kiss and make up? Or hinted about getting hitched now that her nerves had settled?

And what if she didn't?

Again James shook his head, rueful for these and a hundred other questions that had swarmed like bees in his head all night.

From the greenhouse door he heard male voices. The pew wagon was parked nearby, partly filled with the narrow wooden benches that traveled from home to home for Sunday preaching services, weddings, and funerals. James paused in the entry. Plain folks didn't decorate their weddings with cut flowers, but the colorful mums and lacy ferns that Treva grew for her shop had made a fine backdrop for their wedding meal. The glass ceiling and walls gave the place an ethereal look . . . as if a heavenly light glowed around everyone who went inside.

He braced himself for whatever Sam might say to him. He and Sam Lambright had been friends all their lives, but no one's feelings were spared when the storekeeper's dander was up.

What if Sam blamed him for Zanna's running off? Emma and her friends claimed she had been downright giddy about getting hitched—happier than they'd ever seen her. But the men might know different.

"Mornin' to you, James. Didn't figure you'd be over." Matt Lambright set down the end of the pew he'd been moving, and then his dat looked toward the door, as well. In their denim barn jackets, hats, and work gloves, they could have been twins except for Matt's clean-shaven face.

"If you're looking for Zanna, you're in the wrong place." The edge was still sharp in Sam's voice, yet he seemed pleased to see James. "Not much use in asking how you're doing, I reckon."

James shook the hand Sam offered, pleased to feel his usual welcoming grip. "I appreciate all the work you went to, making the place look extra-special for the wedding, and buying all that food."

"And why wouldn't I do that?" Sam asked, shrugging. "We were all so sure Suzanna had met her match and that she couldn't have picked a finer one. I don't know what got into that girl. Can't tell from one minute to the next what's going through that stubborn blond head. I'm sure sorry it turned out this way, James."

"Jah, we feel right bad about the whole thing," Matt chimed in. "It'll take a while for the talk to die down after she gets back. And if she doesn't show up . . ."

The sentence drifted toward the greenhouse's ceiling. Father and son stood silent.

James raked his hair back from his face and replaced his hat. "Let's don't cross that bridge before we get to it," he replied. "Right now, these pews need to be at the Yutzy place for Sunday."

The physical labor of hefting wooden benches, and stacking them in the wagon just so to get them all to fit, gave him welcome relief from all the what-ifs that plagued him. James was grateful for the comfortable way the three of them worked together without the need for chitchat or analyzing a situation that defied male logic. Phoebe and Gail came in to wipe down the long tables, while Ruthie stuffed a plastic bag with trash. Their crowd of nearly four hundred had included dozens of children, so all sorts of food had hit the greenhouse floor. Panda and Pearl, Matt's dogs, snatched up tasty morsels as they trotted around in the big, airy building.

While Matt delivered the pews to their next destination, James and Sam knocked down the tables and stacked them against the wall. "I appreciate your coming over," Sam repeated. "I didn't figure on opening the store this morning, but I've got backed-up bookwork that will make the day go faster. It's better than getting caught up in the clucking and squawking that will likely happen here at home."

James's lips twitched. "Happy to help out, since I'd cleared my calendar of carriage work until after Thanksgiving. If I look too bored, Emma will no doubt put me to work."

"How's hot coffee and warm apple cake sound

about now?" The familiar voice preceded a slender figure silhouetted in the doorway, holding a tray. Abby stepped inside, glowing for a moment as the morning's first burst of sunshine lit the huge room. Her eyebrows rose. "And you're here, James? How gut to see you. And how are your folks and Emma this morning?"

Bless her, the first words out of Abby's mouth weren't about how *he* was doing, or if he'd seen Zanna. "Dat's caught himself a cold with a nasty cough, so of course Mamm's hovering, telling him that's what comes of gathering eggs without his jacket."

"Fresh horehound syrup would be just the thing for both of them." Abby set her tray on the last standing table. "It would give your mamm something to cook up, and after taking it, your dat would most likely nap and feel better, too."

"Gut idea." James glanced at Sam, who'd plucked a thick slice of the fragrant cake from the tray as though he was ready to leave. "I'll come to the store in a bit to fetch the makings."

"I'll be glad to take them over, James," Sam said. "Gut chance to chat with your folks . . . see how they're doing." With a nod the older man walked off, as though taking a bag of dried horehound across the road to the Grabers was just the task he'd been hoping for.

James smiled. Abby had hefted herself onto the table as though to settle in for a cozy chat. She poured two mugs of steaming coffee and placed a slice of cake on a napkin before patting a spot on the other side of her tray.

How did she know he'd thought of talking to her? And with the girls gone inside, it seemed a fine chance to speak of things he couldn't share with just anyone. "Denki, Abby. Awful nice of you," he murmured. He inhaled the aromas of sugar and cinnamon and strong coffee. "Emma's had her hands full dealing with our parents this morning, so breakfast was running late. I didn't want Sam to think I was ducking my after-wedding chores."

"Or that you were too done in to show your face?" she suggested softly. "You're a gut man, James. Sam looks all the better after spending some time with you today. More relaxed."

His eyes widened. Who else would have noticed such a thing? Or suspected the anxiety that had almost kept him home today? "Well, like I told your brother, I'd cleared my calendar of any shop work, so . . ."

"It's the mindless little jobs that save us from ourselves sometimes."

"You've got that right. Mmm—mighty gut cake, Abby," James grunted around the mouthful he'd taken. "Nothing tastes as fine as the fresh apples and black walnuts from your own trees."

"I thought it might sweeten up our morning. Brought it over from home, knowing Barbara and Mamm might not feel much like baking."

James looked at her over his coffee mug. "You must have gotten up awful early."

"And *you* slept last night?" She shook her head ruefully. "I don't need a mirror to see the dark hollows under my eyes."

Abby held her mug in both hands to warm them, looking sadder than James had ever seen her. "And when Zanna comes back and we tell her how disappointed and outraged and humiliated we feel," she continued in a rising voice, "she's not likely to hear that. Not that she's cruel, understand. But she rarely looks before she leaps."

James swallowed hard. He reached for another slice of cake, then thought better of it. Best to get things off his chest before anyone else came into the barn. "Abby, I . . . Now, tell me true, will you? I trust your judgment," he said in a faltering voice. "I can't help wondering if I left something unsaid or undone or—well, Zanna's quite a bit younger than I am, and maybe I courted her too soon after your dat's passing."

"Don't you *dare* blame yourself, James." Abby's expression looked stern despite her pink-rimmed eyes. "Zanna knew exactly who she was hitching up with, and she knew that you could provide her a nice home and a steady income. It's not like anybody twisted her arm to marry you, James. Not like she's in danger of being a maidel at the ripe old age of seventeen."

"Jah, but Mamm and Dat have been wearing on us more this past year," James pointed out. "And Zanna knew that when Emma married, our parents' care would be mostly up to her while I worked in the shop."

"A responsibility—a lesson in love—that we all take on in our families. Just like the care and feeding of kids when they come along," Abby countered sharply. She sipped her coffee as though she needed fortification to discuss her sister. "Truth be told, this disappearing act has me wondering how fit a wife and mother Zanna would make. You can't run off when things don't go the way you planned—and when does that ever happen? While your babies are turning into toddlers and before you can blink, they're getting into rumspringa."

Visions of the children he'd dreamed of having with Zanna made James's mouth go hard. The greenhouse felt chillier now that he wasn't working.

"Sorry I'm ranting at you this way, James. It wasn't my intention to upset you more than you already are."

He sighed. When he went to take another sip of coffee, he wondered how his mug had come to be empty. "I'm grateful to you for the way you're not blaming me. I . . . I had no idea this would happen, Abby."

"None of us did." She tipped the carafe over his

cup again, smiling glumly. "We gave the distant kin something to talk about on their trips home, didn't we?"

His eyebrows rose. "We did." He succumbed to that second slice of warm cake. It didn't fill his emptiness, but the sweet chunks of apple and chewy nuts gave him something pleasant to savor.

James sensed that Abby was gazing at him with something else on her mind. He'd had about all he could handle, however—even though nothing new had come to light. He just felt better knowing the Lambright family didn't blame him for yesterday's fiasco.

"And what will you say to Zanna when she comes back, James? I'm thinking she's got no place permanent to go, so sooner or later we'll hear her story. And we'll have to decide what to do about it." Her voice had lowered again. It soothed him like when he'd been a little boy scared of the dark and Mamm had caressed his hair, convincing him that monsters didn't live under his bed.

Those monsters had matured with him and taken on different forms, though, hadn't they? Right now, embarrassment and betrayal and loneliness loomed large, and he didn't know how to handle them. "I don't rightly know what I'll say to her. Guess I'll listen, and try to keep my sharp remarks to myself while she explains why she ran off. I love her, Abby, *so much,*" James confessed in a tight whisper. "I don't want to think about living without her, after the plans we've made, and yet . . . it'll take some tall talking before I'll take her back, too."

"Anybody could understand that." Abby's answer told him she was near tears—not a state he'd seen her in many times. "Zanna has no idea what she's torn to shreds."

For a few moments the empty greenhouse sighed with their silent anguish—such a contrast to yesterday morning at this time, when he hadn't yet known what a turn his wedding day would take.

"I'd better see if Mamm's going to open her shop, or what all she plans to do with herself today." Abby scooted off the edge of the table, then focused on brushing their crumbs onto the tray so he wouldn't see her tears.

"When Zanna comes home, give her my best, will you, Abby?" he asked sadly. "I can't imagine what's going through her mind. I just hope it's not me she's mad at."

Ever so quickly Abby squeezed his hand. "All right, James. I'll do that."

— Chapter 5 —

Abby entered Cedar Creek Mercantile's back door early the next morning, before daylight had chased the shadows from inside the vast building. Saturday was always a busy day, with more English and tourists shopping, so—family crisis or not—she and Sam would put on their best smiles and conduct business as usual. Mamm planned to be in her greenhouse by midmorning, and Sam's girls would be along to help where they were needed in the afternoon.

Before the store opened, though, Abby had about an hour to devote to her sewing. It was her favorite time, because when her body got into the rhythm of her treadle machine, the fabric moved effortlessly in her hands and her mind became totally absorbed in her work. She hoped to finish the red calico curtains for Mother Yutzy's Oven: Lois Yutzy had expanded her bakery with tables and chairs so folks could chat over their sticky buns, pie, and coffee.

The floorboards creaked as she walked along the side aisle, past shelves of baking staples and fragrant bagged seasonings. She raised the thermostat of the gas furnace, then climbed the wooden stairs to the loft, where her Stitch in Time business occupied one end of the space. She had arranged her nook with a fitting room at the back and shelves for storing sewing notions and her projects in progress. Her sewing machine sat near the loft railing so she could look out over the main level and go downstairs when Sam got too busy helping customers. It was a good system: while she earned a nice income sewing clothes, curtains, and table linens, she could also ring up sales when Sam had to inventory shipments or when he went home for dinner with Barbara and his kids.

Abby stood on a stepstool to twist the handle of the ceiling-hung gas lantern. The area around her sewing machine brightened, and she smiled at the cheerful red calico panels draped over her chair. Then she stooped to pick up a clod of mud, frowning: she hadn't come up here since yesterday, yet here was fresh wet dirt smearing her fingers. Her breath caught.

Under the curtain of the changing booth she saw a pair of muddy tan shoes. Those slender legs could belong to only one person.

"Zanna!" she cried, flinging aside the fabric between them. "Suzanna Lambright, what have you got to say for yourself?"

Her little sister's stricken expression didn't win Abby's sympathy. Zanna looked rumpled from her kapp down to the sag of her grimy stockings, and Abby didn't recognize the jacket, several sizes too large, that drooped from her shoulders. "I—I didn't mean to . . . didn't know what else to do," Zanna blubbered. "Oh, Abby, you've got to help me! Everyone else will hate me so bad they'll not speak to me ever again."

"And why would that be, missy?" Abby still stood with the curtain in one hand. It gave her something to grip as she assessed the situation. Relief rushed through her. Her little sister had returned unharmed, although she looked like a cat left out in the rain. And Zanna had come *here,* believing she'd get the help she needed.

But it was no time to indulge this runaway with favors she didn't deserve.

Zanna sniffled and swallowed, swiped at her red-rimmed eyes.

"I'm listening." Abby relaxed but she didn't let her sister off the hook. "I guess you know Mamm's worried herself sick over you. Not to mention Sam and Barbara and the kids—and all the folks who came clear from Pennsylvania and Ohio and Indiana for your wedding. And then there are the Grabers." She left James out of it. Better to make Zanna ask the biggest questions, to see whether she realized she *should* be concerned about his feelings.

Her sister's face crumpled. Zanna looked pale, and the lavender half-moons beneath her eyes confirmed that she hadn't slept much. "I—I got

myself into a bigger mess than I knew how to—
Oh! I'm going to be sick!"

Abby grabbed her wastebasket and thrust it
under Zanna's mouth just in time. Her sister
retched again and then went into a fit of dry
heaves that made Abby hurt just watching that
young body convulse.

*And what does this remind you of? How many
times have you held a dish tub or the nearest
bucket for . . .*

"Don't tell me you're having a baby!"

Zanna's frightened blue eyes—and another
round of retching—told the tale, didn't it?

*So how will you fix this, big sister? How did
this happen, if Zanna . . .*

When Abby considered what this revelation
meant, her heart pounded. How could James
Graber have acted so betrayed yesterday, when
he'd poured out his soul, if he'd already been
physically intimate with Zanna? Abby had tried
not to think about the man she loved having a
family with Zanna, right across the road, where
the proof of their intimacy would swell with every
new child. She gripped the rim of the wastebasket, blinking back hot tears.

But crying and lashing out wouldn't solve this
problem. Abby reminded herself that she was the
more mature woman here and that Zanna had
come to her for help. Her frustration with James
was another matter entirely. As Abby took in the

anguish on her sister's face, the fear in those watery blue eyes, another possibility occurred to her.

"Zanna, James *loves* children," she pointed out. "He can't *wait* to be a— Why didn't you just keep this little secret by loosening your wedding dress? It's not talked about, but you wouldn't be the first bride whose baby came before the calendar counted up right."

Zanna flushed. She wiped her mouth on the sleeve of that awful jacket and looked away. "You got that right," she rasped. "James couldn't *wait*. And what was I to say? I thought he loved me! And how was I to know . . ."

Abby's throat got so tight she couldn't swallow. She wanted to hear the rest of Zanna's story before she said anything, but her pulse was pounding so hard that it was difficult to follow her sister's low, urgent voice.

"It took me a while to know for sure I was pregnant, and by then . . . Well, I couldn't stand there in church pretending I was pure, could I?" Zanna continued between her sniffles. "And after the way James treated me, I couldn't pretend I loved him or wanted any part of marrying him, either!"

Abby's jaw dropped. This sounded nothing like the tale she'd heard from the man in question.

"I should have called off the wedding," Zanna continued in a rising whine, "but I didn't want to upset Mamm or get Sam all riled up, because he'd already spent so much money, only to figure out I was already carrying."

Abby's patience snapped. She pointed sternly to the chair at her sewing machine. "Sit down, young lady. And don't you dare move." She watched until her sister obeyed, and then carried the vile-smelling wastebasket downstairs to the bathroom.

As she rinsed it out, her mind raced. Zanna's story smelled like spoiled Swiss cheese and had just as many holes. How could Zanna think James didn't love her? Even if he had jumped the gun when the two of them were alone, Abby had never seen him show anything but affection and respect toward her sister. And hadn't Emma and everyone else agreed that Zanna had acted happier than they'd ever seen her, these months when she and James had been engaged?

Abby sighed. If Sam walked in, his temper would further complicate the situation. How could she get this runaway to her house to ask the questions that begged for answers before Zanna told any more bare-faced lies?

Or had Zanna revealed a side of James Graber that no one suspected? Abby's brow puckered in thought as she wiped the wastebasket. He was older than most fellows were when they married . . . and Zanna might have tempted him beyond reason without even realizing it, young and pretty as she was. If James had been having relations with his fiancée, he'd be too much the gentleman to let on about it—especially to a maidel like herself. And what if her own romantic notions about James had fogged her vision of him?

It was all so confusing. *Dear Lord, please don't let me create more problems than I solve,* she prayed as she left the little bathroom. *Please help me say and do whatever will take us along the higher road.*

Abby glanced at the wall clock. First thing, Zanna needed something to settle her stomach. Then they had to slip away—yet the lane to her own little house led right past the homeplace, and they would probably be passing by there right when Sam and Mamm would be coming in to work . . .

Lost in her thoughts, Abby stumbled over a box of discarded clothing left beside the collection bin in the fabric section. The scribbled note on top of it read, *Abby—I need a rag rug for my kitchen, please. No need to hurry. Adah Ropp.*

By the looks of it, other folks had cleaned out some old clothes, as well, because the collection bin overflowed even though the store had been closed since the wedding. The mercantile sat on a county road, so they always locked up—although their close neighbors knew where the key hung in the phone shanty out by the road, if they needed something when the store wasn't open.

As Abby assessed the pile of worn trousers,

59

dresses for doing chores in, and sun-streaked curtains, she grinned. Wasn't this the solution she'd
just now prayed for?

She grabbed a box of graham crackers from the
shelf and hurried up the wooden stairs to the loft.
As Abby entered her sewing nook, she searched
for words that made sense—but then, nothing
about Zanna's story made much sense. Try as she
might, she couldn't tell if her sister was showing
yet, the way she clutched that nasty old jacket
around herself.

"Where did you get that coat?" she blurted
before she thought better of it.

"I found it in the barn where I was hiding."

Abby winced. If she was going to ask the direct,
difficult questions, she had to be ready for
Zanna's answers. Abby opened the box of graham
crackers and handed over a wrapped packet of
them.

"If you think Mamm and Sam would have been
upset about calling off the wedding," she said in a
quiet, purposeful voice, "I promise you, young
lady, you haven't seen *upset* yet. You'd better get
your story straight before you say a word to either
one of them, too, because I'm hearing holes big
enough for a horse to poke its head through."

Cracker poised before her mouth, Zanna
widened her eyes. "Are you saying you don't
believe me? Are you calling me a liar?"

"We don't have time to fight. Sam will be here

any minute," Abby reminded her. "Now that he and Mamm have recovered enough from your disappearing act to open up shop again, you won't be getting their busy day off to a bad start. I'm taking you to my house so you can clean up and get your act together," she said in a tight voice. "*Then* you'll face the rest of your family."

When Zanna glanced out the window, toward home, her blue eyes nearly filled her gaunt face. "And how do you think we'll get out of here without—we *cannot* tell Mamm about the baby, Abby. She'll kill me! And what if James sees us?"

Ah, wasn't *that* the question of the hour? And how did Zanna think she could keep her baby a secret? Abby gestured toward the stairs. "You'll have to answer to all of them—sooner rather than later," she added. "And you owe an apology to James most of all—for spoiling the biggest day of his life. Not to mention breaking his heart."

Zanna stopped short at the top step. She blinked rapidly. "After what he did to me, you feel sorry for him?"

"Move along, missy. While I fetch my cart, you're to gather up all the clothes from the rag bin and meet me outside."

"What are you—"

"Don't stand here fussing at me. Unless you want to meet up with the very folks you betrayed, looking like *this*."

Once they reached the bottom of the noisy

wooden stairs, Abby headed for the shed. Was she wrong to whisk Zanna away to her own little home instead of marching her to the main house to face their family? Would she be able to pull this off without Sam catching her? If he did, he would think she was just as disloyal as Zanna.

Maybe this wasn't the best plan . . . but there was no time to doubt her inspiration. As Abby stepped between the long handles of the two-wheeled wooden cart, used for hauling anything they wouldn't hitch a horse to, she prayed her sister would play along. As she left the little shed, she saw Zanna at the side door and hurried over to meet her.

"Get in!" Abby grabbed some of the worn clothing her sister held. "I'll cover you with these old clothes—like I'm taking them to the house to make rugs. Don't you dare move or make a peep. Understand me?"

With a doubtful glance toward the house, Zanna obeyed. Abby tucked a couple of old dresses around her sister's slender form and then tossed the rest of the clothes on top of her. She would ask God's forgiveness for this little masquerade later, but right now it seemed the best way to avoid a major squabble. It also gave her a chance to set Zanna straight about why her story didn't match up to the truth. Abby stepped between the cart's wooden handles, tipped the cart until it was level, and then trundled off.

Down Lambright Lane she went, over the packed dirt path. If she walked a little faster she could make it past the door before—

Just as she was nearing the corner of the two-story white house, Sam stepped outside. "I got quite a binful of clothes for rag rugs while the store was closed," Abby called out to him. "I'm taking them home so they'll be out of the way once we open. See you in a few."

Her older brother's expression didn't change. Poor Sam had been put through the wringer these past few days and had probably endured all he could handle from his women. Thank goodness he waved and started walking toward the store.

Abby thought her lungs and legs might burst before she got home. As a precaution, she wheeled the cart around to her back door before she slowed her pace. Only when she let go, and the bed of the vehicle hit the ground with a *whump,* did she realize what her concealed passenger might have undergone during the ride.

A gasp came from beneath the clothing as Zanna swatted aside the fabric that covered her face. "Could we do that again so you hit *every* bump in the road this time?" she said grumpily. "I'll have bruises all over my—you *could* help me out of here, you know!"

At the first crack in her little sister's voice, Abby blinked back tears. What an awful ride that must have been. When Abby grabbed Zanna's hands to haul her up, she wrapped her arms around the poor girl. "Zanna, I didn't mean to be so rough. I didn't think about you bouncing against those hard wooden sides—"

"I've got no reason to complain, now that you've got me over here."

"But we've all been so worried about you," Abby finished with a gasp. "We had no idea where you'd gone, or why."

Zanna sniffled loudly, swiping at her red-rimmed eyes. "I've got a lot of questions to answer, I know. And I'm really sorry about cutting up that wedding dress you made me, Abby. Must be the baby that's making me act so crazy, so thankless."

Thankless. Now there was an admission that might redeem a few of the unpleasant moments they'd had over the past days.

Abby drew in a long breath, returning Zanna's worried gaze. "Your wedding dress is the least of our worries right now," she murmured. "Let's get you inside. While I'm working this morning, take a bath, all right? This situation will be easier to handle when we've both simmered down. Then we'll figure out how to tell everybody else what's going on."

Nodding, her sister stepped up the back stoop and into the kitchen. Abby followed, clutching an armful of the old clothing, which she tossed into the alcove where her clothes washer sat. Her pale, blond sister stood in the center of the room, absently munching a graham cracker as she gazed at the glossy wooden cabinets and floors as though she'd never seen them. When Abby noticed how thin and worn-out Zanna looked, she bit back the lecture she'd planned to deliver.

"Make yourself comfortable, sis. Tea and soup and what all are in here," she said as she opened the pantry doors. "Help yourself to clean clothes, and then think about what you'll tell everybody when we take you over home."

Abby turned then, waiting for Zanna to make eye contact. "But you've got to play fair, Zanna. No more of those overblown stories about James—hear me?" she insisted. "For one thing, nobody will believe he treated you badly, even if he . . . made you his woman before you became his wife."

Did that sound as awkward as it felt when she'd said it? Abby fought a surge of anger and impatience when she thought about how Zanna had apparently run away from James, the father of her child . . . the man who'd never seen Abby as anything other than a friend. She sensed Zanna's thoughts were elsewhere, so she kept her personal grievances to herself. "Never, *never* forget that no matter what you do, Suzanna Lambright—or how awful you think things will be when the truth comes out—we're your *family*. We love you, and we'll stand by you."

Abby paused to let that idea sink in. "But things will go a lot easier for everybody if you tell the truth."

Zanna hung her head, her unfinished cracker in her hand.

"Are we gut now, you and I?" Abby asked quietly. "I'd stay, but Sam expects me back at the store any minute."

Her sister cleared her throat. "Jah. I'll be okay now, Abby. Denki."

"I'll come back later to see how you're doing."

Abby closed the door behind her. As she pushed the cart toward the road, the back walls of the mercantile and the glass greenhouse stood as reminders of what would come next. Zanna was right. Mamm's relief when she knew her youngest daughter had returned safely would quickly be overridden by shock and disbelief. Anger and disappointment would raise voices— and issues—such as the Lambright family had never known.

When Abby saw Mamm's shadowy silhouette moving behind the panes of frosted glass, she took a detour. She parked the cart behind the mercantile and tapped on the back door of the greenhouse.

"Jah? Just a minute!" her mother called out, and after a moment Mamm peeked outside. "Oh, Abby—come in! I was just deciding how to price all these ornamental gourds. Might have planted more rows than we should have—" Mamm looked tired, but her eyes never missed much. "And what's on *your* mind, Abigail?"

Abby felt caught up in a whirlwind of emotions, not sure how to break the good news—and the other, more difficult news. The seriousness of Zanna's predicament was setting in now that she was past the shock of finding her sister in her sewing nook. "Well, Mamm, Zanna's back—"

"Oh, thank the Lord! My prayers are answered!" As Mamm embraced her, Abby closed her eyes and sighed . . . hugged her mother and felt her tremble with joy and relief. What a shame, to spoil such a moment by telling Mamm the hard truth. "And where was she? What did she say about—"

"It's not so gut, Mamm. You're not going to like it."

Her mother pulled away enough to search Abby's face for answers. "Now what?" she whispered. "It wasn't enough that Zanna left us all in a pickle . . ."

"She's pregnant, Mamm. Said James couldn't wait, and—"

"And what kind of talk is *that?*"

"—she was too scared to tell you or Sam—or to call off the wedding, or—" Abby stopped to catch her breath as the heat rushed up her neck. "I'm not saying this very well."

Mamm clasped Zanna's hands. "It's Zanna's story to tell, whether she's scared or not. And where is she?"

Abby recognized the tightness in her mother's face. It was the expression she put on to get through a crisis—the expression she'd worn most of Zanna's wedding day. "She's at my house, cleaning up. She smells like she slept in a barn, because she did," Abby murmured. "Zanna knows Sam will get even angrier if he finds out."

"She should have thought of that before— before . . ." Mamm's face crumpled and her whole body sagged. She let out a shuddery breath. "We'll have to find someplace for your sister to go . . . before anyone else realizes she's in the family way."

"But if the baby belongs to James—" Abby shut her mouth. Attitudes may have changed in the English world, but Mamm's generation believed unmarried mothers were not to be seen in public and should not raise their babies out of wedlock.

"Zanna should have thought of that, too," Mamm muttered. "But she obviously did *not* think, so we'll have to make some decisions *for* her."

Mamm put her hands on either side of her kapp as though she was getting a bad headache. "All this turmoil in the past few days. Makes me wonder what the Lord's trying to tell us." She swiped at a tear and smiled sadly at Abby. "I'm going to put up the CLOSED sign before anyone comes in. Let's not let on to Sam about Zanna's condition until she breaks the news herself. I have a lot of thinking and praying to do, and his temper won't help me."

"Jah, I can understand that," Abby murmured. It had always been Mamm's way to deal with problems that arose with her children and the household, and not to bother Dat with them, if at all possible. But Abby knew this situation was too big for her mother to handle alone. "Can I do anything to—"

"Keep your brother busy at the store. And pray."

In the silence of her sister's kitchen, Zanna closed her eyes tightly. *Leave now, before you have to answer to anyone else! There'll be no end to the questions.*

But where could she go? She threw up every little thing she ate—and threw up even when she didn't eat. There'd be no slipping into her room to pack a duffel . . . and truth be told, her condition would soon be obvious to everyone who saw her. She'd kept her secret too long. She was so exhausted, feeling so scared and alone that she couldn't think straight. She felt high and excited one minute and terrified the next.

Zanna sighed, wishing Mamm and Barbara already knew so they could soften Sam before he saw her.

You're going to catch it for running off, and for the expense of the wedding—and then there's that forty dollars he's surely missed from the cash box by now.

And then James will find out. He sounded

worried when he was out looking for you, but that'll change when he hears the truth.

Too upset to think about it anymore, Zanna shrugged out of Mervin Mast's grimy coat and the dress she'd worn these past few days. She washed at the bathroom sink. Then she brushed her hair and rewound it into a bun and tucked it under one of Abby's old kerchiefs. Her sister's oldest gray choring dress—the one Abby wore to help with Matt's sheep or to spend a hot day in the garden —suited her mood perfectly.

The little house was too quiet—and so tidy it looked like nobody lived there. Zanna was too restless to nap. What she *really* wanted was to hear about the wedding! What had happened after her family figured out she'd run off? What had Bishop Gingerich said about her to all their guests? Was James upset and worried? Or did he pitch a fit before he came looking for her?

Zanna turned her thoughts to other wedding details, because thinking about James Graber made her stomach hurt.

Desperate for something to do, she rolled Abby's wringer washer to the sink and hooked up the hose before starting the diesel motor. The clothes in the donation box smelled musty, and it wasn't Abby's way to leave such an untidy pile on her floor. While Zanna worked on the first load, she was more than ever aware of how she hardly knew herself anymore . . . how isolated she felt now. Ordinarily, she would have chatted happily with Gail, Phoebe, and Ruthie while they washed and hung out the family's clothes. But her nieces were working at Mother Yutzy's Oven this morning—and she wasn't ready to face their horrified expressions when they heard her story.

What about her friends Mary and Martha Coblentz? They'd been at the wedding as her newehockers, so surely they'd want to know she was safely home. And what about the girls in her buddy bunch? They could fill her in on the talk from the wedding, and describe James's reaction so she could be ready for it. As her friends' faces flitted through her mind, Zanna blinked back more tears. Nothing would ever be the same with those girls once they found out she was having a baby. But no matter what, she wasn't marrying James.

Zanna wiped her eyes. Enough of these tears and this emotional roller coaster—she had to talk to somebody. That's what friends were for . . .

— Chapter 6 —

Abby's curtains lay unfinished in her sewing nook all Saturday morning as she helped dozens of locals stock up on baking supplies. A busload of English tourists arrived around eleven thirty and swarmed the aisles. Even after Sam called Lois Yutzy's bakery for Phoebe and Gail to come run the cash register and sack the purchases, the crush of customers kept them all going at full tilt long past lunchtime. When the tour bus finally pulled onto the road again, Sam smoothed his graying hair with a sigh before replacing his hat. He looked done in.

"How about if the girls and I head to the house for a bite, and then I'll be back?" he asked Abby. "Fine by me if you take the rest of the day off after that. Looks like you had quite a stack of rags for your rugs."

Abby nodded, hoping he hadn't noticed anything suspicious about the contents of her cart. "That would work fine, Sam. Most likely, folks have done their shopping now and have other places to go during this fine fall afternoon."

Once her brother and three nieces left, the mercantile rang with silence. Abby closed her eyes, drew a deep breath, and caught the scents of bulk spices and the subtle fragrances of Marian Byler's handmade soaps. Nearly two o'clock it was, and she had hoped to look in on Zanna before now—but when Sam returned, she could check on Mamm and then she would have the rest of the afternoon to talk to her skittish sister about the mess she'd created. Abby climbed the wooden steps to the loft, soothed by their familiar creaks. Time to finish sewing those curtains for Lois Yutzy, while no one was shopping.

Her feet slipped into the pumping rhythm that made the treadle machine whir as she guided the hem of the fabric beneath the needle. She seldom made window coverings for Plain folks, but the Mennonite couple who owned Lois's building thought their English customers would like the homier look that ruffled curtains would give to the bakery's new addition. The bright reds and yellows of the calico lifted Abby's spirits—when she was sewing, she became so absorbed in the textures and colors, so deeply satisfied by the way simple seams and stitches created clothing or items folks used in their homes, that she lost all track of time.

The bell tinkled downstairs. Could Sam be back already? Abby looked over the railing to gauge his mood, and then grinned. "Emma! Gut to see you! How's your Saturday been?"

Her best friend smiled up at her and waved a plate of something she'd baked. "I tried a new recipe for pumpkin muffins, with blueberries," Emma said as she hurried up the stairs, "and I thought you'd like one while it's still warm. James and the folks are settling up with Mose Hartzler, now that he's cleaned the chimney and repaired some cracks in the mortar. I've only got a few minutes."

It was a rare treat for Emma to get away, so Abby cleared the curtain panels from her extra chair. "We should probably have Mose sweep our chimneys soon. Winter will be here before we know it."

Emma perched on the edge of the spare chair and unwrapped two large muffins that were still so warm that the berries smeared on her fingers. "Cute curtains, Abby! Who are those for?"

"They're going in Lois Yutzy's shop, where the new tables are."

Emma snickered. "No doubt when Beulah Mae sees them, she'll think her bakery needs fancied up, too. Can't have Mrs. Nissley's Kitchen falling behind Mother Yutzy's Oven, you know."

The two of them giggled and bit into their muffins. As she chewed, Emma glanced around at the finished place mats and dresses waiting to be picked up. "Would you have time to make Mamm a new black dress for church, and another one for every day? Dat needs new pants, too," she added, shaking her head. "I cleared out their oldest stuff—which is why your rag rug bin was so full. They'll fuss at me, saying new clothes are an extravagance, but with winter coming on, they need warmer things to wear."

"I'd be tickled to do that. We can pick out the fabric as soon as we finish our snack." Abby closed her eyes over a big mouthful of sweet, soft muffin, inhaling its cinnamon scent. "Denki for bringing me this nice surprise! I won't get lunch until Sam comes back."

Emma nodded, peering down at the main level of the store to see whether anyone else was around. Then she looked at Abby with wide brown eyes. "Has anyone heard from Zanna? You must be getting awfully worried by now if . . ."

Abby took another bite of her muffin, needing a moment to think. Mamm didn't want anyone to hear about Zanna's pregnancy, but the Grabers—and everyone in Cedar Creek—would want to know her sister was safe. "Matter of fact, Zanna showed up this morning," she replied carefully. "She smelled so bad from hiding in a barn that—"

"A barn? Why on earth—"

"—I told her to clean herself up and get ready to answer a *lot* of questions, once we're all home for dinner."

The tinkle of the bell made them glance down to the main level. The Coblentz twins entered, chattering as they always did. Most Saturday afternoons they wandered the aisles fingering the bolts of fabric and the quilted linens Abby had made, and then they sampled the peanut butter that Sam ground fresh each day before ambling home after their little outing. They always dressed alike, and lately they'd been carrying a cell phone—a sure sign they were pushing their parents to the limit during their rumspringa.

"Afternoon, girls!" Abby called down to them. "What can I help you with?"

Martha and Mary raised their identical freckled

faces, waving. "We've been coming here nearly every Saturday of our lives, you know!" Martha remarked.

Mary added, "Jah, we probably know what you've got better than you do!"

"True enough. Holler if you need me." Abby caught herself before she blurted out that Zanna was back. Such a shame she couldn't share this news with two of her sister's best buddies, the girls Zanna had chosen to be side-sitters at her wedding. Soon, however, Zanna's return to Cedar Creek would become common knowledge. If they were lucky, tongues wouldn't wag for long once—

"Hullo? Jah? Well, where have *you* been hiding yourself?" one of the redheads sang out. "You had a greenhouse full of people—"

"Jah, and when James came back without you, we couldn't help wondering—"

Abby's mouth went sour as she glanced at Emma. The Coblentz twins stood head to head with their cell phone between them, and they could be talking to only one person.

"A *baby?* Oh, my word—"

"Does James know?"

As Emma stared down at the girls in disbelief, Abby rose from her chair. She peered out the store's window toward the phone shanty at the road. It was foolish enough that Zanna would call her friends. Surely she'd not use the phone they

shared with the Grabers, where Sam or Mamm—
or even James—might come upon her at any
moment!

But no, some fellow in a dark hat and a blue
work shirt sat in the little white building, with his
back to her. Maybe James's dat had ambled out
to make a call while Eunice wasn't looking.

Did this mean Zanna had a cell phone, then?
Such a worldly gadget was strictly forbidden now
that she'd joined the church. Was her sister piling
one offense on top of another, knowing full well
she was defying the *Ordnung* with her brash
actions?

"You can't let him get away with this!" one of
the twins exclaimed.

Her sister chimed in with, "What can we do for
you, Zanna? No fella has the right to . . ."

Abby blinked back angry tears. Did Zanna have
no sense of what she was starting as she informed
her friends about her pregnancy? Abby went to
the banister. "Mary and Martha Coblentz!" she
called down. "I'll thank you to keep Zanna's
private business—and your cell phone conversations—to yourselves! We've got enough gossip
flying around town as it is!"

The redheaded sisters gawked up at her,
suddenly aware of how their voices had carried.
One twin clicked the phone off as they both
started toward the front door. Were the Coblentz
girls embarrassed about being overheard? Or did

77

they intend to spread the word about Zanna's situation and how James had figured in it? Abby felt so betrayed she wanted to shake that sister of hers!

Instead she went to the window again. Should she beg poor Emma to keep this overheard conversation under her kapp? Should she rush home to confront Zanna? Such outrageous behavior could not continue.

The door to the phone shanty opened and the man stepped out. His clothing seemed awfully baggy, even for Merle Graber. And James's old dat didn't wear small tan shoes, did he? Abby turned from the window, so mad she was shaking.

Emma's stricken expression tore at Abby as their eyes met. "What's this talk about a baby? Why didn't you tell me—"

"We just found out. And after we break the news to Sam—I'm sorry, Emma!" Abby turned off the light above her sewing machine. "I've got to get home now."

"But James never let on . . ." Emma stood up stiffly and headed for the stairs.

Abby caught up to her retreating friend and tucked her hand under Emma's elbow. "Mamm wants to keep this quiet until we decide what to do. Please don't tell anyone."

Emma pulled her arm from Abby's grasp. Her eyes shone with unshed tears. "And how am I supposed to act like I didn't hear what Mary and

Martha said? Could *you* keep quiet about it, Abby?"

Heartsick, Abby watched her best friend hurry across the blacktop to the Graber home. She turned the sign in the mercantile's window from OPEN to CLOSED and locked the door behind her, not knowing when Sam might be back . . . or whether Mamm had told him of Zanna's return. Abby walked quickly down Lambright Lane and into her house through the front door. She found her little sister lounging on the sofa in a clean dress, sipping a cup of tea.

"So what's all this—your calling the Coblentz twins to tell them about the baby? And sneaking out to the phone shanty in clothes from my rag bin, no less!" Abby's stomach churned, for it wasn't her way to bring things to a boil. By nature she was a peacemaker, a mender of souls, and confrontation had never sat well with her.

Zanna scooted to the edge of the sofa, eyeing her warily. "You couldn't think I'd come home and not tell my friends," she murmured. "I was lonely."

Abby arched an eyebrow. "And how'd you get to the phone without Barb spotting you? Or the dogs fussing over those strange clothes?"

"I tossed them my graham crackers."

Oh, but that was the wrong thing to say. Abby crossed her arms so tightly they ached. "You didn't have to make out like James left you in the lurch. And you could have waited until your own family had a chance to talk to you. Here I thought I'd make things easier by letting you clean up, and you throw your dirt right back in my face."

Zanna's teacup rattled when she put it on the end table. She didn't say a word.

Abby exhaled slowly. She thought about the pointed questions she'd intended to ask, to get at the truth of this situation, and decided her sister needed to answer them for a larger, more critical audience. "I've already told Mamm you're back, and she's plenty upset."

Zanna stood up, her eyes wide. "And why'd you have to—"

"And now it's time to tell Sam and the rest of them you're here," Abby continued, her tone of voice allowing no argument. "You can either come with me and start on your apologies, or you'd better believe they'll be here in a humming-bird's heartbeat to hear what you've got to say. And then we're going over to speak with James."

Abby turned away, heartsick. In all her years as this pretty blonde's big sister, she'd never figured on dealing with this sort of a mess. A baby changed *everything,* for everyone in the Lambright family. The Ordnung spelled out right and wrong: Zanna hadn't learned those lessons very well, but she was about to find out—from Sam, and their mother, and even her unborn child—that nobody dodged a basic responsibility to care for others and to be accountable for themselves.

Out the door Abby went, then down the lane toward the rambling white house that had seen three generations of Lambrights through times of trial and triumph. *Never* had any news like this crossed their threshold, however. At least she heard footsteps behind her: Zanna had chosen to face the fire. Abby slowed down, but her sister didn't catch up.

Then, across the road, the front door opened and Emma Graber came out. She broke into a run, across the blacktop and past the mercantile, passing Abby as though she didn't even see her. James's sister wiped her hands on her apron as she stood in front of Zanna. Her wounded expression left no doubt of what was on her mind. "What's this about a baby?" she demanded breathlessly. "I heard the Coblentz twins talking in the store when you called them. How long have you known, Zanna?"

Abby closed her eyes. Emma's heartbreak came out loud and clear, and Zanna needed to hear it.

A sob escaped Emma as she continued. "And all this time you and James have been doing everything together, planning to get hitched, and—"

"You don't understand," Zanna murmured.

"—you both seemed so *happy!* Yet James has never let on to us about a baby."

81

Emma's sentence ended in a sob, and then there was a painful pause. Abby waited, wondering what would come next. Would this be the part that finally made Zanna realize how she'd stung everyone who loved her?

"James doesn't *know* there's a baby—does he, Zanna?" Emma whimpered and backed toward the road, still wringing her hands. "Don't you be coming over, hear me? Mamm and Dat are still stirred up about the wedding, and *this* news— well, they can't handle it right now. James—"

"Don't you say a word to him!" Zanna cried out.

"—went over past Queen City on a repair call," Emma continued doggedly. "If you're not gonna tell him, then *I* will! How can you think I'll keep such a thing from my brother? From the man who has eyes for nobody but *you,* Zanna Lambright? It'll be all over Cedar Creek in an hour, you know. Mary and Martha probably told everyone they saw on their way home."

When Emma finally realized Abby was there, too, she clapped her hand over her mouth. "Sorry," she rasped. Then she dashed back across the road, the sound of her sobs drifting back to them.

As she focused on Zanna, Abby sighed sadly. "I hope you're ready to own up to what you know —the straight-on truth. You're going to hear a lot tougher talk than this before the night's through."

— Chapter 7 —

"So you're telling me you spent the past couple nights hiding in a barn rather than asking your family for help?" Sam demanded. "And you're saying James Graber took advantage of your innocence and then acted like he didn't care about the consequences?" Their brother glared sternly from his end of the long table, where the whole family waited silently for this discussion to end so the meal could begin.

Not that anyone felt like eating. Matt and the three girls focused on their empty plates while Abby sat with her head bowed, holding Mamm's trembling hand . . . knowing better than to tell Sam how to handle the situation.

"Suzanna, you told better lies than that when you were five," Sam blurted out. "And we'll sit here until we get the truth from you."

Zanna blanched, paler than milk. "I—I just wish I could've talked to Dat, and maybe none of this would've happened," she said, a hitch in her voice. "Mamm never told me how *not* to have babies—"

"Well, wishing won't bring Dat back, little sister," Sam replied. "And frankly, I'm thankful our dat's not here to witness this disgrace. Not so much because there's a baby, but because *his* precious baby is putting us all through the grinder with her whims and her tale-telling."

"Sam, please," Barbara pleaded softly.

Abby tightened her hand around their mother's. While it was true that Mamm hadn't passed along much knowledge of what went on behind a married couple's door, the preachers had made it clear enough that such goings-on were wrong outside of wedlock. Even if they knew little about sexual mechanics, Amish girls clearly understood the sin that such an act involved when they took their kneeling vows to join the church.

Truth be told, Barbara had taken them aside when they'd reached adolescence. As a midwife, she'd made babies her life's work. So Zanna had no call to blame their mother for this predicament. The conversation had looped in this unbearable circle for nearly an hour, all because her sister refused to admit there were gaping holes in her story.

"It's easy to point up the failings of your parents while you're growing up," Mamm said in a low voice, "but let's not accuse your dat of playing favorites, Samuel Jacob. Especially because, as his only son, *you* were the apple of Leroy's eye. You never saw it that way because he expected more of you, preparing you to take his place at the head of this table."

A surprised silence enveloped the kitchen, because Mamm rarely stood up to her son, just as she'd never challenged her husband—or at least not in front of them. Abby was pleased by their mother's remark. It meant Mamm was seeing beneath the surface of this murky situation to what really mattered: the bedrock of love that held them together as a family, through sunshine and shadow.

Their mother sat straighter then, addressing her youngest child across the table. "Go to your room without your dinner, Suzanna, until you can tell us the truth," she said firmly. "That's how we dealt with you when you were little, and it seems you still have some growing up to do. Having a baby won't suddenly give you any more smarts, or rights and privileges, believe me."

Mamm gazed directly at Zanna then, so there would be no dodging the rest of her lecture. "And don't believe for a minute that you'll be staying in Cedar Creek while you're pregnant, or keeping the baby after it's born."

Zanna's mouth opened and then closed quickly. Dropping her napkin on her plate, she rose and walked stiffly toward the stairs, then paused in the doorway and turned toward them. "Come get me when you're heading home, Abby," she pleaded. "Do you see why I can't stay here anymore?"

"Enough out of you!" Sam stood up so fast his chair fell backward. "Your sister and the rest of us have taken all the sass we're going to handle!"

The sound of weeping drifted behind the upset girl, in a kitchen so charged with tension that Abby's heart constricted painfully. Without a word, she and Barbara and the girls fetched the dinner Sam had banished to the oven. The tuna noodle casserole looked brown and too crisp, while the green beans had shriveled in their bowl. But there was no fixing things that had gone wrong this past hour—these past few days—until the right answers came along, at the right time.

It was the quietest meal Abby could ever recall, as though their silent grace beforehand continued while they ate—although the atmosphere in the kitchen felt more frustrated and miserable than grateful. When everyone had finished picking halfheartedly at the meal, Sam and Matt headed outside for the last round of sheep chores. Phoebe and Gail began stacking plates while Ruthie busied herself with the broom.

Barbara let out a long sigh. "All right, then," she murmured, gazing at Abby and Mamm. "It's time we took a closer look at this situation. Best to take Zanna over to your house, Abby. I'll be right there with my medical bag."

"Are you sure you're pregnant, Zanna? Could be that the pre-wedding jitters are keeping you from your monthlies," Barbara said in a quiet voice. "Happened to me, matter of fact—first couple of months after I married Sam, what with all the stress of setting up housekeeping and fitting into a new family. I didn't have any sisters, and with my mamm already gone . . ."

"I used one of those home pregnancy tests," Zanna answered in a tight voice. She was lying on Abby's guest bed, undressed beneath a sheet, as her sister-in-law prepared to examine her. "*Two* of them. Same result."

"And where'd you find out about *those?*" Abby blurted out. What a blessing that their mother had stayed home rather than endure any more startling news from her youngest daughter. Another blessing it was that as a midwife, Barbara knew of store-bought English mysteries and miracles that the rest of them had never encountered, and she was handling the situation with the relative calm of her experience.

"It's not like the mercantile's the only store on earth, you know." Zanna sounded exasperated and angry, like a little girl who'd been tricked into doing something she detested. "And here again, had our mother told us about the—"

"Don't be blaming Mamm for your trespasses," Abby countered with a frown. "It wasn't her fault that some fella went beyond your limits, either, Zanna."

"And speaking of limits, I've about reached mine." Barbara raised an eyebrow in warning to both of them. "If you two can't be in the same room without clawing like cats, one of you has to leave."

"Sorry." Abby sighed, well aware that she was behaving almost as badly as her sister. "I won't say another word. I promise. Not until you've finished with her, anyway."

"Gut." Their sister-in-law focused on Zanna, folding back the sheet and then patting the girl's leg to soothe her. "This will sound way too personal, but we've got to know some things if we're to help you have a healthy baby and stay well yourself. When did you conceive, Zanna?"

Her sister looked mortified. "I—it only happened once, I swear! Back in July."

Barbara nodded, unruffled. "About three months, then. Scoot down a bit more . . . There you have it." She placed her hand on Zanna's thigh, smiling kindly. "This speculum might startle you, but it won't hurt you. Relax, now. We're almost done."

Abby turned away. It felt too much like gawking, seeing her little sister in that awkward position, even if Barbara acted like it was an everyday thing. Zanna's face looked flushed, and it was no time to let another critical remark slip out. From what Abby knew, being around other women who were having babies, things were pretty well set inside them by the time they were three months along.

And how had she—or Barbara, or Mamm—not seen the signs, ever since July? How had she not noticed anything different about her sister . . . who, as Abby thought back, had spent a busy summer helping at Mamm's greenhouse and cleaning homes—and riding out with James after singings and every other night she'd had the chance. Not once had anyone doubted that Zanna was head over heels in love with the man who had lived across the road all their lives . . . a man Abby knew nearly as well as her own brother, because James had confided in her so often. Abby sighed. She'd never had reason to believe James Graber would give in to his physical desires at the risk of ruining Zanna's reputation.

Barbara cleared her throat as she removed the speculum. "It's not James Graber's baby, is it, Zanna?" she asked softly.

Abby turned, noting her sister's stunned expression. Despite the tension in the little room, her heart fluttered.

"You can tell that from *looking?*" Zanna said in a high, tight voice.

Barbara didn't respond right away. She busied herself tending to her equipment. "What you *didn't* say at the dinner table was more revealing than what you *did* say, young lady," she began sternly. Now that she'd completed her examination, Sam's wife seemed intent on getting to the heart of the matter. "Seeing the way James took out looking for you after you disappeared before the ceremony tells me he cares too much for you to dishonor you—or to have premarital sex, breaking the vows you both took when you joined the church."

Zanna sat up, yanking the sheet over her bare legs. "Why's everybody so set on defending James?" she demanded shrilly. "How can you be so sure he's not the reason for—"

"Because he's never given us cause for doubt or second-guessing." In the late-day shadows of Abby's spare bedroom, Barbara looked older, tired of answers that didn't add up, and weary of this young woman's way of dealing with her problems. "You only make this harder on yourself by dodging the truth, Zanna. When you put this baby up for adoption—"

"Who said anything about that?"

"—you'll need to write a father's name on the birth certificate," Barbara continued. She stepped closer to the foot of the bed, so Zanna couldn't duck her intense gaze. "If you don't *know* who the father is, you've not got morals enough to deserve this child—a gift from God—or to saddle your family with your irresponsible ways. And if you do know, you'd better tell him sooner rather than later, Zanna. Paternity issues get sticky in hospitals these days. We don't want a lawsuit—"

"So *you* can deliver it, Barbara. That way I can keep her—I promise I'll take gut care of her," Zanna pleaded. "I *love* this little baby! You'll see what a fine mother I can be."

"You're missing my point." To emphasize her words, Barbara placed her fingertip on Zanna's chest, leaning lower so their eyes were on the same level. "Your brother will have none of this thinking—especially considering how you've already lied to us tonight. And you broke your mother's heart again. That's twice in three days!"

Zanna sat silently. She knew better than to sass back.

"And then there's James, living right across the road," Barbara went on in her no-nonsense tone. "Where's he going to fit into this picture, Suzanna? If you don't marry him, if the baby belongs to another man—"

"She belongs to *me!*"

"—you'd best be confessing it right quick." Barbara stepped back, grasping the handle of her black bag in both hands. "If *my* questions upset you, you've not seen anything yet. When the preachers get wind of your situation, they'll put Sam on the spot—and you know how he'll take to *that!* You'll be shunned, at the very least, not to mention all the talk this will cause in the store. And since I'm the one who has to live with Sam, I'm telling you, Zanna—"

A loud knock on the front door made them all suck in their breath.

"If they're looking for me, I'm not here," Zanna whimpered.

Barbara let out an exasperated sigh. "See there?

When will you learn that you can't hide, little girl? When will you realize you can't tease your way out of this one? Too many lives have been affected by it. We're already tired of paying for this mistake, Zanna—especially since you won't admit you made one."

Again someone pounded on the door. Louder this time.

"I'll get it." As Abby left the spare room, her heart felt like a rock in her chest. They had all figured a runaway bride was the most serious situation they'd ever faced—but that was on Thursday. Now, on Saturday, the stakes had gotten so much higher . . . and it would be spring— another six months—before this baby came. Who could predict what might happen by then?

Abby paused to peer out the little window beside her entryway. She closed her eyes, knowing she must open the door and say what had to be said.

"James." Abby gazed at the angles of his face, sharper and more pronounced beneath the shadow of his hat. *Lord, please don't let me say or do anything to hurt this man any more than he's already been wounded.*

"Abby," he murmured. His eyes looked sad, like an old hound dog's.

"I can guess what you're here for. Come on in, then."

— Chapter 8 —

One look at Abby's splotchy face told James the rumors were true.

And just like that time he'd ridden the roller coaster at the county fair, his emotions flew into a wild spin. From the rising exhilaration of his wedding morning, to the rapid plunge into fear when he went looking for Zanna—and now, his heart raced out of control as he careened around yet another blind corner, hearing about Zanna's return and her alarming news. How many more surprises could he stand?

He stepped into Abby's front room, looking around as he removed his hat. "She's here, then?"

"Jah."

Abby's tone told him she knew more than she would tell—which was only fair, but so exasperating. "Emma told me—they're saying Zanna's in the family way. And so help me, if I get my hands on the fella who did this to her—"

"James." Abby grabbed his clenched fists. Her eyes, usually so shiny bright with cheerfulness, had clouded over. "It's not my place to speak for my sister, but I'm not hearing that the fella forced her into it. And . . . well, she's saying you couldn't wait—"

"*Me? I* couldn't wait? Abby—" Once again his feelings spiraled into free fall, as though the roller-coaster car had jumped the tracks at its highest point. His throat squeezed so tight he could hardly talk. "Please tell me you don't believe I'd do that to your sister."

Abby released his hands. She shook her head, looking as wretched as he'd ever seen Abigail Lambright, the town optimist, appear. *But is she shaking her head because she believes you couldn't sully her sister that way? Or because she can't stand to answer you?*

"It's Zanna you should be talking to, James," she finally murmured, glancing down the hall toward the bedrooms. "I did my best to get her story straight, keeping her here so she could clean up before she faced the rest of the family, but she started phoning her friends. Sam and Mamm are fit to be tied."

"Will you tell her I'm here? And stay with us while we talk?"

Abby's eyes widened as though he'd asked her to chaperone—or referee—their wedding night. "I'm not so sure that's a gut idea, James. She's already peeved me with her dishonesty."

"I trust you to keep us both on the high road, Abby. I'm so upset, I might say or do something I'll wish I hadn't." He fidgeted with his hat, caught between extremes: one moment he wanted to protect his Zanna from all the wagging tongues and take her back, while with his next breath he stood ready to condemn her outrageous lie. Her behavior made a big black mark on both their reputations, even though he'd done nothing wrong.

"Ah. Another one telling me I'm my sister's keeper—and now your keeper, as well." Abby smiled sadly as her sister-in-law came down the hallway with her black bag. "Do you want Barbara to stay, too?"

James shook his head, reading the same resignation—the same verdict—on the face of Sam's wife. "Denki for your help, Barbara. Is—is Zanna all right, then?"

"Better than the rest of us, I'm thinking. I'm sorry this is happening, James. None of us wanted this for you." The midwife paused at the door, studying his face. "I'm going home to pray on it, and trust that God will guide us all toward His way and His will."

The door closed behind her and the front room filled with an awkward silence. James had been here with Emma last spring when Abby had moved into this little place. He liked the way the walls glowed with pale yellow paint in the lamplight, and the simple furnishings made him feel so at home. "Guess I'd best wait here for Zanna. Or has she already slipped out the back way, after hearing my voice?"

Again that sadness hung heavily on Abby's brow, and he was sorry he'd added to it. "I'll get her," she murmured. "We'd best be saying what needs to be said so we can all move forward."

Nodding, James watched her walk down the hall. Such a kind, solid woman, Abby was. Tidy and talented at so many things, yet always giving other folks the credit. He looked at the old oak rocking chair with an afghan folded over its back and then at the sofa, and chose the seat he recalled Sam, Abby, and Zanna's dat resting in most evenings. As he settled against the flat slatted back, James hoped some of Leroy Lambright's patience and wisdom would seep into him. Zanna hadn't been the same since her father had passed, and maybe he needed to address that tonight.

The chair creaked with his weight as he rocked . . . What could he possibly say to right such a wrong situation? To nip this crisis before all of Cedar Creek believed the rumor that he'd dishonored his bride-to-be? Abby reappeared then, watching her sister come down the hall.

James stood up, his pulse kicking in his temples. *Father God, please give me the right thoughts, the strength to listen and forgive . . .*

Zanna didn't look at him. She walked like a wooden doll that needed its joints oiled, then lowered herself stiffly to the edge of the couch. Try as he might, James couldn't see any signs of a baby, but he didn't want to stare. "Zanna," he murmured in a voice that sounded strangely adolescent. "Gut to see you got home all right. We were all worried . . ."

The love of his life focused on the arm of the couch as though some fascinating riddle were written there for her to decipher. When Abby perched on the sofa beside her, James sat down again. The two sisters looked drained, their faces nearly as pale and stiff as their kapps, except Abby's darker brows and hair set off her features more distinctly. As he gazed at Zanna, who'd promised to be his wife, James reached deep inside himself, searching for a solution—a way to persuade the young woman who appeared so distant now. A mere week ago, she couldn't stop smiling at him and talking about the wedding.

James cleared his throat. Best to jump in and hope God put good words in his mouth. "Before you say anything, Zanna, I—I love you," he began fervently. "If we can put the rumors to rest right now—if you'll still be my wife—I'll wipe the slate clean. Then this will blow over, and it will be like it never happened."

Zanna bowed her head. She picked at her fingernails.

Abby grasped her knees, seeming so ready to speak out—yet apparently aware that this wasn't her conversation.

James sighed. He swallowed the lump of

desperation that clogged his throat. "I know it's been hard on you since your dat died, and maybe I shouldn't have courted you so soon after that."

There was not so much as a flicker of Zanna's eyelashes in response.

"And maybe . . . maybe you should've had a little more time for rumspringa before you took your church instruction and kneeling vows. I know your dat wanted the best for you when he convinced you to do that so soon after you turned sixteen," he continued quietly.

Still Zanna seemed lost in her own little world, oblivious to how his soul bled as he searched for the words that would get her talking.

James leaned forward, gazing intently at her. Why would his Zanna not look at him? What else could he say to convince her that he wanted the best for both of them? "I was so happy you wanted to be with me, I probably didn't realize you needed more time for having fun with your friends or . . . for trying things out for yourself."

Zanna fiddled with a loose thread on the sofa, and when she yanked it off, it might as well have been wrapped around his heart. What did a man say to a woman who acted as though he wasn't seated ten feet in front of her, pleading for their life together?

"I'll call the child mine. We'll get on with our lives, Zanna," he rasped. He couldn't miss the way Abby's brown eyes widened gratefully . . .

just as he couldn't ignore the tightening of his fiancée's jaw. "For your wedding present I—I bought you that walnut bedroom set you liked at Yoder's store, so we wouldn't be starting out in a room that looks the same as when I was a kid. Mamm and Dat'll be moving to the dawdi haus—"

Zanna's face was getting red, but he couldn't stop pouring out his feelings and frustrations. At this point, it was in for a dime, in for a dollar. "As far as I'm concerned, Zanna, you still hung the moon and stars! If there's anything at all I can—"

"Stop. Just stop, hear me?"

James felt his body deflate. The voice had been Zanna's, but he hadn't seen her lips move. He rose to stand behind the rocking chair, to grip its sturdy back for support.

So she'd heard enough? He was being a first-class fool, was he? It had been his greatest fear that he'd lash out, or cry, or . . . but he'd never dreamed that this young woman, who threw herself into everything with a bright conviction, would refuse to hear him out. Had she no idea how badly she'd slashed him by running away, and now by *this?*

"All right, then, the stories have to stop, Zanna." James thought the chair back might snap in his grip, yet he felt so powerless. Thank God for Abby, whose wounded expression must mirror his own. "You and I both know I never—*Whose baby is it, then?*"

Zanna's eyes filled with tears. "Mine," she hedged.

"That's no answer, and you know it! How long have you known—?"

"Since . . . July."

A horse might as well have kicked him full force in the chest. When James could catch his breath again, he said, "So we'd been engaged for three months when you—for half the summer you've been seeing another man."

"It—it was just the one time—"

"Zanna, that's enough." Abby grabbed her sister's slender arm, and then released it as though it burned like a blazing log. "Maybe you won't answer to me or to Mamm, but you've got to own up to James about who the father is."

"You could have had the decency to tell me," James said bitterly. Clearly, his turn-the-other-cheek spirit was getting him nowhere except in deeper trouble. "I spent all my time planning and setting up the house. I turned away carriage business for this month so we could have time together. And you went along with those plans. Acted happy. Said you *loved* me, Zanna."

"And what else was I to say? When somebody says they love you, you say it back or they feel bad, ain't so?" Zanna hunched her shoulders. She looked miserable, true enough, yet James detected a stiffness to her features as she pulled herself together . . . as she carefully worded her answer.

"It was gut to see you so happy, James—to see all my family smiling again after Dat's passing. You kept telling me how perfect it was going to be, our marriage, and I wanted to believe—"

"Well, you could have changed your mind before now!" he cried. "If you couldn't tell me you wanted out, why didn't you let Abby know so *she* could've—?" James exhaled forcefully. Abby's alarmed expression warned him he might well break the chair if he didn't get a grip on his temper. He so seldom felt anger, he didn't know how to act when such a wave of it washed over him.

James spun around, spearing his hands through his hair like a crazy man. The sight of the lamp on the table soothed him . . . at least enough to make him realize that no amount of reasoning—no amount of loving Zanna—would save this situation. If she didn't understand how he'd sacrificed his pride to ask her to come back, offering to raise this child as his own, what would be served by putting himself through any more humiliation? Hadn't he endured enough of that in front of four hundred wedding guests?

"You could have said something back in July, too. And obviously you did—but to some other man," he muttered, mostly to get it off his chest. Zanna was beyond hearing his heartbreak, so what was the point of parading it in front of her? "Guess I'll leave it to the bishop, then. There's nothing more I can say here."

James grabbed his hat and left before Abby could see him out. He didn't have the heart to listen to her apologies or explanations, or whatever else she might say to smooth his ruffled feathers or soothe his soul. The autumn evening had a nip to it. Across the moonlit sheep pasture, the gentle roll of the hills—so often a reminder of the Good Shepherd they followed—beckoned him to walk and walk until his legs could carry him no farther. Yet he sensed that even strenuous exercise would bring him no peace.

And what would help you? How can you live with knowing that the sweet Zanna Lambright you lost your heart to not only betrayed you on your wedding day but also gave herself to another man long before that, while you avoided such pleasures out of respect for her?

And Zanna seemed so heedless of the wound she'd inflicted. It had stung him deeply to sense that she felt no remorse, no need to apologize.

From behind the barn, two lithe dog shadows moved toward him, their ears alert as they checked his identity. James crossed his arms tightly. He was too infuriated to scratch behind Panda's ears or to mimic Pearl's soft, conversational mutterings.

What was he to do now? How was he to answer Emma's questions, or his parents', when he got home? Could he attend the preaching at Ezra Yutzy's place tomorrow and endure the endless

102

stares and speculation? Or should he stay away and let folks talk even more harshly about how he'd shamed Zanna and her entire family?

James started down the long lane toward the county road that separated the Graber place from the Lambrights' land; before now the blacktop had never seemed like such a dividing line. Why would Sam's family welcome him here, even if they believed he was innocent of Zanna's accusations? They, too, were in turmoil. If he went inside to make his peace with Sam and Treva this evening, his attempt might well backfire. Better, perhaps, to visit the bishop: to state his side of the story before Vernon Gingerich and the other preachers heard the rumors secondhand.

A steady *clip-clop! clip-clop!* announced a buggy, and it turned to come down the graveled lane, right toward him. When the rig came close enough that he recognized the bearded faces in the glow of its lantern, James sighed wryly at the timing: Bishop Gingerich had already heard the news. He'd never been one to let problems go untended, and he'd brought along Paul Bontrager, another preacher, to assist with this difficult mission. As the horse slowed, James took a deep breath.

"Evening, Vernon. Paul," he said with a nod.

"I guess you know what brings us." In the moonlight, their gazes were fixed on him.

"Jah. I've been here trying to get the full story

from Zanna," he replied with a sigh. He pivoted on his boot heel to hide the sudden crumpling of his face. "I don't know what to make of it, fellas," he rasped. "It's like somebody doused the flame and her lamp went out, as far as how she feels about me."

Vernon leaned forward, his expression grim. "I'm sorry to hear that, James. It's not our intention to rub salt in the wound, but you understand why we need to get this story from the horse's mouth—so to speak—rather than relying on hearsay. And because tomorrow's a preaching Sunday—"

"We figured it best to err on the side of sooner rather than later," Paul added solemnly. "Haven't ever had a wedding go wrong in Cedar Creek, and now with talk of Zanna having a baby, well—it's best to deal with it head-on."

"We can't have our other girls thinking that's the right path to follow," Vernon said. Then he cleared his throat, sounding a bit uncomfortable. "We also need to make it clear about your part in all this, James. If there's to be a confession, and a Members' Meeting about whether to impose a ban, we need to hear from all the folks involved."

"Jah, I understand all that." James closed his eyes to keep his head from spinning. He'd witnessed plenty of confessions and the disciplinary actions that followed, but never had he been directly involved—or been dragged into it on account of someone else's accusations. "Truth be told, I was heading your way, Vernon, to seek your counsel. Zanna's whipped her family into a lather."

"Sam's a pillar. He wants to keep his family in gut standing with God and the rest of the community." The bishop looked beyond James toward Abby's house, and then at the larger white home where lamps lit most of the windows. "Abby's at her place, then? With her sister?"

"Jah. I just came from talking with them, after Barbara gave Zanna a . . . female examination." James sighed, knowing what would come next. It didn't help that the right men were here to steer this matter in the direction it should go; he still felt as if he'd been trampled by a stampede of wild horses.

Vernon nodded. "I'll ask both of them to be at Sam's in a few minutes, and we'll get this settled."

— *Chapter 9* —

A few moments after the bishop left, Abby opened the door and gestured for Zanna to step out ahead of her. "Let's go. We've got a long night ahead of us yet."

Matt's sheep, crowded together along the shadowy pasture fence, murmured at them as Abby and her sister walked past. On the other side of the lane, Mamm's hills of pumpkins and fat jack-o'-lanterns glistened in the moonlight . . . So peaceful, this pastoral setting, yet Abby knew nothing could soothe her right now. Panda and Pearl loped out to greet them, but returned to the barn when neither she nor Zanna patted them.

"Why did James have to go telling tales to the bishop?" Zanna murmured as their footsteps crunched in the gravel. "Bringing all this on before I had a chance to deal with it and—"

"Stop right there!" Much as she hated to harden her heart, Abby recalled the Bible relating how God had done that, too, when He'd been displeased with His people. She turned to face her sister in the driveway. "If there was any *bringing on,* it was you getting on the phone that started this snowball rolling down the hill, Zanna. Had you minded your own business— talked to Mamm and your family instead of the twins—the bishop would still be involved, but we might be working things out differently. Ain't so?"

Zanna pivoted, crossing her arms. Despite her defensive stance, tears were streaming down her moonlit face alongside the strings of her kapp. "Why do you hate me so, Abby?" she rasped. "I thought you of all people would understand why I couldn't marry James Graber!"

And what was that supposed to mean? Best not to go down such a trail right now while their family had so many other matters to settle. "If I hated you, would I have offered you my home as a hideaway today? Would I be so upset about the choices you've made?" Abby asked softly. "Problem is, you have *no idea* what you've gotten yourself—or the rest of us—into."

At the main house, Abby held the screen door to let Zanna enter the kitchen first . . . Was her sister upset enough that she might run off again? Now or after they met with Vernon Gingerich? It wasn't a happy thought, but it made Abby aware that she was indeed her sister's keeper.

Zanna paused to smooth her apron, listening to the quiet voices that drifted in from Sam and Barbara's front room. She entered ahead of Abby then, walking between the preachers, the family, and James with her head lowered and her hands clasped. She took the place beside Barbara on the sofa.

"Evening, everybody," Abby murmured. The only seat left was the ottoman between Sam's recliner and the platform rocker James sat in, so she took it. She placed her hands on her knees and waited for Vernon Gingerich to begin.

"Let us start by asking for the Lord's assistance and wisdom," the bishop said as he rose from his wooden rocking chair. Everyone got quiet and bowed their heads.

You know how we need Your help, Jesus, Abby prayed. *Help us to listen to Your still, small voice instead of to the confusion and chaos in our hearts.*

After a moment Vernon cleared his throat. " 'The Lord is my shepherd; I shall not want,' " he began in a low, clear voice. " 'He maketh me to lie down in green pastures . . .' "

With her head still bowed, Abby followed the ancient psalm in her mind, anticipating the familiar words and feeling the deep comfort they always brought her. In her mind, she saw the Lambright land and imagined Matt's sheep whenevcr she heard these verses.

" 'He restoreth my soul: He leadeth me in the paths of righteousness for His name's sake.' "

The front room took on a whole new atmosphere as everyone around her breathed deeply, silently following along as Vernon rendered the passage in his unhurried, steady cadence. Abby felt better. The bishop had set the tone for the way they would handle Zanna's predicament.

" '. . . and I shall dwell in the house of the Lord forever.' " Bishop Gingerich sat down, leaning forward in his rocking chair, and looked at each of them in turn. Bathed in the soft glow of the oil lamps, he appeared as serene as always, yet his expression reflected the magnitude of this situation. "It's good you've came back, Suzanna. This tells us you haven't forgotten the promises

108

you made when you took your vows earlier this year, about following our beliefs . . . about confession and repentance. About right living. About putting faith in God before family and all other worldly concerns."

Zanna kept her head bowed. She knew better than to answer until she was asked a question.

Paul Bontrager spoke then, his eyes alight in a face weathered by a lifetime of farming. "We heard the story being spread by some of our girls—your friends, Suzanna—and we came here for the truth of it, as you've joined the church and they haven't." With a sigh, he added, "This seems another example of how telephones become the Devil's own mouthpiece when they're used for spreading gossip."

From across the room, Abby glanced at Zanna's face. Her sister's cheeks were flushed, and she'd pressed her lips into a tight line. She looked ready to cry again. And she clearly intended to let everyone else do the talking.

"From what we've heard today, this is what we believe has happened," their mother stated, eyeing Sam when he seemed ready to jump in. "Suzanna's carrying a baby. And James Graber had nothing to do with that. Ain't so, Suzanna?"

Zanna closed her eyes. She nodded.

"We want to hear you say it." Mamm sounded resolute now. "There's no hiding from a truth that affects every one of us in this room, daughter."

A forlorn sigh filled the rough circle they formed. "Jah," Zanna murmured. "There's a baby. I was wrong to blame it on James."

"And we fully intend to uphold whatever discipline you call for, Vernon," Sam chimed in. "If it's a kneeling confession tomorrow, a shunning to follow that, we believe it's for the best."

Zanna's face fell as she glared at her brother. "I'm trying to say I'm sorry," she whimpered. "Sorry for the way I made you all worry when I ran off—"

"And will you confess this at a Members' Meeting after the service tomorrow morning?" The bishop leaned his elbows on his knees, trying to get Zanna to look at him. "It's all well and good to apologize here amongst family, but true repentance is to be shared with every member. It's a reminder of how we every one fall short, and need to be guided back to God's path."

"She'll do whatever is required, Bishop," Mamm reconfirmed. "If it means she'll be living with my aunts in Indiana until the baby's born, so be it. Sam and I will see that she carries out whatever you and the others decide."

Zanna's eyes widened like a spooked mare's, but she held her tongue. With the bishop and Preacher Paul present, she knew better than to protest Mamm's declaration. She swiped at a tear, then looked away as though to keep from crying more in front of them all.

"I prefer to hear *your* reply, Suzanna," Vernon insisted. "When it comes to confession and repenting our sins, no one else can speak for us."

A little sob escaped her. "Jah. I'll be there tomorrow. Ready for confession."

The others in the room shifted in their seats, as though relieved that Zanna was contrite. Abby felt grateful that such difficult issues arose so seldom, because gatherings like these took their toll on everyone's emotions.

"Do you have anything more to say, Suzanna?" the bishop asked. "We should discuss the fellow who fathered this baby."

"James." Zanna inhaled deeply as she fixed her gaze on him. "Did you mean it when you said you'd still marry me?" she asked in a faltering voice. "When you said you'd clear the slate and raise this baby as your own?"

James stood up suddenly, as if irritated that she'd put him on the spot in front of their church leaders. "And did you mean it when you said you loved me each time I said I loved *you?*" he rasped. "Did you *mean* it, all those times you kissed me and acted so excited to be getting married—even though you gave yourself to somebody else in July?"

Zanna's head shot up, her resentment matching his.

When Vernon rose, the only sound in the room was the rocking of his empty chair. The old fellow straightened his stooped shoulders, a reminder of the weight he bore as their district's bishop. "Once again, Suzanna, you were not alone in this sin," he insisted quietly. "The man in question needs to make it right—to come forward and confess along with you, so—"

"But that will never happen!" Zanna looked at the family members around her, entreating their support. "Even if I thought it could work out, you'd never agree to me marrying him."

"Is he English, then?" Mamm's face clouded over, as though this might be the greatest disgrace of all.

"Is he married?" Sam demanded. "If you got yourself involved with—"

"No."

Abby recognized the set of her sister's jaw. Zanna had assumed that look, that tone, when she was a child who'd been cornered by the adults. And James? He was a man aghast at Zanna's unwillingness to reveal the rest of her unpleasant secret.

"He's not marrying or settling down anytime soon; I can tell you that," Zanna replied. She crossed her arms protectively over her mid-section. "I've done a lot of thinking about it, and I—I'm taking full responsibility for the mistakes I made. And for raising this baby, too."

"You have no idea what you're saying," Sam said, exasperated. "No idea about taking on—"

"Hush, Sam! Let her say what she will," Mamm insisted. "We're all here listening, as witnesses. You've always said Zanna needed to be held accountable, ain't so?"

Abby shifted in her seat, trapped between two angry men. On her left, James sat down again as though he regretted seeing this side of the girl he'd loved, while on her right, Sam bristled at their mother for overriding his authority. This sort of confrontation was rare, as it went against the principles of their faith.

Abby's stomach knotted. *Let Zanna speak her mind carefully, Lord, and guide the bishop as he directs her fate,* she prayed quickly. *Help us to wrap our arms around this difficult situation and see Your will at work.*

Zanna sighed, lowering her eyes. "You're my family. I came home because I knew I couldn't do this alone. God saw fit to make a baby, and I intend to keep it—to raise it rather than give it up for adoption," she added, with a purposeful look at Barbara and Mamm. "If you can't help me with that, then I—I guess I'll have to find some-where else to go . . . some other way to support myself and my child."

Abby closed her eyes, while her brother rose from his chair as if to signal the end of this discussion—and his patience. This sounded like another of Zanna's uninformed decisions, a fantasy she had no practical way to carry out. Yet

Abby detected the steely determination of a young woman who would make good on her veiled threat to leave. At seventeen, her youngest sister had no idea of what complications she faced.

Then again, what young mother did? Even longtime wives confided that, while raising a family might be their highest purpose in life, there were no easy answers when it came to handling each baby—prioritizing the usual work to be done while dealing with feedings and fatigue and sickness and all the other demands a newborn made on their time and energy. Not to mention what husbands and other family members expected of them.

Bishop Gingerich fixed his gaze on Zanna until she looked at him. "Suzanna, your attitude does not become you. It's not for you to decide your punishment or the fate of your baby. As a member of the church, you must submit to the decision of the other members tomorrow. Do you understand this?"

Zanna pressed her lips into a tight line. She nodded.

"If you'll excuse us for a bit, Bishop—" Sam motioned for his wife and Mamm to follow him into the back bedroom. "This whole ordeal sprang up so sudden-like—just this morning—so we've not had a chance to discuss alternatives amongst ourselves."

Bishop Gingerich watched them leave, and

then resumed his seat. Abby tried to relax on the backless ottoman. How long might their impromptu conference last? This endless day was wearing on her . . . There was no appropriate chitchat to fill in this awkward gap as it stretched into five minutes . . . ten. The mantel clock struck another quarter hour, then marked more silence with its loud, steady ticking. Pale and scared, Zanna looked ready to pass out as she stared, unseeing, at her lap. Beside Abby, James gripped the arms of his rocking chair and let go, gripped and let go.

Finally Mamm and Barbara returned and took their seats, with Sam following behind them. Abby couldn't read her brother's expression, but she sensed that some tall talking had been done on all sides. As head of the Lambright family, Sam made all the big decisions—or had to be convinced that anyone else's idea was something he could enforce. Something he could live with.

"We appreciate your patience, Bishop," he said. "Since Barbara's birthed a few babies in similar circumstances, I'm going to let her say what we came up with. Knowing, of course, that we'll abide by whatever the church members decide tomorrow."

Bishop Gingerich nodded. "Let's hear it, then."

Zanna's face tightened. She eyed her mother . . . then studied her brother and his wife.

"We realize, Vernon, that most pregnant Amish girls stay with someone away from home and then give up their child for adoption," Barbara said quietly. "Yet, in some ways, it seems such a tradition relieves the young woman of responsibility—gives her a clean slate when she comes home, if she and her family can keep the baby a secret. It also takes away the lifelong accountability that comes with raising a child—especially one conceived outside of marriage."

"Jah," Sam joined in, looking at Zanna. "We're not happy about this situation, not one little bit, but Zanna's got to face the consequences of her actions—and the way this child will change the rest of her life, and her family's, too. It would be too *easy* to let her give up this baby, especially now that she's told her friends about it. I can see that now."

"You realize that if you keep the child, the whole family suffers the shame, then. The Grabers do, too," Preacher Paul added with a scowl. "Besides that, Zanna's got no way of supporting a child—"

"She's said she'll find one. And we'll hold her to that. It won't leave her much time to get into any more trouble, ain't so?" Sam looked at Zanna to drive home the fact that they intended to carry through. Beside him, Mamm nodded her agreement.

"So be it, then." Vernon glanced at Paul, who stood up beside him. "We'll see you all tomorrow." He donned his broad-brimmed black

116

hat. "You're making a big mistake, keeping the baby's father a secret, Suzanna—letting him off the hook while you shoulder the whole load. But as I told your brother when you fled from your wedding, we all make our choices. And we face the consequences for a long, long time."

Zanna had never felt so humiliated or so helpless, with no say in the way she would spend the rest of her life. After the meeting she hurried over to Abby's house, and then—late as it was—she returned to Sam's before he and Barbara went to bed. "Here!" she said, tossing the two twenties on the kitchen table. "I was wrong to take this money from the store's cash box, and wrong to run off, and—well, it seems that everything I do or say is just wrong, wrong, wrong!"

Sam lowered his face to the same level as Zanna's. "Don't be getting me started up again."

"I gave back what I took and I'm sorry, all right?" As she turned toward the door, Zanna fully expected a big hand to pull her back into the kitchen for another talking-to. But only the night wind whipped her, coming around from behind the sheep barn with a whistle that hinted at winter and smelled like rain.

She went into Abby's house again, to pull another coat from the closet. Her older sister had put on her nightgown and was letting down her rich brown hair to brush it.

Startled, Abby looked at her. "Zanna, don't tell me you're running off again, after you promised to—"

"Here's Mervin Mast's barn coat, all washed and clean," Zanna said, hanging it on the doorknob. "Jah, it would be the better thing for me to return it to him myself, but since I'll most likely be put under the ban tomorrow, he couldn't accept it from me. Will you see that it gets to church, so he can have it?"

Abby gripped her hairbrush. "Jah, I can do that."

"Never let it be said that I added stealing to my long list of sins." Zanna exhaled loudly, not that it made her pulse slow down. "Don't wait up. I've got a lot of walking to do. A lot of thinking."

"Praying helps," Abby reminded her in a choked voice. "That's what I'll be doing for you, Zanna."

"That's all well and gut," Zanna muttered as she opened the front door again, "but I'm thinking God's not in much of a mood to listen to *me* right now."

Why did she feel so scattered? What was this tingling, tight energy that forced her to keep moving? As Zanna strode down Lambright Lane, she had no idea where she was heading. How could anyone be expected to go through all that she'd endured today?

No rest for the wicked, her thoughts taunted.

But she didn't feel wicked. *Terror* better described her emotion: outrageous fear about what would happen tomorrow nipped at her heels as she hiked along the dark, windswept country roads.

The thought of becoming an outcast, a misfit—not a girl anymore but not a wife, either—loomed like a huge black hole in front of her. Would she ever have *fun* again? Who would want to bc her friend? Zanna yanked off her kapp and unpinned her hair to let the wind whip it around her face. Loneliness gripped her heart and she couldn't stand to think about such total isolation. So she kept walking even though her shins ached.

What would happen tomorrow? Kneeling confessions were required for those who had blatantly strayed from the path, but most folks simply sat with their heads bowed as they admitted their wrongdoing. Ezra Yutzy had used his boy's cell phone to arrange delivery of some deer he'd raised to stock the woods at a Minnesota hunting lodge. Zeke Detweiler had hauled hay with a modern tractor, while Bessie Mast had bought new dishes without first asking permission of her husband, Mervin. *Piddly* sins, compared to hers!

Folks in Cedar Creek might go through the motions of forgiving her premarital relations, but they'd be reminded of her trespass every time they saw her baby. Hers was not a forgive-and-forget kind of sin, and her child, too, would grow up in its shadow. And then, after she'd served out her punishment, what man would want her for his wife? They'd never forget how she had betrayed James Graber.

Maybe you should have gone along with the bishop's way. Sounds a whole lot easier to let somebody else raise this baby.

The thought made her double over with pain. She stepped off the blacktop, bracing herself for another vomiting fit, but nothing came up. After she caught her breath, she took note of her surroundings.

How had she made it clear out to the Ropps' dairy farm? When had it started raining? Nearly two miles she'd traveled, yet she hadn't gotten rid of that jittery craziness that made her pulse pound so hard.

There's the highway—your chance to keep on walking. Might be the best thing for everybody.

But Zanna turned toward home, hunkering down against the wind as the rain fell in sheets. She gasped at a lightning flash, wishing she'd paid more attention to the weather when she left.

When it rains, it pours. And this is only the beginning.

Abby jumped at the first bright flash of lightning. She didn't feel right, being here in her cozy little home while her sister was out in this oncoming storm, but Zanna could have taken any of a dozen back roads or shortcuts across neighbors' places. Finding her in the darkness would be nearly impossible. Maybe she had taken shelter in a barn . . .

A flapping sound, and a motion outside her kitchen window, made Abby lift her lantern to see outside. How had laundry gotten hung on her clothesline? As she rushed outside to rescue the dresses and pants that danced crazily in the wind, she realized Zanna had washed the clothes from her rag bin when she'd laundered Mervin's coat. Abby raced back inside and shut the door against the first drops of rain.

"Oh, Zanna," Abby murmured as the shower pelted her roof. "It seems like nothing's gone right all day, and tomorrow isn't likely to get much better. I wish I knew what to do for you, little sister."

She dumped the contents of her laundry basket on her table and began to fold the pieces. Here were faded dresses she'd seen Eunice Graber wearing for years, worn thin at the elbows . . . three pairs of broadfall trousers with hems that had tattered from dragging on the ground. Abby had noticed how Merle seemed to be shrinking with age.

How would Eunice and Merle feel, watching their grandchild grow up across the road without a dat, instead of in their home with James? And how would they and Emma and James handle unkind remarks from folks around town who didn't think Zanna should be allowed to keep this baby?

Abby folded clothes that Adah Ropp must have donated—drab dresses she and her two girls had worn, as well as her husband Rudy's old shirts, which were stained and torn from working with his dairy herd. There was plenty of fabric for a large rug, even if it wouldn't be a very colorful piece.

A loud rumble of thunder reminded Abby that Zanna was out there in the darkness somewhere, probably feeling lost and alone. She closed her eyes as she clutched the last wrinkled shirt to her chest. "Lord, I'm tired and I'm at a loss for answers," she prayed above the patter of the rain on her roof, "but I can't just stand by while my sister and James—our two families—flounder in the storm that's blown into our lives. What would You have me do?"

For several moments she heard only tree branches tapping her window to the rhythm of the rain. It occurred to Abby then that while the Ordnung cautioned against interpreting Scripture, the best advice could be found in the Good Book. She went to her bedside table, where she kept her grandmother Abigail's Bible, and opened it to her bookmark at Isaiah 61, where she'd left off reading.

" 'The Spirit of the Lord God is upon me,' " Abby whispered, " 'because the Lord hath anointed me to preach good tidings unto the meek; He hath sent me to bind up the broken-hearted . . .' "

She felt tingly with goose bumps. There was no question about who was feeling meek and broken-hearted—and right now Zanna was out there getting drenched. Abby rushed to her closet for her raincoat, chiding herself for not going after her sister at the first rumble of thunder. She had no idea where to look, but she trusted God to guide her along the dark, wet roads. Wouldn't life be so much simpler if she always had such faith?

"Zanna! Zanna, come here and get in!"

Zanna turned. Was she hearing voices now, truly going insane? Shielding her eyes from the rain, she saw the lanterns of a closed carriage as it approached. How had she gotten so lost in her fear that she hadn't heard the horse's hoofbeats? Who would be out in this storm, offering her a ride?

"Get in, before you catch your death! Something told me to turn down this blacktop, or I might never have found you."

"Abby!" Zanna clambered into the carriage. All this way she'd walked, determined to fight this battle alone, yet the sound of her sister's voice—the proof of Abby's unconditional love—broke down her defenses. She bawled like a baby as the carriage lurched forward, until the sound of the rain on its roof and the muffled *clip-clop! clip-clop!* of the horse's hooves lulled her into a sense of peace.

She was safe. She would soon be dry and warm,

in a cozy bed. And she was *not* alone. All that inner struggle . . . what had it accomplished, except that she felt as worn as an old choring dress?

Zanna sighed. "I can't thank you enough, Abby."

Her sister turned, smiling tiredly in the darkness. "You've got that right," Abby teased. "We don't want you to feel thankless ever again, ain't so?"

— *Chapter 10* —

"Sister Suzanna, the members have heard your confession and have decided upon a six-week ban." Bishop Gingerich's voice resonated in the Yutzys' basement as he gazed solemnly at the young woman who knelt with her head bowed and her hand over her face. "We're not to shake your hand or eat with you, nor can we accept your gifts or assistance. We separate ourselves from you to show our love in Christ Jesus, that you might think on your sin and fully repent when your shunning has run its course."

As James focused on the knees of his black pants, his insides twisted tighter than a pretzel. During the Members' Meeting he'd been cleared of any blame for Zanna's pregnancy, yet he felt no joy in it. Before she'd left the crowded room, Zanna had tearfully confessed to her sin of the flesh, but that didn't fill the emptiness that yawned inside him.

"Do you understand the serious nature of this discipline?" the bishop continued. "Do you realize, Suzanna, that we all pray you'll return to the fold, submitting fully to God's will and ready for right living again?"

She sniffled loudly. "Jah, this is the punishment I deserve," she murmured. "I was wrong to defile the love James Graber has always shown me."

James squeezed his eyes shut, stabbed by a pain like none he'd ever endured. He'd known Zanna had a willful streak—a tendency to work things around to her own way—but never, never had he anticipated her unfaithfulness. Since he had no carriage orders lined up for the next couple of weeks, it might be best to visit kin, as he'd planned. He wouldn't collect any wedding presents, of course, but time away from this humilia-tion would do his heart good.

His dat leaned into him, talking louder than was polite because his hearing was almost gone. "Ain't that the Lambright girl, son? The one you just married?" he asked in a thin voice that carried above the crowd. "Why's she confessin' to havin' a baby? Ain't that the natural way of things?"

James clenched his jaw against a bad answer: Dat's memory had grown dimmer, and because he

125

hadn't seen for himself that the wedding was canceled, it wasn't real to him. "We'll talk about it in a few, Dat," he whispered against his father's gnarled ear. "For now, we want to be quiet so the meeting will be adjourned. Time for dinner."

"Could be Merle's seeing things clearer than we give him credit for," a voice came from the women's side of the room.

The crowd went quiet. Vernon and the two preachers tried to identify who had spoken: such an utterance was highly uncommon once the verdict had been announced. "Please stand and state your meaning," Abe Nissley insisted.

"Jah, we'll not be having any discussion after the fact," Paul confirmed. "It's not right to undermine the bishop's decision, now that we've voted."

James's temples throbbed. The Yutzys' basement was stuffy, and a lifetime's training in patience wasn't making this extended meeting any easier to endure.

Finally a lone figure rose on the far side of the room. "It's all well and gut to put the ban on Zanna," Adah Ropp ventured, "but she shouldn't bear the punishment alone."

James groaned silently. Rudy Ropp owned a large herd of Holsteins while his wife worked at the Mennonite cheese factory where they sold their milk, north of Clearwater. Some said Adah secretly favored electricity and other progressive ways because of her association with these

126

folks—even though everyone agreed you couldn't buy better cheese anywhere.

Bishop Gingerich cleared his throat. "And what are you suggesting, Sister Adah? You could have spoken up during our previous discussion."

Adah clasped her hands in front of her black apron. "Rudy and I are raising two girls near the same age as Zanna, still in their rumspringa," she said. "Plenty of parents here want to know about the fella their daughters ought to steer clear of."

Kapps bobbed. Whispers hissed among the members on both sides.

"What's Adah sayin'?" Merle demanded in a loud whisper. "Why's she askin' who—"

"Shhh!" James placed a finger on his father's lips, wishing the bishop had stifled this nonsense. "Mamm'll be giving you the *look* for talking out of turn."

Zanna's face flushed as she turned to face the women's side. "You'd better be sure you want that answer before you ask such a question, Adah Ropp."

The crowd sucked in its breath. Zanna still stood before the bishop and the preachers, and while she had appeared contrite during her confession, the headstrong young woman James knew so well had just met Adah's challenge with one of her own: another unheard-of disruption of order.

And why would that be?

James's stomach clenched again as he considered the possibilities. It was no secret that the two Ropp sons had scattered—left Cedar Creek rather than join the church or go into their dat's dairy operation. His nerves jangled. Even though he secretly wanted to confront the man who'd shamed his fiancée, a part of him didn't want to know which fellow Zanna had fallen for. After he'd waited all these years to find the right wife, losing her to a moment of misplaced passion made him feel . . . lacking, even though the situation was clearly wrong.

"What are you saying, Zanna?" Adah replied tightly. "It's not proper for you to protect that fella from your shame. And it's not right to raise a child without its father."

"Tell that to Jonny, then!" Zanna blurted out. As gasps and murmurs rose among the members, Zanna clapped a hand over her mouth and ran from the crowded room, a retching sound drifting back through the door before it could close.

Jonny Ropp, was it? What did she see in that defiant, no-account—

James crossed his arms hard, feeling trapped on that runaway roller coaster again. He wanted to chase after Zanna and demand the truth. He wanted to hitch Jonny Ropp to a carriage and make him haul the weight of this shame and humiliation.

Not that Jonny would care about what he'd done to Zanna, or to the relationship James had cherished with her. Last he'd heard, the younger Ropp boy had jumped the fence and never looked back. No one seemed to know where he was or what he was doing—

But Zanna knows. And she doesn't want to tell anyone else. Why isn't she hauling him into this ring of fire—making him own up to that one time he took advantage of—that one time she let him—

Too agitated to sit any longer, James stood up. At the same time, Abby Lambright rose from her tightly packed row of women to excuse herself, probably to go help her little sister. Adah, too, pushed sideways between female knees and the next bench, as though *she* intended to be the first to reach Zanna.

"We'll not be going anywhere until this meeting is finished and we've blessed the meal we're about to share," Vernon announced firmly. "Sit down. All of you."

With a sigh, James obeyed. Abby and Adah eased back into their places.

"We'll adjourn with no further discussion here —or any gossip about this situation once we leave," the bishop added sternly. "It's unfortunate, the way we've learned more about Suzanna's situation. But because Jonny's not joined the church, we have no means of persuading him to come forward unless he confesses of his own free will."

Vernon looked at the women and then at the

men. "So we're leaving this matter to the Lord and we'll wait and watch for His guidance. As the Good Book says, we are to be still and know that He is God. Are we in accord about this?"

Heads nodded. "Ayes" were murmured.

James closed his eyes. His temples throbbed. The airless basement was closing in on him, and he knew he couldn't sit there much longer.

"So be it, then."

As Vernon called for a moment of silent thanks for the common meal they were about to share, James felt anything but hungry. Had Zanna taken off again? Now that the rest of her secret was out, would she go elsewhere and find a way to support herself and her baby? She'd threatened to do that last night, and it wouldn't surprise him.

Or was she on her way back to Jonny?

Abby rushed out the basement door and broke free from the crowd of chatting women. Across the Yutzys' yard she raced, gazing beyond the pens of chickens and ducks, and then past the enclosures filled with the young deer that Ezra raised for northern lodges, to stock their forests for hunters. How had Zanna disappeared so quickly when she was sick to her stomach? It wasn't until Abby hurried past the large building that housed Ezra Yutzy's wooden pallet business that she heard muffled weeping.

"Oh, Zanna!" she murmured as she wrapped her

arms around the most forlorn figure she'd ever seen. "You might be under the ban, but you'll never be alone. The worst is behind you now."

Abby tucked her little sister's head against her shoulder and swayed slowly, rocking her in that ageless, instinctive rhythm, the same way she'd soothed this little soul since the day she was born. She'd been the one to comfort Sam and Barbara's little ones, too—Aunt Abby had always loved holding these children close as their breathing fell into rhythm with hers. Zanna's arms encircled her shoulders and for several moments she sobbed out her frustration and pain . . . the weight of confessing her activities as well as the name they'd all been waiting to hear.

Jonny Ropp. You had to pick the most unlikely candidate for a dat on the planet.

But wasn't it Zanna's way to leap at an enticing challenge before she considered the consequences? Abby understood Jonny's allure. Last she'd heard, the youngest and best-looking of the Ropp family had taken to driving fast cars and reveling in all the English ways he'd been denied as a child. A dairy farm's success revolved around a milking schedule that made the daily routine even more restrictive than most Amish observed, and Abby hadn't been surprised when Jonny left Cedar Creek on his sixteenth birthday without a backward glance.

Some said he'd gotten such a wayward streak

while helping Adah at the cheese factory store, where English tourists and the Mennonite owners put worldly ideas in his head. He'd toed the mark at home to avoid Rudy's discipline, but he was gone like a shot first chance he got. His brother, Gideon, left soon after that.

But what did all that matter? Right now—even though it went against the strictest sense of shunning—Abby held a young mother-to-be who felt more alone and terrified than she could admit. Zanna was under the ban, so she was to eat at a separate table at home and would remain in social quarantine until her six weeks' punishment had passed. For this energetic, sociable young woman, the members' imposing such seclusion would be akin to plucking a butterfly's wings or silencing a robin's song. Sam had said he'd make their little sister suffer for her sin, and now that they knew who'd led Zanna down the path to perdition, he would surely see that she felt the full brunt of her shunning.

Abby sighed, still rocking Zanna's shuddering form. "You're sure Jonny Ropp's the father?" she murmured. "I'm not doubting you or putting judgment on Jonny's head, understand. Just hoping you didn't blurt out his name to spite Adah for raising that question."

"Is it any wonder he left home? And Gideon, as well?" Zanna swiped at her eyes. "Can you imagine how that woman's tongue shredded her kids' confidence? And Rudy spanked them with his belt, out in the barn!"

Abby cringed. While good parents made a point of disciplining their children, Rudy Ropp's punishment seemed more heavy-handed than what most dats would do. She thought back to the Members' Meeting, when Adah Ropp had spoken out of turn. It wasn't so much that Jonny's mamm was hateful. She was just more insistent on being heard than was common among Plain women. "Some would say Adah spared the rod . . . let her younger boy pick up on those Mennonites' progressive ideas," Abby remarked quietly. "We never see our parents in the same light others do. But I believe it's a gut thing, the way you turned loose of Jonny's name."

"How can you believe that, Abby?" Zanna raised her tear-streaked face, looking wretched. "He's no more inclined to act like a dat than he is to join the church! I—I haven't even told him about the baby, knowing he'd rather run the roads with his taxi service, chattering on his cell phone, than settle down with a wife and child. Not that Mamm or Sam would let me marry him."

Abby absorbed as much of this as she could while watching the emotions shift on Zanna's pale face. Before long, Adah or Barbara or Mamm would find them here, and this heartsick young girl would clam up again. "So he drives, does he? For the Amish?"

"Jah, or whoever will hire him." She swiped at her eyes, smiling in spite of her pain. "He's on call with a couple of retirement complexes, taking folks to doctor appointments. Does a gut business carrying Plain folks to weddings and funerals at a distance, too. Makes enough that he's bought a used stretch limo for those trips."

Abby smiled. Now that Zanna was talking about Jonny, her sister had perked up and was in a frame of mind to move forward, to deal with her situation—and it seemed a fine time to glean as much information as she could. "So . . . what on earth might a stretch limo be?"

Zanna's blue eyes sparkled in spite of their red rims. "Oh, Abby, it's the loooooongest car you ever saw! The front and back ends are joined together by a stretched-out middle section that holds a lot more folks, in wider seats. Mighty fancy inside. Makes you feel like royalty, riding in it!"

And how would you know what royalty feels like? Abby heard footsteps, and she wanted to avoid any more confrontations. "Let's get you home," she suggested. "You won't be eating with us today, and I bet you're half starved—"

"Oh, Abby, I'm so hungry, I could eat my fingers!"

"—but we've got to figure a way . . . maybe Matt could drive us." They rounded the far corner of Ezra's pallet factory and saw the long tables where folks were sitting down to the sandwiches and pies the women had set out. "There, I see him."

"Jah, but he's sitting right next to James."

Abby closed her eyes against a welling up of emotions so mixed she wasn't sure what to make of them. Zanna would have to speak to James sooner or later—just as she'd have to face up to Adah Ropp and Jonny. It was their brother, Sam, who rose from his seat, however. His stride was long, as though he intended to prevent Zanna from approaching those who had just banned her.

"There'll be no more skulking about, missy!" he declared in a low voice. "Now that your carryings-on with the Ropp boy are common knowledge, everyone in Cedar Creek will be watching to see that you make gut on your promise to repent."

"Sam, she's feeling puny and I'm taking her home," Abby insisted quietly. "We wanted to see if Matt could drive us."

"And what's wrong with walking? Zanna had no trouble getting herself out of the house before the wedding, now, did she?" In the midday sun, their older brother's face looked ruddy, more etched around the eyes and where his mouth curved downward toward his beard.

When Zanna drew in a breath to protest, Abby squeezed her arm in warning. There was no point in challenging Sam's perfectly valid statement,

135

or in getting him peeved at *her.* "Jah, there's that," Abby murmured. Never mind that Indian summer had set in and the day was unseasonably warm, or that the two-and-a-half-mile walk home might make their younger sister woozy or dehydrated. "We'll go along, then. Enjoy your dinner, Sam."

Zanna's wretched expression nearly made Abby cry. One of the pies Barbara had brought was peach, Zanna's favorite, and she could use a piece of that sweet goodness herself after the morning they'd all endured. Sam returned to his seat, and there was nothing to do but head on home—or risk having Adah make another spectacle.

"All right, then," Abby murmured. For appearances' sake she stepped farther away, because the rules of shunning required her not to be in close contact with her sister. "We'll start home, and if you need to sit down, just say so. We'll find a hydrant for a cool drink, and plenty of folks between here and home would be happy to let us pick an apple from their trees."

Down the gravel driveway they walked, with Abby slowing her pace to match her sister's. The sun beat down on the backs of their necks, and the weed heads in the lane's center strip of green brushed their skirts. At the county road they turned left, and once they were walking on the blacktop, the waves of heat felt more intense.

"Do . . . do you think I'm a bad person for letting Jonny . . . do what he did?"

136

Abby smiled sadly. "I think you're young and you're human—and Jonny is, too," she added with a hopeful rise in her voice. "Maybe you're both getting your wayward streaks behind you now so you'll have an easier road later on."

"It won't be *easy,* raising a baby by myself."

"Do you really think I'd make you do that?" Abby asked gently. "Barbara and even Mamm will come around once that little punkin's born. Suckers for the wee ones, they are."

They walked for a while before Zanna stopped in the shade of an old oak tree. Her face shone pink with sweat and she looked done in. "I made a mess of things with James, Abby. How can I ever make amends?"

"Well, you could start with an apology. And follow it up with the truth." Abby smoothed her sister's kapp into place again. "James suffered a big hit. It may take him a while to come around."

"He won't want to hear about Jonny and me. What else is there to tell?"

Abby shrugged. "All you can do is apologize. You can't make him accept it, or expect him to be your gut friend again—leastaways not in the near future. For now, you have to keep yourself healthy, and serve out your six weeks so you can be reinstated in gut standing."

Zanna nodded forlornly. "It's all so scary now . . . and my feelings jump around like grasshoppers, sky-high happy one minute and lower than mud the next. Just when I decide something would be a gut move, everything changes. And then I do something stupid. Or I throw up."

"Oh, Zanna, I can't imagine what your body's going through, not to mention your mind." Abby looked around, but the nearest hydrant was at the Detweiler place a half mile down the road. "Do you want to wait here in the shade while I fetch you some water? Or can you—"

"Don't leave me, Abby. *Please.*" Zanna's eyes widened as she clutched Abby's hands.

Where had such fear come from? They'd walked this road since they were kids—knew every place around Cedar Creek and all the families who lived there. Did the poor girl think Adah or James had followed them to lecture her some more?

"I'm right here," she replied. *Please, dear Lord, let me see the next right thing to do so Zanna doesn't collapse before I get her home.*

Her sister nodded, and then tilted her head. "There's a buggy coming. Hope it's somebody likely to give us a ride."

"And who wouldn't?" Abby gazed back the way they'd come, hoping the driver would be sympathetic to their plight. She, too, had grown weary of raised voices and constant stress. Some quiet time in her porch swing with a glass of cold lemonade would bring her closer to God than she'd felt all day. And how she needed that chance to listen for the still, small voice of calm that might guide her in the coming weeks.

"Well, now, would you look at this," Abby murmured. "It seems our Phoebe has hitched a ride with Owen Coblentz."

"High time, too." A sly grin brightened Zanna's face. "All the while Owen was building your new place, Phoebe could hardly keep her eyes in their sockets."

"Took Owen a while to figure that out, did it? He seemed mighty intent on his work all those months—like maybe he felt her watching but didn't know what to do about it." Abby stepped closer to the road, waving happily as the buggy halted beside them. "Going our way?"

The young couple's two bright smiles lifted her spirits. "When we noticed how puny Zanna was looking, I took it as my cue to leave—not that I told anybody we were coming after you two." Phoebe scooted closer to her handsome driver, reaching for her younger aunt's hand. "I tucked some sandwiches and a couple slices of pie into the basket for you, and Owen poured a big jar of water."

"Best news I've heard all day—right, Zanna?"

"Jah, I'm parched and starving after all the goings-on at the service," Zanna replied as she clambered into the backseat. "I wasn't going to make it one step farther. Denki for thinking of us."

"Jah, double that denki." Abby joined Zanna in

the back and then lifted the picnic basket between them. "Just goes to show how the Lord truly does provide. You've got to love a cold drink, fresh pie, and a ride home—and gut company. Ain't so, Phoebe?"

Her niece's cheeks turned a pretty pink. "You and Zanna are the *best* company, Aunt Abby," she teased. "Owen's a lucky fella to have the three of us along."

— *Chapter 11* —

Monday afternoon James slipped into the back room of his carriage shop. The CLOSED sign would stay in the front window because he wasn't ready to deal with people, but coming here to work offered his only chance at regaining some peace . . . some perspective, after all the surprises of the past weekend. Running the Members' Meeting through his mind again and again was driving him crazy, yet he couldn't stop. Zanna's confession filled his memory: the way her hand shook as it covered her face . . . his name on her lips as she admitted she'd been wrong to betray him, to forsake the love he'd shown her.

Jonny Ropp. Jonny Ropp! Of all the fellas she could have chosen . . .

James walked through his large back room, where he parked wagons awaiting repair and the buggies and carriages that he was constructing for customers. It was a senseless exercise, second-guessing why Zanna had succumbed to such a hellion as Jonny Ropp. What James needed was work to occupy his mind, his hands. He perched on the stool at his workbench, where a large piece of creamy white upholstery leather awaited the clear beads and fake jewels that would transform a basic rig into a carriage fit for an amusement park princess.

Lo, I am with you always, even unto the end of the world.

James frowned as he tried again and again to thread a large needle. "So why weren't You with Zanna, that moment when she forgot her promises?" he muttered. It was wrong to challenge the Scripture that ran through his mind—probably a form of blasphemy akin to contradicting Christ—but the words had come out before he could stop them.

It might have happened just that fast for Zanna, too. In the heat of the moment with a silver-tongued devil, she forgot the Old Ways she'd been raised with—just as Eve succumbed to the serpent.

James blinked. He was no more immune to a lingering kiss and deep eye contact than Zanna was. And had he been alone with her when he was Jonny's age, before he'd joined the church . . . oh, temptation would have been so easy to fall into.

The memory of Zanna's kiss made him knock the open box of beads off his workbench. He cried out in frustration as dozens of shiny fake diamonds rolled all over the floor and underneath his equipment. What he didn't need was another mess to clean up—and was that someone tapping on the window?

He looked up to see Abby . . . dear, dependable Abby Lambright, peering in at him. He wasn't in the mood to talk, but he could hardly send her away, either. He opened the side door. "Be careful as you come in," he warned her. "It's one of those days when every little thing's getting on my nerves. A whole box of beads just scattered all over the floor."

"Goodness, James, I've never seen your shop when it had such a sparkle! Here." Abby handed him a small brown bottle and then laid aside the clothing draped over her arm. "I'm on my way over to see Emma, with a couple of new dresses I've started for your mamm. I noticed you hadn't come to the mercantile for your break this afternoon, and I thought some homemade root beer might hit the spot."

"No need for a break when I haven't been working—and my shop fellas are on paid vacation for a few more days yet." He tipped the bottle to his lips to savor the cool, spicy sweetness of a beverage Barbara Lambright was especially good at making; at any given time, several bottles of root beer sat brewing in Sam's cellar. "How'd you know I'd be needing this?"

Abby snatched the whisk broom off his workbench and began sweeping beads into the dustpan. "Even without what's been going on with Zanna, it's a mighty warm Indian summer day. I'm hoping this heat won't come between us, James."

James blotted his mouth on his shirtsleeve. He admired her for being the one to offer an olive branch, even though he certainly didn't blame Abby for her sister's waywardness. Before he'd downed half the root beer, Abby had plucked a polishing rag from his shelf and emptied most of the beads onto it. With quick, efficient grace she rolled the fake gemstones up in the cloth and used the bundle to wipe the dust from his floor. "You're a saint, Abby."

Abby's face turned a pretty pink. "Nah. Just your average garden-variety sinner. I've made plenty of mistakes in my day and I'll make lots more." She smiled up at him, looking so serene and wise. Her gentle friendship, along with the sight of her glossy brown hair, tucked neatly under her kapp, and her sparkling brown eyes made James feel a lot better.

"Well, if you're a garden-variety sinner, you must be a daisy or one of your mamm's mums," he remarked. "Me, I'm surely a weed. Pesky as a dandelion."

She shrugged. "Dandelions make mighty gut wine, they say—and greens—you know. And truth be told, there's nothing that brightens a spring day like a hillside dotted with those little yellow flowers." Abby picked up his needle and threaded it without a second thought. She studied the crisscross of lines on the white leather, which marked where the beads should be stitched on the back of the carriage's seat.

Her smile soothed him. James exhaled some of his tension, realizing he felt better just being in her presence. Wasn't it just like Abby to see something as lowly as a dandelion in such a positive light?

"And I reckon Zanna's like a morning glory," Abby continued in a wistful voice. "Lovely and fresh. Able to take hold and grow just about anywhere."

James swallowed more of his root beer. He had no idea where Abby was going with this line of thought, but he allowed his mind to follow her easy talk because it surely was an improvement over his previous fretting. She pulled the needle up through the leather . . . dropped two of the sparkly hollow beads down the length of thread, and then poked the needle through the heavy upholstery material again.

"But like the morning glories out amongst our

crops," Abby went on, "Zanna tends to grow best where she's not supposed to, and twines herself around every plant and post until it's a real effort to get rid of her." Her smile went lopsided. "Not that anyone wants to see Zanna gone. Even if she's caused us more trouble lately than we'd like."

And didn't that perfectly sum up Suzanna Lambright? James sighed, aware of how Zanna's blue eyes brought to mind the shade of the morning glories his mamm trained up the trellis alongside the porch. "You make it hard to hate her," he murmured, "even if I want to."

"So maybe you can find it in your heart to forgive her?"

James pressed the cool glass bottle against his lips. *Abby nailed you with that one,* his conscience taunted. "Doesn't she have to ask me to forgive her?"

"Why?" Again Abby shrugged. James didn't see how she could have planned this conversation, but she was playing it to her best advantage. "It's up to us older ones to lead by example. It's a bothersome thing my sister's done, throwing her life and everyone else's into such a tailspin, but in six months it'll bring us a miracle. Maybe God thought we needed one."

His jaw dropped. Once again Abby had brought him to a point he couldn't refute, and while he didn't feel overjoyed, he was at least more settled and able to see beyond his wounded pride.

After all, hadn't he been proven innocent at church yesterday? And while Zanna had ripped out his heart with her unfaithfulness, at least she hadn't married him and then tried to pass off the baby as his. She'd called the wedding to a halt in her own way. And once he got past this wild ride, driven by such intense emotions, he might find out it was the best thing that could have happened to him.

"Did I say something that rubbed you the wrong way, James? That wasn't my intention." Abby looked up from her sewing. Somehow, while he'd been lost in thought, she'd covered an entire diagonal line with beads. She knotted the heavy thread and began on the next line over.

"No, Abby," he murmured. "You just gave me plenty more to think about. I guess we'll see how it all works out as time goes along." James found a smile for her then. "Thanks, Abby—for the root beer and your quick stitching, too. I'm not nearly as handy with a needle and thread as you are."

"Do you suppose that's why I call my business Abby's Stitch in Time?" she said in a teasing tone. Her brown eyes sparkled, and in a few more minutes she had completed a job that would probably have taken James the rest of the day. "I'd best be getting over to visit with Emma about these clothes for your folks. She'll wonder what's happened to me."

And what's happened to me? James thought. Whereas he had been feeling antsy and out of kilter, mad at the world, he now had a more positive outlook, a reason to let go of his anger—or at least some of it.

"Have a gut afternoon, James." Abby picked up the clothing and started for the door. "Just leave that empty bottle at the store—or bring it over to the house. We'd still enjoy seeing you, you know."

He returned her smile. "Denki again for the root beer—and the gut advice," he called after her.

As Abby waved from the doorway, it seemed he should be saying something more to such a fine friend. But he couldn't think what it would be, or how to say it the right way, as Abby would. So he left it alone.

As Abby stepped onto the front porch at the Graber house, she hesitated. She'd spent a lot of time here with Emma, especially in their growing-up years: the gray enameled porch floor and the wooden swing hanging to her left seemed as familiar as those at her own home. She prayed that she and Emma would remain gut, close friends again. They had parted under a cloud, and a lot more of Zanna's story had come to light since then, too.

She knocked loudly, and then waited to hear footsteps coming through the house. No doubt

Emma was trying to catch up on her afternoon chores now that the four Grabers had eaten their noon meal. As her best friend opened the door, Abby smiled warmly.

"Emma! I picked out some fabric, and then I cut pattern pieces to fit your mamm, from the clothes you put in my rag bin," she ventured. Abby patted the partially sewn dresses that were draped over her arm.

"That was fast work—especially considering what all happened with Zanna over the weekend." Emma held open the door. The Grabers' front room seemed a little more cluttered than usual, its cream-colored walls a little more scuffed than Abby recalled . . . but it was her cluttered, scuffed conscience that concerned her now.

"Emma, I'm always happy to sew for your family," Abby began, "but Saturday when you were up in my sewing nook, I felt awful bad about—"

"Oh, Abby, I'm sorry I got so huffy!" Emma grabbed her in a quick hug, her eyes shining with tears. "There wasn't a thing you could do about the way the Coblentz twins and your sister spread that story about Zanna's baby. I—I was just shocked and I felt bad for James, not mad at *you!*"

"Sorry I snapped at you, too, Emma." Abby shifted the pieces of fabric on her arm to show her best friend the colors she'd chosen. "They're basted and ready to try on, if you and your mamm have a minute."

"I don't know how you get so much done, Abby. Come to the kitchen," Emma added as she walked in that direction. "The light's better in there at this time of day. I'll get Mamm."

Abby followed Emma between the two upholstered rocking chairs, past the long sofa in the front room, and then into the Grabers' kitchen. While her friend went down the cellar steps, Abby smiled at James and Emma's dat. "How are you today, Merle?" she asked.

He was seated at one end of the big table, intent on picking the nutmeats from cracked black walnuts. He popped a chunk of walnut into his mouth as though he had no idea Abby was there.

Abby smiled and laid the clothes over the back of a chair. "Those are gut-looking nuts in your bowl, Merle," she said in a much louder voice. "Did your trees put out a lot of walnuts this year?"

"Hmm?" He blinked and then grinned at her. "Abby Lambright! Didn't hear you come in. Eunice keeps me mighty busy, you know."

"Helps you stay out of trouble," Abby teased. She was used to the way Merle didn't always answer what she'd asked him.

Eunice's reedy voice came up the cellar stairs then. "Jah, and we can keep an eye on him better when we sit him there, too," she remarked. When she reached the top step, Emma's mamm peered across the kitchen, adjusting eyeglasses with thick, pointy-cornered lenses. "Some days we can't tell from one minute to the next what Merle might take a notion to do. Now what's this Emma tells me about you sewin' up some new dresses? I wasn't any too happy about her clearin' out my old ones, you know."

Abby smiled patiently. "Jah, it's hard to let go of our favorite clothes," she said with a nod, "but the snow will be blowing soon. We can't have you shivering in dresses that are worn thin. If you'll try this on for me, Eunice, I can get the sizing right for the black church dresses—"

"Now, Merle, are you paying attention to what you're doing?" Eunice crossed the linoleum floor, making a racket in her sturdy, hard-heeled shoes. "If I bake these walnuts into a coffee cake and somebody bites into a piece of—look at that shell!" She plucked a large dark shard from the nutmeats her husband had sorted on a dinner plate. "I would've lost a tooth if I'd bit into that! And the dentist would've cost a pretty penny, too!"

"But that didn't happen, Mamm," Emma pointed out with a patient smile. "And that's because you and I always sift through Dat's nut chunks after he's finished."

"He's not paying one bit of attention," Eunice continued, throwing up her hands. "Some days I don't know why I bother talking to him! Now, what've you got here, Abby?"

When Emma raised her eyebrows and gave Abby an apologetic look, Abby smiled back. It was a wonder Emma wasn't going a little crazy, dealing with her difficult parents day in and day out. As she held up one of the basted dresses so Eunice could see it better, Emma's face lit up. "Look at this pretty teal fabric, Mamm!" she said, her voice rising with excitement. "And this cranberry dress reminds me of the Christmas quilt you and I made a few years ago."

Eunice's eyebrows flickered above her glasses, as though she were about to make another critical remark, but then she blinked and ran her fingers over the deep red fabric with a sigh. "I miss sewing, you know it?" she murmured. "Used to make all our clothes, but I can't see gut enough to thread a needle anymore. Makes me cranky sometimes, gettin' old does."

Abby's throat tightened. What a blessing it was that her own mamm was still able to cook and sew—and that running Treva's Greenhouse gave her days a purpose and kept her in contact with other people. "We all take our turns at being cranky, Eunice," she remarked quietly. "I picked these colors from the new fabric we just got in. And the way this polyester crepe washes up, you can dry these dresses on hangers and they won't need to be ironed."

Behind her mother, Emma flashed Abby a thumbs-up sign and a grateful grin. "We'll be right back after Mamm tries on a dress."

As the two women left the kitchen, Abby took a chair across from Merle. The kitchen looked clean, but not as tidy as Barbara kept hers—probably because Emma had plenty to do without cleaning every little corner of it each day. Maybe it was best that seventeen-year-old Zanna had realized she wasn't cut out to care for James's aging parents . . .

"I put that big piece of nutshell in there to see if Eunice was payin' attention, you know." Merle smiled sweetly, and Abby couldn't help laughing with him. She'd never once heard James and Emma's dat lash out in anger, and it was good to see his sense of humor had remained intact.

"That *is* a mighty fine shade of red, Abby. Like a Red Delicious apple." Merle's wrinkled face lit up with a boyish grin. "Takes me back to when we were courtin', and Eunice had more spring in her step—and more smiles on her face, too," he added in a wistful tone. "She wore red quite a bit back then. One time she made dresses for herself and the three oldest girls that got Beulah Mae Nissley and the other gals talking about how colorful they were. Worldly and immodest, they said."

Abby smiled. Merle Graber might be slipping a little memory-wise, but when he recalled his past he always got such a glow on his face.

"I put a stop to that nonsense," he added with an emphatic nod of his head. "Asked the bishop if Beulah Mae and the others might be showin' signs of covetousness. Pointed out how God had made cardinals and dark cherries and poinsettias that shade of red. Vernon agreed with me, and that ended that kind of talk."

"I remember those dresses you're talking about," Abby replied with a grin. "My older sisters and I wanted dresses from that same bolt of cloth. That was back when Dat was running the store—"

"And how is Leroy? Haven't seen him around much." Merle peered intently at her, perfectly sincere.

Should she correct Merle . . . remind him of Dat's passing? Or should she humor him? Abby felt a pang of sadness for the cruel way old age was treating James and Emma's parents, and she was glad when Eunice returned to the kitchen wearing the basted teal dress.

Emma came around from behind her mother, smiling. "I told Mamm how awfully nice she looks in a dress that has some perk to it. Reminded her that it's no sin to replace worn-out clothes—especially since you make them into rugs, Abby."

"Not much goes to waste," Abby agreed. She moved quickly around the older woman, checking to see that the sleeves joined the shoulder seams at the tops of her arms rather than sloping down too far. "How do you like it, Eunice? Does it fit the way you want it to?"

Emma's mother smoothed her wrinkled hand over the fabric. "I like it fine," she replied with an edge to her voice, "but it's such an extravagance, havin' you sew me four new dresses at one time, Abby."

Abby had a feeling Emma had gotten a talking-to while she helped her mother try on this dress. She considered her reply as she knelt to look at the length.

"A three-inch hem should be gut," Emma suggested purposefully. "I'm thinking you can use this dress as the guide for the other ones, Abby. And as long as Dat's trousers follow the same size as the ones I pitched out—but an inch shorter—they'll be fine, too."

Abby heard her cue to leave: her friend was trying to prevent another unpleasant lecture from her mother. "Jah, I can do that. Thanks for checking the hem size for me."

"We sure do appreciate such personalized service," Emma added. "I bet you've got lots of orders to sew up, so we shouldn't be taking any more of your time." She turned to her mother then, her smile looking a little weary. "Let's get this dress off you, Mamm, so Abby can take it back with her."

As she waited, Abby watched Merle pick out a few more nutmeats. He was meticulous about it, seeming engrossed in his work and happily occupied. There was no missing how he and

James resembled each other, the way they both held their mouths just so as they concentrated, and the matching noses and strong, broad hands—though Merle's fingers trembled slightly as he held the metal pick.

When Emma bustled back into the kitchen, Abby gathered the clothing she'd brought over, glad that her friend wanted to escort her to the door.

"Bye, Abby!" Merle called behind her. "Tell your mamm and Barbara I'd be happy to pick out their walnuts, too. I know they're busy, and it helps me pass the time."

"I'll do that, Merle. You take care, now."

As she and Emma stepped out onto the front porch, Abby lowered her voice. "Do your folks need to be careful about the money? If you can't pay what I usually charge—"

"Puh! Abby!" Emma grabbed both of her hands, her eyes wide. "The farm's crops and James's business are doing better than ever. Lately Mamm's been pinching pennies until Mr. Lincoln yelps, and there's no need for it. It's not like we're extravagant, and we're certainly not poor."

"Thrift and frugality are habits we all learned from our mamms—and they learned from their mamms. I just didn't want to cause a problem for you."

"Denki, Abby. Those dresses are just what she needs, maybe to feel better about herself." Emma gripped Abby's fingers before letting go of them. "Some folks have a hard time being happy about anything."

"There's that," Abby agreed. "We're most of us about as happy as we decide to be."

Emma cleared her throat as she looked past the mercantile to the big white house across the road. "And what about Zanna? Is *she* happy now, Abby?"

How could she answer that? Abby let her gaze follow two black and white dogs as they herded a cluster of sheep toward the sheep sheds. "I believe my sister's done the right things, taking on her shunning and deciding to raise the baby," she replied quietly. "Sometimes we've got to wait and see how the Lord works it all out, and be happy that He's in charge instead of us."

As Abby left the mercantile late Tuesday afternoon, she felt the heaviness of an approaching storm: the sky loomed gray in the distance and she smelled rain on the breeze. The sheep huddled near the fence, bleating and bawling as they nudged toward the trough. Customers had chatted about the season's first real cold front bringing a heavy frost and maybe some snow this evening.

Abby stepped into Barbara's kitchen and inhaled deeply. "Smells gut, girls! What're you cooking up?" she asked Gail and Phoebe. Ruthie grinned at her from the far end of the table, where she was setting places for dinner.

"Had some day-old dinner rolls at the shop, so we baked a hen. Creamed the meat with celery and onions to ladle over top of them," Gail replied. "Mamm got called to help with a birthing—"

"Marian Byler's having her twins, more than a month early," Phoebe added in a concerned tone.

"—so it might be a while before she gets home."

Abby washed her hands. Marian had been a classmate, and now she supplied the mercantile and area gift shops with her handmade soaps. She'd been feeling poorly for most of her pregnancy. "How much of Zanna did you see today? It's too bad she's not allowed to keep cleaning her houses—at least until she's showing more," Abby remarked. "The six weeks of her ban will drag by, especially since she needs to earn money for baby things. But Sam said she wasn't to be out and around—"

"And you'll not be changing my mind about that, either," her brother said, coming through the kitchen door along with a gust of chilly wind. He glanced around the kitchen. "And where might your mother be, girls?"

"Off to Bylers' for a delivery." Gail stood straighter at the stove, stirring the creamed chicken to keep it from sticking to the pan, while Phoebe arranged rolls on a cookie sheet for warming.

Sam's eyebrow rose. "We won't wait for her.

Matt's got a couple ewes needing attention, and what with it getting dark earlier, he and I will be going to the barn as soon as we eat." He glanced out the window, toward the road. "Here comes Mamm, finally. She needed help covering her plants before tonight's frost, but Zanna was nowhere to be found."

Gail and Phoebe exchanged a glance. Their smiles faded as they looked to Abby for support. "She's napping, Dat," Ruthie replied quietly. "Been feeling puny ever since she tossed up her lunch."

Sam hung his denim coat onto a peg behind the door. "Might as well call that sort of behavior to a halt right here and now. I'll be back in a few, when I've rousted her out of bed. Then we'll eat."

His boots clomped heavily on the plank floor, and Abby knew better than to plead on Zanna's behalf. She swung open the door, smiling at her mother. "And here you are, Mamm! Busy day at the greenhouse?" she asked cheerfully. "Looks like you ducked in just ahead of the rain."

"Jah, and now we know why folks have been snippy all day, too. Big changes in the weather coming, they say." She removed her shawl, her gaze lingering on the tiny table set off about ten feet from the main one, where Zanna would eat as part of her shunning. "Why do I have a feeling Sam's gone to fetch your sister, Abby? He's been none too happy since he heard a truck of baking supplies from Lancaster overturned. Icy roads out that way."

"Jah, we'd promised Lois Yutzy a crate of flour," Abby replied. "She didn't help his mood much, saying she'd have to buy her supplies at the store in Clearwater—"

"I'm walking as fast as I can, Sam! If it were *you* feeling pukey—" Zanna's voice cracked as she preceded their brother into the kitchen.

"I wasn't the one who broke my promises by running around with Jonny Ropp. You had your dance and now you're paying the piper, missy."

Biting back an attempt to smooth things over, Abby stepped to the stove to help her nieces. Her heart ached: Zanna looked wretched, with dark crescents under her eyes and her kapp askew from being put on in a hurry. Matt came inside then, and they all sat down at the big table—everyone but Zanna, who slumped at the small folding table, all alone. They prayed silently. Zanna waited until all the dishes had been passed around before she came over to fill her plate.

"Better take more than half that roll, Zanna," Mamm urged gently. "And as gut as this creamed chicken smells, it'll set just right in a jittery stomach. This stage will pass."

Zanna shrugged halfheartedly. She took two spoonfuls of the chicken mixture and returned to her place. Sam and Matt ate heartily, discussing the ewes, while the rest of them remained silent.

Abby had no doubt, however, that the topic would change before long: her brother had allowed Zanna to sit in uneasy peace yesterday and at breakfast, but it wasn't his way to let important questions go unasked.

As Sam took the first slice of apple pie, he gazed pointedly across the kitchen. "And how did you spend your day, Suzanna? Mamm could have used your help with covering her hanging baskets—"

"I'm sorry, Mamm," Zanna murmured.

"—and when I said you weren't to clean houses anymore, I didn't mean you could spend your days in bed," Sam went on. "We've got another six weeks of your ban—and six months of this *situation*. So we'd best settle some things here and now."

"It's not a situation, Sam," Mamm remarked. "It's a baby, and we're to care for it as one of God's children—"

"So where's Jonny Ropp, now that he's caused such a ruckus?" the man at the head of the table asked. "And why on earth did you hook up with *him?*"

The kitchen rang with an uneasy silence. Zanna swallowed, her head hung low. "He and I were scholars together all through school, you know," she murmured. Her fork clattered to her plate and she left it there. "It wasn't like I took up with a stranger."

"Well, hasn't Jonny always been stranger than most?" Sam glanced around for acknowledgment of his play on words, but everyone else remained focused on the pie they were passing. "What's *strange* is that you knew better, Zanna. I'm figuring you hadn't been engaged to James but three months—not to mention how your kneeling vows from joining the church should've still been fresh in your head. Does your faith mean nothing to you?"

Abby's eyes widened. Their brother didn't need to be such a bully with his words, but there was no telling him that. When she opened her mouth, Mamm squeezed her wrist, reminding her to keep her opinions to herself. A silence darker than the storm's clouds filled the kitchen. They all jumped at a sudden crack of thunder, which seemed to further inspire Sam's tirade.

"So now that you're catching the brunt of the trouble, little sister, what's Jonny planning to do about this baby he's made?"

A sob escaped Zanna and she curled over until her face nearly touched her plate. She didn't speak for a long moment. "I . . . haven't told him. Haven't seen him since—"

"Well, then, it's time to pay that boy a visit. Or, since you're so chatty on the phone," her interrogator added wryly, "you might want to call his cell and fill him in. If he won't stand by you, it tells the tale about what a fence jumper he is—seeking out selfish pleasure rather than taking responsibility for what he's done to you."

Sam paused to shove a large bite of pie into his mouth. Abby fidgeted with her napkin. Matt eased his chair back from the table. "Got to see to those ewes," he murmured. "May I please be excused, Dat?"

Sam dismissed him with a wave. "I'll be there in a few. Soon as your aunt Zanna gives me some answers that mean something."

Zanna's whimper tore at Abby's heart. Through the window she saw the dim lanterns on the front of a carriage, and hoped it was Barbara—or anyone else who would give Sam a reason to stop hounding their sister. True enough, he was asking questions that needed to be addressed, but he'd never known how to deal with women when their emotions came into play.

"I told you, I'm raising this baby!" Zanna insisted in a shaky voice. "I've saved away most of my cleaning money, and I'll be a gut mother—"

"You have no idea, missy," Sam replied. "And why you humiliated James is beyond me, too. Such a dependable, steady man he is. You could've been making a new home with him instead of putting us all through the wringer over a no-account—"

"All right, then! Here's an answer for you!" Zanna rose, composing her thoughts as she braced herself behind her chair. "There's nobody I'd rather be living with than James," she began. She was glaring at Sam, continuing while she still had her nerve up—before he could challenge her again. "It's Eunice I can hardly stand to be in the same room with! What with her constantly fussing at Merle, and him not responding, it's like a—a circus gone haywire over there."

Abby glanced at Mamm. This revelation came as no surprise, as Eunice had stung them all with her tongue over the years. But what a sad truth Zanna had confessed—the real reason, at last, for her unthinkable behavior.

"They're James's parents." Sam stood up, as well, wearing a look of total disbelief. "James can't help who they are—or the *way* they are as they get up in years. He and his sister are doing their best."

"Eunice has never liked me. She thinks I'm not gut enough for her son." Zanna swiped at her eyes but managed to keep talking. "She never thought I should be cleaning houses, either, when you and Mamm have work in your stores I could be doing."

Mamm sat forward to comment, but Abby nudged her under the table.

"That's not Eunice's concern, is it?" Sam pointed out. "We've known all along storekeeping's not to your liking when things get slow. You have to ignore what other people think."

163

"Well, there's no ignoring the way Eunice gawks at me through those awful old glasses," Zanna cried. "And she talks about me like I'm not even in the room. And the way she squawks at poor Merle for every little thing—why, it might've been her constant yammering that made him have that breakdown. That voice of hers could wake the dead."

Sam's girls glanced at each other, their lips twitching. Abby had overheard other folks say those very things about the decline in Merle Graber's health, but this was no time to point it out to Sam.

"Merle had a stroke," their brother stated emphatically. "It's not our place to speculate about why—"

"Can you imagine living with that racket day in and day out?" Zanna grimaced as tears streamed down her cheeks. It took her a moment to find her voice again. "I—I feel real bad about the way I treated James, but I don't see how he and Emma stand it. I knew if I married him, I'd be saying things I shouldn't—or going crazy myself. And I didn't know how to tell him."

Mamm sighed sadly. "Well, there it is," she murmured.

Nodding, Abby noted that Zanna looked so young and so devastated, gripping the sides of her chair as though to hold her life together. Her head hung so low that the strings of her kapp dangled above her untouched dinner. It didn't help to know that James had probably been counting on Zanna's sunny personality to brighten that household across the road. And her sister's admission, while more complete than what she'd confessed in church, didn't really solve anything, did it?

Sam slid his chair under the table with a *whack,* preparing to leave. "That's the most useless, juvenile excuse I've ever—why, if my kids hinted they felt that way about me and their mother—"

"You know that's not true, Dat!" Phoebe exclaimed.

"We'd never feel—it's a whole different life in this house," Gail chimed in.

"—I'd order them out," Sam continued sharply. "They've been raised to respect their elders, just like you were, Suzanna, and—"

The kitchen door blew out of Barbara's hand and banged against the wall as she stepped in out of the storm. Her black bonnet dripped and her wet coat clung to her shivering figure as she bent to take off her saturated shoes.

"Let me help you." Ruthie jumped up from her chair, as eager as the rest of them for this diversion. While Barbara's youngest took her bonnet, Gail and Phoebe draped her soaked coat over the pegs and put a towel beneath it.

The lines were etched more deeply than usual in Barbara's face. Her eyes, normally a sparkly brown after a delivery, somberly took in the scene as she stood on the rug. Clearly, the nasty weather had been the least of her worries.

"Let me reheat the rest of this creamed chicken and fix you a plate," Abby said as she took the serving bowl to the stove. "Looks like things didn't go so well with Marian."

"An ambulance took her to the emergency room. The babies are early, but I think the first one will be fine." Her pause—what she didn't say—made everyone's eyes widen sadly. "The second twin's cord got tangled while the first one was coming out, and . . . well, there's no telling how much brain damage happened when her oxygen got cut off. No way to anticipate such a trauma," she said with a sigh, "nor do I think a hospital team could have done any better. Even so, I'm feeling mighty low about it."

Lord Jesus, I ask Your comfort and tender mercy for poor Marian and Carl and their babies—and Barbara, too, Abby prayed as she stood at the stove. Babies had a lot of folks in an uproar lately, it seemed. And in a way, she was grateful that her maidel status meant she'd not endure the risks and discomfort of childbirth.

Which means it's your calling to comfort those who face such trials and heartache . . . to bind up the brokenhearted.

The thought came at Abby from out of nowhere, but she recognized that still, small voice, didn't she? She stood for a moment, her head bowed over the pot she stirred.

Barbara cleared her throat. She took in Zanna's tear-streaked face and Sam's high color as they stood across the large kitchen from each other. "I heard your raised voices as I was coming in, and I'm saying right now that I've had enough conflict and despair for one day," she stated solemnly. "Life is precious. We shouldn't waste it making other people feel small and worthless, nor should we cry over spilled milk and make endless excuses," she added. "We should love each other. We should do the work God's given us. It's as simple—and as complicated—as that."

— *Chapter 12* —

The next morning, Zanna moved her clothes into Abby's spare bedroom before breakfast. No one consulted Sam about her change of residence, but he made no fuss about it: Abby thought her brother seemed quieter, maybe because Barbara's request for less disagreement and despair was sinking in. The cold drizzle kept traffic in the mercantile to a minimum, so Abby decided to spend the dreary afternoon at home working on the rag rug Adah Ropp had ordered before all the hoopla about Zanna's baby had kicked up.

"Will you be needing anything before I leave?" Abby asked her brother.

Sam had arranged a big display of apples from Mose Hartzler's orchard, and he was filling the shelf alongside it with jars of apple butter that Mose's wife, Hannah, made to sell in their roadside stand and local stores. "Nope," he replied. "Unless you've got answers to all those questions concerning our sister."

Abby smiled gently. He looked older today, yet he seemed drained of the temper he'd spewed last night—maybe because he enjoyed this physical work in the store. "It's not what you want to hear, Sam, but sometimes—like Vernon said on Sunday—we have to watch and wait. We can't always know what lies ahead, and we've got to have faith that the right things will happen for Zanna—and for Jonny Ropp and James and the rest of us, as well."

"Easier said than done."

"I'll keep praying on it." She tugged his beard affectionately. "Your name will come up when I do. Did I hear you say another truckload of flour and spices is on its way from Lancaster?"

"It's arriving tomorrow afternoon, they tell me."

"Gut. I know a couple pairs of hands that will be happy to bag those for you."

As Abby stepped out the front door of the Cedar

Creek Mercantile, she noticed that a light burned inside the carriage shop across the road. It meant James was working on that glittery white carriage again, and for that she was thankful. Next door, at Treva's Greenhouse, Mamm's silhouette moved inside the fogged glass walls as she tended houseplants and the potted mums she'd brought inside when the weather had turned colder.

Before long, snow would be clinging to the hillsides. No matter what sorts of trouble people caused, it was comforting to know that the seasons would still come and go. Fall would be followed by Thanksgiving and Christmas, with all their extra baking and celebrations, and for that Abby was grateful, too. The upcoming holidays were a reminder that no matter how unsettling their daily life became—mostly because of the mistakes folks made, thinking they knew best— God was in charge. The trick was to accept this, to submit to His higher wisdom, and to patiently believe that all things were possible for Him, even when all hope seemed lost.

As Abby entered her house and walked through the kitchen, she felt a welling up of gladness. Zanna sat at the table by the window. She looked rested, and she was ripping out the hems and seams of the old clothing they'd collected at the store. "I figured you'd be starting a rug soon, and I'm in the mood for ripping strips," she announced.

"That's gut," Abby replied with a wry smile, "on

account of how I need to write up my piece for the *Budget*. But jah, I'll be needing a rug soon, and yours are just the hands I want working on it, too."

Zanna's brows rose. "You realize it's been a while since I made a rag rug, ain't so? I hope it's all right that I want to use your big crochet hook rather than braiding coils and then stitching them together."

"I like that method best myself. The rug's easier to handle as you work, and it'll hold together better." Abby went to the cabinet in her front room and came back with a large box. "I've got some fabric scraps left from the last quilting frolic, too. Adding in these new prints will brighten up those old clothes—because we want this to be a special rug, Zanna," Abby added in a thoughtful tone. "A true work of your hands and heart."

Her sister glanced up warily from a faded brown dress she'd cut some notches in. "And why are we saying this piece will be any different? Your rugs always turn out better than anyone else's, Abby. Mine won't be as flat and even and perfect as yours."

Abby smiled, and then took her writing tablet from the kitchen drawer. She put on a kettle for tea. "It's for Adah Ropp. She ordered a rug while you were away."

Defiance clouded Zanna's blue eyes. "If you think I want to—"

"I think you'll see this as a way to mend some

170

fences. To offer up a gift that says you can rise above Adah's sharp remarks," Abby replied. "Adah's none too happy about what her boy's done this time—on top of jumping the fence and not associating with his dat these past few years."

Abby wasn't surprised to see the resistance rising in her sister's face, but the more she thought about it, the more perfect this idea seemed. "Consider it a peace offering, Zanna—a gut thing to work on while you're under the ban, don't you think?" she murmured. "When you do your best work for somebody who rubs you the wrong way, you show the kind of love Barbara was talking about last night. And besides that," Abby added with a grin, "when we deliver the rug, it'll be you Adah's paying."

Zanna's shoulders were rising like a cantankerous cat's. "Maybe this isn't such a gut idea, Abby. Adah's sure to find all sorts of things wrong with a rug *I* make—"

"That's why it has to be the prettiest, sturdiest rag rug anybody's ever made for her."

"Maybe I could work it up and we'll say *you* did." Zanna widened her eyes, pleading like a little girl.

"Then the money will be mine, sister. Think on it while you're ripping those strips."

Abby poured boiling water into two mugs, added tea bags, and then sat at the opposite end of the table from Zanna. Through the back window,

171

the view of the brightly colored maple trees and sweet gums usually inspired her—except last night's wind had stripped off most of their leaves. It was yet another reminder that winter would soon arrive . . . and watching Zanna rip strips gave her an idea for the piece she'd write.

It was a mysterious process, putting words on paper. Abby had found that composing her thoughts for a *Budget* article often clarified her feelings about the events she reported. And if ever she had needed more clarity, the time was now. So much had happened so quickly this week, she'd had no time to ponder what it all might mean in the grander scheme of things . . . in the way the Lord wanted her to live her life for others.

Here in Cedar Creek, life has been a lot like making a rag rug, Abby began. She sipped her tea and then let her thoughts guide her pencil without interrupting their flow. The good ideas often got lost when she imposed judgment too soon.

You start by washing old, faded dresses and shirts, thinking how you can bring new life—new usefulness—to this castaway clothing. Rag rug making involves tearing garments apart, then working in strong, brighter fabric left from other projects so as not to waste the materials you've been given. Sometimes you must rip out stitches that become too tight—or add in extra stitches to ease your way around tricky curves. This is never something you can plan ahead of time.

Only working your way around by feel and instinct, adding in your love with each and every stitch, will make a rug that lies flat and holds together well. When you've finished, you've created something new and beautiful from materials that had been discarded.

Folks here in Cedar Creek are especially sorry for Marian and Carl Byler: their newborn, Elizabeth, is doing well in the medical center after an early arrival but her twin sister, Esther, lived only one day on account of severe trauma during the delivery. It's another way life brings us strips that aren't always bright and perfect and beautiful, while God provides ways to stitch in strength and fresh hope so our rug holds together anyway.

Abby paused. The Bylers' story, while tragic, had been the easier one to report: who wouldn't feel sympathy for Marian and Carl? But she couldn't skip over Zanna's canceled wedding—kin who'd come from Ohio, Indiana, and Pennsylvania would be wondering what had happened since then. Friends and family hereabouts would read her account with interest, as well, because of the rumors that had run rampant before Zanna's confession on Sunday. Even now, folks speculated about what would happen to this misbegotten child: they all recalled how Jonny Ropp had left town on his sixteenth birthday only to return a few days later, showing off his fancy van and his cell phone. He'd openly belittled his parents' dairy farming and their out-of-fashion faith.

Make believers of them.

Abby dimpled her cheek with the end of her pen. That still, small voice was reminding her that a higher good could be served with every word she wrote. As Cedar Creek's scribe for the national Plain newspaper, she was to present local events so that all would be informed—and none would be misrepresented. The canceled wedding and Zanna's confession were only part of the picture: she had to consider James, too. His hopes and dreams had been ripped to shreds. His family had been humiliated, and the revelation of another man's baby had only rubbed salt in their wounds.

Abby recalled James's stunned silence, the pain on his handsome face when she'd told him Zanna had disappeared . . . and his anger when he'd heard that the woman he loved was carrying Jonny Ropp's child. No good would be served by spelling out these details for the Amish across America —especially since many women in Cedar Creek would report their versions of this local scandal in letters to their kin back East anyway. Better to give this situation no more space than she had allotted the announcement of Marian Byler's unfortunate birthing . . . best to write it the way Zanna would form the rows of her rug with the big crochet hook: loose and even, with love and care.

Once again Abby put her pen to the paper:

As many of you know, the marriage of Suzanna Lambright to James Graber was called off. As with that rug I mentioned earlier, sometimes you're crocheting along on a fast, easy straightaway and then you come to a curve: if the stitches don't fit right, no matter how much love and effort and patience you apply, there's nothing to do but tear out that section so you can rework it. We must believe that when our plans—for rugs, or lives—don't happen the way we'd hoped, it's because God has a better idea, a different path and purpose for us.

My wish for you this week: never give up or give in to despair and stuff your unfinished rug in the trash. Keep thinking on it, praying over it— as we ask you to do for the Bylers, the Grabers, and the Lambrights. ~Abigail Lambright

Abby reread the piece, smiled, and wrote a neater copy of it to send in the mail. She kept her drafts in a loose-leaf notebook, a sort of diary of her life since she'd volunteered to be the town scribe a couple of years ago—right around the time she'd turned twenty-five and realized James Graber would never see her as a potential wife. Now *there* was a sorry state she'd been in! A time when the rag rug of her life seemed ugly and puckered and beyond fixing. What young woman dreamed of living alone?

Yet once Abby had declared herself a maidel,

175

she'd immediately become closer to Sam's children at an important time in their young lives, and she'd created her Stitch in Time business. She also cherished the time she'd spent helping Dat plan her house so Owen Coblentz could build it . . . a cozy home that would be Zanna's haven while she reconsidered her future, as well. Had Abby married, none of those things would have happened.

And whom had she considered for a husband? No one but James. He alone had made her heart sing. *So why waste another man's life—or your own—settling for less of a marriage than you dream of?* This was the thought that had run consistently through her heart when she prayed on her unmarried state a few years ago, until she'd begun to trust the Lord's truth for her life. This inner guidance had been a beacon ever since, and now Zanna's situation again proved the wisdom of listening to it, and sharing it.

Abby went to the kitchen for an envelope and a stamp. It pleased her to see her sister sitting at the kitchen table with strips of fabric draped over the chairs according to color. Zanna was patiently removing the hem from a floral print dress— something she wouldn't have spent her time doing when she was younger.

Zanna looked up, the seam ripper poised at the next stitch. "Gut thing Adah's Mennonite friends donated their old clothes so we have different colors and more patterns. And you know," she continued in a pensive tone, "I'm thinking the royal blue of my wedding dress would set off a lot of these quilting scraps—if you won't be upset at me for using it that way."

Abby hugged her sister's slender shoulders. What a good sign, that Zanna was thinking beyond her earlier excuses for not making Adah's rug. "Since you already snipped it into ribbons," Abby teased, "this might be the perfect way to reclaim a dress that will never be worn. And with those shirts in the darker blue, you've got a nice contrast to the faded browns and grays from the donation box. Adah will be tickled."

Zanna's smile curved wryly. "Jah, that's why I want to make a really fine rug and then deliver it, like you said. To see the look on her face."

Abby heard a bit of payback in that remark, which defeated the whole principle of having Zanna make these rugs. As she thought about her response, she watched her sister cut more strips, about two inches wide and the length of the broadfall trousers she held. "If Adah's rug turns out gut, you might make one for James and Emma's mamm," Abby suggested quietly. "All the rugs in their house are looking worn, and if anyone could use a gift, it's Eunice Graber. I don't expect she gets many."

The slight rise of Zanna's eyebrows told Abby she'd gotten the hint about her attitude. Zanna

177

yanked a long section of thread from another hem, smoothed the fabric flat with her hand, and then snipped it at two-inch intervals. As she ripped the long strips, a sigh escaped her, yet she didn't seem as hopeless or helpless as she'd been these past few days. "I could make rugs until the day I die and not repay *you,* sister," she murmured. "Denki for putting up with my moods, and for helping me out of this tight spot. I don't *intend* to be thoughtless or rude or—and I never in a million years wanted to hurt Barbara or Sam or Mamm. Sometimes I just don't pay attention. I run off at the mouth without thinking."

Abby leaned over her sister's chair to hug her shoulders. It might not be the way the Ordnung said she was to treat her shunned sister, but wasn't affection the better alternative to emotional distance? Weren't approval and encouragement the quicker ways to persuade this young woman to show that same kindness to others, now that Zanna could see where she'd fallen short?

"I'd rather hear you talking this way than have you making me rugs any day," Abby whispered. "I'll fetch that wedding dress. Then I can be stitching the ends of your strips together so you can get a gut start on your rug before dinner."

Zanna blinked back tears. "You're the best sister ever. You know that, Abby?"

And wasn't that about the nicest thing anyone had ever said to her? Abby went to fetch the ruined wedding dress before this conversation turned into a crying match. The day might be blustery and bleak, but it was warm as toast in her little house. And wasn't that something to celebrate?

A few days later, Zanna sat at Abby's table stitching around the oval rug's next curving edge. She carefully inserted her big crochet hook into the previous row, feeling more than counting how many extra stitches would keep the rug loose enough that it would lie flat. She'd had to rip out plenty of places and redo them to get the rug started right, yet it measured nearly three feet wide now. This project had been a better way to fill the long hours than she had anticipated: while Zanna had watched Abby make plenty of these sturdy floor mats, handwork had never been her cup of tea. She had always had someplace more fun to go, some buddy to giggle with.

But her life would never be that way again.

As she glanced out at the falling snow, Zanna sensed it would be a long winter. Boring. Too quiet. Afternoons, she got so lonely she couldn't wait for Abby to get home, or for Barbara to suggest she come over and help with the baking or cleaning.

At least the gossips and finger-pointers have stopped. And come April—

It seemed so far away, the month her baby was

due. Yet as Zanna realized how much she needed to learn about childbirth, and how much money she had to tuck away these next months, her heart raced in panic. How could she possibly earn enough money—any money at all—if Sam made her stay here, out of sight?

Stop it! Just leave it be.

Zanna left about six inches of the floral strip hanging loose and picked up the last length of blue fabric that had once been her wedding dress. As she worked in the new color, carefully tucking in the edges, her mind wandered.

If you'd worn this pretty blue dress—gone through with the wedding—you'd be Mrs. Graber now. And if you hadn't gone to see Jonny that one last time . . . ridden on his new Harley, hanging on to him for dear life while you couldn't stop shrieking and laughing . . .

Zanna sucked in her breath. There it was again, that little tickly feeling.

Might be a sign you're to stop thinking about Jonny and that wild ride . . . and what came after. It only makes you feel lonely, missing what you can't have.

Zanna sighed. She crocheted around the small end of the oval until she reached the straight edge again. It wouldn't be long until she presented this rug to Adah—and informed Jonny's mamm that she'd made it especially for her. Zanna wasn't so sure how Adah might react to that, but she wanted to see the outspoken woman's face. She hoped Abby might say something to fill in the awkward pauses, to keep stupidity from coming out of her own mouth. Her sister had said that thinking positive thoughts, believing good things would come of this awkward situation, was the best way to handle discouraging moments. Some days she had a lot of those.

A knock at Abby's kitchen door made Zanna turn around to see Mamm coming in, stomping the snow from her boots. "How are you, Zanna?" she asked cheerfully. "Gail brought sandwiches home from the pie shop. You might be under the ban, but you and the baby need to eat lunch, I figure. And how's that rug coming?"

"It's nearly finished." Zanna closed her eyes. Things had been none too cozy between her and Mamm since she'd made her confession. She would rather eat alone . . . but the scent of Lois Yutzy's fresh bread, melted cheese, and grilled onions reminded her how hungry she was.

"It's time I closed up the greenhouse for the winter. Not a soul has wandered in there today, what with this snow." Mamm padded over in her stocking feet and set the fat white bakery sack on the table. "Why, Zanna, what a wonderful mix of colors you've got in this rug! When Abby told me you were making it, and who it's for—well, I . . ."

Her mother sat in the chair across the little table. Her chin quivered, and then she made a fuss of getting out the sandwiches, rattling the sack. "Mostly, I want to apologize for acting so stand-offish. Making it sound like this baby is to be your punishment, or a burden you have to bear all by yourself, instead of the most wonderful blessing."

Zanna sucked in her breath and sat up straighter.

Her mother studied her. "Need a dishpan?"

"No, no, it's . . ." How did she describe this sensation without sounding ridiculous? "It's this little tingly, feathery feeling. Probably nothing, but—"

Mamm counted on her fingers, and grinned when she got to four. "Well, now! It's a gut thing your mamm came over today, because that's the baby moving, Zanna," she exclaimed. "It'll be real to you now, letting you know it's growing like it's supposed to."

"Oh!" The most deliriously happy moment she'd known in months made Zanna clap her hands together.

Mamm hopped up from her chair to hug her, laughing, rocking her from side to side. "Best news I've heard for days! It's always a big moment, no matter how many children come along." Her blue eyes shone as she smiled; her happiness made her look downright girlish again.

Zanna grabbed the nearest sandwich and unwrapped it. Ravenous, she raised it to her lips—but then she smiled at her mother and they bowed their heads. *Lord, I thank You for this happy moment. And for bringing my mother here, like You knew I needed her today.*

After Mamm opened her eyes, she took such a big bite of her sandwich, the melted cheese gushed out. It plopped onto her apron, yet she giggled hysterically. Zanna caught the giggle bug, too, and for the next few minutes they chewed and covered their mouths and laughed until tears streamed from their eyes.

"Ach, child, you were always the one," Mamm said when she could string the words together. "With your older sisters, Irene and Louise, I was so set on getting everything right, doing things just so for your dat—proving myself as a young wife, you know. And then along came Sam and Abby, and I had more children than I had hands to hold onto them. And then," she continued with a teasing smile, "there was you."

Zanna paused with her sandwich near her mouth. "Always trouble, was I?"

Mamm squeezed Zanna's knee. "It must have felt that way, all the times we kept after you to sit quiet in church and sent you to your room for smarting off. But you know what?"

Mamm swiped at a tear left over from their giggling spree. "You turned out to be the child who made me let go of trying to be perfect, Zanna. You made my heart skip rope to hot peppers and then jump out of the playground swing when I was flying higher than I was supposed to. Even

183

on days when nothing was going right, I could laugh and go on—because of you, Suzanna."

Zanna sat absolutely still, amazed by what Mamm had just said. Was this her own mother talking?

"And don't you forget I said that, either, when I seem all cross and bothered." Mamm smiled, dabbing at the gooey yellow cheese on her apron. "But don't you tell Sam and Abby I've said that about you! They think Dat and I let you get away with too much when you were little—and they'd be jealous as all get out, hearing me carry on this way."

Zanna smiled, just as the baby tickled her insides again. "Jah," she murmured, still grinning. "We shouldn't make them covet the way you've spoiled me, Mamm—as though you love me best. Can't have them breaking the Tenth Commandment on *my* account, can we?"

— Chapter 13 —

A week later, when Abby returned from delivering Eunice and Merle's new clothes, she glanced into the back room of the mercantile, where huge bags of flour, rolled oats, and other staples were stacked on the shelves. Her younger sister sat at the table with a scale, surrounded by dozens of small baggies full of nonpareils, sanding sugars, and candy sprinkles in a wild array of colors. Abby loved to fill and label those little bags, as it lifted her spirits to work with the bright yellows, greens, pinks, and reds—made it feel like Christmas was right around the corner, to work with toppings that looked like holly berries and snowflakes and tiny stars. Zanna had volunteered for this job, and that was a step in a positive direction.

"Are you doing all right with those sprinkles, Zanna?"

"I've got a few more labels to stick on, and then I'll put them on the shelves." Zanna popped a pretzel-shaped cookie into her mouth. "I've got to head home to make supper soon, though. These cute little graham crackers won't hold me for long."

"Leave whenever you want, sis. You've been hard at it all afternoon." Abby looked around the main room of the mercantile for their brother. She waved at Merle Graber as he followed Eunice past the refrigerated cases with a shopping cart . . . saw Beulah Mae stocking up on supplies for Mrs. Nissley's Kitchen. "I might stay longer, while Sam checks in more boxes off the truck," Abby remarked to her sister. "This cold snap's bringing lots of folks into the store."

The bell on the front door jangled as Adah Ropp came in, looking flustered as she grabbed a shopping cart. "We're in for a blizzard tonight," she announced. "The television at the Clearwater Cafe was saying five or six inches, with a winter weather advisory through the weekend." Adah hurried down the first aisle and tossed packages of macaroni and rice into her cart as though sleet were already nipping at her sturdy black heels. "Gut thing I worked at the cheese store today or I wouldn't have known to stock up. I might not make it in to work tomorrow—"

"And there again," Sam chimed in with a chuckle, "we might see nary a flake! Seems to me television gets folks all riled up by constantly repeating weather predictions that are about half right. I'll stick to the almanac, thanks," he added as he set out the last of the new snow shovels.

"I'm with you, Sam!" Merle said from the candy aisle. "Got plenty of achy joints to tell me the weather's a-changin'. No need for a TV."

Eunice's head had bobbed as she followed this conversation from aisle to aisle. She pushed up her thick glasses. "Nothing gut comes of watching TV, Adah," she declared from halfway across the store. "Maybe your boys would have stayed on the farm if you hadn't taken up English ways."

Over in the bulk cereal section, Beulah Mae Nissley hefted a big bag of egg noodles into her cart with a decisive nod of her head. "Could be James would be settled in with his bride by now if you'd applied a firmer hand to Jonny's backside—and stayed home to raise him, Adah. Nothing gut's to be gained by going against the Old Ways."

Abby stood aghast, stock-still beside the storeroom door. Was the change in the weather making these women bicker from different parts of the store? Or had last month's gossip at church, squelched by the bishop, finally popped a seam to spew out? Abby glanced at Zanna, who still sat at the storeroom table but was nearly ready to stock shelves . . . unaware of how the talk was heating up among Cedar Creek's more outspoken neighbors. What a shame if her sister walked into the middle of this conversation, now that she'd acquired a more responsible, happier frame of mind.

"And who are *you* to tell me this, Mrs. Nissley?" Adah's sharp reply rang out. "You've been running your business on the highway, depending on English tourists for years!"

"Using gas ovens and deep freezes, too, so I'm not on the electrical grid like those Mennonite cheesemakers," the bakery owner shot back. "Walking to work, not three minutes away from what my kids were doing while they still lived at home, instead of driving to another town. And let's not forget—"

"Adah! Beulah Mae—please, let's not bicker," Abby spoke above their squabbling.

"—that my pies and breads and carryout lunches also bring folks to other businesses here in Cedar Creek," Beulah Mae continued in a rising voice. "Which means *my* day's work doesn't contribute to another town's prosperity!"

"Let's cool your tongues, ladies," Sam warned. While he sounded calm and in control, his voice carried to every corner of the store. "I didn't make my remark about weather forecasting to spark such a hot conversation."

"You're a fine one to talk, Sam Lambright!" Adah stopped her cart not five feet from Abby, pointing her finger toward the storeroom. "Letting your sister work here when she's under the ban. And her carrying a baby while she's unmarried, too. *She's* the root of this whole conversation, ain't so? Had she left my Jonny alone and been faithful to James, we'd none of us be talking this way!"

Abby's face went hot and then she turned. Zanna had just come out, holding a shallow box stacked with bags of sanding sugar. Her flushed cheeks and shaking arms announced her agitated state, and she looked ready to blurt out a retort.

"Has anyone else here never made a mistake?" Abby asked pointedly. "Or never confessed to a preacher or at a Members' Meeting? We're supposed to be setting an example of compassion and forgiveness for Zanna."

A whimper rose above their heated conversation. With a *whump!* the box of baking sprinkles hit the plank floor, and Zanna raced down the nearest aisle, awkwardly dodging a cluster of

English ladies before she ran out the front door.

So much for her attempt at peacemaking. Abby grabbed the front end of Adah Ropp's grocery cart, wishing she could take everyone back a mere two minutes, to when they were all shopping before they went home to dinner with their families. Sam strode purposefully toward Mrs. Nissley's cart, and then motioned for Adah to join them at the checkout.

The mercantile got very quiet. Abby released Mrs. Ropp's cart, happy to let Sam deal with this situation, as the male in charge—not that their neighbors' opinions of Zanna would improve any time soon. She went to where the box of toppings had landed, and then fetched a broom from the storeroom. Not many bags had spilled, but it was a mess no one should walk in.

"It's not just a matter of how our English customers will perceive this sort of behavior," Sam said in a low voice as he totaled Beulah Mae Nissley's order. "It's the rift I see getting wider, right here amongst us Plain folk. There needs to be a whole lot of thinking about our own shortcomings, and more forgiveness toward those who are struggling to make gut on their past mistakes."

"Tell it to the bishop, then!" Adah flashed a resentful look at Beulah Mae as the bakery owner set her items on the counter. "This isn't the first time I've been blamed for my boys taking off, and I'm getting right tired of it!"

"I'll meet with Vernon about this matter if you will." Sam gazed at each woman until her eyes met his and were lowered. "These catfights have got to stop, or by the time Zanna has that baby none of us will be on speaking terms. That's not the right way to go, and we all know it."

Adah Ropp pinched her lips together in a tight line.

Beulah Mae Nissley focused on her coin purse, picking out the correct change.

Abby stood back, allowing Sam to restore order. Eunice Graber gripped the handle of her shopping basket, closely observing the conversation at the checkout, while Merle seemed to have retreated into his own little world. True enough, Abby had overheard similar remarks spoken behind hands at a recent quilting frolic, and it was time to call such talk to a halt—for Zanna's sake, as well as for the good of Cedar Creek. Her sister had confessed and accepted her punishment. Weren't these other folks keeping the sin alive by talking it up?

After a few moments of uncomfortable silence, Sam said, "All right, then, I'll ask Vernon to set a time, and we'll meet together. Seems my house is as central as anybody's. And from here on out, I want no more of your backstabbing in my store."

James turned the sign in his shop window from OPEN to CLOSED. He stretched wearily. Even though today he'd nearly completed the white custom-order carriage for the amusement park in Orlando, the hours had dragged.

Was the change in the weather making him feel so down and dissatisfied? Or had so much time alone made him dwell on the fact that Zanna would never be his wife . . . and that he had no taste for starting all over again, courting other women? He'd learned his lesson so far as falling for a girl several years younger than he went, yet the women closer to his age were all married or they'd crossed that invisible line that made them maidels. At twenty-nine, he was beyond attending singings . . . Would he have to venture over to Clearwater or beyond Bloomingdale to find a wife?

James gazed at the carriage he was making and sighed. With its lustrous white leather upholstery, accented with beaded jewels, and strands of tiny lights strung all along a gridwork of clear, spherical supports, it would be the most wondrous —and the most expensive—vehicle he had ever created. How was it that he could build a coach befitting a fairy-tale princess, yet he had lost all hope of making his own love story come true?

He'd worked through lunch today . . . didn't drink much water. He'd neglected his basic needs, and now he had this bad attitude to show for it.

When James stepped outside, tiny pellets of hail pinged against his face. The gray sky matched his mood, too, so he decided that before he went home he'd go across the road to the mercantile. If he drank a bottle of juice and chatted with Sam Lambright, maybe he'd feel better.

James was strolling across Sam's gravel parking lot, considering what little gift he could take home for Emma, when a familiar figure shot through the mercantile door. Zanna was as upset as he'd ever seen her, her head lowered and blubbering, not watching where she was going—

"Ooph!" She butted right into him and then wailed all the louder. James lapsed into old habits, better days: he wrapped his arms around Zanna's trembling shoulders . . . felt the bulge of her belly and imagined how beautiful she'd be as her pregnancy progressed.

"Ach! James!" Zanna jerked away, shattering the spell. Her eyes streamed with tears and her chin quivered while her face flushed with embarrassment.

Or was that regret he saw?

There was no use in wondering. Although . . . if she said the right words, made the promises his heart yearned to hear, he might—*might*—consider taking her back. Then again, she'd caught him in a weak moment. He had known so many of those lately, he couldn't recall how it felt to be strong and confident.

Zanna mopped her face with her sleeve. "I'm so mad at that woman, I could—"

"Which one?" No need to guess, however: Adah Ropp had swung open the mercantile door and was marching toward her buggy while Beulah Mae Nissley huffed off down the road on foot. This wasn't the first time they'd stirred up trouble with their tongues.

Zanna glared after both of them. "It'll never be enough that I confessed—that I took a shunning as my rightful punishment. She'll keep picking at me like I'm a nasty old scab, and—well, so will Beulah Mae, for that matter. And I'm sick of it!"

Zanna dashed around the side of the mercantile, toward Abby's little house at the far end of the lane. When she veered off the driveway and bent over to vomit, James's heart went out to her. Had he stuck with that pie-in-the-sky plan to claim the baby as his own, Zanna wouldn't be the object of such scorn. But then he remembered the cold hard truth of her words when the bishop and Preacher Paul had talked with them . . . how she'd only repeated that she loved him because he'd said those words to her first.

Matt's dogs trotted from the sheep barn to look after her, so James did not. Behind him, the mercantile door opened again and out stepped his parents, each carrying a small parcel. Mamm's eyes darted warily behind lenses that enlarged them, and Dat . . . well, Dat appeared oddly amused. He approached James and patted his arm.

"She's stickin' out with the baby, son," he

confided. "I'm guessin', by the way she's carryin' it, you're gonna have a little boy!"

His mamm grabbed Dat's arm to steer him toward home. "That's nonsense and you know it, Merle. Why do you carry on so?"

"See you for dinner, James." His father smiled and then walked beside her, docile as a lamb.

"Jah, Dat. Be there in a few." James waited until his parents started across the road to let his mask slip. No matter how often he explained, his father's muddled mind hadn't held on to the fact that the wedding had been canceled. Dat was still living in anticipation, with everything rosy and sweet and joyful. He'd always adored Zanna's pert sense of humor and the way she lit up a room.

So who was the wiser? His father, for insisting it was all going according to his original happily-ever-after? Or him, for thinking he'd never love again?

— *Chapter 14* —

A few evenings later, Abby hung her damp dish towel to dry and joined the group in Sam and Barbara's front room. The mood felt only slightly different from when the family had originally gathered there with the bishop to discuss Zanna's confession.

"We're all here now, Vernon," Sam said. "Thank you for setting up a time to meet with us." He surveyed the folks, seated with their chairs in an uneven circle. "We need to settle this bickering once and for all. Not just for business, in front of our customers, but because this concerns the fate of our families and our faith."

Abby noted who had come on this snowy November evening: at the head of the circle, to her left, sat Bishop Gingerich, and on his other side Preacher Abe Nissley occupied the recliner beside his wife, Beulah Mae. James had driven his parents across the icy road, and the three of them filled the green corduroy sofa. Adah Ropp was perched on the ladderback chair to Sam's right, and Sam had claimed his favorite platform rocker. There were nine of them, all told. Barbara, Mamm, and the girls quietly finished the dishes in the kitchen. At Sam's suggestion, and quite willingly, Zanna had stayed at Abby's house. She'd had no desire to endure yet another round of public scrutiny.

"We'll begin with prayer, asking for God's guidance," Vernon intoned. After their moment of shared silence, he glanced at Sam. "Will you fill Abe and me in on what happened the other day? I don't believe James was in your store at the time, either."

Sam clasped his big hands over his crossed knees. Now that this meeting was under way, he seemed more settled than he'd been for the past few days. "When Adah remarked about seeing a winter storm advisory on the TV while working at the cheese store in Clearwater, I said I preferred the almanac's weather predictions. From there, Eunice and Beulah Mae lit into Adah for working away from home, and—"

"Did we come here to talk about the weather—which, by the way, ended up bringing us that big snow the TV predicted?" Adah interrupted archly. "Seems to me the whole argument centered around how *your sister* should not be seen working in public."

Just that quickly the gloves came off. Abby leaned forward to catch Vernon's eye. "In all fairness to Zanna—"

"Abby, you were working at the store when this happened, while not being involved in the exchange of words, correct?" the bishop cut in. "Is Sam telling it the way you recall? Did you notice anything else that might shed light on this incident?"

Abby sat straighter. She was here to see that Zanna was treated fairly, but she also had a responsibility to present the truth as she knew it. It was the Plain way to put faith above family, no matter how badly she wanted to stick up for her sister.

"Jah, Bishop, Adah was in a stew about the weather report, and then Eunice remarked about how Adah was taking on too many Mennonite ways, what with watching the TV and all," Abby recounted quietly. "Then, from a few aisles over, Beulah Mae joined in. She said none of this trouble would have started had Adah stayed home and raised Gideon and Jonny with a firmer hand."

"Is that how you remember it, Adah?" the bishop asked before she could protest. Beside him, Abe Nissley scowled at his wife while Eunice focused closely on the conversation so she wouldn't miss her turn.

"Pretty much, jah. But I'm telling you it all goes back to Sam allowing his sister to work in the mercantile and parade around in public view. Especially now that she's showing," Adah added. "And her under the ban, no less!"

"All the while you three women were kicking up a fuss, Zanna was working in the back room, out of sight," Abby pointed out. As she saw the rising color in Adah's face, she reminded herself to remain calm and keep her voice low. "Folks are quick to mention Zanna's mistakes, but when she's being useful, helping Sam in the store without pay, they find fault with her, too."

Abby paused, hoping to word her next comment in a way that wouldn't spark more conflict. "And that's exactly what you did, Adah, the minute she stepped out with a big box of cookie sprinkles.

No matter what Zanna does, it seems to be wrong. Is it any wonder she's upset?"

Bishop Gingerich held up his hands to silence any further remarks. "It has always been difficult for Suzanna to sit still and stay out of sight—"

"High time she learned," Adah piped up.

"That's why it's called the *ban,*" Eunice joined in. "The whole point is to make her feel removed from the rest of us while she serves out her penance."

"Don't we believe that the Lord helps those who help themselves?" Abby pleaded. What they'd said was correct, according to the Ordnung, so she kept her voice low. This was no time to escalate their discussion into another bickering match. "Last time we all met, the night before Zanna's confession, folks criticized her for not helping at Mamm's greenhouse or the mercantile, and now they're calling her on the carpet when she *is* working. What's she supposed to do, Bishop?"

Beulah Mae sat with her arms crossed, looking straight over at Adah. "It's not fair that Zanna's shouldering this load alone, either. If your boy would own up—"

"Jah," Eunice exclaimed. "Not fair to anyone, seeing how this problem is partly Jonny's doing."

"Nobody asked for your opinion, Beulah Mae," her husband said sharply. "As a preacher's wife, you're to be setting a better example. You women are getting way out of hand."

"Jah, and when it happens in the store, with other customers and English there, it's a problem for every one of us," Sam remarked. "It's not a gut reflection on our ways or our faith. Not a proper picture of submitting our wills to a higher power, either."

Eunice and Beulah Mae sat back, chastened, while Adah appeared prickly around the edges yet. Abby wondered why her husband, Rudy, hadn't come with her tonight, but asking that question might well kick open a whole new hornet's nest.

Vernon Gingerich took advantage of the pause to glance around the room. "James, you mostly just brought your folks over on this wintry night, but how do *you* see all this? It's affecting your life in ways we're not touching on here."

From his seat on the sofa between his parents James rested his elbows on his knees. His brown hair looked longer than usual and a little unkempt. To Abby, he lacked his usual sparkle —and why wouldn't he?

"It's not been the happiest of times for me," he confirmed in a low voice. "And while I wasn't in the store during this exchange of words we're talking about, I did see how upset Zanna was afterward. She was crying and running at the same time—and she ran smack into me."

Abby felt the blow against her own midsection as though her sister had rammed into her instead.

She and Sam had both noticed how James hadn't been coming into the store lately for his afternoon package of sweet potato chips or jerky. Was it because he'd seen Zanna go in to work? Or was he isolating himself, allowing his emotions to heal?

"And while I don't feel real gut about the way Zanna left me in the lurch," he continued in a strained voice, "I felt worse after hearing how she'd been talked about and pointed at, with other folks in the store to witness it. That's not a very kind or Christlike way to treat a girl in trouble, seems to me."

Abby's pulse pounded. James wore his heart on his sleeve for all to see, and once again she wanted to say an encouraging or comforting word to her longtime friend. But this wasn't the time or the place.

"Seems to me the wagging tongues and pointing fingers are becoming as troublesome as Zanna's situation," Abe Nissley observed as he scowled at his wife and Eunice. "But there *is* that matter of shared responsibility for her being pregnant, and it'll keep coming around until something's done about it." Preacher Abe focused on Adah Ropp then, his expression softening as though he suspected the answer before he asked his question. "What do you hear from Jonny these days, Adah? And why is Rudy not here with you tonight?"

Jonny's mother crossed her arms. Her face went

tight. Adah wasn't accustomed to being asked such direct questions, even though that was *her* way of dealing with people. Abe hadn't made any accusations; as a matter of fact, his tone suggested a situation that might not be common knowledge. And Adah's hesitation . . . her changing expressions . . . suggested that the preacher had found a soft spot beneath her starched kapp and stiff chin. But then, wasn't it harder to remain calm and strong when folks were being *nice?*

Adah's facade crumbled. "No matter what you think about my working at the Mennonite cheese shop, I'm doing everything I can to keep the dairy profitable," she replied in a tiny voice. "What with the two boys leaving home, Rudy's got more than he can handle, keeping the cows milked . . . getting the milk and cream sold."

She let out a long, shuddery sigh, as though she'd been holding her worries in for a long time. "Neighbors don't buy it all up on a regular basis," Adah continued. "So when the Mennonites over at the cheese factory offered us a contract, we couldn't afford to say no. My income from clerking and wrapping the cheese helps make up the difference for the lower milk prices and higher feed bills we dairy farmers deal with these days. Our friends have their opinions about that, but they're not paying our bills, either."

Adah Ropp inhaled deeply to settle herself. Now that Abe had put her on the spot, she'd lost her vinegar. "This isn't something Rudy wants talked about," she continued in a pleading tone, "but it about broke him down when Jonny and then Gideon jumped the fence soon as they finished school. And when Jonny rubbed his dat's nose in it by buying a van to drive for Amish all around Clearwater—well, Rudy's been mad at the whole world ever since."

The silent front room echoed with Adah's heartbreak. Nobody knew what to say, and they didn't want to interrupt her sad tale now that she was pouring it out.

Adah looked away. "Rudy says that because the boys up and left—turned their backs on their family and their faith—he wants nothing to do with them. Refuses to speak to them, and forbids me to contact them, too." Her choked sob grabbed hold of everyone in the room and refused to let go, like a hand closing around their hearts. "I thank the gut Lord for my girls. How could I keep the house running without my Becky and Maggie? But . . . but I feel so alone at times—"

"Oh, Adah, we had no idea!" Abby leaned forward and reached across Sam. "Everyone figured Rudy was awful disappointed about the boys, but we didn't suspect the extent of it."

"This is something we must speak to Rudy about," Vernon agreed solemnly. "It's not good for his soul—or his body—to hold such anger inside. It's not good for you, either, Adah, being denied your sons and your love for them." He looked around the circle, hoping everyone would see his important point. "Even if they jumped the fence, you need to know how they're doing for your own peace of mind."

Adah nodded, tears streaming down her face. She briefly gripped the hand Abby had offered her, and then plucked a handkerchief from her skirt pocket.

"And no matter what you might think of Zanna, that baby she's carrying is your grand-child," Abby insisted softly. "It would be a gut thing for you and Zanna both if you could love that little baby for who she is."

"Oh, it's a boy," Merle countered with a decisive nod of his head.

Adah blew her nose, not responding to this new thread of talk.

"Carry on all you want about that baby," Eunice cut in, "but it's still not fair to my James that Zanna and Jonny were carrying on behind his back whilst—"

"Mamm." James slipped an arm around his mother's shoulders to silence her. "We've been chewing on this like a cow working its cud, and it'll do none of us any gut if we don't see the bigger picture. Maybe—just maybe—all this ruckus is meant to wake us up," he suggested. "Maybe we're supposed to see that when the storm's whirling around us, like that snow and sleet Adah heard predicted, the one we can truly rely upon is God. Even when family lets us down. Even when . . . even when we learn our dreams aren't going to work out."

Once again Abby's heart pounded. She gazed at James, seated across the room between his elderly parents. If only Zanna had sensed how wonderfully strong—how steadfast—this man was. If only she'd realized how much he loved her.

"Seems to me we've each got our work to do, and we're getting by as best we can," James continued earnestly. He looked around the room at the circle of friends he'd known all his life. "Adah's selling her cheese while Rudy keeps the cows producing the milk for it. Beulah Mae brings in new customers for us all with her pie shop while Abe tends his crops and serves as one of our preachers. Sam provides us the supplies we can't grow ourselves, and he's trying to keep Zanna on the right path, as best anyone can. And Abby . . ."

Abby held her breath as James met her gaze. What was he going to say in his low, compelling voice? His brown eyes softened. He smiled for the first time she could remember since Zanna had run off with his hopes and dreams.

"Abby's caught smack in the middle," he went on, entreating those around him to listen. To *believe*. "She sews for every one of us, brightens our dark days with her kindness. She wants the best for her sister, jah, but I've never doubted she wants the best for me, too—for all of us—no matter how things seem to be unraveling. I wish we could all be more like her."

Abby felt light-headed from lack of air. Had anyone ever paid her a higher compliment? If only . . .

There was no use in wishing for what would never be, far as her future with James went, she reminded herself.

Abby managed a smile, aware of how flushed her cheeks felt. "Believe me, Adah—and Eunice and Beulah Mae," she entreated them, "my sister's working out her penance, and she's feeling the effects of this ban. As far as I know, she's had no contact with her friends since she knelt before us at the service—and that's a hard thing for a chatty girl her age."

She paused, hoping they'd all understand Zanna's decision to keep her baby a choice that didn't mesh well with Plain tradition. "Zanna's trying to spend her time well, learning from her mistakes and planning what comes next for her and this child. She's not keeping it just to go against the grain, understand. She *refuses* to give her baby up for adoption because she believes that's no way to treat someone you love."

Abby looked at each of the women in turn, to share something that hadn't occurred to her before now. "For a girl who's just seventeen, that seems a big, responsible step to take," she ventured. "I'm not sure I could have done it at that age."

She sent a silent apology across the room to James, and then looked at Adah. "So, jah," she added softly, "Zanna knows all about feeling alone, too. Not a one of you seems to see her side of things. All you see is her sin."

The room grew very quiet. The clock on the mantel struck nine in slow, sonorous tones.

Sam cleared his throat. "So what would you have us do now, Bishop?" he asked. "All our talking does no gut if we don't back it up with action. I'll do whatever you ask of me."

As Vernon looked around their circle, other heads nodded. At last it seemed as if everyone had released their resentment and complaints, and they were ready to be in harmony with one another again. Abby was pleased that Sam had set aside his previous disapproval of their sister—no small miracle. He was willing to move forward and help everyone else along that path, as well. It was powerful, what friends in the faith could accomplish when they set aside petty gossip and aspired toward the ideals that the bishop, Abe Nissley, and Paul Bontrager preached.

"I believe we've worked out our differences now," Vernon replied. His round face resumed its usual ruddy glow. "I admire young Zanna for working, but I feel you and Abby should limit her to tasks in the storeroom or in your homes, out of the public eye," he said to Sam. "But you who gossip and place blame—whether upon

Zanna Lambright or each other—stand just as guilty in your own way."

He paused to let this declaration sink in. Adah, Eunice, and Beulah Mae lowered their eyes and listened to Bishop Gingerich's decision without further protest.

"After all," he continued, "we're quick to consider adultery a *big* sin while we minimize the sin of gossip and speculation. Truth is, bearing false witness is breaking one of God's commandments, same as if we engage in infidelity or lewd behavior. Confession would be the first step toward reconciliation with our friends and our faith—whether that be after the service next Sunday, or right here and now."

The room remained quiet as they awaited a decision.

Dear Lord, we say we're trying and soon as You know it, we're back to our old habits. Help us make our positive intentions stick this time. Abby kept her head bowed. Sometimes it took a moment to decide between an immediate opportunity to confess and the need to bring it before everyone. It depended on how deep the misstep went, and how the spirit prodded one's conscience.

"I'm sorry I've been so cross and contrary. I'll try to do better, with your help," Adah began. She looked at each of them, awaiting acknowledgment, before focusing on the bishop. "And I'd be grateful if you'd speak to Rudy,

Vernon. He's wearing himself awful thin, what with just the young Bontrager boys to muck out the barns every now and again. Rudy's too stubborn and proud to hire full-time help, you see." She smiled ruefully, swiping a last tear from her face. "And I know he'd feel better, getting such resentment against our sons off his chest, too. But don't tell him I told you!"

They all nodded, knowing that Rudy was a man of few words and fewer requests for help.

After another moment or so, Beulah Mae Nissley released a sigh. "I'm quick to jump in where it's none of my business," she admitted, reaching for her husband's hand. "I'm sorry I put you to the test, Abe, as I don't know where I'd be without you. And, Adah, I didn't mean to upset the apple cart, as far as saying you'd taken on too many Mennonite ways," she went on. "And Sam, there's no excuse for how we forgot ourselves and carried on like pecking, squawking hens in your store, either. You're exactly right. We all need to put our faith into practice while we're doing everyday things."

Eunice smoothed her navy blue skirt over her knees. "I—I don't mean to keep fretting about Zanna and Jonny, worrying over the situation like it's white lint on a Sunday black dress." She adjusted her glasses to look at Sam. "Mostly I can't let it come between us as friends and neighbors, like we've been for all these years.

And I shouldn't be making this any harder than it already is for you, son," she said with a sad smile at James. "You've got plenty on your plate, keeping track of your dat and me, and seeing after Emma, without me adding more."

James's lips quirked. "It's all right, Mamm. You just want the best for me, like always. It hasn't been easy for any of us since the wedding got called off."

Abby's shoulders relaxed. It always felt better, once the apologies were made and accepted, even though this topic of conversation would come up again: Zanna's pregnancy and then her baby would remind them of it.

"Pass along our best to your sister, Abby." Adah Ropp was leaning around Sam. Her pink-rimmed eyes made her age more apparent, but there was no mistaking her sincerity.

"I'll do that, jah," Abby replied.

"I'd go over and apologize to her right now, except she's being shunned."

Abby heard a dodge in Adah's remark: it was perfectly acceptable for folks to visit her sister if they did so to encourage her to keep the faith. But if the bishop thought Mrs. Ropp was ducking her responsibility, he didn't say so.

"I can't make up for what Jonny's done to your sister, or to your families," Adah said as she looked at Sam and James, "but I'll pray on it. I'll try to change my attitude about Zanna, too—and about that innocent child being born into such uncertain circumstances."

"We can't ask any more than that," Sam replied with a nod. "And we'll keep Zanna more confined—as best we can, anyway. She's got an ornery streak every bit as strong as your Jonny's."

"Jah, there's that." Adah chuckled, prompting everyone else around the room to smile, as well.

"Let's all pray about the intentions we've just stated," Vernon suggested. "We all sin and fall short, and we owe it to each other to forgive and truly forget—knowing that someday it'll be our turn to ask forgiveness."

After they bowed for a moment of silence, the bishop donned his broad-brimmed hat. "Thanks for coming together to settle these disagreements, friends. Be safe as you're going home. It gets tricky out there on that dark road."

— Chapter 15 —

Zanna appeared sleepy-eyed but rested when she came to the table the next morning. As she stretched her lithe body and yawned, her pregnancy appeared more obvious—which meant the baby was growing like it should, at nineteen weeks.

"Thought you might snooze the day away," Abby teased as she divided a steaming cheese omelet between their two plates. "But it's gut you're resting better. I was late enough getting back last night that I didn't want to wake you."

The blue eyes across the table widened. Zanna nibbled a corner of toast. "So how'd that go? I suppose those biddy hens thought I should have been there to—"

"Ach, now! They talked it out and got past pecking at each other. And you should, too." Abby sat down at her place and bowed her head briefly. "Truth be told, Adah sends you her best. Come to find out, she's feeling low about her boys leaving home. More so because Rudy doesn't allow her to make contact with them."

Zanna listened with her gaze fixed on her omelet. "Jonny told me his dat ordered him off the farm, last time he showed up. Rudy said any boy who'd smart off about honest farming and then go acting English, jumping the fence and driving a car, was no son of his."

Abby's eyebrows went up. She could well imagine Rudy Ropp making such a statement. "Can you understand how that made Adah feel?" she asked softly. "As if losing contact with her boys wasn't bad enough, she told us she took her job at the Mennonite cheese store to help pay their bills. With the cost of feed going up—"

"So you're taking her side now?"

Zanna's wounded tone didn't surprise Abby, and the question gave her the opening she'd hoped for. After she'd come home last night, she'd thought a lot about what had been said, and the bishop's good-bye had stuck with her, as well.

It gets tricky out there on that dark road.

She studied Zanna's face, pleased with how her cheeks were abloom today. Her kapp was fresh and her hair and dress looked clean and tidy. It wouldn't be easy to break all the necessary news or to change her sister's attitude, but Abby considered it her mission—her new calling—to see Zanna down this dark, tricky road to the light that came, like God's grace, every morning.

"I'm not taking anybody's side," Abby replied with a shrug. "I'm just saying that none of us knows what sort of load another person's carrying. In a lot of ways, you and Adah are alike."

As she'd expected, Zanna looked at her in utter shock. "How can you compare me to that—"

"Well, we all know how Adah Ropp speaks her mind," Abby began with a wry smile. "And when she's got an idea, or something she wants done, there's no telling her otherwise and just no stopping her. Ain't so?"

"You're saying these are her finer traits?"

Abby laughed and reached across the small table for Zanna's hand. "You don't see yourself in that description?" she asked with a grin. "There's nothing wrong with determination and a can-do attitude, little sister. It's something I've always admired about you, truth be told. Those are certainly traits any young mother needs."

"Oh." A grin flickered on Zanna's lips.

"Adah breaks the mold by working over in Clearwater, too," Abby continued quietly. "She catches a lot of static about working away from home—and you know how *that* feels, when folks don't approve of your decisions. And, like you, she latches onto more modern attitudes, yet she stays with her faith." Abby paused, reflecting on how last night's conversation had gone. "I had a better appreciation for Adah Ropp after I learned she tolerates so much criticism because her job away from home keeps the dairy—and her family—afloat."

"So you don't think working around the Mennonites cost her those two boys?" Zanna quizzed. "That's what folks always blame their leaving on. But I'm saying Jonny and Gideon skedaddled out of Cedar Creek on account of their dat's attitude. His meanness, mostly."

Not wanting to comment—because this young lady had certainly accused her own dat and older brother of being too strict—Abby steered the conversation back to where it needed to go. "We all get notions about folks, and sometimes we have no idea about the way their lives really are," she remarked carefully. She smiled at her sister, hoping her words would have the desired effect.

"When I told them you refused to give up your baby because it's no way to treat someone you love, it made them reconsider the Old Ways a bit. You have to remember that when they were your age—"

"A hundred years ago?"

"—girls had no choice in the matter," Abby continued earnestly. "They got shipped off to distant kin, or a maidel aunt in another town took them in until the baby came, and by then the adoption was already set up. When the girl was as young as you are, the parents hoped to get her married off without anyone being the wiser about her past. Including her new husband."

"That's a pretty big secret to keep, isn't it?" Zanna reflected aloud. "And . . . what of the baby, then? How's a girl supposed to start fresh with a new husband without wondering every single day about the little one she gave away? That would *kill* me, Abby!"

Abby smiled at the love ablaze in her sister's blue eyes, and prayed it would guide Zanna down some very tricky dark roads. "I'm just reminding you how hard it is for the women hereabouts to accept the way you're doing things—and I'm suggesting you appreciate Sam for not whisking you away, out of sight."

Zanna chewed her toast, considering. "I told him I'd run off again if—"

"And we'll have none of that." Abby paused

until her sister looked at her straight on. "But you know another way you're like Adah Ropp? She admitted how lonely she was without her boys around."

"But she's got Becky and Maggie—"

"Sure she does. But losing your own flesh and blood after they're nearly grown isn't much different from acting like you never birthed them." Abby let this idea soak in a bit. "What I'm saying is that Adah might warm up to being a grandmother if you'll let her. It would be a gut thing for the both of you, and for the child, too."

Zanna's expression said it was time to move on; her sister was a good one for pulling down an invisible window shade between them when she didn't want to hear difficult truths.

"So what else went on? Surely it didn't take all night to hear about Adah Ropp." Zanna glanced at Abby from the corner of her eye. "What did Beulah Mae and Eunice have to say? And James? I saw him bringing his folks over."

Abby bit her lip to keep from praising strong, mature, compelling James Graber. She would sound like a lovestruck fool, no doubt. "He was concerned about you being so upset when you came out of the store, same as Sam was. James isn't real happy, all things considered, but he'll forgive you. If you ask."

Again Zanna's blue eyes widened. "We'll see

about that. What about his mamm and Beulah Mae?"

Abby knew a dodge when she heard one. "All three of them apologized and admitted their wrongdoing at the end of the discussion, rather than waiting for a preaching Sunday to confess."

"I can see where they'd do that," Zanna remarked, probably recalling her own more public confession. "So now everybody's righty-tighty? Gut to go?"

Abby held back a remark about Zanna's irreverent attitude. "Sam asked what he and I could do to improve the situation, as well."

"And?"

Zanna's one-word response rang with a challenge. Abby knew better than to stall, so she replied as gently as she knew how. "We're to keep you out of the store's main room. Working here at the house might be best—"

"But haven't I stayed out of the phone shanty? And stayed away from my friends?" she shot back. "And wasn't I helping Sam, like folks said I should, instead of cleaning houses? Never mind that Phoebe and Gail and Ruthie work at Lois Yutzy's shop instead of at Mamm's greenhouse."

"The very things I pointed out to them, jah." Abby sighed, knowing how frustrated her sister must feel. "But when we ask, and the bishop answers—without declaring that we should

216

make you disappear and give up your baby—it's gut to go along with what he says."

Zanna stood up. She went to the table in the front room to run her hand over the rag rug, which had finished out at nearly four feet long. The two shades of blue made a colorful contrast to the duller strips and brought out the brighter hues of the printed fabrics she'd worked in.

Abby cleared their dishes without saying anything more, letting her sister chew on Vernon Gingerich's decision.

"So . . . have any more clothes landed in your donation box?" Zanna asked with a loud sigh. "Sounds like I might be making rugs all winter."

"Lots of gals would enjoy having that option." Abby knew all about that edge in Zanna's voice: her sister hadn't finished expressing herself.

Zanna threw the rug to the floor and stomped on it. She put her hands on her hips, looking like she'd bit into a lemon.

Then she relaxed . . . appeared to be contemplating her options in a more mature way. With a bare toe she stroked the rug she had made for Adah . . . focused on the royal blue fabric that had been her wedding gown. "What if I called Jonny to say his mamm wants to see him real bad? He had no hard feelings against her when he took off. It was his dat he couldn't be in the same barn with."

Abby sensed something fishy was going on,

but she took the bait. "You know where he is?"

"Well, jah!" Zanna laughed as though the answer—her condition—should make that obvious. "I know his cell number, anyway."

Abby kept her smile to herself. She prayed the Lord didn't let her play the fool too long. Zanna knew exactly where Jonny Ropp hung his hat—if he wore one anymore.

"And why would you be calling him?" she quizzed her little sister. "Rudy's told Adah she's not to speak with those boys, so some folks might see your call as meddlesome, at best. Leading Adah into temptation, against her husband's wishes."

"It's a sin for her son to come back and see her?" Zanna asked. "What if I set it up to surprise her? Or what if Jonny comes back without telling her first, so Rudy can't say—Oh, forget it! This is insane!"

Zanna glared at her, exasperated. "Honestly, Abby, do all the Old Ways—the old rules—seem *right* to you? The Ordnung says we can welcome family members who haven't yet joined the church—because they still might take their vows. Is it a crime to bring a family together again?"

It was a good question, and there was no satisfying answer. "Some folks think that when somebody jumps the fence rather than taking his vows, he's forsaking his family as well as our faith. And along with that, the Bible says wives are to submit to their husbands." Abby joined her sister in the front room, careful not to step on the new rug. "So if Adah goes against Rudy's saying she can't see the boys—"

"Oh, all right! So my calling Jonny has nothing to do with Rudy and Adah, or rules and regulations, or—" Zanna turned away. Her fists clenched and unclenched at her sides.

"Maybe I just want to hear his voice again. Maybe I can't stay mad at him because—because I *miss* him, Abby," Zanna wailed. "You don't know how *awful* it feels, to love somebody when it'll never work out. Not just because of all these stupid rules, but because . . . well, he doesn't have a *clue*. Jonny has no idea how much I love him." Her voice had trailed off to nearly nothing. Zanna hung her head and let her tears plop onto the rag rug.

Abby clenched her eyes shut. Oh, but she knew *exactly* how awful it felt to love someone who didn't know about or return that love! Once again, however, she set aside her feelings for James. Zanna had just made several revealing statements that needed to be clarified while it was just the two of them talking.

"Are you sure it's not your loneliness speaking, rather than love?" she asked gently. "It's not your way to isolate yourself, and you've been so gut about not running with your buddies."

"Not by choice, exactly." Zanna shrugged

forlornly. "Last I heard, the Coblentz twins were forbidden to come to the store, and their folks took their cell phone." Her eyes misted over. "Lots of the other girls are helping their mamms . . . probably being told to stay away from me. Like I'd be a bad influence."

Abby sighed along with her sister. This was all part and parcel of shunning. Although folks were encouraged to visit a member under the ban to show their support, it was difficult for teenage girls to show that support, and difficult for the girl being shunned to lose contact with her friends. "So," Abby began, hoping the right ideas would come to her, "now that you've told James why you can't marry him—"

"This isn't about James." Zanna sniffled loudly, shaking her head. "Oh, I tried to love him, Abby. He's a gut man, like all of you say, but he's too old for me. And I finally figured out I was making everybody happy about that marriage except for me."

Her blue eyes, full of tears, tugged at Abby's heartstrings. Anything she said, as a maidel, would hit Zanna the wrong way, so she kept quiet. Instead, Abby opened her arms and hugged her sister close, like they did far too seldom these days. Zanna swayed with her, sniffling against her shoulder, soaking in the warmth they both needed right then.

"Oh, Abby, what should I do?" Zanna sobbed.

"When I ran into James coming out of the store—when I saw the pain in those brown eyes, and knew I put it there—it hurt so bad I couldn't look at him. I didn't call off the wedding to spite him, you know. Truth is, I'd been seeing Jonny Ropp for a long while."

"Jah, we figured you'd been slipping out with him before your rumspringa, even though Dat said you were too young," Abby replied. Most young folks kept their courting a secret, and most parents went along with this Plain tradition, but Zanna hadn't always been quiet enough when she came home from her dates with Jonny.

"Oh, jah. We were sweet on each other all through school, too. He's like nobody else I've ever met. Jonny makes me laugh—at myself, even. He has a gentleness about him even if everybody's always figured him for a trouble-maker, but when he asked if I'd jump the fence to live with him, I couldn't do it. I just wanted to see him one last time, and . . . I didn't tell him I was engaged to James."

"Sounds like you had a notion you didn't want to be Mrs. Graber, even then."

"Jah. But I was too scared to tell anybody. Then later, I couldn't tell Jonny about the baby, either, though that was my intention when I ran off the morning of the wedding."

Zanna eased away to look at Abby, sighing sadly. "I've joined the church, so marrying

Jonny's not an option. And he'll think I'm forcing his hand if I lay on the blame for the baby to lure him back to Cedar Creek." She shook her head. "That's no way to catch a man if you want him to love you of his own free will—not that Jonny would figure out that *love* part, the way I did a long time ago."

Abby ached for her little sister . . . ached for the young woman so caught up in a fellow that Mamm and Sam would never approve of. But the situation made more sense now; she understood that Zanna hadn't acted on a moment's compulsion on the July day when she'd conceived Jonny's child.

And just as Jonny Ropp had no inkling of the depth of Zanna's love for him, Zanna had no idea how deeply committed James had been to her. What a sad triangle, where none of the emotions and intentions matched up, so all three parties were left unfulfilled, hurting, and lonely.

Oh, Abby knew how *that* felt, too!

"So what I'm saying is . . . calling Jonny might turn into a gut thing for Adah and me, and for Jonny, too." Zanna was reasoning aloud, although she didn't sound convinced. "Maybe hearing his voice will give me the courage to tell him about the baby—or at least tell him how bad his mamm's missing him. If he can't hook up with me and his child, maybe at least he can come see Adah—or meet her somewhere."

Abby raised an eyebrow. "I can't think you want to tell Jonny about the baby over the phone, Zanna. That's kind of personal—and who knows how he might react?"

Zanna shrugged as though she had no further ideas. She looked young and vulnerable, a far cry from the raging, protesting teenager who hated rules and regulations.

"Do you want me to drive you to where Jonny is, then? Maybe if—"

"No! I don't want to get *you* in trouble, too, Abby. It'd look like you were going against the limits of my shunning, and—" She let out a short sob. "I—I don't know what I want anymore. Or what to do. I'm so confused about everything."

"Comes with being pregnant, they say."

"But I know if there was a way to marry Jonny, a way for him to really love me, and for me to stay in gut standing with our family and the church," Zanna added tearfully, "I'd jump through a hundred hoops to be his wife. To raise this baby with him."

Abby's heart swelled. Zanna hadn't sounded this certain about anything in a long, long time, even if some of the logic didn't add up. But then, when had love ever been logical? In a perfect world, Abby could see things coming together for the best, for Zanna and Jonny . . . for her and James . . .

But the world wasn't perfect, was it? Abby

223

recalled being Zanna's age and believing things could work out the way her heart wanted them to, if only she believed strongly enough. "Well, then, sister," she murmured, thumbing the tears from Zanna's sweet face, "hold on to that thought and that hope, that things will work out. Because if you give up hoping, it's for sure and for certain you won't find what you're looking for."

Zanna nodded. She looked drained. Resigned.

"Tell you what." Abby glanced out the window, and was surprised to see snow falling in thick, fat flakes. "I've got some nice-size scraps left from Lois's curtains, and some of Sam's fabric bolts are low enough to be discounted as fat quarters, like we sell for quilting and other projects. There's no rule saying a rug has to be all rags, you know!" She ran the toe of her shoe along the edge of the oval on the floor. "This rug you made for Adah is one of the best I've ever seen, Zanna. Your stitches are relaxed and even, and you balanced the colors so well. And it lies flat, too."

"Denki for saying so—"

"Maybe rug making's not the most exciting way to pass the time, but it's something we could sell in the store so you could put the money toward baby things." Abby smiled at her. "Think about it, all right? I'll fetch those other pieces of fabric from the store, in case you decide to start a new rug."

— Chapter 16 —

Just after midnight that evening, Abby heard her sister slip down the hall and then out the front door, closing it very quietly behind her. Abby sighed. It was so tempting to throw the quilts over her head, but being her sister's keeper was a full-time job—like parenting, or caretaking for an elderly relative.

In her urgency, Zanna didn't realize how visible she was on this clear, moonlit night: a figure cloaked in black, slogging through the eight inches of snow that had fallen since mid-morning. And at seventeen, she didn't realize how transparent her ideas and actions were. Down the lane to the road she went. Moments later, the pale glow of her flashlight lit the phone shanty.

Abby watched from the window near her bed. Such a beautiful night it was. The snow had stopped, and the frosted branches of the trees and evergreens glowed in the moonlight. The world felt hushed, and Abby could see the rolling white pastures beyond Sam's house and the Grabers'. Courting couples would be out in sleighs, cuddled beneath layers of blankets as Belgians pulled them across pristine white pastures—

but that wasn't Zanna's option right now.

The poor girl had shared so many of her feelings that Abby hadn't slept soundly, as she ran the revelations through her mind again and again. Together they'd ripped bright, colorful strips of new fabric for another rug, but her sister had much larger projects in mind . . . bigger dreams and bolder ideas. And rightly so.

Abby slipped into her flannel robe and went to the front room to wait. Again, it was tempting to allow Zanna her secret trip to the phone shanty— even though everyone in Sam's house would see her tracks, come morning. By the time Abby peeked out the window beside her favorite sewing chair, Zanna was already heading back to the house.

Not much of a phone call. Had Jonny not answered? Or had he yanked the proverbial rug out from under Zanna again, giving her a reaction she hadn't counted on? The girl was head over heels, no doubt about it. Abby hoped, what with all the other disappointments Zanna had faced lately, that the most daring and dashing of the Ropp boys hadn't taken her heart for a wild ride.

Help me say the right things, Lord, she prayed as she waited in the dimness. *Help me to be the blessing Zanna needs right now.*

As the door opened, Abby held her breath. Zanna slipped out of her black coat and bonnet and hung them back in the closet. It would be easy to stay still, and maybe her sister would return to bed to ponder whatever she'd heard on the phone. But why should she lie awake herself and let her sister get all the sleep?

"And what did Jonny have to say?" Abby asked quietly.

Zanna jumped, her hand flying to her chest. "Scared me half to—what are you doing, Abby? Spying on me?"

"I had a lot on my mind. I was awake when you passed my room." Abby chuckled, making her hair shimmy down her back. "It's not like Sam and the others won't know where you went. Your footprints will be visible in the snow."

Zanna slumped in the chair on the other side of the lamp table. "Jah, I figured that out halfway to the road. But I couldn't get him off my mind. Does that make me wicked? In need of another confession this Sunday?"

Abby detected just enough sarcasm that she left that remark alone. No good would come of pressing Zanna for details she didn't want to share. Silence was the best way to make folks squirm, and then spill out what they were thinking.

"He didn't answer, so I got his voice mail. Like you said, it didn't seem right to say how bad his mamm missed him, or to tell him about his baby, over the phone—much less by leaving a message." Zanna let out a short, mirthless laugh.

"So I dialed again, just to hear Jonny's voice saying to leave my name and number and he'd call back. I couldn't do that, either, though. Does that make me a coward, Abby?"

"It just means you're nervous and scared, as any girl in your shoes would be."

Zanna let out a long, sad sigh. "And I keep wondering, too, how I'm supposed to—how I'll ever manage to be both a mamm and a dat to a newborn and still earn enough to keep us going like I told Sam I would."

"Zanna. You can stop that kind of thinking right this minute." Abby rose to wrap her arms around her sister, who seemed to be on the verge of another crying fit. "Did you really think we'd shut you out? Make you raise this baby all by yourself?"

Zanna hugged her harder. "But I told everybody . . . I didn't know what I was letting myself in for when I . . ."

"Can you name me one Amish woman who's ever had to raise a baby all alone?" Abby lifted her sister's face, which still felt chilled from her walk outside. "Your family wouldn't do that to you, Zanna. Even Sam agreed to stand by you, knowing full well what that would mean. Knowing how folks will talk and tell him he should have done things different."

Zanna's breathing became deeper as she considered these things.

"And then there's this: you know how many little sets of clothes are tucked away in the attic at Sam's. How many diapers and bibs and booties." Abby smiled as she recalled the births of Sam and Barbara's four children . . . and the way they'd all welcomed this girl in her arms, seventeen years ago. "And you can't think Phoebe or Gail or Ruthie will let you keep this baby all to yourself, once it's born. Not to mention Mamm and Barbara."

"Jah, there's that." Zanna looked up at her, smiling as best she could. "Sometimes my mind whirls in useless circles, ain't so? Like when your sewing machine belt snaps and no matter how hard you pump the treadle, the needle won't go."

Abby chuckled. "But we know how to fix that. And we've got plenty of folks living right here on Lambright Lane wanting the best for you, and for this baby—even if it's a situation that none of us has taken on before," she added. "We've just got to have faith instead of fear. We've got to believe that somehow this will work out for the gut in every one of our lives, in ways we can't know about. That's God's job, to understand how it'll all fit together."

Zanna stood up then, allowing her weariness to take over. "Maybe what I need is a gut night's sleep, now that you put all these wild notions to rest for me, Abby."

Her sister removed her kapp and let down her

hair, so pale it glimmered in the moonlight coming through the window. She'd gotten her looks from Mamm's side . . . the longer facial structure and fair skin and blue eyes. At times like these when Zanna let down her guard she seemed as fragile, as lovely, as any angel. "How is it you came to be so kind and wise, Abby?" she whispered. "I don't seem to have a brain in my head some days."

"And how is it you got the flawless skin and golden hair while I came out looking like Sam?"

Zanna laughed. "Just lucky on that count, I guess."

"We're every one of us blessed." Abby hugged her once more, savoring this moment when all was well once again. "Night, now."

"Night, now." Abby watched Zanna amble to her room, and then went over to the table where their afternoon's rug strips hung over three spare chairs. Her sister had begun the center of this new rug, which had already taken the shape of a rectangle, in a bolder mix of prints and colors than her first project.

And just like they chose the prints and the plain colors—the curves or the squared corners—it was God's doing that all the strips worked into something useful and all of a piece. And if Zanna thought Abby was kind and wise, that was God's doing, too. If only she could live up to that when the road got bumpy again.

• • •

Early the next morning, James settled into the phone shanty's rickety chair. Time to call that amusement park fellow to say the white princess carriage was on its way, and tomorrow being Thanksgiving, he wanted to get a jump on any customer calls that needed his attention. The little red button was blinking, which meant messages were waiting for him, or for the Cedar Creek Mercantile, Abby's Stitch in Time, or Treva's Greenhouse—or any members of their two families.

The Grabers and Lambrights had shared this phone ever since the previous bishop had allowed their businesses to have one: Emma and Sam's girls had insisted they get a new message machine where everyone punched in a personal code, but Sam was having none of that. He had informed his daughters they could do their courting in person if they didn't want anyone else to listen in on their love lives.

James punched the PLAY button. A Stoltzfuz gal from over west, in Jamesport, needed Sam to call her about carrying some of their jams and pickled veggies in his store . . . Treva's Aunt Mattie from Indiana wanted to pass along some family news . . .

"Zanna, you called me twice last night, after midnight, but left no message," a male voice rumbled in his ear. "Missing me again, babycakes? Been

231

w-a-ay too long since I've seen your pretty face."

James exhaled like he'd been sucker-punched.

"So if you want me to swing on by for you, gimme a call. You've got my number, girl. Bye, now."

"Jah, and I've got your number, too, you dog-gone—" James smacked the top of the old table. Why had Zanna called Jonny Ropp? And why at such a late hour?

Sneaking a call . . . Not that it was any of his business. Not two weeks ago, Preacher Abe spoke about how it was wrong to listen to other folks' messages.

But this *was* his business! Zanna was the woman he'd vowed to marry, and she had contacted that no-account bad apple who'd taken advantage of her.

Old news, remember? She confessed and now you're to forgive and forget.

James winced. His conscience was right, but it still burned him that Zanna and Jonny Ropp were apparently *not* old news. If he'd wanted proof that she didn't love him, and that he should move on, here it was.

The realization still left him feeling battered. Just when things had gotten easier because Sam had declared Zanna wasn't to work in the mercantile anymore, he'd heard *this*.

Why not cut my heart out with your sewing scissors, Zanna? It'd be a lot less painful.

James inhaled deeply, aware that his pulse was racing. He needed to finish this inner drama, somehow. Over the past five and a half weeks that he'd been working on that white princess carriage his raw feelings should have had time to heal. Sunday marked the last day of Zanna's ban. He was to forgive her in his heart even if she didn't ask him to—even if her swelling belly didn't let him forget what she'd done.

Yet in lonely moments James still recalled the laughter in her eyes after he'd teased her . . . and the sweetness of her eager kisses . . .

He jabbed the ERASE button.

James closed his eyes then, groaning. While he didn't want to hear Jonny Ropp's voice ever again—nor did he want Zanna or Emma or anyone else to hear Jonny's message—it wasn't his place to delete it. He knew better! Yet in a heartbeat his despair had gotten the best of him and had taken control of his finger.

Well . . . if she called and didn't leave Jonny a message, she had nothing important to say to him anyway, ain't so?

That wasn't a good excuse. If he were truly a mature, forgiving man, he would tell Zanna that Jonny had called, and he would apologize for erasing a message meant for her.

With a sigh James pressed the PLAY button again and jotted down a couple of numbers so he could call back about two new orders for courting buggies. It would be good to have his two employees, Leon Mast and Perry Bontrager, returning after Thanksgiving, so he could get the shop back into full production again. He felt grateful for work that would keep him busy as winter set in, yet at this moment he was just peeved enough to walk away—start over someplace far, far from Cedar Creek. The work would follow him, for he'd built up a fine reputation and every Amish community needed carriages.

"James? You done in there?"

He blinked. Emma was peering in the frosty window.

Slipping the phone numbers into his coat pocket, James stepped outside. "Sorry. Just thinking my thoughts." He put on a smile for his sister, who was shivering as the bottom of her coat flapped in the brisk north wind. "Is everything all right?"

"I've been to the merc. I need a hand getting some crates of canned peaches and baking supplies home when you get a minute."

James raised his eyebrows. "Dat's not feeling up to that today?"

"Mamm's got him bringing up jars of grape juice and whatnot from the cellar, packing them to go to Iva and Daniel's for Thanksgiving tomorrow," she replied, shaking her head. "She doesn't want Dat out walking in this snow, for fear he'll fall—not that he's happy about being cooped up." Emma cleared her throat purposefully as they stood beside the road. "And what's on *your* mind, James? You looked ready to punch your fist through something."

She'd caught him on that one. But did he really need to admit what he'd done . . . what he'd heard? Would it count as his confession if he told his sister instead of confronting Zanna or bending Preacher Paul's ear?

James considered what Emma had just said about packing for the trip. For the first time in their lives, Thanksgiving dinner would be someplace other than here at home: at the wedding, their older sister Iva had realized that Mamm was getting to be more of a hindrance than a help in the kitchen. So tomorrow, early, they were driving the ten miles to Queen City in time for the big family dinner and then staying over for a couple of days. Had Zanna been here to help Emma cook, the plans would no doubt have been different.

But that wasn't going to happen.

His parents were agitated about the trip tomorrow—another change in their lives—and they were wearing Emma thin with their fretting, so his frustration about Zanna and Jonny seemed petty in comparison—not a burden his sister needed to bear right now. "I was a little peeved about a message, jah, but I'll get over it," James hedged. "I'll go fetch those groceries for you and be right back."

Emma raised an eyebrow, as though she intended to wait him out.

"Go on, now," he prodded her. "Mamm will fuss at you for staying out here in the cold too long."

James headed back toward the mercantile, thinking again about Jonny's message for Zanna, and his anger which had flared so suddenly. He'd better get over Zanna's calling Jonny and move on. She had her own life now.

He stepped onto the mercantile's porch, past the display of sleek wooden sleds Ezra Yutzy had made, and entered the store. The bell above the door still thrilled him—as it had when he was a kid, until Mamm had scolded him about going in and out just to hear it jingle. The aroma of dried spices and freshly ground peanut butter soothed him, the plank floors were swept clean, and the shelves were arranged so Sam could see over the tops of them from wherever he was working.

Sam waved at him from a bin near the back, where he was stacking big bags of road salt. "I loaded your sister's crates into a wagon," he said, pointing toward the side door. "Easier than wheeling a grocery cart over the road. Got a few icy patches out there."

"Denki, Sam. I appreciate that." James took a deep breath, happy that while so many things he'd taken for granted had changed recently, the

Cedar Creek Mercantile remained the same as when Leroy Lambright—and Leroy's dat before him—had been running it. James started over to where the wagon awaited him, passing the same sorts of men's hats, suspenders, and work gloves that had been for sale there all his life.

"Emma says you folks are heading to Iva and Daniel's early tomorrow," Sam remarked. "Have a gut trip. Travel safe."

"It'll be a new adventure, for sure," James replied. "A break for Emma, too, since Iva's in charge of the cooking."

The wooden stairs creaked and he looked up to see Abby coming down from her loft, smiling at him. "And speaking of Emma," she said, "I have a little surprise for her. Let me grab my coat and I'll walk over with you."

James smiled to himself. It was just like Abby to sense when Emma was feeling frazzled. The two of them hadn't buddied back and forth as much since Zanna had moved into Abby's spare bedroom, and James understood how they could miss each other's company, now that so many of their other friends were married. He picked up the wagon handle, and when Abby came out of the back room in her black coat and bonnet, he pushed open the side door for her. She was carrying a long, dark garment bag on a hanger, holding it high so it wouldn't drag on the ground.

"And are you all packed and ready for your

trip, James? Hope the weather holds for your drive over to Iva's," she said brightly.

James chuckled. "Doesn't take much packing for Dat and me, you know, and Emma's packed an extra dress or two for her and Mamm. It's the other boxes—jars of canned vegetables and jellies, and bags of sweet corn and peas from the freezer—that has them in a dither, I think."

"Deciding what all to share?"

"Figuring out how to fit all those boxes in the carriage and still have room for the four of us."

Abby's laughter blew away on a gust of wind as they paused at the side of the road to allow a pickup to go by. Her cheeks had turned pink and her brown eyes sparkled as though whatever she carried in that bag was something mighty special. James glanced inside the empty phone shanty . . . and wondered if he should admit to Abby that he'd erased that message from Jonny Ropp. As he thought about it, Jonny hadn't relayed any impor-tant information, as such. He'd only returned Zanna's call and teased her about missing him.

Abby might be happier not knowing about that call, especially when she was bursting with the anticipation of giving Emma her surprise. He decided to deal with deleting that message—and his feelings about it—himself, for now.

As they entered the snowy lane to the house, Abby dashed ahead of him, her sturdy boots crunching in the snow. "I'll get the door for you, James—"

"I've got a piece of plyboard under the porch," he called out, chasing after her. The heavy wagon clattered on the hard-packed snow. "I'll lay it on the steps and wheel the wagon right on up to the door. Saves me hauling up several armloads."

Abby seemed invigorated by the cold weather, and it lifted his spirits to be spending these few moments with her even though it was Emma she was coming to see. He propped the plyboard to one side of the three steps, like a ramp, and up he went with the wagon. As Abby held the door to let him precede her inside, her smile took him back more than a decade, to when they were scholars together in the one-room school. So carefree and happy she seemed right now, despite all that was happening with her younger sister.

You could take a lesson from Abby Lambright. Attitude is everything.

James was about to say how much he had enjoyed her company, but the way Abby was smiling up at him, her wind-flushed face framed by her bonnet, left him temporarily speechless. For fear of sounding juvenile, he merely murmured, "Denki, Abby. Mighty kind of you."

"You're welcome, James." She nodded and let him pass in front of her. Was that a sigh he heard, as though she'd been hoping he'd say more?

When Abby saw Emma at the kitchen table,

loading quart jars of vegetable soup and apple pie filling into a milk crate, her excitement filled the room. "I brought you a little something," she said with a big grin. "An early birthday present—and a Thanksgiving gift. Because I'm ever so thankful you're my friend, Emma."

Emma's eyes widened. Her mouth made an O as she held the sides of the garment bag that was suspended in Abby's hand. James thought his sister might cry. "Now what did you go and do?"

"Open it and see."

Emma glanced at James, as though asking if he knew what the dark bag concealed. James shrugged and took the first crate of canned peaches from the wagon. It wasn't even a gift for him, yet he vibrated with anticipation. If Abby had chosen it—or made it—whatever it was would be nothing short of wonderful.

"Oh, Abby! A dress—"

"Couldn't let your mamm be the only one at the table tomorrow wearing something new."

"And made from this gabardine I spotted from clear across the store the minute I walked in last week."

Abby chuckled slyly. "Didn't I tell you I see everything that goes on from my little perch? I thought this rusty red color was the nicest of the lot—different from anything you had. And different from the ones I made your mamm."

Emma grabbed her in a hug and held her for

several moments. "You have no idea, Abby, how you just brightened my day—my whole week," she murmured. She pulled away so she could smile into her best friend's eyes. "And I'll have you know, Mamm's wearing the cranberry dress tomorrow. I saw her looking at it this morning, grinning like a kid at Christmas."

"Happy to hear that," Abby replied. "I know she was perturbed at you for clearing out her old ones."

Emma released her to hang the new dress on a peg where it wouldn't get wrinkled. She ran her fingers over the fabric . . . a new dress, the matching V-shaped cape, and a crisp white apron, as well. The expression on her face made James realize how perfectly Abby had pleased his sister. Emma had so little time to sew, and was so used to putting Mamm and Dat's—and his— needs before her own, he couldn't recall the last time she'd worn something new.

And wasn't that one of the things Abby Lambright did best? She quietly watched, and waited for just the right time to share her love and her talents . . . the way she had taken Zanna into her home and then convinced the naysayers around Cedar Creek that her sister should keep her baby because she loved it.

"I'll miss coming over tomorrow night for a piece of your pumpkin pie, Abby," Emma said. She reached into the box on the table and handed Abby a jar of strawberry-rhubarb jam.

"You'll have a gut day with Iva and Dan and the rest of them," Abby assured her as she tucked the small jar into her coat pocket. "We've got the whole holiday season now to enjoy pumpkin pies—and we will!"

— Chapter 17 —

As Abby and Zanna stepped into the kitchen where Mamm, Barbara, and the girls bustled about, Abby closed her eyes in sheer delight. "I don't care how much gut food we cook, week in and week out, nothing else smells like Thanksgiving Day!" She set down her pie carrier to remove her coat while Zanna closed the door against a brisk wind.

"That comes from not eating all morning, waiting for the feast." Mamm finished rolling out the whole wheat dough so Ruthie could cut circles with a biscuit cutter and then fold them into a "pocketbook" shape.

"It's the stuffing," Phoebe declared. She and Gail stirred dried bread cubes into the Dutch oven, where they'd simmered chopped celery and onions. "Why don't we make this for every day, instead of just for turkey and filling pork chops now and again?"

"That's what keeps stuffing special. It's not like we ever go hungry, you know." Barbara emptied two quart jars of green beans into a glass casserole dish. "Me, I'm just thankful Abby made the pumpkin pies. What with checking on Marian Byler, I ran short of time yesterday—and nobody else makes pumpkin pie as spicy and tasty as Abby's."

"And how's Marian's baby, then? Home from the hospital, I hope?" Abby asked.

Barbara added a quart of drained tomatoes and spoonfuls of Italian seasonings with the green beans and then stirred them all together. "Elizabeth's as perky as you please," she said, shaking her head. "Marian's another story, grieving the one she lost. The doctors agreed there was nothing we could have done—that Elizabeth's cord cut off Esther's oxygen for too long before we knew about it. It would've been a hardship had she lived, on account of the brain damage. But it's a sad story no matter how you look at it."

"Can't wait to see them later today. They're calling her Bessie!" Ruthie piped up.

Even with that cheerful remark, a cloud hung in the kitchen for a moment. Zanna stirred the homemade noodles, maybe a little faster than she had to. "It's got to be hard, carrying babies to term, hoping and dreaming for them—"

"Suzanna, there's no call to worry yourself,"

Mamm insisted gently. "Your baby will be just fine. You come from hardy stock—just look around you."

"And like we talked about," Abby reminded her, "it's not like you're doing this all by yourself. We'll get you through it, little sister."

Happier chatter resumed then, as slices of acorn squash went into the oven beneath a huge turkey. In the other oven, a duck roasted in a blue enamel pan, and Mamm flipped it expertly with a spatula and a meat fork so the skin would get crispy. "Awful nice of Carl Byler to dress this bird for you, Barbara. He's certainly had other things on his mind."

"He said it was the least he could do for me." Barbara sprinkled shredded mozzarella over the bean casserole, covered it, and then stuck it on the rack under the duck. "We'll put half of that duck and some turkey aside, to take over later. They won't have much dinner on their table after Carl's family goes home to Ohio tomorrow."

By the time Matt and Sam came in from the sheep chores, the meal was nearly ready. In from the porch came a bowl of cranberry sauce that glimmered like a ruby, along with the apple-walnut salad Dat had always loved. The fridge had been too full to hold those two dishes.

"It's a wonder the table doesn't collapse," Matt proclaimed after they'd prayed. And because he'd said it in just the way his dawdi had, for as many years as they could recall, everyone fell silent in remembrance.

"Jah, Leroy's right here with us," Mamm said in a voice that quivered a bit. "He wouldn't be missing a Thanksgiving dinner. And he wouldn't want us getting all teary-eyed, either. Start that turkey around, son."

As their plates filled and then their stomachs, Abby savored the talk as much as the sage stuffing; she laughed until she shook at Ruthie's account of ice skating with the wobbly-legged Detweiler girls. All around the long table, the faces she loved most glowed with goodwill, not to mention the glory of having three kinds of dessert. Mamm's gooseberry pie suited those with a taste for tartness, while Matt raved over the apple-raisin crisp Phoebe had baked. When they could hold no more, however, it was Abby's pumpkin pie pan that had nothing but a few crust crumbs left in it.

"Sure thankful you brought another one of those, Abby," Sam said as he pushed himself away from the table. "I can't do it justice yet, what with sampling the other two sweets. I'm saving my favorite for later."

Abby beamed. What a wonderful meal! Even though it was a few days before Zanna's shunning ended, Sam had put away the separate table before they'd arrived, and Zanna sat with the rest of them. No one had mentioned any gossip the neighbors were spreading about her, either, so their conversation had been pleasant. With all of the women and girls helping, washing dishes and redding up the kitchen went quickly.

"We're going for a quick check on the Bylers," Barbara reminded Sam, while Mamm wrapped up generous portions of their meal to take along. Sam and Matt talked of driving over to see cousins north of Bloomingdale after the women returned.

Zanna smiled shyly. "Abby's taking me to deliver Adah Ropp's rug. We're hoping nobody will see that as a violation of my ban, what with only a few days left of it."

"It's a generous gesture," Barbara confirmed. "I've got to think Adah misses her boys most of all on the holidays. And such a lovely rug will surely convince her you wish her the best."

"That's the idea," Abby said. "She can't fault us for having gut intentions, anyway." As they said their good-byes and then walked over to fetch the rug from Abby's house, she smiled at her younger sister. "Are you feeling all right about this visit? Seems to me you've come a long way in the six weeks since you let out Jonny's name."

"It'll be fine." Zanna's black bonnet concealed her expression as she hunkered down against the cold wind.

"It'll be easier to do this and not have it on your mind anymore," Abby remarked gently. "And what can Adah possibly say but gut things?

246

She's getting a finer rug than I would have made her—and I'm not just saying that, either."

"I'm glad you're going along, Abby. In case I trip over my tongue."

"It'll go fine. Maggie and Becky will be glad we stopped by, too." Abby headed toward the stable to hitch up a horse. "Think of it as spreading sunshine where it's needed most. Put on your cheeriest smile, sister, and I'll see you in a few."

They were rolling down the road shortly, huddled together in a buggy beneath a heavy blanket so the rest of the family could use the closed carriages. Abby smiled despite the wind that nipped at her cheeks. The world looked like a picture postcard: smooth, perfect snow blanketed the pastures, and the evergreens wore special dresses of white lace. A cardinal warbled above them, and from across the road came a reply.

As they drove over the Ropps' cattle guard, their wheels rattling on its frozen steel pipes, a grizzled German shepherd woofed at them. This raised the alarm for two beagles to run from the barn, baying as though the sky were falling. Folks joked about Rudy Ropp's four-footed security system, but out here where there wasn't another farmstead in sight—near a highway that carried a lot of traffic over the Missouri-Iowa line—it was wise to have such noisy greeters.

When Abby caught sight of Adah's face at the front window, she waved, her heart beating faster. "Since we won't be staying all that long," she murmured to her sister, "we'll leave Tucker hitched."

Nodding, Zanna eased down from her side of the buggy. Abby was about to shoo the barking dogs when the Ropp girls stepped out onto the porch, grinning. "Happy Thanksgiving!" Maggie called out.

"Jah, Mamm's hoping you brought her new rug," Becky chimed in. "I dropped a cherry pie on the old one—"

"Upside down!" her little sister added gleefully.

"—so now it's out in the barn for the dogs."

Adah stuck her head out the door and waved. "Don't keep them out here in the cold with your chatter, girls! Bring them on in."

Zanna clutched the rug, wrapped in a long plastic bag, as though using it for a shield. She climbed the uneven wooden steps and went into the kitchen, with Abby right behind her. Leftovers from the holiday meal cooled on the countertops. It was a cozy room but in need of fresh paint, and the gingham curtains above the sink were streaked where the sun had faded them.

Adah seemed genuinely pleased to see them, but she raised a finger to her lips. "Rudy's snoozing after his big dinner," she murmured. "Early as he gets up of a morning, it's best to let him nap when he can. We'll visit here in the kitchen."

Abby nodded as the girls took their coats and pulled out kitchen chairs for them.

"Shall I brew up some tea?" their hostess asked. She paused, gazing at Zanna. "It's gut to see the both of you. I'm guessing that's the rag rug I asked for a while back?"

"Jah." Zanna grinned timidly before handing her the long roll. "Abby asked me to make it, what with the time I've been spending at home—"

"And look at all the colors!" Maggie cried when her mother unrolled it. "Better keep Becky and her cherry pies away from this one."

"Almost a shame to put it on the floor." Adah held the oval rug close to study it. "Such nice even stitches, too. The crocheted kind holds together so much better than—"

Rudy Ropp cleared his throat noisily, scowling at them from the doorway. "You can't accept that rug, Adah. And you know quite well *why.*" His hair stood up on one side, but there was nothing sleepy about those eyes; they bored right into Zanna, as though he were looking straight through to her soul and believed the worst about her.

Abby cleared her throat. "Gut afternoon, Rudy. This would be the rug Adah ordered from me several weeks ago, so—"

"But Zanna made it. And Zanna's handing it over to her," Rudy interrupted, "and we're not to take anything from the hand of one who's been shunned. Considering her circumstances, and who she claims fathered that baby, I'll have nothing she's touched coming into my house. Not even if she's welcomed back into the fold on Sunday."

Adah and her girls looked horrified, while Zanna began to tremble. Abby slipped an arm around her sister's waist. "That's mighty harsh condemnation, considering how my sister confessed before the membership and has nearly served out her shunning."

"Jah, I heard that confession," Rudy replied brusquely. "And, frankly, I don't believe a word that comes out of her mouth. Anybody who'd betray James Graber and then try to blame her baby on Jonny, after all the wildcatting she did before she took her instruction . . ."

"That was during her rumspringa, Dat," Becky mumbled.

"Don't you talk back to me, daughter!" His words echoed in the low-ceilinged kitchen as his face turned as ruddy as a fall apple. "The brothers you once had never grew out of their running-around phase, and I'm saying Zanna's a bird of that same feather. Even though she joined the church and went through the motions of confessing."

Abby's heart skittered in her chest. She felt awful for poor Adah and the girls. "You've got it all wrong about Zanna seeing a lot of fellas before she said her vows. And if you had doubts during that Members' Meeting, Rudy, you should have said something then."

"Don't tell me what I should or shouldn't do," he blurted, crossing his burly arms over his large stomach. "You and Adah have too many notions in your fool heads about having your say and doing as you please. And then there's Zanna," he added, his voice rising. "Anybody who's courted as many fellas as she has, batting her big blue eyes at them, has nothing but trouble on her mind!"

"Rudy!" Adah exclaimed. "How can you say—"

"We'll be going, then. Didn't mean to disrupt your day." As Abby slipped into her coat, Zanna hurried out the door without putting hers on. Abby glanced apologetically at Becky and Maggie and then took the rug Adah thrust at her.

"And don't be telling the bishop he needs to visit again," Rudy called after them. "Can't get my cows milked with Vernon chewing his cud at me."

By the time Abby stepped into the carriage, Zanna had the reins in her hands. Abby let out the breath she'd been holding. "That was the saddest, most awkward—I'm so sorry he said those awful things about you, Zanna. I had no idea that was coming."

Zanna focused on the snowy road, sitting stiffly and staring straight ahead.

"Do you see now why Jonny and his brother left?" Zanna asked in a choked voice. "If I were

Becky and Maggie—and Adah—I'd go to work at the cheese factory one day and never come back. They're afraid he'll come after them, though."

"Jah, that was fear on their faces. The three of them look too scared to leave and too scared to stay." Abby spread the rug across their laps so she could roll it up. "I'm sorry that happened to you, Zanna. Rudy had no call to—it would be a gut idea for Preacher Paul and Preacher Abe both to go along when Vernon visits again," she mused aloud. "Surely the bishop realized something wasn't right, last time he was there."

Abby put her hand on Zanna's back and rubbed it. "Would you feel better if we went to see the cousins with Sam and Matt? Might help you get that nasty voice out of your mind."

Zanna shook her head, looking miserable. "I just want to work on my rug. When my hands are busy and I'm thinking about what color will look best for the next row, I forget about what all's happened of late." She looked at Abby, her eyes glistening with tears. "I'm trying to think mostly positive thoughts. They say it's as important for the baby to feel love and happiness as it is for me to eat healthy foods."

"Jah, there's that," Abby murmured as they approached Lambright Lane. "Every one of us needs to feel loved. Most especially Rudy Ropp, I'm thinking."

— *Chapter 18* —

Fresh snow had fallen late Saturday night, after James and his family had returned home from their Thanksgiving visit at Iva and Dan's, so the ride out to Mervin Mast's for the Sunday preaching service took a little longer. From Nissley's Ridge, the view of all the farmsteads beneath their fresh blankets of white ordinarily took James's breath away. Last time he'd been here was on his wedding day, when he'd been searching for his bride. A lot had happened these past seven weeks, and he'd made his peace. With most of it, anyway.

James felt edgy, though. He hadn't seen Zanna since before the meeting at Sam's place and he'd tried to put her out of his thoughts ever since he'd heard Jonny Ropp's phone message. There would be no avoiding her today, however: she'd be seated up front, awaiting reconciliation with the members after the preaching. She'd still be having Jonny Ropp's baby, but her sin with that man would be forgiven—erased as surely as he had deleted Jonny's message on the machine four days ago.

How many times had she checked the phone after he'd hit the ERASE button? Did she figure

Jonny was ignoring her message? Did she call him back? Why couldn't he get that whole thing off his mind? Only one way to quit stewing about it . . .

James stopped the carriage near Mervin's big white house and hopped out to assist his parents. While Emma escorted them inside, he parked the carriage and let his bay into the barnyard with the rest of the horses. While erasing a phone message was a minor offense, he'd decided to confess to Vernon or Paul, and follow their counsel about whether he should admit his misdeed to Zanna.

As James approached the house, however, he saw that Sam and Abby were speaking with the bishop in low, earnest voices. Vernon Gingerich's round face was creased with concern as Abby related her story, while Sam nodded beside her. He saw no sign of Zanna.

Has she decided against coming back? James scanned the crowd of women in their black bonnets and coats filing inside to get warm. He returned Mamm's little wave, noting how much shorter she looked these days, standing beside his sister.

". . . just thought you should be aware of the situation out there," Abby was saying. Vapors of her breath encircled her rosy cheeks before vanishing into the cold air. "Rudy's as angry a man as I've ever seen, and it's not just his interfering with today's meeting I'm concerned about. Adah and the girls won't tell you about his temper, on account of he'll get back at them. It seems like a powder-keg situation."

James raised his eyebrows. While Rudy Ropp had never been a cheerful sort, he seemed stable . . . usually worn to a frazzle, but keeping his dairy afloat and his family fed. The economy had been rough of late—for English as well as Amish—yet he sensed Abby's concerns had nothing to do with the Ropps' financial situation.

Vernon nodded and thanked the Lambrights for keeping him informed. He gazed around, gave James a quick wave, and then went inside to shake the hands of all who'd come to worship today.

James sighed. He'd have to wait until after the meeting to speak with the bishop or Preacher Paul. He gazed at the line of bearded, black-clad men filing into the Masts' front room . . . waved at Leon Mast, Mervin's son, who worked for him in the carriage shop. Then, when James didn't spot his father, he followed a hunch. Sure enough, a lone figure ambled through the snow toward the pasture fence where the horses stood shoulder to shoulder, snorting and shifting to stay warm.

"Dat!" he called out. "We can't be dilly-dallying. The singing's about to start."

His father kept walking, as though he hadn't heard. *Or he's strolling down his own little memory lane. Time to be getting him checked again.*

As James ran out to fetch him, a rapid-fire *clip-clop! clip-clop!* came down the snow-packed lane behind him. When he got his father turned toward the house again, he saw Adah, Becky, and Maggie Ropp scrambling toward the kitchen. Their expres-sions mirrored what he'd overheard moments ago: a sense of agitation that didn't come from being a few moments late for church. As Rudy raced the carriage toward the corral, James yanked his father off the driveway for fear they'd be hit.

And what sort of bee is up Rudy's bonnet, that he's driving so reckless?

"Watch out, there!" Dat hollered, scowling at the carriage behind them. "What's the world comin' to when a fella nearly gets run over goin' into church?"

"I don't have an answer to that," James murmured, hurrying him along. "Let's get our trousers brushed off and take our seats, so Mamm won't think we're playing hooky."

A boyish grin lit his father's face. "Used to do that now and again, when I was a scholar in the lower grades," he admitted in a conspiratorial whisper. "Your mother took it upon herself to be sure the teacher knew it, too."

James grinned in spite of his mood. How amazing, that his father so vividly recalled details from seventy years ago but probably couldn't say what he'd eaten for breakfast. As they entered the crowded room, which had been expanded by removing the partitions to the bedrooms and kitchen, James pointed his dat toward the waiting ministers. They all shook hands before taking the last spaces on the back bench. He nodded across the crowd at Emma, who'd been watching for them to come in.

And then he saw Zanna. Seated in front of the other women, with her head lowered and her hand over her face as was the custom for one under the ban, she still made his heartbeat skitter. Her belly was bigger . . . and he had mixed, wistful feelings about that.

His musings were cut short when Rudy Ropp slammed the door and squeezed in beside him as the hymn leader sang the first note. The dairy farmer's breathing was labored after rushing in from the corral. Rudy focused on the page of the *Ausbund* James held for the three of them, but he didn't sing. Several minutes later, as Abe Nissley read the Scripture and began the first sermon, Rudy shifted like a restless child. James felt anything but worshipful, caught between a fidgeting Ropp and his dat, who needed elbowing now and again so he wouldn't doze off.

Rather than settling as the service stretched into its second and third hour, the man on his left raked his beard or sighed loudly or shifted. James considered what Abby had been saying to Vernon, about how things were not ideal at the

Ropp place: a powder-keg situation, she'd called it. And, indeed, Rudy's fuse seemed to grow shorter as the service lengthened. It was as though someone were winding a spring inside him tighter and tighter with each verse of the final hymn, until—when Bishop Gingerich called Zanna to come forward for her confession—Rudy popped up like a jack-in-the-box.

"This is wrong, I tell you!" he blurted. "What we did, agreeing to let that—that Jezebel—remain amongst us while she's carrying a baby, goes against all the Ordnung says. We must get back to the Old Ways."

"Brother Ropp, you've spoken out of turn," Vernon replied firmly. "You were here when we voted on Suzanna's shunning six weeks ago and you made no complaint."

James closed his eyes; Zanna's expression was too much to bear. It was difficult enough for her to kneel before this gathering of members once again, to confess her sin and await a unanimous acceptance, let alone endure another outburst of name-calling.

"My wife spoke up, however," Rudy pointed out, "concerning the influence that Zanna's example — and the man who shared her sin—would have on our own two daughters. Yet no one stood by Adah to support her plea, not even after Zanna accused our son Jonny of being the father. I don't believe a word of *that,* either," he exclaimed vehemently.

"You took her at her word without a shred of proof."

Rudy sucked in a breath and continued his tirade before anyone could interrupt him. "But I can tell you that Zanna came to our place Thanksgiving with a rug. Said she'd made it," he added with a sneer. "Treating it like a peace offering, she was, yet expectin' to be paid for it—and leadin' Adah into temptation by handing it directly to her. And Zanna was still under the ban, no less."

Vernon pressed his lips into a thin line, a sign he was searching for the best way to regain control of this meeting. Paul Bontrager rose from his place on the preachers' bench and gazed sternly at Rudy.

"Brother Ropp, you had a chance to discuss these matters with the bishop when he went to your place earlier in the week," the preacher pointed out. "Vernon told me you all but chased him out of your barn. Not very neighborly. Nor proper."

The folks in the crowded room looked at one another in dismay. James sensed that many of the oldest members probably shared Rudy's misgivings, but in the interest of encouraging Zanna to remain a faithful member of the church, they had set aside their objections.

"I was trying to get my cows milked," Rudy protested. "He came at the busiest part of my day—and he didn't offer to help, neither."

"All that aside, Brother Ropp, let's show some respect for the man who's taking responsibility for your soul," Abe Nissley remarked. He, too, had stood up and the three preachers made a formidable sight in their black vests and stern expressions. "If you want to abide by the Old Ways, you'll be apologizing right now to Bishop Gingerich—both for your behavior last week and for this disruption of a Members' Meeting."

Rudy drew himself up in a huff, looking ready to spout off again, but the bishop beat him to it.

"I heard a different version of Zanna's Thanksgiving visit, Brother Ropp."

The house got quiet. Vernon's eloquent voice carried easily over the crowd. "I understand your wife ordered a rag rug several weeks ago, and Abby Lambright invited her sister to make it because folks insisted that Zanna remain out of the public eye. Abby saw this as a good way to mend some fences."

"Who're you going to believe, Bishop? Abby Lambright, who took Zanna into her house so she wouldn't be so *embarrassed* by folks like Adah, who call this situation as disgraceful as it is?" Rudy demanded. "Or will you stand with the man who kept a more Christian home by making his sons clear out when they refused to join the church?"

James let out an exasperated breath. "Rudy, sit down, man," he insisted in a hoarse whisper.

"Kids born Amish are family—children to be loved—even if they go their own way."

Rudy turned on him like a cornered animal. "And who are you to talk, James Graber? You who condoned the behavior of the woman who ran out on you, by voting she could stay here amongst us and raise that baby?" he challenged. Then he pointed toward Zanna, who was still kneeling. "What kind of man would tolerate such a betrayal?"

Several folks sucked in their breath while kapps bobbed across the room. James felt the heat rise into his cheeks, but he held his tongue.

His dat, however, popped up off the bench. "You've got no call to speak to my James in that tone. It's that kind of meanness that made your own boys leave home, and you can't tell none of us any different."

Bishop Gingerich was making his way between the men's benches, in an unprecedented trip away from the preachers' position. His face looked tight with the effort to remain patient. "The Old Ways tell us how a Members' Meeting is to be con-ducted, as well, Brother Ropp," he said in a deceptively calm voice. "You are clearly out of order. You will sit down now. We shall proceed with Zanna Lambright's confession and the vote, and then we shall address *your* concerns. Following procedure is part and parcel of the Old Order, is it not?"

Rudy Ropp's breathing became more pronounced. His tall, bulky body shook and his cheeks became the color of raw beefsteak. "If that's the way it's to be," he rasped, "then I can't belong to this church—nor this community—anymore! It's like in the Gospel of Matthew when Jesus called the Pharisees hypocrites for shutting the kingdom of heaven—not going in themselves, nor letting anybody else in, either."

Rudy's hand swooped down to grab his black hat and then he strode toward the door. He pivoted to scan the crowd. "Come along, Adah! Girls!" he commanded. "We've got nothing in common with these folks anymore."

Adah's face paled. She stood up among the women, looking unsure of what to do and very frightened. "Rudy, the bishop said you can have your say after—"

"Are you going to stand by me? Or will you betray me the same way Zanna Lambright treated the man she was promised to?"

The room got deathly still. Nobody breathed, watching the emotions play on poor Adah's face . . . and feeling Becky and Maggie's terror when they slowly rose, back among the younger women. The Old Order taught that obedience to God and the church came before allegiance to family, so Rudy Ropp's demand was no small matter.

James recalled the way Adah had disrupted the

meeting six weeks ago, when Zanna had made her confession and admitted who had fathered her child. He had resented the way their outspoken neighbor had humiliated Zanna, yet now he felt compelled to offer poor Adah and her girls a place to stay until this matter got sorted out. It made better sense now, what he'd heard Abby telling the bishop before church. And it was a situation unlike any he'd ever seen in the peaceful town of Cedar Creek.

With a whimper, Adah hung her head. But she stepped carefully toward the aisle, around the other women's knees and feet, as though she dared not defy the man who had so blatantly challenged her. Maggie and Becky followed, too shaken to do otherwise.

"Let's offer up a prayer," Vernon said as the doors closed behind the Ropp family. "Lord God, we ask Your presence with a troubled family, just as we require Your assistance to know how we, as Your church, should deal with this situation. We trust You to guide us in the way we should go."

After this rare prayer spoken aloud, the bishop's footsteps were the only sound as he returned to his usual position. He paused in front of Zanna, as though composing his thoughts, while everyone else watched. And waited.

James held his breath. After two outbursts during meetings—both on account of Zanna and her decision to keep her baby—would Bishop

Gingerich insist that she leave Cedar Creek? Four months remained before she delivered, and if her presence sparked such unheard-of controversy, Vernon might decide to remove the source of their troubles. James placed his elbows on his knees and put his head down. He wasn't praying, exactly, just putting his thoughts into more meaningful order.

"Sister Suzanna, I commend you for remaining on your knees, in the faith—not only during this distressing turn of events today, but throughout these weeks you were under the ban," Vernon finally said in a low voice. "We'll continue now, by hearing your confession and then asking you the time-honored questions that follow it."

Folks relaxed visibly. Shoulders loosened . . . scowls eased. Although James had a hard time hearing it again, Zanna's clear, compelling account of her wrongdoing seemed to purge everyone of the tension Rudy Ropp's outburst had caused.

Dat leaned closer to whisper in his ear, "Did I do the wrong thing, tellin' Rudy to zip a lip?" His father's eyes widened and he quivered a little. He suddenly seemed so old . . . so fragile. "Didn't mean to make things harder for you—"

"Oh, Dat . . ." James hugged his father until their foreheads met. It wasn't proper behavior for church, but what else could he possibly do? "I'm grateful you took my side. Grateful you've shown me so much more love and kindness

264

than Rudy Ropp gave his boys. Sad story, that one."

His father clapped him on the back. "Proud of you, son. You're a gut man."

The world went still. Time crystallized. James suddenly saw this moment through the bright shine of sunlight on an icicle. True enough, the bishop was asking Zanna if she believed in the salvation of Jesus Christ, but something told James to cherish this fine moment when his father was mentally clear—and to believe every word Dat had said.

A sweetness flowed through him. For the first time in weeks, James felt peaceful and right with the way things were. Sometime soon he'd know God's purpose for putting him through these tough months with Zanna Lambright.

Stewing over that erased phone message suddenly seemed petty. And as James saw how Abby gazed at her kneeling sister with steadfast, unconditional love, it became clear to him how he should handle that erased phone call. The answer rang with the solid clarity of the Old Ways, yet gave him the hope of a new understanding about Zanna and his feelings for her.

James grinned despite the solemnity of the occasion. It felt so good to *know* how to proceed: God the Father had spoken to him through his own earthly dat, and despite Dat's infirmities, the message resonated loud and clear. It was another case of how the Lord worked out His purpose even through people who were imperfect—and usually unaware of the parts they played in the bigger picture.

As Zanna left the room so the members could vote, her face shone with the relief of having completed her part of this ancient ritual: confession and penitence. Forgiveness and acceptance would follow if everyone believed she had truly turned herself toward the right way again.

"Jah!" James affirmed when his turn came to vote. Dat nodded and said the same.

The vote went quickly. As Zanna returned to hear their positive verdict, sunshine beamed through the windows as though the whole world shone with the happiness James felt. Renewed. Reaffirmed. After Bishop Gingerich adjourned the meeting by suggesting a silent prayer for the Ropp family, and thanks for the meal about to be served, what a wonderful moment it was. The younger women flocked forward to hug Zanna, exclaiming over how they had missed her and saying that she looked like a rose in bloom.

James agreed. His heart thrummed when Mary and Martha Coblentz linked arms around Zanna. When Zanna gazed at Emma and then beckoned her to join them, a circle of lifelong friendship was renewed. His sister's joy brought tears to his eyes. She had missed her friend more than she'd been able to admit. The older women then encouraged Zanna, too, complimenting her behavior in light of the way the Ropps had tormented her.

And wasn't that something? This was the same girl who had defied the rules and acted on impulse for most of her life.

James considered this revelation, yet another gift on this day that had started on such a sour note. He rehearsed what he might say about the phone message—yet this was not the time to address his own need for forgiveness. He could wait for a quiet, more ordinary moment when Zanna would truly hear what he needed to say.

When he stepped up to her, James reached for both of her hands rather than settling for the customary handshake. This was the woman he'd planned to marry, after all: he loved Zanna even if that emotion had changed shape and meaning over these past couple of months. Her hands still felt so tiny in his; those bottomless blue eyes still swallowed him whole when Zanna focused on him.

"It's a wonderful day," he murmured, aware he was talking yet not sure what words were coming out.

"Jah. Denki for your kindness, James. You could have acted a lot different."

Again he considered the change in her tone, her response. This ordeal was making a woman of her, even if she was no longer *his* woman. "I hope we can talk soon, Zanna. I—I have things to tell you."

Her eyes widened. "That would be fine," she replied, glancing at the others who were waiting to greet her. "You know where to find me."

"Jah." He gently squeezed her hands, aware of how others were following their conversation. "Take care, now."

"You, too, James."

— Chapter 19 —

What had James meant by his mysterious remarks? All afternoon Zanna replayed the feel of his hands holding hers, the expression on his face . . . the light that shimmered in his deep brown eyes. *I hope we can talk soon, Zanna. I have things to tell you.*

As the common meal progressed, she reminded herself that he had nothing romantic in mind: James Graber wouldn't be proposing again, nor did she want to marry him. Raising her baby would be so much easier with a husband, though —not that she'd called Jonny back to tell him he was going to be a father. The table talk reminded her of something else Jonny should probably know, however: his mamm needed Gideon and him more than ever now that Rudy's temper had boiled over for all of Cedar Creek to see.

"Never heard the likes of such talk in church,"

Nell Coblentz remarked as she passed along a relish tray. Like her twin daughters, she had auburn hair, and her fair complexion colored with her emotions.

"And while Rudy was never one to visit much, who would have dreamed he had such a temper? And who could bclicve Adah's been living with it—and her being so outspoken," Lois Yutzy joined in. "Here—I brought these candied fruit buns for you to try before I bake them for the shop. Got the starter from a gal over in Jamesport."

"Jah, I've been eyeing those," Mamm said as she snatched one from the basket. "The way Abby told it, she and Zanna couldn't leave fast enough when they took that rug to Adah on Thanksgiving Day. Do you suppose he's really leaving the church? Or moving to another settlement and taking his milk cows with him?"

"I don't think Rudy's got the money for a move like that," Bessie Mast remarked. "But one thing's for certain. Adah and those girls don't want to go with him. And that opens a whole new can of worms."

"Jah, the bishop's got his hands full."

Zanna finished eating her slice of red velvet cake and excused herself. After the common meal, the younger people usually planned activities for Sunday evening. As she approached the barn, where they went when it was too cold to stay outside, it felt good to spend time with her buddy bunch again—to speak freely to them now that she'd submitted to the shunning and restored herself to full membership.

She paused inside the door. The volleyball nets were set up and they were choosing teams. Physical exercise would do her good, but did expectant mothers play such boisterous games? What if the baby got hit by a spiked ball? If she jumped up and then landed wrong, would the baby be jarred loose? Her arm curved protectively around her belly.

Zanna realized, too, that most of these friends were still enjoying their rumspringa . . . and were probably a few years away from taking their baptismal vows. And while some of them had paired up—like Phoebe and Owen Coblentz, who were sharing a huge gingerbread man over in the corner—she didn't feel comfortable with the courting crowd, either. She'd known Mamm's friends all her life, of course, but they were, well—old. They talked of their adult children and their grandkids; the frustrations of aging and husbands set in their ways like mailbox posts in concrete.

So now that she'd been welcomed back . . . where did she fit in? While Mose and Hannah Hartzler and Perry and Salome Bontrager were close to her in age and expecting their first children, it wasn't like they'd be including her in any of their activities. They had married last spring and were set up in new homes. She would be the only one without a partner.

Is this how it feels to be a maidel, like Abby?

For a scary moment, Zanna envisioned herself at twenty-one with a school-age child but no prospects for marriage. A lonely future of either supporting herself and her baby or remaining dependent upon Sam loomed ahead, and what a bleak existence that would be. And while Abby insisted she had remained unmarried by choice, and she'd done very well with her Stitch in Time business, she was the exception to the Amish tradition for women. After you were a daughter and a sweetheart, you became a wife and a mother, or you were just . . . odd. Undesirable.

Abby's not odd! the voice in Zanna's head countered.

Abby doesn't deserve to grow old alone, either. Is that what you want for a future?

Zanna hurried from the barn, stung by the way no one had noticed her standing at the door. With heartsick clarity she saw how much she'd forfeited when she left James Graber at the altar. She'd burned her bridges, too, telling him she'd only mimicked his affections and didn't love him enough to marry him.

I hope we can talk soon, Zanna. I have things to tell you.

James's words still teased at her. She'd seemed

so sure she was head over heels with Jonny when she'd poured out her heart to Abby, but what did it say about her commitment to him—to his unborn child—if she couldn't pick up the phone again and leave him a message? Even so, Zanna sensed she was more in love with Jonny than he would ever be with her. And while the Ropps' dramatic exit from church—and maybe from Cedar Creek—had obviously distressed Adah, calling Jonny to say his mother needed him was a lame way to get his attention again.

Zanna sighed. She had felt so overjoyed only an hour ago, yet now all she wanted was to go back to Abby's.

The following Thursday night Abby sat at the little table with her sister long past the time they should have been sleeping. "Zanna, you need your rest," she pleaded, reaching over to still the slender hands that crocheted as though Zanna's life depended on it. "It's all well and gut to be earning an income, but the baby wants you to sleep sometime."

"The baby has *no idea*," Zanna replied in a desperate whisper. Doggedly she slipped another strip of fabric into the row she was working, to begin a new color. "What else is there for me to do, Abby? Sam still doesn't want me working in the store, and Mamm's closed her shop for the winter." Zanna's hands dropped into her lap, and she looked up sadly. "Do you know how it felt to be surrounded by my best buddies again after my confession, only to be invisible by the time we'd eaten? To become a nobody who belongs nowhere in Cedar Creek?"

"Oh, Zanna, that's not so!" Abby gripped her sister's trembling hands. She'd suspected all week that something had upset Zanna last Sunday, and here it was, at last. "Your friends were glad to have you back amongst them. And Barbara says this flu season's the worst she's seen in years, so it's just as well you're not working in the store, exposed to those germs from all the folks going in and out."

"But when will it end?" Zanna blurted. "When do I get to have fun again? Never?"

Abby hugged her sister's shaking shoulders. "I think that between being so dog-tired and having this extra helping of hormones, you're riding a roller coaster, Zanna. If it makes you feel any better, I can remember how jumpy Mamm got while she was carrying *you*. We all walked on eggshells those nine months—"

"That wasn't my fault, you know."

"Of course it wasn't, and nobody blamed you." Abby smiled tiredly at Zanna, whose belly seemed to grow visibly each week. "You wanted out of Mamm, and we all wanted to meet you, too. But we had to wait for your time. Just like we're waiting for this wee one you're bringing us, Zanna."

Her sister hung her head. "But once the baby's born, all I see is this endless stretch of . . . nothing except baby tending. And nobody to share it with. Making rugs keeps me busy, but . . ."

Abby chuckled. "Oh, there will be all manner of special new moments and smiles—first times. And all your friends—and Mamm's—wanting to hold your wee one and coo over it, when they bring a gift." She paused, feeling her sister's pain. Her desperation. Abby had been in this same desolate frame of mind when she'd watched her friends Marian and Eva get married and start families; there were no right, comforting answers to the questions that plagued Zanna. "How about if I make us some cocoa and then you can stretch out on the sofa for—"

The cry of a siren made them look up. They listened for a few more moments as the wail continued.

"That's quite a ways off," Abby murmured. "Coming from east of town. Can't tell if it's the police chasing a car, or an ambulance."

Zanna closed her eyes, concentrating on the sound. "Way out by Highway 63, maybe? It's harder to tell with the snow muffling the sounds."

"Wait—is that the fire bell I'm hearing now?" Abby listened more intently: it seemed a second siren had started wailing, and then came the *clang-clang-clang!* of the big bell Mervin Mast rang when someone spotted a fire, or when his

Mennonite neighbors got the call from the Clearwater fire station.

Abby and her sister rushed to the window as loud honking and another siren approached Cedar Creek on the county road. Lamps were lit at Sam's and the Grabers', and by the time a fire engine stopped out front, its red lights flashing, Sam and Matt were rushing from the house. The dogs were barking excitedly, but they sat down in the snow when Matt ordered them to stay put. The two men and James hopped aboard the truck before it sped off down the blacktop.

"Mighty gut thing the bishop allowed our fellas to have scanners," Abby remarked as she gazed after them. "Think of the places that would burn down if our firefighters didn't get notified in time."

Zanna tossed her half-completed rug onto the table and stood up. "Barbara will most likely follow them to see if anybody's hurt. I'm putting on my boots and going with her."

"Jah, it's not like we're getting any sleep," Abby remarked. She was pleased to see that Zanna had come out of her low mood. As she and her sister hurried toward the big house, they found Barbara and Mamm hitching Tucker to a carriage. Abby urged Zanna in ahead of her and then pulled a blanket around the two of them in the backseat. They reached around Barbara's medical bag and some big bottles of water to turn on the flashing lanterns. A pile of blankets and a bag of clothing took up a lot of the space she and her sister shared.

"It's not gut that it's gotten so much colder," Mamm remarked, shivering. "Makes it harder to pump water out in the country."

"And if it's a house afire at this hour, it's likely the folks inside got caught by surprise." Barbara stopped the horse at the end of the lane so three more pickups with flashers on their dashboards could speed by: their county road was a main route from east to west. "Looks to be serious, with so many volunteers being called out."

Abby peered ahead through the carriage's windshield, which was quickly fogging over. A few English had hobby farms out this way, but mostly it was Amish who raised livestock and crops. Other carriages were joining them, keeping to the shoulder so wailing police cars could whiz past them. When a column of smoke and angry orange flames lit the distant sky, they all gasped at once.

"That's got to be the Ropp place—"

"Jah, it's their house that sits on that hill," Mamm murmured.

"—and if they don't douse those flames soon, they'll lose their barns and their milking machines, too," Abby added. "Looks like the old shed where they kept their buggies and wagons is already gone." She glanced at her sister, who was staring at the flames in horrified fascination.

Zanna shook her head as though she were clearing away a bad dream. "You don't suppose Rudy finally got so mad . . ." She couldn't seem to complete the thought.

"Oh, Zanna, let's hope he didn't do something stupid. Or desperate," Barbara added in a tight voice. "It's been one thing after another for that family. When I was looking in on Marian Byler, Carl mentioned that the last time he helped with the chores there, Rudy didn't offer any pay. Not that Carl wouldn't have helped anyway, but a new father can use some extra cash."

Abby considered this as they turned onto the lane where the Ropps lived. "That matches up with what we saw in the house, I'd say. Adah really did need that rug. Her kitchen could have used some paint and fresh curtains, too."

"Jah, and then there's Jonny," Zanna mumbled. "Driving a stretch limo and a Harley, along with his van."

Their mother glanced back at her, smiling despite her concerns. "Care to translate that for me?"

Zanna focused on the leaping flames, her hand at her throat. "It's a really long car and a really fast motorcycle. Would you look at—oh, that wall's falling over!"

They all grimaced as the front of the Ropp house slowly caved in to be consumed by the fire. Firemen dashed around with hoses, while the police kept curious, concerned neighbors a safe distance from the blaze. A fellow in a bucket suspended above a fire truck shot a powerful stream of water toward the side of the house nearest the outbuildings. Terrified bellows came from the barn and the acrid smell of smoke seeped into the carriage.

"Look—over there by the garden!" Zanna exclaimed. "It's Adah and the girls. Must be in their nightgowns, from what I can tell."

"You'd better get them wrapped in these blankets while I check on the firefighters. That bag of clothes has socks in it, too. I bet they're barefoot," Barbara said as she set the brake. "Bring them over to sit in the carriage where it's warmer. Can't have them getting frostbite on top of losing everything." She reached back for her medical bag, her expression grim. "Come get me if you see somebody hurt."

The night wind whipped their coats and bonnets as they stepped out of the carriage. The roar of the flames was unlike anything Abby had ever experienced. The heat from the blaze gusted around them as they hurried toward the Ropps with an armload of blankets and clothes. "Here—wrap yourselves up!" she called above the racket of the firefighters and their radios.

Zanna rushed over to help Maggie and Becky, hugging them as she asked what had happened. Barbara dropped her bag to embrace Adah while

Abby wrapped the poor woman in an afghan. "Are you burned anywhere?"

"No, we got out through the windows," Adah rasped. Her face was blackened from smoke and her loose hair blew wildly around her shivering body. "We were all sleeping and next thing I knew, the girls were thundering down the stairs screaming about a fire."

Barbara was examining Adah's face and hands while she listened. "Where's Rudy, then?"

The stricken woman nodded toward the house before bursting into tears. "He's over there helping the firemen, but—but—" She swiped at her face with the sleeve of her black coat. "Well, I couldn't say this to *him,* but my first thought was that the Lord's paying Rudy back for the way he ranted in church last week."

Mamm threw an arm around her. "Now, Adah, don't go thinking such things!" She crouched in the snow then, to ease a pair of Sam's heavy socks over Adah's cold bare feet.

"But it was so awful, the way he talked! He's been impossible to live with ever since, until— well, I just don't know what the girls and I are going to do." Adah buried her face in Barbara's shoulder and sobbed. "He got so he didn't trust the bank. A while back he pulled out all our money and—and—"

Abby's stomach soured as she mentally finished that sentence.

"Don't you worry about that," Mamm insisted as she steered Adah toward the carriage. "Let's get you back to the house, out of the weather. We'll put you in Zanna's room and figure everything out when you're warm and settled."

"You go on back with them," Barbara agreed. "We'll get rides with these other folks."

"Zanna, you'd better come along," Mamm called over her shoulder. "We can't have you catching your death out here."

"Gut idea." Barbara put a no-nonsense arm around Zanna's shoulders. "You've got a couple of friends who could use an ear right now. Denki for coming along to be their blessing."

Abby could see her little sister wasn't too keen on leaving, but Zanna knew she'd been outvoted. After the carriage left the driveway, Barbara went around checking the men for injuries while Abby poured fresh water into plastic cups for them. The fireman in the suspended bucket had drenched the house enough to keep the blaze from spreading to the barns, and the other high-pressure hoses had almost doused what flames remained.

As Abby stood beside Matt, Sam, and James, she asked, "Did any of you hear what caused the fire?" The wind nearly blew her words away, so she leaned closer to James as he sipped his drink. He smelled of sweat and smoke, and his eyes were bloodshot in his sooty face.

James shook his head sadly. "The fire marshal

will have to figure that one out. But when your house and buggies are gone, and the stuff you've had all your life, it doesn't much matter how it started."

"We saved his herd, though," Sam remarked. He downed a whole glass of water in a few gulps before wiping his face on his coat sleeve. "Rudy swears he's not leaving the place. He says they can live in the barn, so he can keep up with the milking while they figure out what to do next."

"Sam, that's crazy talk." Abby shivered just thinking about Adah and the girls—or anyone—staying in a barn with the cattle, in December. "They've got no way to cook, and no clothes or—"

"Jah, he's half out of his head. I was thinking he wasn't quite right when he was acting out at church." Her brother glanced around at the fellows who were winding up the hoses. "Did I see Mamm taking Adah and the girls home with her?"

"Jah. She told them they could have Zanna's room."

Sam nodded. "I'll tell Vernon about how Rudy's planning to rough it out here . . . see if the bishop can't convince that fella to come in out of the cold—in more ways than one." Her brother's expression sobered. "I can't help wondering if he might have caused the fire—either on purpose, for some desperate, crazy reason, or because he got careless. Or just mad. He's been awful hot-headed lately."

"Zanna had the same thought."

James's eyes widened as he surveyed the watery heap that had once been the Ropp farmhouse. Embers still glowed here and there, and steam rose from the ruins. "If the inspector points a finger at Rudy, things will get a lot worse before they get better. It's probably a gut thing you got his family tucked away safe."

"Lots of things to consider." Sam handed Abby his glass. "I'll see you at home, sister. We've done all we can do until daylight."

Zanna sat at the window of Abby's spare room, looking out into the cold, starry night. As she brushed her hair, images of the fire refused to leave her mind . . . the brightest glaring orange she'd ever seen giving off such intense heat . . . the fluttering of fabric and paper scraps that glowed around the edges as the wind whisked them off . . . the terror on Adah's face as she said they had no money in the bank.

The Ropp girls hadn't said much during the ride back, but Zanna knew how it hurt to need so much help from other people . . . how their dat's behavior in church had exposed more than they'd wanted folks to know. They were still in shock from watching as their home was swallowed up by those raging flames, but soon enough the hammer would hit the nail.

Had all of Rudy and Adah's savings been stashed away in that house? What had happened to Jonny's dat, that he'd turned in on himself and couldn't trust the bank—and had nothing but mean, critical words to say to his wife and daughters?

Before she'd made a conscious decision about it, Zanna's feet were taking her back down the hall. She shrugged into her coat. It was crazy, thinking Jonny would answer his phone at this hour—or believing her call would influence him—but somebody had to tell him about his family's catastrophe. Even if he'd vowed never to return to Cedar Creek, maybe he'd pass the word and his brother, Gideon, would respond to the news differently.

And maybe he'll punch the ERASE button when he hears the sound of your voice. Not like he's ever called you back after last time . . .

Zanna hurried down the long, snowy lane, burning with the certainty that she had to do *something* for the three women staying at Sam's. Adah Ropp might not be her favorite person, but maybe . . . maybe Jonny's critical, busybody mamm had been trying to help her by insisting that the father of this baby be held accountable. Amazing, how six weeks spent mostly by herself had changed her thinking.

She slipped into the little white shanty and

283

shut the door against the bitter wind. Before she lost her nerve, Zanna punched the numbers . . . waited during the first ring, and the second one, knowing Jonny probably had his cell phone turned off at this predawn hour.

"Yeah—hey, it's Jonny Ropp. If you want a ride to town—or need a driver for long-distance trips—I'm your guy!" his recorded greeting said in that breezy way he had.

Once again the sound of his voice did crazy things to her. The baby kicked her, and she nearly slammed down the receiver before the *beep* prompted her to record her message.

"I—Jonny, it's Zanna, and you've got to come home," she said into the phone. "Your house just burned to the ground. Your mamm and sisters are staying at Sam's, and . . . well, we're thinking all their money got lost in the fire, too, and—just do the right thing, okay?" she added in a faltering voice. "You and Gideon and the girls are all your folks have now."

She hung up, feeling scared and nervous yet exhilarated. Maybe Jonny wouldn't call back, but she'd sent him word, hadn't she? She'd done what she could to help friends who couldn't help themselves.

Zanna stepped out of the phone shanty, noting the edge of crimson-peach along the horizon. As she hurried toward Abby's house, the fierce wind blew her hair back from her face; she hadn't bothered with a bonnet because it was a nuisance while talking on the phone.

Just for a moment, she recalled the same sensation of freedom—the sense of dangerous, delicious exhilaration—she'd felt while riding on the back of Jonny's Harley with her hair down, the last time she'd seen him . . . the way her body had tingled whenever he'd held her hand as they'd walked through the moonlit countryside so many nights with the crickets serenading them. Jonny Ropp's smile and sweet affection, all those eve-nings they'd slipped away together, had proven that beneath his handsome bad-boy mask, he was more gentle and sincere than folks knew, despite the way he'd left Cedar Creek.

Just for a moment, Zanna allowed herself to admit she was crazy in love with that fellow even if it would come to nothing. She slipped back into her little room at Abby's and slept better than she had in weeks.

— Chapter 20 —

James stood near the door of his carriage shop's big back room early on Friday morning, mentally taking attendance of the folks gathering for this special meeting. The pew wagon had arrived days earlier for Sunday's preaching service, so his place was a logical spot to discuss how to help after last night's devastating fire. He and his employees, Perry Bontrager and Leon Mast, had moved the carriages they were working on in the main shop area to make room for the benches, which were now nearly full of folks talking about the fire.

"That's the craziest thing I ever heard! Why would a man stash all his money away in his house?" Beulah Mae Nissley demanded. "If he got upset with a teller here in Cedar Creek, he could have banked in Bloomingdale. Matter of fact, that's where my bakery account is, while Abe keeps his crop money here in town. It's just safer, having your money in more than one place."

"A lot of things Rudy's done of late strike me as out of kilter," Mervin Mast replied in a low voice, and his son, Leon, nodded emphatically beside him. "And his bad moods started back a ways, long before he spoke out of turn in church."

"That's another thing we need to discuss," Vernon Gingerich agreed as he rose in front of the crowd. "Folks only get into trouble when they pull away and keep to themselves, thinking they can handle their troubles alone. Right now, though, we've got more basic concerns to deal with."

The bishop held up his hand. "Let's get started here, folks," he called out above the chatter.

"We've got a lot to cover, and we'll begin by asking God for help with it."

James bowed his head along with the others, waiting by the door to admit any latecomers.

After their silent prayer, Pete Beachey stood up. As their deacon, he led discussions involving members with hospital expenses or other emergencies they couldn't pay for on their own. He looked older and sadder than when he'd taken James on as an apprentice, probably because he'd never really recovered from his wife's passing a few years ago.

"As you know, we've got funds laid away for such times as this," he began in a reedy voice, "but money's not the immediate cure. The Ropps lost all their clothes and furniture and whatnot, plus the food they'd put up. Treva Lambright took Adah and the girls home with her last night, but Rudy's got a herd to milk—"

"What if the fire marshal says Rudy started the blaze himself?" Amos Coblentz interrupted.

"And what about the way Rudy said he was leaving the church?" Ezra Yutzy joined in. "It's one thing to set a family back on their feet again, but it's a horse of another color if they want no part of us, or our help."

"Jah, I went over on Wednesday to service his milking equipment," Zeke Detweiler chimed in, "and he sent me packing. I've seen to Rudy's mechanical stuff ever since I installed his new bulk tanks and agitators, so it wasn't like I was selling him something he didn't want."

Again the bishop raised his hand for silence. "We're jumping ahead of ourselves. I've asked Ferris North, the fire marshal, to inform me of his findings—and to keep this catastrophe out of the papers. We take care of our own, and right now Rudy Ropp is still one of us."

"Bishop, may I say a word?" Abby Lambright stood up, surveying those who sat around her. "Let's not forget that Adah, Becky, and Maggie can't replace what *they* lost, either. I'm gathering up donations of clothes for all four of them, and Mamm said she wanted to head up a food drive with everybody kicking in a few jars of canned goods or packages of meat from their freezers, when the Ropps are ready for that."

"Those are good, practical ideas, Abby," Vernon agreed with a smile.

"And sewing frolics!" she continued, her voice rising with excitement. "I'll provide the fabric for anybody who will make quilts and table linens, so tell your wives to sharpen up their scissors. But first thing, of course—they'll need a home to put this stuff in, fellas."

James chuckled to himself. Leave it to Abby to jump in feetfirst and offer up her time and resources, regardless of how the men quibbled.

"They'll need a place sooner rather than later," Sam remarked over the crowd's chatter. "Rudy

288

figures on living in the barn so he can keep milking. Have you heard anything more on that, Vernon?"

The bishop shook his head ruefully. "I went over there as soon as I heard the sirens last night, same as Pete and Abe did. When Rudy began talking that way, we each offered him a place to stay in our homes."

"Told him he could bunk at my place, too, since I'm just half a mile down the road," Mervin remarked. "Offered him the use of whatever wagons and clothes I have, too, but Rudy called me a busybody do-gooder. Well, those are the *polite* words for what he said, anyway. He had a wild look in his eyes that warned me not to offer him that help again."

The crowd got quiet and looked to the bishop and Pete for what came next. James couldn't recall a time when so many in Cedar Creek had expressed dismay over a member's attitude—nor had a member ever provoked such controversy by acting so uncharitable. Ordinarily, the families here visited back and forth and helped one another during harvest or when somebody passed on. Their community of faith was the family of God here on earth. So why—especially only three weeks before Christmas—was neighbor speaking out against neighbor, or protesting the way they'd been treated?

This all started when Zanna ran off. And

that all started with Jonny Ropp. Kind of comes full circle, doesn't it?

James frowned. He'd slept so much better since he'd put such thoughts behind him, but the conversation around him was fueling that same negative mind-set. Folks were fidgeting on the benches, whispering among themselves as though Abby's enthusiasm and helpful ideas had blown away like snowflakes in the wind.

"Lots of you fellas and I have raised barns and rebuilt homes together," Amos Coblentz said as he stood up to address them. He was a master carpenter who'd apprenticed with Vernon years before he'd become Bishop Gingerich, and Amos was molding his boy, Owen, into a remarkable builder, as well. "But why would I want to commit my time to a house for a fella who says he's leaving Cedar Creek? Why would Sam or James donate materials, like they have so many times before, when one of this family's sons has caused them so much grief of late—and when Jonny and Gideon are nowhere to be seen when their family needs them?"

James couldn't miss the way Abby glanced at Sam and then turned in her seat to observe his own reaction. He couldn't forget her suggestion that *he* should be the mature one; *he* should offer forgiveness to Zanna rather than waiting for her to ask. It was a sorry thing for these old friends to dredge up all these feelings again—and so soon after they had welcomed Zanna back into the fold in the spirit of love and compassion.

"We should put our money where our mission is," James heard himself declaring. His conscience and his heart had spoken for him, perhaps prodded by Abby's intense brown eyes. And he couldn't back down now, could he? "Can you imagine how bad Adah and the girls must feel, losing their home? Losing all their savings? It's worse because it's so close to Christmas, too.

"And maybe," he continued, hoping he sounded convincing, "when Rudy sees us building a new place for him and his family, he'll realize he belongs here amongst folks who care what happens to him. Who else will help him, if we don't?" James asked, his voice growing stronger. "Yet if Rudy came in here and heard the way we're jawing about him, he'd walk right out. And I can't say I'd blame him."

The big workroom went quiet. James's friends, whom he'd known all his life, were glancing at him, and then at one another, to consider how this idea fit with their own. James relaxed all over, going with the flow to redirect this energy— mostly because Abby's beaming smile told him he'd said the right thing.

"Going along with Abby's spirit of giving, I'll replace the carriage and a buggy that got burned up in the Ropps' shed," James continued. "And if somebody else will spring for the wood and materials, I'll build a wagon or two, as well. As far as I can see, this has nothing to do with Jonny and Zanna. It's about neighbor helping neighbor —doing rather than just saying. It's taking Christmas out of the pretty cards and putting it into practice."

"I agree with that a hundred percent, James," the bishop said, seeming to gauge the group's mood. "I've always believed God gave me carpentry skills so I could build things up rather than tear them down. When the lot fell to me to be your bishop, I saw it as another way all the pieces fit together," he added. "Building lives and a community of faith. Repairing and patching, too. We have a brother who's in need of a lot of prayer and patching."

Vernon smiled kindly at Amos Coblentz, who had taken his seat again. "I understand your hesitation to pitch in for Rudy, after the way he talked at our last service. And I know how we hate to waste anything, be it effort or materials," he added matter-of-factly. "It won't be an easy task, clearing away the rubble of the fallen-down house to build a new one. The foundation's a block of ice and debris from all that water we poured on it last night."

The bishop straightened his stooping shoulders, as though bearing up under yet another burden. "We'll vote on this, as always. But my recommendation is that we build the

Ropps a new home because it's how we take care of each other. If Rudy moves on, that's his choice," Vernon added quietly. "Maybe Adah and the girls will stay, in which case they'll be needing a place. As will any new family coming to Cedar Creek—or any of our members looking for a different home. Whatever we build is bound to be stronger than what burned down last night."

"Jah, there's that," Beulah Mae murmured. "Adah had been stuffing folded newspapers into the cracks where the chimney was pulling away from the frame, rather than fussing anymore for Rudy to fix them. The papers made the fire burn all that much faster, no doubt."

From his spot by the window, James saw a familiar pickup truck pull up to the curb. "Ferris North is here," he announced. "Maybe he'll have a report for us."

Folks turned their heads to watch the local fire marshal, a man they all knew because he inspected their businesses and advised them about how to prevent property loss. Ferris North was English, but he made sure the volunteers in their Plain communities had warning systems that fit with their beliefs.

"Morning, folks," he said, nodding as he approached Vernon. "I want to thank all of you who helped last night. The house was nearly gone by the time we arrived, but we saved the barns and Rudy Ropp's livelihood—which certainly counts for something."

Everyone nodded, watching him intently.

"Let this be a lesson to any of you who still don't have smoke alarms—like the Ropps didn't," he continued sternly. "The fire started in their chimney, because of the buildup of creosote inside it, and then blew up into the attic. A good cleaning every fall—the most basic of maintenance—could have prevented last night's disaster. And some tuck-pointing and masonry repair would have kept the drafts from feeding that fire once it started. Mose Hartzler does this kind of work, and for a very reasonable price."

"Just like I was saying," Beulah Mae muttered. "It's a crying shame Rudy didn't look after—"

"Thank you, Ferris," Bishop Gingerich said pointedly. "This lays some rumors to rest, and we appreciate your diligent work—and your understanding that this remains a Plain concern, rather than an opportunity for the media to sensationalize our tragedy."

"It'll go no further than my report." Ferris nodded at them all again. "Merry Christmas, folks. And don't forget—those smoke detectors Sam sells in his store would make fine, practical Christmas gifts."

Most of them chuckled. Everyone appeared relieved that while Rudy had been negligent with his repairs, he hadn't set the fire because he was angry or to attract attention to his grievances.

"All right, then," Amos said. "If we're moving forward with this, I'll be happy to lead the on-site building crew, Vernon, if you'll round us up some carpenters from Clearwater and coordinate the other help. Owen and I just finished a place similar to the Ropps', north of Queen City. If we all agree to use that floor plan, we can get started as soon as the site's cleared."

"I'll be happy to do that," Bishop Gingerich said. "Several seasoned builders live in my Clearwater district, and those who don't do construction work anymore can get started on furniture."

"I've got Mennonite cousins with heavy equipment who will help clear away the mess around the foundation," Preacher Paul said. "And I'll build your cabinets and handle the trim work, if you'll have me."

James and the rest of them laughed, getting caught up in this rush of goodwill; Paul Bontrager had extraordinary talent with wood and was in high demand for his custom shelving and display pieces.

Sam stood up then, nodding his approval of how folks were jumping in to help. "Count on me for your supplies, Amos. I'll have the lumber delivered as soon as you tell me what you'll need."

"And I'll bring in extra help to make meals for your crews, Amos," Beulah Mae chimed in. "It's never a problem, getting our women to cook for a project like this."

"And never a problem getting us to eat it," Amos replied. He smiled across the crowd at James and said to him, "I'll have my Noah gather up the boards and odd pieces left from our last couple of houses, for those wagons you said you'd put together. Noah's been saying he'd like to make carriages someday—like you, James— so maybe you could put him to work on this project? See if he's got any aptitude for it?"

An apprentice? James hadn't considered that. Noah Coblentz was a lanky, loose-limbed kid with red hair like his sisters, so he was the target for a lot of teasing. James raised his eyebrows, glancing at Leon and Perry to gauge their reactions. "Send him over," James replied when he saw his men nodding. "What with the shop being busy again, I could use another fella making these rigs for the Ropps."

Vernon was beaming, clasping his hands before him. "Shall we vote and make it official, then? All those willing to move forward on replacing the Ropps' home—"

"AYE!" The thundering response rang in the rafters of the workshop, so loud that everyone laughed again.

Folks clustered together to make their plans, and later as they were leaving, James appreciated their thanks for the meeting space and for steering them toward a positive goal. Abby's smile wrapped him like a warm blanket as she bundled up to cross the street and begin her day at the mercantile.

"Fine job, James," she said. "Only takes one or two to rise above, and the rest will generally follow."

"Jah, it's gut to scc everybody coming together. And this new project gives them something more worthwhile to talk about than me and Zanna." He glanced across the road, his heartbeat quickening with an idea. "Is your sister doing all right? Feeling better these days?"

"Barbara pronounced her fat and sassy yester-day during her checkup, jah. She keeps herself busy making those rugs, mostly." Abby smiled up at him, her face framed by her black bonnet. "I put Zanna in charge of raising her friends' spirits, so she's bringing the Ropp girls to my sewing shop to make clothes this morning. With Zanna and Maggie cutting the pieces and Becky stitch-ing the seams on my machine, they'll all have dresses and aprons, and a shirt and trousers for Rudy, by tonight."

"Nice of you to lend them your workspace."

Abby shrugged and pulled on her gloves. "I'm thankful it wasn't my place that caught fire in the night. We can all do our part to provide them a house, but Adah and her girls have the harder job, making it a home again."

James nodded at this insight. Abby always

considered underlying issues that others missed. "There's no telling how Rudy will react to our help. Let's hope he doesn't take all our gut intentions and pave himself a road to hell with them." He glanced across the blacktop again, where three figures were walking along the snowy lane with two dogs frolicking around them. "Here come your girls now. Have a fine day, Abby."

"You, too, James." She stepped out into the wind, then glanced at him over her shoulder. "Every day's a fine day if you believe it is. Ain't so?"

He didn't know how to reply to such optimism. He could only smile as he watched her step nimbly toward the county road. When he focused on Zanna, walking between her two friends, something prodded him to grab his coat from beside the door. Zanna rarely got out these days— and never worked in the mercantile now, to keep peace with the folks who didn't wish to be reminded of her pregnancy.

Across the road he dashed, aware that those leaving the meeting would see him with Zanna and might speculate about that. But he had a debt to settle. The time seemed right, while he was riding the waves of excitement generated in his shop this morning.

"Zanna!" he called, breathless from his sprint ahead of an oncoming car.

She stopped and looked at him full-on with those blue eyes. "James. Gut morning." Her gaze flickered to the folks getting into their rigs. "Looks like you had quite a crowd for your meeting."

"Jah, and we got positive results, too." He willed his heart to stop hammering. This was a matter to be discussed calmly and without anyone else listening in. "Can I have a word with you, Zanna? It won't take but a minute."

— *Chapter 21* —

Zanna's eyes widened. Her cheeks tingled, more from curiosity than the cold. Here it was, the moment she'd wondered about since last Sunday, when James had said he needed to talk. "Jah. Um—" She glanced at Becky and Maggie Ropp, who watched with eager interest. "Have Abby help you choose the fabric for those clothes we'll be making. I'll be there in a few, all right?"

Becky and her sister raised their eyebrows at each other, but they went inside. No doubt they would quiz her about this conversation all day while they sewed. James leaned toward her, his eyes shining like hot coffee. "Zanna, I did something that demands an apology. I've got no excuse for it, except that I lost my head for a bit."

And what could this be about? She watched him, waiting.

"Remember a few weeks ago, when you dialed Jonny Ropp's number twice and hung up?"

How did he know about that? Zanna shifted her weight, suspicious now. It wasn't as though she'd said anything indecent for Jonny to respond to on the message machine—and it wasn't James's business if she had!

James sighed. "Well, he called you back. It took me by surprise, sitting there at the phone and hearing his voice mail message. It hit me all wrong, that you'd be in touch with him, and before I thought about it, I erased Jonny's message. And I'm sorry for that, Zanna." He rushed on in a whisper. "I hope you can understand. And forgive me."

Jonny had called her back? *Jonny called me back! And James is saying—*

Zanna forced her thoughts to stop swirling in her head. She desperately wanted to know what Jonny had said. But it didn't feel right, asking James about that. "I'd called to tell him his mamm could use his—well, what with his dat acting so—oh, never mind!"

Jonny called me back! So maybe when he hears that last message I left him—

James stood rooted as though he had no intention of ending this conversation. "I didn't feel right, letting it go by without saying something," he explained. "I hope you feel as gut as you look, Zanna. Hope things are going well for you."

While James had spoken to her with this same consideration after her confession last Sunday, she hadn't expected him to keep wishing her well. "Doing okay, all things considered," she murmured.

Zanna noticed the softness of his brown eyes . . . the laugh lines that deepened when he smiled at her. While James Graber would always be considerably older than she, and his parents would only get more difficult to deal with, for a fleeting moment Zanna wondered why she'd thrown away their relationship. "James, I—"

A dark red van pulled to a stop in front of them. The driver rolled down the window and grinned at her. His blond hair fell in unruly waves around a face that shot her pulse into a panic.

"Zanna!" Jonny Ropp looked her up and down as though James weren't standing beside her. "Hey—got your message from last night. Thought I'd check out what you said about that fire. Hop in," he coaxed, nodding toward the passenger seat. "Fill me in, will you? It's not like I'll be staying long, if Dat's out there."

Zanna suddenly knew how Lot's wife must have felt, being transformed into a pillar of salt, unable to think or speak. The dimple in Jonny's cheek winked at her. "Sorry! Gotta go!" she rasped, clutching her coat around her, and then realizing how that accentuated her belly.

Into the mercantile she dashed, as though one of Mervin Mast's bulls were chasing her. She beelined toward the back room, where she might get hold of her runaway thoughts in the peace and quiet. From the aisles where the yard goods were displayed she heard familiar voices, Abby's among them as she encouraged Jonny's sisters to choose fabric that was warm and sturdy for their new winter dresses.

I saw Jonny and ran like a scared rabbit, while he gawked at my belly . . .

"So there you are, Zanna. We were thinking James must have had something awfully interesting to say—" Abby stopped in the storeroom doorway. "You look like you just saw a ghost. Are you feeling all right?"

She forced herself to breathe. She made herself drape her coat over a peg as though it were an ordinary day and nothing extraordinary had just happened. "I—I called Jonny's voice mail again last night," she confessed in a halting whisper, "to tell him about the fire. He just now pulled up in his van. Asked me to ride out there with him, to see the house."

Abby's eyes nearly filled her slender face. "Jonny came *here?*" She glanced into the main room of the store, where Maggie and Becky were choosing their dress fabric. "Shall we tell the girls? Or will they only get more upset if he doesn't want to see them?"

"I was so shocked I didn't tell him they were here. I don't know." Zanna grabbed for the back of the chair where she usually sat to fill bags with spices and cookie sprinkles. "Honest to Pete, Abby, I don't know anything right now. My brain's whirling so fast it might spin right out of my head!"

James reminded himself that he was wiser and more mature than Jonny Ropp, the hellion who'd taken advantage of his fiancée. Of course, this kid in the van didn't know any of that—did he? Unless Zanna had told Jonny about her engagement, and told him he was about to become a father, Jonny probably assumed that Zanna had been chatting with James Graber as she had all her life, because he lived across the road. Yet something in Zanna's expression when he'd mentioned Ropp's phone message suggested she hadn't spoken with this fellow since last July . . .

It would be so easy to give Cedar Creek's most flamboyant smart aleck an earful about what Zanna had *really* gone through of late, and then send him packing. Jonny wore a black leather jacket, but no hat. The shiny ring in his ear boldly announced that he hadn't joined the church and never intended to.

"So . . . there really was a fire?" Jonny demanded as he gawked out the window of his rumbling van. "How come I didn't see it on the news?"

James saw no reason to get chatty. After all,

Jonny hadn't asked how he was, or what was up with Zanna, or anything else that would reconnect him to anyone here in Cedar Creek. "Bishop Gingerich didn't want reporters and TV cameras—"

"Oh, that's right. Amish are good at keeping their secrets."

James clenched his jaw. *Jah, like when Zanna didn't tell you she was marrying me last July.*

"Secrets aren't always a gut idea, you know," Jonny said. "They make it easier for folks to get away with stuff—to sweep problems under the rug, like they never happened." He turned off his ignition and opened the van's door to step outside. "If people knew what my mother's had to put up with in the name of *submission* to the Old Order's ways—" He bit off his sentence as though he'd revealed more than he had intended to. He leaned against his van and crossed his arms as though he didn't quite trust James. "So is the house totally gone or did Zanna exaggerate about that in her voice mail? Did everybody make it out okay?"

James scowled. "Why would she exaggerate about your house burning down?" he demanded. "If the fire trucks hadn't arrived when they did, the milking barn and all the other outbuildings would've burned, too, you know." James was familiar with folks who started talking about one thing and then swerved into a different subject. As far as he was concerned, it was rude—and it led folks to believe things that weren't true.

At least Jonny looked more concerned now. His eyes widened and he raked back his hair as he considered what he'd just heard. The Ropp boy stood taller these days—their eyes were on the same level even if the two of them didn't see eye to eye—and it seemed Jonny wanted to prove to James that at nineteen he was a man. And a man of means, as well.

"Jah, the girls came downstairs, hollering about the fire, just in time to get out through a window, along with your folks," James explained. "The house and the shed burned to the ground, though." Something made James want to lay it on with a heavy hand, to see what Jonny Ropp was really made of. Was he still the loudmouthed daredevil who'd sped through Cedar Creek full tilt on a motorcycle, scaring the sheep and cows? If so, he had no business—no right—to raise Zanna's child.

"They lost all their savings, too," James added. No sense in leaving out this very important detail, considering Jonny supported himself quite well by driving—or that's what folks said, anyway, and that's what his big van and that flashy motorcycle suggested. "Guess your dat got into it with a teller a while back and then pulled their money out of the bank. Stashed it in the house."

"He yanked out *all* of their—you can't be

serious!" Jonny paced to the front of his van and back again, as though deciding what to say next. "When Zanna left a message that they'd lost— Well, a lot of that money was what Mamm earned at the cheese factory. But Mamm's all right? And the girls, too?"

"Jah. The three of them are staying with the Lambrights." No need to reveal how the locals had voted to rebuild their home, at least not until he heard Jonny's own plan for helping his family. "The girls are at the mercantile now."

"Lemme guess," Jonny interrupted in a tight voice. "Dat wouldn't leave the place. Would rather hole up with those blasted cows, wallowing in his mucky moods and blaming everybody else for his troubles."

"Far as I know, he's still out there, jah." James smiled, waiting for whatever other axes this troublemaker might grind . . . whatever he might reveal about his feelings toward Zanna, too. Jonny had filled out some; he had more of a man's body now. But he still didn't seem inclined to take on adult responsibility.

"So what started the fire?"

Jonny's tone told him Rudy was the first suspect who'd come to this kid's mind. James saw no good reason to let this disgruntled son mistakenly believe that, however. "The fire marshal said too much creosote had built up in the chimney. When the wind whistled through the cracks, sparks flew right on up into the attic and caught fire."

An odd look crossed Jonny's face. He looked James over, as though deciding how much to say. "You probably heard all sorts of stories about my running off a few years back," he began in a defensive tone, "but I was putting distance between me and Dat after I told him I wasn't gonna spend my life being a slave to his dairy. Where's the future in that—for him and two sons, no less? The county extension agents gave him suggestions about how to get more milk from his herd and make a better living at it—and he told *them* where to go, too."

James had no trouble believing this about Rudy, but he merely nodded.

"And then he'd sit in church—or wherever anybody else was watching," Jonny went on in a rising voice, "and make like he was living right with God while, in reality, he was treating our mother worse than the dirt he walked on. Talking to her like nobody deserves to be talked to. And at all hours of the night, when we kids were trying to sleep.

"And Mamm kept *her* secret, too," Jonny added angrily. He dug his boot heel into the snow, shaking his head in disgust. "She went along with his bad-mouthing because wives are supposed to sub-mit to their men. She acted like she was fine and dandy so her friends wouldn't know how Dat slapped her around when he was in one of his moods."

James regretted hearing this. Rudy's ways with Adah didn't completely surprise him, but such violence went against the faith in the most fundamental way. Still, he had just been offered another avenue of discussion, and he meant to take it.

"So why didn't you stay to look after her?" he asked pointedly. "Why'd you run off and break her heart? It was bad enough that Gideon left, but you were always your mamm's favorite."

Jonny leveled his gaze at James the same way Matt Lambright's dogs stared down a contrary ewe. "I'm *back*. Ain't so?"

"Are you?" Jonny was still pretty good at dodging questions and tricky situations that put restrictions on him.

"I've done right well, driving for Amish and making trips back East with them." Jonny pressed on proudly. "Sounds like it might be a gut time to load Mamm and my sisters into the van and take them away with me."

Jonny crossed his arms again, leaning against his van as though he might be mapping out such a plan . . . or might have other subjects to catch up on yet. Even though James was getting cold, he sensed it might be worth his wait to stand there a few more moments.

"So . . . were my eyes fooling me," Jonny ventured in a quieter voice, "or is Zanna in the family way? She must have gotten hitched a while back without telling me."

Oh, James could think of answers for that question! But he knew better than to air his own grievances—especially to *this* fellow. "You'd better ask her that yourself. Girls get touchy when you talk about their personal business."

Jonny's pale brows rose. He smiled slyly. "So . . . Abby Lambright hasn't caught you yet, Graber?" He glanced pointedly at James's clean-shaven chin, a sure sign that he wasn't married. "I remember the way she used to gawk at you during church and the common meals."

The question caught James by surprise, though he kept it from showing on his face. Was this kid smarting off, trying to rile him up? Or had Jonny seen something in Abby's expression that he'd missed? Had other folks noticed her watching him, too? James shifted, uncertain. Why hadn't he picked up on any feelings Abby might have for him? Then again, why would he discuss it with Jonny Ropp, of all people?

"Abby's a maidel—by her own choice," James replied. This was common knowledge, after all, made more apparent when her dat had built her a home and she'd opened her sewing business in Sam's store. But two could play this game. "So how about you, Jonny? Have you joined up with the Mennonites by now? Got yourself a wife?"

"Hah! That noose won't go around *my* neck!

Saw enough of what marriage is about while I lived at home. Well—" Jonny glanced at his fancy wristwatch. "Guess I'll run out past the farm. Gut talking to you, Graber."

"Don't be a stranger," James replied. "Your Mamm would be awful glad to see you. And the girls are in the mercantile—"

"Jah, I'll catch up to them. Later, dude!"

James shook his head at that one. "Dude" had never set well with him, maybe because it went against the grain of everything Amish . . . which described Jonny Ropp pretty well, too, didn't it? He stepped back as Cedar Creek's most notorious fence jumper opened the door of his shiny red van and swung back into the driver's seat. It didn't sound as though things had changed much with Adah's younger son, nor did James hold out a speck of hope that Zanna might receive any help from the kid who'd always seemed to be moving on to bigger and better things. *Just passing through.*

With a grin, Jonny revved his engine, as though to race down the curving county road with no regard for the slick spots. Behind James, a door slammed and footsteps clattered on the mercantile's porch.

"Jonny! Jonny—wait for me! I'll go out there with you!"

James turned. Zanna was picking her way between the cars and carriages in the snow-packed parking lot. In her black coat and matching Plain bonnet she didn't look like the type to be hurrying toward a fellow like Jonny Ropp, but James set aside his conflicted thoughts. When she nearly slipped, he caught her by the arm.

"Denki, James." Zanna looked nervous and scared . . . flustered that he was here while she was riding off with the father of her baby. Truth be told, James felt some concern for her safety, but he had no say over whom she rode with or how she behaved, did he?

"Be careful," he warned Jonny sternly. "The road home's more slippery than it looks."

— *Chapter 22* —

Zanna settled into the front passenger seat of Jonny Ropp's van, aware that riding with him went against the Ordnung . . . aware that the safety belt made her pregnancy very visible. She couldn't let such concerns stand in her way, however; she'd called Jonny to convince him he should come to Cedar Creek, and here he was. It might not be the best time to discuss the baby, now that his house had burned and his family had been displaced, but when would the perfect opportunity ever arrive?

As the van turned down the county highway toward the Ropp farm, every nerve in her body jangled and she felt even more nervous than she had the morning she'd confessed her sins at the Members' Meeting two months ago. What if Jonny didn't believe the baby was his? What if he told her it was all her problem—that she was on her own raising his child?

"So what made you change your mind and come along?" he asked in that carefree tone she remembered so well. "From the look on your face when I pulled up to where you and Graber were talking, I thought you were scared to get in the van with me or something."

"Your sisters and I—well, we didn't think you should go out to your farm alone," Zanna blurted out. There was no sense in disputing how startled she must have looked when she saw his face.

"But Becky and Maggie didn't come. Only you, Zanna."

Oh, but that smooth, musical tone of his voice made her tingle all over. Zanna forced herself to focus on the topic at hand. "Maggie and Becky don't want to go, Jonny. Your family barely got out of the house alive. They were barefoot in the snow, shivering in their nightgowns when the walls of their home—your home—collapsed into the flames. I—I felt so helpless. I've never seen anything so scary."

She made herself take a deep breath. Recalling last night's disaster made her feel the heat and the terror and the devastation all over again. Zanna clasped her hands in her lap and looked at the familiar snow-laced trees along the shoulder of the road. "I was helping your sisters sew some clothes in Abby's shop today because they lost *everything,* Jonny. That . . . that's why I went back inside the mercantile when you rolled down your window. I had to tell them I wouldn't be helping them for a while."

Well, that was partly the truth, anyway. Zanna inhaled again, wishing this conversation didn't feel so strained.

"So what did you want to tell me, those two times you called but didn't leave a message?" Jonny asked.

Zanna closed her eyes. Why couldn't she just tell him the baby was his and get it over with? Her pulse throbbed all over her body and her throat tightened until talking felt impossible. As Jonny drove slowly around the last curve before they reached the Ropp farmstead, where the plows had piled the snow into a high bank that blocked their view of the house, she took hold of his wrist. His leather jacket under her fingers felt soft and supple. His muscles tensed as he started to turn in at the Ropps' lane.

"Jonny, the only home you've ever known burned to the ground last night," she whispered. "Three fire trucks and all the fellas from around Cedar Creek were fighting it, and it was the most awful thing I've ever—" Zanna turned her head suddenly as the bleak, black remains of the house came into view. "It's even worse in the daylight. Jonny, I—I'm so sorry."

Jonny made a choking sound and then exhaled loudly. He pulled the van off the road, stopping short of the cattle guard.

Zanna found the nerve to look toward the house site again. Jonny gripped the wheel, staring at the frozen lake of ice where blackened timbers and the tumbled remains of the chimney jutted out at odd angles. The concrete stoop looked totally out of place: three steps and a short, square landing that led nowhere. Adah's bushes and shrubs were gone, except for ice-covered stubs sticking up from the ground.

Jonny appeared more stunned, more dismayed, than she'd ever seen him. "Graber said the wind blew through the chimney cracks. Told me too much creosote had built up—" He smacked the dashboard with his palm. "You could have cleaned it after I left, Dat," he muttered, his voice high and adolescent.

Jonny turned to Zanna, his expression vacillating between anguish and anger. "Clearing the chimney with the long wire brush used to be my job," he said, his voice raspy, "because I thought it was great fun to climb to the roof, like a monkey, even while Mamm was hollerin' that I'd fall to my death if the shingles had frost on them."

Zanna nodded miserably. Nobody would be

cleaning that chimney again. It was charred rubble, along with all the other nooks and crannies of the white house that had been added on to over three generations, same as Sam's house had been. The Ropps had never been as prosperous as the Lambrights, and their house had always seemed sort of dingy and sad when she visited with Becky and Maggie. They more often came to her house, maybe because they enjoyed her cheerful home.

With a heavy sigh, Jonny eased the van over the noisy metal pipes of the cattle guard and up the rise in the lane. "You know, Holsteins have been grazing that pasture since way before I was born," he said, pointing at the vast fenced area to their left. "All day they just chew their cud, watchin' the traffic go past with those brainless expressions on their faces. Look at them," he said, gesturing toward the door to the milking barn. "Bumping against each other, waiting to get inside out of habit, because it never occurs to them to do anything different."

Zanna watched his face: his mouth had tightened into a harsh line and he was blinking a lot to keep from crying. It wasn't easy to see him so upset, criticizing the cows to keep his shock from swallowing him up, but it was better than looking at the blackened foundations where the house and shed had stood. Only the metal skeletons of a carriage and a buggy remained. The two beagles and Shep, the German shepherd, raced around the side of the barn, barking wildly, as they did whenever anyone entered the yard. Jonny paid them no mind.

"I didn't take to animals the way most Amish kids do," he continued in a low voice as he slowly followed the driveway around the milking barn. "Gideon used to remind me how once when I was four I wandered into this barn and yanked on a cow's tail while Dat was milking it by hand. Got kicked nearly to Kingdom Come," he said with a sad laugh, "and when I came to, I was smeared with manure. Mamm was cryin' over me, the cows were in an uproar—and Dat was madder about that lost pail of milk than I'd ever seen anybody get."

Jonny looked at Zanna and sighed. "That's when I knew I'd never be a dairy farmer."

"Jah, that would make an impression on anybody," she replied.

The milking barn looked shabby. A thicket of dead weeds poked up through the snow along the fencerows. And still those cows stood there, some of them beginning to bawl. They stomped the frozen ground, their breath escaping in clouds of vapor.

"That was the main reason Mamm got me a job at the Fishers' factory with her, maintaining their cheesemaking equipment," Jonny went on. The van was moving very slowly along the part of the lane that cut behind the outbuildings. "I was about fourteen then. That mechanical stuff came easy for me, and so did running the cash register and waiting on customers. And once Gideon hooked up with a well-off Mennonite family in Blooming-dale, working in their commercial poultry opera-tion, Dat just snapped," he said, emphasizing the words with a click of his fingers. "He disowned us—for leaving the faith and our family to make our fortunes, he said. But Mamm was always proud of us."

Zanna smiled. Adah Ropp had never lacked for good things to say about her boys, even after they had left home. She let Jonny talk without interrupting him because his voice soothed her . . . and recalling his past was his way of coping with the present devastation. It also kept him from asking what she'd been up to these past five months.

"Gideon and I have been buying cheese from Mamm at Fisher's every now and again, but she doesn't let on at home about our visits." Jonny stopped the van on the road between the Ropp farm and Mervin Mast's place, and they saw the fire's devastation from another angle: heavy tire tracks and blackened timbers covered with ice. In her mind, Zanna heard the sirens again and saw the flashing lights of the fire trucks that had arrived too late.

Jonny turned the van around and drove slowly back toward the milking barn. He frowned at the dashboard clock. "If the cows are still waiting to be milked at nine thirty, where's Dat?" he asked. "He's up before the sun."

Zanna sat straighter, picking up on Jonny's concern. She'd been so engrossed in his nostalgic chatter, she hadn't thought about why the milking hadn't been done. "Even if he'd burrowed into the hay to keep warm last night, all that bawling would have wakened him by now."

As he sped up the van, Jonny focused on the barn. He scowled when Shep and the two beagles rushed right at them this time, barking and circling the van so it was hard to see where they were. Their ruckus sounded even more urgent than the lowing of the cattle.

Jonny stopped the van beside the milking barn. "Why aren't you mutts milkin' those cows?" he teased as he stepped outside. He sounded worried, though, and when Shep headed back around the side of the barn, looking over his furry shoulder at them, Zanna got a nasty knot in her stomach. She eased out of the van, relieved when Jonny came around to grab her hand. Together they hurried cautiously over the snowy ground while the beagles raced ahead of them.

"Dat?" Jonny called out. When he opened the barn door, it sounded way too quiet inside. No gas lanterns were lit. No milking apparatus stood at the ready for the morning's work. Zanna shivered, pulling her coat closer around her. Why weren't

318

the heaters on? The dogs had slipped inside through the door flap in the back wall, which allowed them to sleep in the barn and also to rush outside whenever they heard a suspicious noise. They sniffed her anxiously and nosed at Jonny.

"Dat? Dat, are you in here?" Jonny hollered. His gaze darted around the metal tanks and the rows of stanchions where cows should have been fed and milked hours ago. Shep barked insistently and retreated to a back corner as fast as his old legs would carry him. Jonny and Zanna followed.

"Dat!" Jonny cried.

Rudy Ropp lay sprawled on the barn floor. Suddenly wishing she had paid more attention when Barbara had demonstrated resuscitation techniques, Zanna knelt beside the pale, grizzled man. She strained to hear his faint, irregular breathing despite the bawling of the cattle. When Jonny grabbed his father's shoulders, she took hold of his hands. "I don't think you're supposed to move somebody who's unconscious."

"We can't get him to the van anyway. He's bigger than we are and . . . dead weight." Jonny grimaced at the way that phrase had come out. He grabbed his cell phone and jabbed 9-1-1, then waited breathlessly for what seemed like forever.

"Not many cell towers out here," he mumbled. "Might mean we don't have enough signal to— Jah! Send an ambulance to the Rudy Ropp place on Route E!" he said in a nervous rush of words.

"I found my Dat passed out cold in his barn. No idea how long he's been this way, or . . . Jah, thanks."

Once Jonny received assurance that help was on the way, his shoulders relaxed but his expression remained grim. "If Mamm's at your house, what's the best way to reach her? I hate to leave you here while I run back for her—"

"Best thing is to call the phone shanty and hope somebody's close. Or we can follow the ambulance through town and pick her up." As Jonny punched numbers on his cell phone again, she peeled off her coat and laid it over Rudy. It didn't cover nearly enough of the tall, burly man, but it was better than nothing in this cold, drafty barn.

Jonny immediately shrugged out of his jacket and handed it to her. Zanna caught the warm scent of his cologne in the leather even as she prayed that someone in the phone shanty would pick up.

"Come on, now—please, God, let somebody answer!" Jonny whispered as he paced in a tight circle. "Surely somebody hears the phone ringin' and ringin'—jah?" he rasped. "Jah, this is Jonny Ropp and—Graber, is that you?"

Thank goodness James had answered. Sometimes an older fellow knew more about what to do in an emergency.

"James, I've called the ambulance," Jonny was saying. "Dat's collapsed on the barn floor—will you let Mamm know?" Jonny closed his eyes, as though he was grateful for a calm, familiar voice asking reasonable questions. "He's breathing, jah. No sign of blood but he's a mighty funny color . . . okay, so you'll let her and the girls know to be ready when I swing by for them? Denki, James. I owe you one, big-time. Jah, Zanna's fine. Mighty glad she was along when I found Dat this way."

Something warm inside Zanna fluttered, but as he ended the call, she kept her focus on his dat. She placed her hand on Rudy's neck to reassure herself there was still a pulse, faint and erratic but definitely there.

"Gut thing I learned how to drive," Jonny remarked in a nervous voice. When he exhaled, his breath rose in wisps of vapor. "You know, as many times as I've taken folks to hospitals, I . . . I've never been farther than the front desk."

"Not what you bargained for when you came to Cedar Creek this morning." Zanna forced a smile, wishing she could wipe the worry from Jonny's handsome face.

"I've never seen anybody lying so . . . still," he finished in a barely audible whisper. He looked like a scared little boy, at a loss for what to do next.

Zanna stood up and took his hands, looking up into his eyes and hoping she sounded encouraging. "But you're handling things just fine, Jonny, and we got here in time to call for help. I'm thinking God had a hand in that."

As a siren sounded in the distance, he wrapped his arms around her. Zanna reminded herself that he was shivering with cold and fear; she told herself not to get her hopes up about this young man getting attached to her in a permanent, romantic way.

"If something happens to Dat," Jonny said in a faltering voice, "what will become of Mamm and the girls? Especially now that the house and all their clothes and food and furniture are gone? How will the herd get milked, and the milk get delivered?"

Jonny released her to grab his phone again. He closed his eyes with the effort of remembering. "Sure hope I've got this right. It's been a long while since I called Mervin." He punched the numbers and waited, sighing impatiently when the phone in the Masts' shanty kicked into message mode. "Mervin, it's Jonny Ropp, and I'm headed to the hospital with Dat. If you could see that his cows get milked, I'd appreciate it. Oh, here's the ambulance! Thanks, Mervin."

Zanna waited beside Rudy as Jonny and the three barking dogs went outside to signal the driver. Moments later, the paramedics came in. She got out of their way and stood to one side with Jonny. He answered as best he could when the paramedics asked him questions and watched as they checked Rudy's vital signs and hooked up an IV. She'd never seen Jonny looking so helpless. After the EMT fellows quickly carried his father out on a stretcher, he grabbed for her hands.

"I—I've not thought much about the end of Dat's life, but I never saw it happening like *this,*" he said, shaking his head. He looked at her as though holding her gaze might keep him grounded and rational. "Maybe if I wouldn't have left home . . . Zanna, how'd you handle it when your dat got sick?"

"Jonny," she said, grasping his hands more firmly, "you *don't* handle it by blaming yourself or assuming he's not going to make it. You take a lot of deep breaths, and you say a lot of prayers, and then you keep doing the next thing that has to be done."

She smiled up at him, hoping she sounded braver and stronger than she felt. "By now, James has told your mamm and your sisters what's happened and that you're coming to pick them up. You're in the driver's seat, Jonny, because none of the rest of us can be, jah?"

He blinked, then seemed to gather himself together again even though his smile looked uncertain. "Jah, you're right, Zanna. We'd better get going."

Zanna sat in the hard plastic hospital chair that afternoon, wishing she were invisible. When she'd arrived with Mamm, Adah, and the girls this morning, they'd gone through the usual exclaiming and explaining. In a tearful reunion, Adah had hugged her Jonny for dear life. Rudy had regained consciousness and was stable, but waiting for the results of many tests had worn them thin. Stress and exhaustion had silenced them as the last rays of afternoon sun slanted through the windows.

Zanna felt as frayed as a worn-out dishrag. Rather than make eye contact with any of them—because the subject of her and Jonny *would* come up—she studied the dust on the fake plant beside her chair. When James Graber had appeared around two o'clock and then pulled up a chair beside Adah for an update on Rudy's condition, all the air had seemed to leave the already stuffy room.

Could there be a more unbearable situation? Because the waiting area was so crowded, Zanna sat beside Jonny, while Mamm, James, and Adah faced them from across a coffee table strewn with old magazines. Becky and Maggie shared an issue of *People*, but their peeks over the top only made Zanna feel more like screaming. And all the time her baby—Jonny's baby—kept kicking and fussing inside her, with Jonny none the wiser.

"I'm thinking a cup of tea might perk us up, Adah," her mother said. "And the walk to the cafeteria would be gut for us, too. You girls want to come along?"

Maggie and Becky hopped to their feet, eager for a change of scene. The four females weren't out of sight before James rose, as well. "I need to let Amos Coblentz know I'm not in my shop, in case Noah figures to start working on those wagons."

Jonny smiled tiredly. He'd been very quiet since they had arrived—nervous about being in a hospital and what the doctors might be doing to his dat. As James's footsteps faded down the hall, Zanna felt as if someone had grabbed the waistband of her apron and was pulling it tighter and tighter.

"Awful nice of you to come along, Zanna," Jonny said. "I don't know what I'd have done without you, back at the barn."

His voice held a hint of that sweet-talking he was so good at, but she told herself not to fall for it. If there was to be any release of the tension in this airless waiting room, she had to find a way to tell Jonny he was the father of her child.

"I remember how awful it was to bring my dat here, first of the year," she murmured, wiping away sudden tears. "He passed here, you know— not that your dat will do the same," she added quickly. "If you hadn't called the ambulance, he would have been gone by the time Adah took out that casserole she was making him. And finding him *that* way would have been even more horrible."

"I still feel pretty low. As I watched him lying there on the barn floor, I kept thinking about all the times I couldn't wait to have that man out of my life."

It was the most somber she'd ever seen him: Jonny Ropp slumped in his chair without any hint of the daredevil who'd roared along the road on his motorcycle. "Well, we've all noticed lately how upset he gets, over the least little thing," she said softly. "Your mamm told us he'd get up at all hours of the night to roam the house, then be dozing off at dinner, or while she was talking to him."

"Guys have a way of tuning out the wife's voice, you know."

It was meant to be funny, but Zanna stiffened. Was telling him about this baby a waste of her time? She shifted in her hard seat, wishing she'd gone for tea with the others.

But you've got to talk. It's now or never—no matter how distracted he is by his father. Jonny might not come back once Rudy's up and around.

Zanna drew in a deep breath. "Jonny, I've got to tell you—"

"So, Zanna, if you're not married, how is it you're—"

His gaze locked onto hers. Jonny was asking a sincere question, puzzled rather than poking fun at her. The baby kicked, telling her to get on with it. Zanna's throat felt so tight she could hardly breathe. "I was—engaged. To James. Before July."

Jonny's jaw dropped. "You were going to marry James Graber?"

"This past October, jah."

"And he backed out on you, after he got you—" He stared at her belly. "So how are you still living in Cedar Creek, right across the road from him? And you've been talking to him today as though everything is fine between you."

Zanna's face prickled with heat, but she made herself look him in the eye. "I was with *you* in July, Jonny," she reminded him. "So I was the one who backed out on James, the morning of our wedding day."

Jonny's eyes widened. He leaned closer, as though he didn't quite believe her. "And he's still speaking to you? And Sam lets you stay at home, when everybody can see you're—"

"James and Sam are special men," she murmured. Why on earth wasn't Jonny making the obvious connection? Zanna closed her eyes and willed herself to tell the rest of the story. "The baby's yours, Jonny. So I couldn't marry James and pretend—"

"What?" Jonny's outburst made the folks around them turn to gawk. He flushed, and then looked away, gripping the arms of his chair. "But . . . it was just that once."

Zanna scowled. "Jah, well, I've said that a hundred times, but that didn't make it go away," she said. "You think it was easy, telling everybody? You think I *liked* it, going through two confessions—before and after being shunned? And meanwhile keeping your name out of it until I couldn't hold it in anymore?"

Jonny went very still. "So everybody knows? Even Mamm?"

Zanna let out a wry laugh. "She's the one who stood up in church and said I should reveal the father so she'd know who her two girls should stay away from. The preachers—everybody—had been saying all along that this child's dat should be confessing right along with me," she added in a hoarse whisper. "I was so peeved at your mother's tone—her attitude—that I spat out your name to rub her nose in it, mostly."

He swallowed hard. "And she's . . . okay with it?"

"She refused to believe it at first. And your dat called me a liar—threw a big fit after the preaching service, the Sunday before the fire." Zanna made herself take a breath. The last scrap was out of the box now, and she had the advantage of knowing how this crazy quilt would fit together. "But Adah's made her peace with it. The baby's her grandchild, Jonny. *Your* child."

He stood up suddenly, thrusting a hand through his collar-length blond hair. "I can't believe they didn't send you off—like they did my cousin Ann—to keep you out of sight. And then make you give it up for adoption."

"Nobody on God's green earth could make me

give up this baby, Jonny. I told them I'd leave if they did." Zanna stood up beside him, sensing she had only a few moments to make him understand exactly how she felt. "I knelt in front of the whole church and asked forgiveness for my sin, but I told them I *would* raise this child—by myself, if need be—because God brought it to me for a reason. I don't know for sure what that reason is just yet, but I *love* this baby, Jonny. No matter what *you* think."

His face reddened as reality sank in. "You could have told me . . ."

"Your feelings about joining the church and getting hitched have always been obvious," she pointed out. "Meanwhile, James offered to marry me anyway, and to raise this child as his own. But I said no."

"I would have taken you to a clinic to—would have paid for it, so you could have married Graber and no one would have been the wiser."

Zanna's heart slammed in her chest. She wrapped her arms around her belly, willing herself not to cry. "You haven't heard a thing I've said, Jonny. It's just like I figured, ain't so?"

He stuffed his hands in his jeans pockets. "I'm out of here. Have to walk this off while I think about things." Jonny stalked down the hall, his body as stiff as a stick figure. His boots clattered on the tile floor, telling the world he couldn't get away from her fast enough.

329

Zanna eased into her chair again, forced herself to take a deep breath and let it out slowly. So now he knew. And see there? It hadn't changed a thing, no matter how much she'd helped him with his dat that morning. So she'd better forget that lovey-dovey happily-ever-after stuff and get on with her life.

She picked up a magazine. She couldn't read the words for the tears in her eyes, but it gave her something to hold on to.

"How are you, Zanna? Looks like Jonny didn't take to your news so well." Mamm eased into the chair where Jonny had been sitting and clasped Zanna's hand. "James told me it was a gut time to come back. He stayed just around the corner from you, in case things got out of control."

James had watched out for her? Zanna smiled, even though it would be a while before she felt happy again.

"We've got some better news, though," her mother went on in a hopeful tone. "The doctor's been talking to Adah about some of the tests. He says Rudy had a heart attack in the barn—and that if Jonny hadn't called for help when he did, his dat would have been gone. Just goes to show you how a cell phone—and God's gut timing, getting Jonny out to the farm—worked together in the best possible way today."

"Jah. Jah, it did," Zanna agreed quietly. She felt all done in.

"Shall we start for home?" Her mother stood and coaxed Zanna from her chair. "James went to call the driver who brought him in, so we can go with him. Adah and the girls need to spend more time with the doctors and seeing after Rudy, and then they'll catch a cab."

And Jonny? Where did he fit into this scenario?

Jonny always found a way to get where he wanted to go, so she'd best not lose any more sleep over him. It wasn't like he was worrying about her.

— *Chapter 23* —

Abby took up her pencil, grateful for this quiet time on Tuesday morning to write her article for the *Budget*. Events in Cedar Creek had been more sensational than anyone wanted, what with the stir caused by Zanna's pregnancy and confession, but this fire . . . the Ropps' losing all they had. It wasn't the kind of news she enjoyed reporting at Christmastime, yet maybe some good could come of it.

She said a prayer, asking that her report would be a blessing to those who read it. Then she began to write, relying on God to supply the words. Her articles were often more like essays than what most scribes sent in, but folks told her she was an inspiration. And wasn't it her calling, to be a blessing to Plain folks across the nation?

Cedar Creek has seen more than its share of tragedy this week. Rudy Ropp's family barely escaped when their house caught fire and burned to the ground, all the contents lost, last Thursday in the wee hours. The fire's cause was too much creosote that had built up in the chimney. (If you don't recall the last time you swept your chimney, and if you don't have smoke detectors, let this be a word to the wise. An ounce of prevention means you won't be fretting over how to replace all the furniture, clothing, and preserved food the Ropps have lost—not to mention the mementos that make a house a home.)

Abby paused, gazing out her window at Sam's two-story snowcapped home. How fortunate they were that special quilts and chairs enriched their lives, gifts passed on to them from Mamm and Dat's parents and grandparents. She didn't want to report as though she wore rose-colored glasses, but what would she accomplish if her readers felt depressed by what she told them? How did she write about the fire's devastation, followed by Rudy's collapse in the barn, in a way that would not only inform her Amish audience but inspire folks, as well?

Yet we've seen God's hand at work even after such a terrible event. When Jonny Ropp learned of his family's loss, he returned to the dairy farm and saved his father's life. Rudy had fallen to the barn floor after a heart attack, but Jonny summoned the ambulance in time. Rudy's heart disease was diagnosed, along with a chronic case of sleep deprivation. We expect Rudy home in another week, with a high-tech pacemaker in his chest. Adah and the girls have stayed in a hospital guest room to help with his therapy and daily care.

We neighbors met in James Graber's carriage shop and response to this critical situation has been heartwarming. Thanks to donations of carpentry expertise, lumber, and supplies, the Ropps will have a newly furnished home as well as a new shed, complete with replacement buggies and wagons. Through sewing frolics and food drives we will gather the everyday things it takes to run a household. And all of this, according to our master carpenter, Amos Coblentz, will be completed by New Year's Day!

We invite your prayers for Adah and Rudy Ropp and their children: Gideon, Jonny, Becky, and Maggie. And we wish you a blessed Christmas from Cedar Creek, Missouri!

At the chiming of her kitchen clock, Abby quickly wrote out her good copy of the article. Today was the first of several sewing frolics, and she'd received a rush shipment of especially cheerful prints for quilts along with solid broadcloth colors for curtains. Amos had given her all the window dimensions, so she and the other women would complete most of Adah's new curtains today. Now *that* was something to celebrate!

Tuesday morning, James began to make the wheels for the Ropps' new carriage. He had set the fiberglass body and the undercarriage, pieces he had acquired from other Amish shops, beside the workbench in a back corner of his main building so he could work on this special project while Perry Bontrager and Leon Mast kept up with the ongoing repairs and orders. Wheel making was a basic skill he would soon be teaching to Noah Coblentz, but today the repetitive work of securing the sixteen wooden spokes in each of the four wheels would keep his troublesome thoughts from circling like buzzards. Ever since Jonny Ropp had rushed away from the hospital after Zanna told him he had fathered her child, James had replayed the scene and its dialogue in his mind far too many times.

No woman deserved to be abandoned by the man who had placed her in such a precarious position.

But what could he do about it? Not much, because Zanna had chosen to keep her child, and she'd also rejected his second marriage proposal. James had stopped being angry with

Zanna, but he still cared what happened to her.

He had completed the first wheel and was positioning the spokes in the second one when a tapping on the window glass made him turn. The last person he'd expected to see peering in at him on this blustery day was Jonny Ropp. Even though the wintry wind whistled outside, the kid's blond hair framed his face in a sleek English style. When James motioned for Jonny to come in through the shop's back door, the younger man's sparkly earring winked as he chewed insistently on a wad of gum.

"Hey, Graber."

"Jonny," James replied with a nod. Never mind that Ropp's timing was uncanny: James wasn't in the mood for friendly chitchat after what he'd witnessed in the hospital waiting room on Sunday afternoon. He began arranging the wooden spokes around the center steel hub of the wheel he was making. "What can I do for you?"

Jonny's expression shifted between boldness and uncertainty, and other emotions James couldn't read. "I came to see what you can tell me about Zanna's . . . situation. She's told me about confessing and being shunned, yet still she's raising this baby in Cedar Creek—and her brother's going along with it." He focused icy blue eyes on James. "Something's wrong with this picture. Why hasn't Sam Lambright shipped her off to a distant relative's house? And why is the bishop allowing Zanna to keep the kid and raise it by herself? And why didn't somebody tell me she was pregnant?" he said in an exasperated tone. "Do you know how it feels to be the last one to find out you're about to become a—a *father?*"

James let out a sigh, reminding himself that he was the older, more mature man here. Jonny's attitude irritated him, but getting sucked in by this fence jumper's insensitivity wouldn't make the situation any better for either of them—or for Zanna.

James cleared his throat. "Why are you asking *me* these questions?" he demanded. "If you'd cared enough about Zanna after having relations with her—or if you'd visited with your mamm and sisters—you'd have known those answers a while back."

Jonny pivoted on his heel, his eyes flashing. "It's not something a fella expects to find out about in a waiting room after he's found his dat almost dead!" he replied sharply. "You'd think she could've said something earlier—like when she first found out about the baby, or when we drove out to the farm the other day."

James bolted a spoke at the wheel's center hub, making Jonny wait . . . giving them both a chance to cool down. Finally he pondered aloud. "Do we ever have control over when we receive life-changing information? And since Zanna didn't figure to have a future with a fella who'd left the Amish life behind, it took more courage for her to tell you about the baby than either of us can imagine."

Jonny's brow furrowed. "How can you stand up for her, after the way she left you on the morning of your wedding?"

James managed a smile despite the way this worldly blond was wearing out his welcome. He deftly measured and marked the ends of the wooden spokes that would be fitted into the wheel's rim. "We defy logic—forget common sense—when we forgive someone we love, ain't so? Or would you know anything about that?"

"Hey, I came here asking you legitimate questions. I don't need your holier-than-thou attitude!"

James raised an eyebrow. Such a rude remark didn't deserve a response, so he flipped the switch of the pneumatic saw that would shape the spokes' outer ends into cones, like pencils in a pencil sharpener. Wood shavings flew as he guided the end of one spoke . . . two spokes, into the whirring machine.

Jonny shifted, stuffing his hands into the pocket of his sleek jeans. "Okay, sorry. My bad," he said above the noise of the air-driven saw.

My bad? What on earth did that mean? At least Jonny hadn't called him *dude,* but James still felt no need to answer him. If he'd come here to say something, he needed to get on with it. James continued rotating the wheel and whittling the ends of the spokes until he'd completed all sixteen of them.

"So is it true, what Zanna told me? That you said you'd marry her anyway when you found out about the baby?" Jonny blurted out when the saw fell silent.

"Why do you think she'd lie about that?"

"I didn't say she'd lie! I just—" Jonny let out a frustrated sigh as he stepped out of James's way. "I can't feature you raising another guy's kid, let alone marrying a woman who got herself pregnant while she was engaged to you!"

"She didn't do that to herself, Jonny," James snapped. "And, here again, if you have to ask such a question, you have no concept about what it means to truly love someone." He drew in a deep, steadying breath and then fitted a dowel cutter on the end of his saw. "Why are you here? I'd like to finish this carriage for your family."

Jonny's stiff shoulders dropped. He studied the dark gray fiberglass body and the assembled undercarriage with new interest. "That's another thing I don't get," he remarked in a quieter tone. "Why did the Lambrights invite my mamm and sisters to stay there, after the way Mamm badgered Zanna about having a baby? And now you're replacing the carriage that burned up because Dat didn't clean the chimney?"

"Jah, because it's the right thing to do. Like I've told you before, we Amish look after each

338

other." James positioned the first spoke so he could cut the cone-shaped end into a dowel peg that would fit into the outer rim of the wheel, but he held off on flipping the power switch. At least Jonny seemed to be listening now. "Is there anything else you want to know?"

The iciness in Jonny's blue eyes melted a bit. "Okay, so maybe I'm being a pest and getting way too personal," he admitted in a lower voice, "but now that the shock of Zanna's big news is wearing off, maybe . . . maybe I'm trying to figure out if I could ever be the man she could marry. I—I have no idea how to be a husband, or a father."

"And you're asking me?" James drew another deep breath to still the painful throbbing of his heart. Jonny's question had struck a deep nerve, reminding him again of how much he'd lost when Zanna left him. "I was ready and willing— twice—to take on those roles. But now?" He sighed. "That opportunity has passed me by. Maybe you should ask somebody with more experience. Seems to me Sam Lambright knows what it takes to hold a family together."

James guided the first spoke into the dowel cutter, easing his ruffled emotions with the steady, systematic rhythm of a job he'd done hundreds of times. Abby was right: work was the cure for a lot of ills because it gave his mind something productive to focus on. He had, indeed, forgiven Zanna for the hurt she'd caused him these past couple of months, but dealing with Jonny Ropp's questions was another challenge altogether.

At least the kid was considering Zanna's needs now. It was an improvement over roaring through Cedar Creek on his noisy motorcycle, stirring up the chickens and the sheep. James continued cutting dowels, wondering how long Jonny would hang around watching him. When he had completed that task, he reached for two arcs of wood on the workbench, which would form the outer rim of the wheel.

"Okay, well—sorry to be a bother," Jonny murmured as he glanced toward the door. "I figured you'd be the easier one to ask about all this stuff, after the way I skipped out on Zanna at the hospital. Maybe it's her I should be talking to."

James felt a smile warming his face. "Sounds like your best idea yet. Gut luck with that."

Jonny's lips twitched. "Yeah, I'll need it, probably. Later, dude."

Resisting the urge to protest that slang label, James picked up his pneumatic drill to make the holes in the outer rim of the wheel, where the doweled ends would fit. The wind whipped into the shop, blowing wood shavings around his feet, and he glanced toward the door. Jonny was looking at him with a softer . . . downright grateful expression as he stood half in and half out of the shop.

"Thanks, Graber. For everything."

James nodded, struck by what a decent kid Jonny could be when he gave it a shot. "You're welcome. I hope it all works out, and I hope your dat's feeling better soon."

A week later, Abby sat at their second sewing frolic, where several of the women and girls had gathered around Barbara's big kitchen table to make a crazy quilt. With tea, cocoa, and Mamm's sticky buns on the sideboard, quilting for the Ropp family was a perfect way to spend a snowy mid-December afternoon. Abby and Emma sat together, and Marian Byler had joined them today, bringing baby Elizabeth in a carrier. It was good to see Zanna and the Coblentz twins, Mary and Martha, huddled together, too, over the odd-shaped scraps of calico and twill they were arranging on squares of quilt backing.

"Sleep deprivation? You're telling me that missing out on a few hours' sleep was what was making Rudy so crazy?" Bessie Mast paused to thread her needle, which allowed Barbara to explain the diagnosis.

"It's a serious situation if it goes on for long— and you know how men tend to ignore the signs that their body is out of kilter," she added with a wry grin. "The surgeon said Rudy's pulse was so low, a part of his mind was *afraid* to go to sleep for fear he wouldn't wake up. So he wasn't getting much oxygen, either, which made his heart condition worse."

"So that pacemaker will fix him up?" Eva Detweiler had been following the conversation closely while she'd featherstitched over the seams of a pieced square. "Could be my Zeke needs to get checked. He's not old enough to be feeling so tired—and his dat passed from heart failure at an early age."

"What we need at our house is a cure for Abe's snoring," Beulah Mae chimed in. "If he'd quit sawing logs all night, I'd get so much beauty sleep, why, who knows what a kind, polite—and gorgeous!—gal I might become?"

Abby laughed along with all the other women. She and Emma glanced over to where Eunice sat at a small table with Eva's two little girls, cutting the larger fabric scraps into pieces for the rest of them to stitch together. "It's gut that your mamm's helping us even if she can't see well enough to sew," Abby remarked quietly.

Emma smiled as she seamed a scrap of red gingham to a piece of yellow twill. "Jah, she was happy to get out today—and the way Eva's girls, Polly and Laura, are chatterin', Mamm can't dwell on her aches and pains," she added. "James took Dat to the shop today to count out bolts and whatnot for the wagon they're making the Ropps."

The kitchen door opened and Lois Yutzy

stepped in, her black coat speckled with big white flakes. "Well, I wouldn't believe it, except I've seen it with my own eyes," she exclaimed as she hung her bonnet on a peg. "I took the stew and biscuits out for the men's dinner, and they got the Ropps' new roof on this morning. They'll have the house enclosed by tonight."

"Jah, when Amos and the bishop take charge of a project, you'd better believe it'll scoot along ahead of schedule," Mamm said, sipping her tea and nodding in approval. "Awful nice of those Mennonites to bring out a generator and lights so the crew can work longer hours on these short days."

"Well, the Fishers appreciate Adah's working there as much as she and Rudy depend on selling their milk to the cheese factory." Lois eased into a chair Abby had pulled up to the table for her. She glanced toward the end of the table, where Barbara's three daughters, as well as Zanna, Mary, and Martha, sat. "Also a nice surprise to see Jonny there, putting his mamm's new cookstove together," she remarked brightly. "Amos told me Jonny drove past the farm last week, and when he saw how the fellas were building a new house, he stayed to help them. Guess he did some tall talking, and Gideon's come back, too, to keep the cows milked while their dat's laid up."

"Well, *that's* a gut sign," Abby replied. This information was such a positive surprise that it took her two tries to thread her needle. "Maybe it's finally dawning on him that he could've lost his family in that fire."

"Goodness, how long has it been since we last saw Gideon?" Bessie asked.

Eva snipped the end of her embroidery floss. "Wouldn't it be a wonderful-gut thing if those boys came home to stay?"

"You know it'd be a load off Adah's mind, having them back," Barbara remarked.

Abby glanced up in time to see Zanna nip her lip. A week had passed since her sister had told Jonny about the baby, and he'd made himself scarce ever since. Abby's heart went out to Zanna as she remained focused on her sewing. Why was it, when Zanna did what was right, the wrong things happened next? If Zanna's expression was anything to go by, hearing that Jonny was working in Cedar Creek only made her feel worse, even though everyone was pleased that he was helping with the new house.

"Just so happens I'm signed up to deliver their noon meal tomorrow," Gail said with a sly smile. "I could use a hand, Aunt Zanna. If you get my meaning."

Emma giggled. "What *you* mean, Gail, is that you're going out to see if Gideon Ropp's as fine and feisty as you remember. No secret you were sweet on him before he left town to tend all those chickens."

The Coblentz twins snickered, elbowing Zanna and provoking a smile from her. Abby felt grateful to Mary and Martha for pitching in on these sewing frolics, and especially for their acceptance of Zanna now that her life had spun outside the lines that defined their own futures. As she looked around the table, at familiar faces lined with love and laughter, Abby realized that gatherings like these were the batting and backing that held the crazy quilt of their lives together. Every one of these women had her own talents and strengths—added her own colors to the community—yet despite differences of opinion and age, they fit together all of a piece, like the multipatterned squares of this crazy quilt they would complete today.

Gail grinned. "Jah, well, the fella you're setting *your* hopes on smells like sheep most of the time, Emma. And Matt's no more aware of how you feel than Gideon's thinking about me."

"Got to poke men with a crochet hook to get their attention, most days," Phoebe remarked. She smoothed the large square she'd just completed, smiling at the way the colors and patterns went together. "I might go with you tomorrow—"

"Ooooh, going to gawk at Owen, swinging that hammer with his sleeves rolled up," Mary teased.

"Jah," said Martha, her freckled face alight with mischief, "but instead of that crochet hook, I'd take a big pan of cherry cobbler. Owen's holding out for a girl who's as gut a cook as our mamm—"

"And who picks up after him, same as she does," Mary added with an emphatic nod. "Wants his things all neat and tidy—shirts pressed just so—but he shows no inclination to lift a finger when it comes to keeping his room neat."

"Blames it on Noah, that their room is such a sty."

Abby and the older women smiled at one another as the Coblentz twins chattered on. Hadn't they all had similar conversations when they were girls gathered around a quilting circle?

Abby wondered if things would be different now with James if she had baked him more cherry cobblers—or poked him straight out with a crochet hook of words about her feelings for him?

Thoughts like that took her nowhere, of course. The last time Abby had spoken with James, he'd shared his frustration over the way Noah often showed up tardy and sleepy-eyed—sure signs that the young redhead was out late, pushing his rumspringa to the limit. James felt Noah showed an aptitude for painting and restoration, though, and he had a good eye for welding. It had hardly been romantic talk.

But James was moving forward. He'd adjusted the expectations he'd had about being married two months ago, just as Abby had reached that moment last year at about this time, when she'd asked Amos and Owen Coblentz to draw up plans for her house. If folks were to find any contentment in life, they had to stop looking wistfully backward so they could forge ahead with a clear vision.

And how could she help Zanna move on, too, now that Jonny Ropp seemed to be ignoring her?

"I don't see how taking these rugs over with the men's dinner will change anything," Zanna protested as she dressed to go with Phoebe and Gail the next day. "I made that first one with the blue dress fabric for Adah, jah, but the rest were for selling in the store."

Abby gazed into her sister's cornflower eyes, wondering how best to explain her theory. "Six rugs you've made over the past couple months, but you're keeping them around . . . like you can't quite let go of them. Maybe because each one turned out prettier than the last," she added with a smile. "Maybe if you consider this your goodwill offering, and let Jonny and the other fellas see how you're giving the work of your heart and hands, just like they are, it'll show how far you've come in forgiving the woman who railed at you the loudest when you decided to keep your baby."

Zanna considered the suggestion, looking doubtful. "But isn't that being prideful?"

"No more prideful than those men sharing their best talents, knowing they're good at what they do," she said with a laugh. "Maybe Jonny will realize how much Sam and James and the others are donating—not because Rudy's been nice to them but because they believe in helping folks who are in a bad way. Your rugs would be especially for Adah, too. More personal than a house, even though that's the bigger gift."

Zanna said thoughtfully, "Like the woman in Jesus' story who put in the two coins, and He said it was the greater gift because it was all she had?"

"Jah, that's a gut way to think of it—as long as you don't go telling folks about it. That's where the prideful part would come in."

Zanna went to her room and came back with three of her rugs rolled up. She picked up the tin of decorated Christmas cookies she'd made the day before. "I'd better be scooting along. We've still got to stop by Beulah Mae's café to pick up the roast beef."

As she walked down the path that Abby had shoveled to Sam's house, Zanna hoped her older sister was right: maybe donating her rugs would show Jonny that her heart was in the right place. And if he didn't take the hint, or wouldn't talk to her, well . . . she had planned to live without his help, anyway. For all she knew, he would disappear again after his dat came home from the hospital.

When she reached the carriage her nieces had loaded, Zanna tossed the rugs into the backseat and then climbed in beside them, careful not to disturb the two pans of cobbler on the floor. "Morning to you, Aunt Zanna!" Gail said from the front.

"Ready to see the new Ropp house—oh, and Jonny, too?" Phoebe teased as she took the reins.

"I suppose." Zanna shrugged. "Not counting on a lot from him, considering how he hasn't said boo since he learned the baby was his." The two girls in front got quiet then, and she was sorry she'd dampened their mood.

"So, these are what you've been making, all those days you've been holed up at Aunt Abby's?" Gail reached back for the smallest rug and untied the string around it. "Ooh, sister, would you look at the way Zanna worked in all these bright colors! Red, gold, and rust calicos, and ginghams that go with them."

Phoebe let Tucker make his own way down Lambright Lane. Once they were on the county road, she ran her hand around the crocheted rows that formed the rug's circle. "All these years, we had no idea that Zanna had such a way of turning rags into rugs—and riches," she said with a laugh. "If Owen finally takes the hint and we get hitched one of these days, will you make me one big enough for a front room? Anybody's home would look cozier with rugs like these."

Zanna's eyes widened. These pieces had mostly been a way to pass the long afternoons, and maybe make some money. She'd had no idea her nieces would be so excited about her work. "Jah, I suppose—"

"And you can't make a special rug for Phoebe unless you make one for me, too," Gail chirped. "Start on it anytime, and I'll tuck it away in my cedar chest. It'll be special because *you* made it, Aunt Zanna."

As they stopped by Mrs. Nissley's Kitchen for a large catering pan of sliced roast beef, Zanna reminded herself not to get carried away on this tide of excitement. It was natural for Sam's girls to make a fuss over her handiwork, but it was another thing altogether to hope Jonny would speak to her today. It had stung like a wasp that he'd been more willing to pay for an abortion than to help her raise his baby, and it went against all the values they'd been raised with, too.

"And would you look at that," Gail crowed as they rounded the bend of the county road. A new two-story house of fresh lumber stood where the old place had been, with the milking barn behind it. "Except for the black spots in the snow, you can't even tell there was a fire."

"And they've put on one of those fancy metal roofs, too. That's a wild shade of copper."

"Looks like a big autumn leaf. Or a giant metallic pumpkin rind, all flattened out." Phoebe halted the horse, and then they picked up the cobblers and the Dutch oven of green beans.

"We'll let the men carry the meat and that box of plates. You're not to be lifting anything heavy, Aunt Zanna."

Amos Coblentz came over to help them. "Better come on down and get dinner while it's hot," he called to the crew atop the house. "Gut as it all smells, it won't last long, fellas."

Owen's father grinned at them and then lifted the hot catering pan as though it weighed nothing. "What do you think of that fancy roof? A company in Kirksville donated it to get some free advertising. Figured folks driving along the state highway would see it, along with their sign down by the road."

"It looks like it ought to outlast a shingle roof. More fireproof, too," Zanna said. She grabbed her tin of Christmas cookies and the three rolled-up rugs, thinking to stick them someplace where they'd stay clean and out of the carpenters' way. She heard the whine of pneumatic drills and the *rat-tat-tat* of air hammers as she and the girls made their way carefully along the icy path.

As she followed Amos through the side door, however, another one of the crew hollered, "I'll go fetch the rest of our dinner." Before Zanna knew what hit her, her rugs flew out of her arms and the cookie tin fell to the floor. Frosted stars, Christmas trees, and angels spilled out onto the gritty subflooring—all yesterday morning she'd spent decorating them, too!

351

Jonny Ropp backed away, startled. "Zanna! I'm sorry for not watching—are you okay, girl?"

The roomful of men and tools fell silent.

She blushed, nodding. "Jah, I'm fine."

"Ten-second rule!" somebody across the room hollered.

"Been eatin' sawdust all day, anyway. What's a little more?" Mose Hartzler teased.

"That yellow star with the sprinkles has *my* name on it." Owen Coblentz and the fellows closest to Zanna snatched up the cookies at their feet while an older hand retrieved the tin. The room—what was to be the kitchen—filled with exclamations over her goodies as the shiny red container got passed from one tool-belted carpenter to the next.

"Life's short, eat dessert first," Abe Nissley declared. The silver-bearded preacher grinned at her, gesturing with a gingerbread house that had a big bite out of it. "If you made these for Jonny, he'll just have to come see you to fetch his own, ain't so?"

Jonny still looked stunned. Was it because he'd run smack into her, or because he hadn't expected her to come to the site? He went outside then, while other men laid a couple of unfinished doors across sawhorses to use as tables. Zanna and the girls set out plates and silverware, and soon the other food and the big coffee urn had been carried inside. The crew of a dozen found

352

crates and step stools to sit on, and then bowed their heads for a moment of silent prayer.

"Dig in, fellows. I'll be right there. I want to admire these rugs Zanna brought in."

Zanna's eyes widened when Bishop Gingerich picked up the rag rugs and spread them on a cleared worktable for all to see. This was not what she'd planned.

"Here's another example of how the answer to our dilemma often appears if we ask for heavenly direction," Vernon went on. "We were discussing what colors to paint these rooms, as Adah's still at the hospital with Rudy, and her boys said they'd rather not second-guess their mamm's preferences."

Laughter rang around Zanna, and the men's faces lit up. Jonny and Gideon chuckled sheepishly as they tucked away gravied roast beef and mashed potatoes.

"I suggest we paint the kitchen cream, to go with this one," the bishop said as he held up the first oval she'd made. "And this round one's just right for stepping out of the shower, so maybe the bathroom should be pale yellow? And wouldn't any of us want to sink our feet into this rectangular green one when we get out of bed on a cold morning?"

The men were nodding, following the bishop's conversation as they ate. Phoebe was spooning up a big bowl of cherry cobbler, smiling at Owen, while Gail poured hot coffee for Gideon Ropp. Eager to be out of the spotlight, Zanna fetched more of Mamm's warm rolls from their insulated bag.

"Is one of those the rug Rudy was all upset about during church?" Preacher Paul asked her as he reached into the bread basket.

Zanna's cheeks went hot, recalling the strain of those moments, both here at the Ropp house on Thanksgiving Day and again at preaching the next Sunday. "Jah, the first one, with the blue. I—I brought along a couple more, thinking how Adah's lost everything she had in the fire."

Vernon raised an eyebrow. "You were making these rugs to sell, weren't you? Part of your way to support your baby?"

She closed her eyes. Could this questioning possibly get any more public—any more embarrassing? What must Jonny and Gideon think, now that the bishop was revisiting the issues their parents had raised about her pregnancy? "Jah, but—I can make more," she added on sudden inspiration. "They go together fast."

"I'll be wanting a couple for Eva," Zeke Detweiler exclaimed. "Make them mostly red— her favorite color—and about the size of that big oval one."

"Lois just finished a flower garden quilt, so she'd be tickled to have new rugs for both sides of our bed!" Ezra Yutzy called out.

"Well, if Beulah Mae hears your wife got two new rugs, she'll have to have three!" Abe chimed in with a chuckle. "Zanna, those are wonderful-gut rugs. You've been hiding your talent under a basket all these years."

Zanna's jaw dropped as every married man in the room called out a rug order. "Wait! I'll never remember who wants what."

"I'll write them down for you." Phoebe playfully snatched a carpenter's pencil from Owen's shirt pocket. "And if you fellas are looking for a special Christmas present for somebody, you could write out a gift certificate for a rug and put Zanna's name and number on it. Then whoever gets it can call her and order exactly the right colors and size."

"Now that's a fine idea," the bishop replied with a big grin. "My mamm and her two sisters are shut-ins now, but wouldn't they love to have new rugs to brighten their rooms in our dawdi house?"

Who could have believed this overwhelming response to her rugs? While Phoebe wrote down the orders, Zanna and Gail passed around the remaining cobbler and poured coffee. The bishop came up beside Zanna then, looking mighty pleased. "It's a pleasure to see you helping with our meal—and even better to see how everybody wants your work," he said as he held his mug beneath her carafe. "Don't shortchange yourself, come time to decide on a price for those rugs.

We all want you to succeed, Zanna. You've gone against the grain a time or two, but your heart's in the right place."

"Denki for starting that—that avalanche of rug orders," she murmured happily.

Vernon smiled as his gaze wandered over to where Jonny rose from the table. "The Lord helps those who help themselves—and those who help their parents, too," he replied. "James Graber mentioned how you'd called Jonny after the house burned down. And that led to him saving his dat's life, and then calling Gideon home to keep the dairy running. There's no end to what can come of one good idea put into action, Zanna. Faith truly can move mountains."

Had her phone call to Jonny been an act of faith—or of desperation? As she and Sam's girls stacked the dirty dishes, Zanna hoped the bishop's remark would hold true as far as how Jonny responded to fatherhood. The men rose from the makeshift tables, their thank-yous filling the room before they went back to work. When Zanna glanced around, she saw that one particular blond and his brother had made themselves scarce already.

No sense in getting upset about it. Hadn't all those rug orders given her better things to think about—so much work that heartache couldn't worm its way into her Christmas season?

"Don't leave without me," Gail whispered as she slipped into her coat. "Gideon asked me to meet him out in the barn for a minute."

Zanna's smile felt lopsided. "Jah, Phoebe's touring the rooms here with the fella who helped put them together. We can't leave if we don't have a driver, ain't so?"

And meanwhile, she might as well make herself useful. No courting for her today, it seemed.

Zanna stacked the dirty plates in the box and laid the silverware alongside them. The Dutch oven had barely a cup of green beans left in it, and nearly all the roast and potatoes were gone, too. The pans were now light enough that she could load them into the carriage, so she and the girls would get home sooner to eat their own lunch. The air hammer started in the room above her as she went to the door, balancing the bean pot inside the two cherry-smeared glass pans.

A hand reached around her and clamped over the doorknob. "You've got no business carrying that, girl. Stack the rest of the stuff so I can do the walking over that ice out there. Then I'll help you over the slick spots."

Jonny stood beside her, his face mere inches from hers—but only for a moment. Zanna surrendered her dirty pans, mumbled her thanks, and returned to the table to do as she'd been told.

Since when do you jump just because he says so?

That voice in her head made a good point, yet it seemed the smart thing for a girl in her condition to consider. After he'd carried the catering pans out, Jonny Ropp stood in the doorway looking her over. It was then that Zanna realized he was wearing broadfall work pants instead of designer jeans . . . and suspenders over his blue shirt instead of a belt with a fancy buckle. As the baby fluttered inside her, Zanna reminded herself not to get too excited: a change to Plain work clothes didn't commit him to Plain ways—or to her.

He glanced around the unfinished kitchen. "I nearly fell on my butt just now," he remarked, "so we're taking no chances with you, missy. This box Mamm's new stove came in looks like just the sleigh we'll be needing."

Zanna looked at the beautiful new cookstove in the corner—a far nicer one than anything Adah could have hoped for before the fire. "And it came in pieces? You put it all together?"

Jonny shrugged. "It was simple, really." They slid the box through the door to the snowy path outside and Zanna sat down in it, feeling very awkward. Jonny started pushing her toward the carriage that awaited them on the icy lane. She hoped Gail and Phoebe wouldn't be long, because sitting out in the carriage sounded like a cold, lonely wait.

Next thing she knew, Jonny was laughing. He shoved her box across the slick ice toward the slope that had frozen when the fire trucks doused the flames. When he hopped in beside her, Zanna shrieked—right before they swooped down the hillside at a crazy speed while Jonny threw his weight against his side of the box to make them spin.

She began to giggle and couldn't stop. The sheer exhilaration of careening across the pasture, watching the white world and the farm buildings whirl around them, sent her heartbeat into high gear. By the time they leveled off at the bottom of the hill, Jonny's arm had slipped around her. They came to a gradual stop, but Zanna's pulse kept right on racing.

"I shouldn't have done that," Jonny muttered. "We could have hit a tree, or—if the box had come apart, you'd have been—" He gazed intently at her, shaking his head. "I seem to be real gut at doing all the wrong things, and I'm sorry."

"Don't apologize for having fun. I haven't laughed this way since—" Zanna closed her eyes, wondering if she dared finish the sentence. "I haven't felt so dizzy—so crazy—since you took me for that ride on your Harley, back in July."

Jonny caught her gaze and held it. "Hear me out, will you? I haven't had much practice at apologizing." He crammed his stocking cap farther down over his ears, gathering his courage. "It was exactly the wrong thing to do, walking out on you at the hospital last week. Just like it was a bad idea to talk like I'd rather get rid of the baby than have it."

He let out a long sigh. "I've made a mess of your life, Zanna. Yet you're working it out, facing up to the folks who put you down for doing what you believe is right. Mamm told me all about how folks stayed away the whole time you were under the ban. That had to be hard, thinking your friends wanted nothing more to do with you."

Zanna's heart thudded harder. She'd never seen Jonny so serious, had never heard him admit to making a mistake. His gaze remained riveted on hers, as though this impromptu sleigh ride had cleared his vision and firmed his resolve.

"And you helped me more than you know when we found Dat on the barn floor—even though I'd already done you so dirty," Jonny went on in an insistent voice. "You're making those rugs to support yourself, when you could have kept this whole thing under your kapp and married Graber."

"I don't love James enough to marry him," she said. "If I'd been truly committed to him, I wouldn't have been seeing you that one last time. And I wouldn't have known that I had to raise your child."

Jonny looked away. But here within the confines of their stove box, there was no escaping. No second-guessing when it came to bringing another life into the world. "You're so strong you make me look like a coward, running off just because Dat and I couldn't get along."

"Nobody else had any idea about his temper, until lately."

"Jah, well, I was just looking for an excuse," he admitted. "And when I saw how run-down the equipment had gotten while I was away, how old Dat was looking and how frazzled Mamm seemed —well, I can't explain it. When I found him face-down in the barn, I knew I was partly to blame. It was a wake-up call. And then when you said the baby was mine—"

"It was a lot to pile on you, all in one day," Zanna murmured.

"Phooey on that! Don't make excuses for me, Zanna, because I'm plenty gut enough at making them for myself." He looked at her with a fierceness in his eyes . . . something akin to fear and determination and anguish all mixed together.

And she knew how that felt, didn't she?

Zanna cleared her throat. If she didn't say this now, while Jonny couldn't run from it, she might not find the nerve again. "I didn't marry James," she said, "because I love *you*, Jonny. I'm not saying you have to love me back, or *do* anything about my feelings, but—"

He grabbed her face between his hands and kissed her, hard. "I'm not going to listen to that kind of talk."

And what did that mean? Would he climb out of the box and leave her? Would he escort her up to the carriage and then never speak to her again?

The emotions on his face ran the full range, from anger to exhilaration, fear to despair—and Zanna wasn't sure where she fit into that mix.

Jonny sighed and glanced up the hill. "We'd better get you back to the carriage. Seems you've got a lot of rugs to make and me, well . . . I'm still figuring out where I fit in—or *if* I fit in. Hang with me while I get it all straight in my head. Will you do that?"

Zanna's heart fluttered—or was that the baby, doing a little dance? She nodded, suddenly hopeful.

"Understand," he went on, "that I will *not* come back to the same sort of stuff Dat dished out before. Nor will I let him treat Mamm that way again, either. And who knows?" He went on in a lower voice. "Maybe Dat wants no part of Gideon and me coming back. He sounded pretty set about it when he told us we weren't his sons anymore, for not joining the church or wanting to run the dairy."

Zanna couldn't imagine how much the words must have hurt Jonny and Gideon, even though they'd put up a tough, rebellious front. All in all, she felt very fortunate that folks in Cedar Creek —and her own family—had accepted her decision to live outside the lines. "Maybe that will change when he sees how you boys came back to help rebuild your homeplace. From what I've heard, he was more seriously ill, and for a longer time, than any of us realized."

Jonny chewed his lower lip as though he hadn't heard her. "I know that puts you in a bind, girl—what with you already being baptized, and all. But don't write me off, okay? I'm not making any promises, but I'm starting to see things in a different light now."

Did she dare to hope for the best? As she and Jonny walked uphill through the powdery snow, his hand felt strong and purposeful, wrapped around hers. His mood lightened as he talked about working with Gideon again: his brother milked the cows and arranged the milk pickups, while Jonny had been repairing the machinery. He'd even improved some of the dairy's equipment in ways he'd learned about while living among the Mennonites in Clearwater.

Zanna soaked up his confidence as they topped the hill. She caught the looks Gail and Phoebe gave her as the bishop was loading the last of their boxes into the back of the carriage. Vernon Gingerich didn't seem surprised to see her and Jonny together. His face glowed with the cold air and his usual goodwill as he smiled at them.

"I was just telling the girls how delighted I am with our progress here," he said, "and how surprised Adah and Rudy will be when they come home from the hospital. They still don't know about the new house, or about these carpenters' goal to have them in it by the first of the new year."

"How's that possible?" Zanna blurted. "New

Year's Day is less than two weeks from now."

"The work is mostly indoors now. That makes it a lot easier—and warmer—for everyone who's helping." Vernon focused on Jonny then, as though assessing the youngest Ropp's attitude about their project. "Our concern is that your dat will go back to working eighteen-hour days too soon," he remarked. "Rudy's not the sort to let other folks help him. Nor does he want to feel like a charity case."

"You've got that right," Jonny said with the hint of a smile. "Gideon and I have been fixing a lot that went undone, as far as his buildings and milking equipment go. But that's not to say we'll stay on once he gets home. Dat may not want us to, for one thing."

The older man nodded. "Most of us didn't understand that side of the situation, son. We all assumed you and your brothers were full of yourselves—rebelling against your father's authority. But your mother set the other preachers and me straight on that score when we visited with her at the hospital."

Jonny looked surprised that such an understanding had been reached . . . that the leaders of the church seemed willing to listen and to accept another side of the story.

"Matter of fact, your mamm asked us to hear her confession, there in the hospital chapel," Vernon went on in a softer voice. "She said she was real sorry for being so thorny and opinionated—and that she'd laid it on a little heavy with you, too, Zanna. She sincerely hopes everything will be different now that Rudy's on the mend."

"She's not the one who needs to be apologizing," Jonny protested. Then he got his attitude under control. "What I mean to say is, they might've put a new gadget in Dat's chest to keep him ticking, but it's his attitude that needs an adjustment."

Zanna turned to hide her smile. "The pot's calling the kettle black, maybe," she murmured.

The bishop squeezed her shoulder, smiling with her. "It's all about forgiveness, in the end. And sometimes the forgiveness has to come from the one who feels he or she should be receiving it," he said quietly. "It would do your dat, and your mamm, a world of good if you stopped by the hospital to see him, Jonny. Our talking to him, as preachers, can only go so far."

Vernon turned when somebody hollered for him to help set the bathroom cabinets in place. "Well, they're saying I've lollygagged long enough. You two have a good day—and Zanna, I'm tickled to pieces about all those rugs you'll be making. You do wonderful work. And you're more of an inspiration than you know."

"Well, there you have it," Gail said as the bishop stepped inside the house. "And, Zanna, it's all fine and dandy if you want to stay here flirting with

Jonny, but I'm going home to have some lunch."

"I've got to get back to work myself," Jonny said. His expression suggested he was pleased . . . maybe a little amazed. "These older fellas kinda like it that us younger guys can crawl around on the floor to reach under pipes and behind tight places. I—I had no idea they'd be so generous, or so glad to have Gideon and me helping."

"It's your home they're building," Phoebe reminded him gently.

"Don't be a stranger, Jonny," Gail said. Then she made a point of getting inside the carriage, ready to go.

But Zanna stood watching Jonny as he walked back along the icy lane . . . the lanky body, stronger than it looked . . . the swagger in that walk, even though his talk had toned down as much as his clothing had. The blond hair hanging out the back of his stocking cap caught the afternoon sun and had a glow about it. Would her baby—his baby— look anything like Jonny Ropp? Would there come a day when she wished Jonny hadn't left his stamp on the child she'd vowed to raise?

Or would Jonny come around?

"Aunt Zanna!" Gail cried. "Are you going to stand there in the cold watching Jonny's backside, or shall we get on home so we can start ripping strips for those fifteen quilts on your list? Christmas is a-comin', you know—and it won't wait around for *you*."

— *Chapter 24* —

After a Christmas Eve supper of vegetable soup, Emma's fresh bread, and gingerbread cookies she and Mamm had made, James went into the front room with his dat. A fire burned brightly in the fireplace. Emma had arranged an evergreen bough on the mantel and displayed some of the pretty Christmas cards they had received from family and friends. As he always did, Dat picked up the Bible for their nightly devotional and dropped into his favorite upholstered chair. After he had thumbed through the Good Book's pages, he looked up at James.

"My eyes aren't what they used to be," he said. "How about you read for us tonight, son? It being time for the Christmas story, I don't want to mess it up and get your mamm in a dither. She knows all the words by heart, you see."

"Jah, there's that. I'll be happy to read, Dat." James settled into the chair on the other side of the small table, aware once again that his father wasn't as active or as confident as he'd been even a few months ago. He glanced at the page and looked up. "You're wanting Matthew's version of the story, rather than the second chapter of Luke?"

"Jah. The part about the angel coming to Joseph, before the trip to Bethlehem," his dat replied with a decisive nod. "Luke doesn't go into that part."

Emma came in from finishing the dishes then. She raised her eyebrows when she saw that the Bible wasn't in their father's lap. "James is reading tonight? You're not feeling up to it, Dat?" she asked as she took her seat on the sofa.

"I'm perkin' along all right, I reckon. And after that fine soup for dinner, I'll be ready for bedtime so's we can leave for Iva's gut and early tomorrow." Their father shrugged, glancing at Mamm as she, too, emerged from the kitchen. "We've been talking this over, your mamm and I, thinking it's time to move into the dawdi haus, come the new year. No steps to climb that way. Easier on all of us."

Emma glanced at James and he shrugged slightly. Although they'd talked of their parents shifting into the rooms built onto the back of the house when he and Zanna were to get married, James sensed it wasn't a good time to quiz them about this decision. Mamm was wearing the new teal dress Abby had made her last month, and looking happier than she had for a while. And wasn't that a Christmas gift in itself?

"Whenever you're ready, we'll move your bedroom furniture and your clothes downstairs," James replied. Then he focused on the page in the

Bible, getting himself into the proper frame of mind. "Dat asked for the first chapter of Matthew, starting with the eighteenth verse, which comes a bit before Mary and Joseph's trip to Bethlehem."

He cleared his throat and began to read. " 'Now the birth of Jesus Christ was on this wise: When as his mother Mary was espoused to Joseph, before they came together, she was found with child of the Holy Ghost. Then Joseph her husband, being a just man and not willing to make her a public example, was minded to put her away privily.' "

"Just like you, James," his father remarked with a decisive nod. "Not wanting to make a spectacle of Zanna. Tryin' to keep things decent and low-key even when Adah and Rudy raised such a ruckus in the mercantile and at church."

"Hush now, Merle," Mamm insisted. "It's not right to interrupt while somebody's reading God's word."

James glanced at Emma, who was looking frazzled after a day of packing for tomorrow's trip. In some ways, going to Iva and Dan's made the holiday more difficult, what with the extra planning and dealing with Dat's forgetfulness and Mamm's moods—and little offshoots of conversation like this one. "Thanks, Dat," he said quietly. He didn't care to draw too many parallels between Joseph's behavior and his own because Zanna's situation was different from Mary's. "I'll go on with Joseph's story now, all right?"

His father nodded, satisfied. Mamm adjusted her glasses to focus on him again.

" 'But while he thought on these things, behold the angel of the Lord appeared unto him in a dream saying Joseph, thou son of David, fear not to take unto thee Mary thy wife: for that which is conceived in her is of the Holy Ghost,' " James read with expression. " 'And she shall bring forth a son and thou shalt call his name JESUS, for he shall save his people from their sins.' "

Mamm's eyes widened and she sat forward. "Haven't had any dreams like that, have you, son?" she queried in a nervous voice. "None of us are thinking Zanna's gonna bear another child who'll change the whole world like Jesus did, but . . . well, we wouldn't want to miss any signs like Joseph got in his dream, either."

Emma's eyes widened. She looked at James as though to ask where on earth this line of thought was coming from. "Mamm, we're all tired and we need to pray before we get you off to bed," she suggested.

"What're ya sayin', Eunice?" his dat blurted. "Zanna's baby has already changed the whole world, on account of how not a one of us'll be the same because of this child. Ain't so, son?"

James blinked. Dat had said a mouthful there, hadn't he? And once again, in that inexplicable way his unpredictable mind worked, their father had made the Scriptures fit their situation more closely than they could have imagined. And he had put James on the spot with his question, too.

"I believe," James said slowly, hoping not to bungle his answer, "that God has a reason for the way things are happening for Zanna—and, jah, for me, too. And while I haven't heard angels in my dreams, telling me how things will work out, I trust Jesus to help us make sense of how our lives are supposed to move forward."

As he looked at his parents, who seemed to be shrinking into fragility as the months passed, he had a fleeting thought that a Christmas would soon come when they wouldn't both be conversing this way. "Shall we pray and then call it a day?" he suggested quietly.

After they had all bowed their heads in silence, Emma went upstairs with their parents to be sure their clothes were laid out for the early trip tomorrow.

James went to the front window. Across the road, lights shone at the Lambright house, and a little farther up the lane at Abby's little place, too. Otherwise, the twilight had wrapped around Cedar Creek like a thick blanket of deep blue, embedded with stars above serene, snow-covered pastures that rolled beyond the mercantile, Treva's greenhouse, and the sheep barns. While he was grateful that Ida and Dan were hosting the big family gathering tomorrow, it saddened him that Christmas as they'd known it had slipped away like Dat's memory and Mamm's patience. Tomorrow, he would be driving them to Queen City in the sleigh. No doubt, it would be a sedate, careful ride, totally different from the wild sleigh rides he and the neighbor kids had enjoyed on several Christmas afternoons of their youth.

As Emma's footsteps clattered on the wooden stairs, James remained focused on the rolling hillsides, chuckling over the memory of one particularly eventful outing the Christmas he had built a sleigh in Pete Beachey's shop and given it to the family as a holiday present.

"Well, now," his sister said as she came to stand beside him, "you're wearing a different expression altogether from when Dat had you playing the part of Joseph."

James nodded. "Jah, I was remembering that Christmas afternoon when you and Iva and Sharon were in the backseat of the sleigh, and we'd stopped by to pick up Abby—"

"Because the Lambrights have the biggest, best pastures for sleigh riding, so we almost always went over there," Emma said, joining in eagerly.

"—and we'd ridden just beyond Cedar Creek, when up over the hill popped the Ropp brothers in their sleigh."

"Jonny couldn't have been more than eight or nine," Emma recalled in a faraway voice, "but he wasn't about to let Gideon drive."

"Jah, and he was egging me on to race," James continued as the scene played out in his mind. "I was old enough to know better, while you and the older girls were hollering to stop that nonsense, on account of how we'd get in trouble if anything happened to the new sleigh."

"And Iva was just the one to tattle on us, too."

James laughed and slipped his arm around Emma's shoulders. "And Abby was sitting up front with me, saying 'James, can your mare go any faster in this snow? We've got to show those Ropp boys a thing or two!'"

For a moment they were silent, reliving the sleigh race that had crossed the unfenced back acres of the Lambrights' farm. James remembered the shine in Abby's eyes and the way her cheeks glowed in the cold air as her laughter rang out. He had urged Peggy to gallop faster, aware that he was playing a dangerous game yet loving the look on Abby's face.

Had Abby been sweet on him then, as Jonny had hinted the other day? Or had she mostly been excited by their race against the daredevils of Cedar Creek? James smiled at how she'd radiated such joy as the sleigh raced across the snowy knolls, and he couldn't help wondering if things would be different this Christmas if back then he had really noticed Abigail Lambright.

"Jah, you showed them some snow when they turned over their sleigh on that big hill," Emma quipped. Then she shook her head. "We were lucky nobody got hurt."

"Lucky the horses weren't any worse for the wear, too. But none of us were thinking about safety at that age," he replied. "We helped Jonny and Gideon turn their sleigh right-side up while they brushed the snow from their clothes, and everybody went back home like it was no big deal."

Emma rested her head on his shoulder. "Nothing seems that simple anymore, ain't so?" she asked wistfully. "As I recollect, Zanna had measles that Christmas."

"And I was just as glad she did, because back then I considered her as pesky, in her little-girl way, as Jonny Ropp was." He laughed ruefully. "Who could have known that she and I would get engaged? And that it would be me who got dumped this time around, instead of Jonny?"

His sister raised her head to look at him. "Maybe it's a gut thing we can't see into the future," she murmured wearily. "I'm headed for bed, James. Don't spend the night stewing over Zanna and Jonny and wondering how it'll all turn out this time, okay? Night, now."

"Night, now." He watched his sister start up the staircase, but it was Abby on his mind. Calling up her gentle smile made him feel better about this evening's devotional reading and the way his parents seemed to be aging before his eyes.

And wasn't it Abby's way to play the part of that angel in the passage, telling folks not to be afraid because whatever happened was in God's hands? Now, that was something to ponder . . . a true gift that Abby shared with every one of them.

"Merry Christmas, Abby," James whispered. And although he still didn't know how everything would play out for Zanna or himself, he went to bed a happier man.

" 'And they came with haste, and found Mary and Joseph and the babe lying in a manger,' " Matt read with enthusiasm. " 'When they had seen it, they made known abroad the saying which was told them concerning this child. And all they that heard it wondered at those things which were told them by the shepherds. But Mary kept all these things and pondered them in her heart.' "

Abby sighed with the wonder of this passage. "Every Christmas we hear these words, yet this year they seem extra-special." She slipped her arm around Zanna, who sat beside her at the big table in Sam and Barbara's kitchen. "Think how Mary must have felt, carrying a baby all those months, having to explain that she wasn't married to Joseph, and that it was God's own child."

"And Joseph, too—having to take an angel's word for it that he was supposed to go ahead and marry her," Mamm said as Matt put away the big family Bible. "Not a lot of men would have had faith enough to go along with that, or to raise God's own son. It just goes to show you what wonderful-gut things can come from situations that don't fit the rules, if you believe the Lord's behind them."

"I'll agree with that, as long as you don't write Jonny Ropp into the part of God." Sam, at the head of the table, smiled wryly as he focused on Zanna. "And you, little sister, have taken on your responsibilities a lot better than I figured you would. You made the right decision, keeping this baby. I'm glad you convinced us to go along with it."

Grinning, Abby raised her eyebrows. Their brother was truly feeling the spirit of Christmas, to admit such a thing. How well she recalled Sam's anger and accusations when Zanna had revealed her pregnancy back in October. And what a blessing, that her sister was blooming like a pink poinsettia now that morning sickness was behind her. Barbara's regular checkups indicated that mother and child were blessedly healthy.

As they bowed for a silent prayer before their Christmas dinner, Abby smiled with her eyes closed. After she said thanks for their special food, she added, *We thank You, too, Lord, for the way the bishop and our friends have come together in Your love and forgiveness. It's another Christmas miracle that except for a little redding up, the Ropps' new house is finished.*

"Merry Christmas! And God bless us, every one!" Sam declared. "Let's do all this gut food justice."

He took a slice of pineapple-glazed ham and started the platter around while everyone else reached for the steaming bowls in front of them. Mamm and Barbara had cooked everyone's holiday favorites: candied yams with marsh-mallows for Matt, corn casserole studded with chunks of red and green bell pepper for Gail, and festive red applesauce cooked with red-hot candies for Ruthie.

Abby grinned as she picked up the platter of roasted duck with apple-pecan stuffing. "You outdid yourself, Mamm. This is the only Christmas present I need, right here."

"Gut," Matt teased around a mouthful of food. "Because we didn't get you anything else."

The meal was one of the merriest Abby could remember. They recalled walking their hillsides with Dat to find just the right Christmas trees, and sleigh races with the Graber kids on Christmas afternoons. Even back then, Abby had been so certain James was the man for her.

Reality had worked out differently than her dreams, yet Abby felt fulfilled and content. Had she been married with children, she couldn't have devoted so much time to their recent sewing frolics. Nor could she have provided the fabric, because her Stitch in Time business wouldn't exist. And as she smiled at Zanna, Abby sensed she was able to be a more supportive sister because she was single, too. Zanna had certainly needed that.

Over warm gingerbread drizzled with Barbara's special lemon sauce, Abby saw that even though they'd stuffed themselves silly, a lot of their dinner was left. They had decided days ago to share it with the Ropps. "Hospital food can't measure up to this feast," she said. "And Adah's got to be feeling low because with Rudy still there, their family can't share Christmas dinner at home. She and the girls are probably awful tired of staying in that hospital guest room."

Barbara nodded, her eyes sparkling. "We've got plenty to share, so we might as well start wrapping them up a care package."

Abby turned to Zanna, excited by a new idea. "Why not call Jonny? Ask if he wants to go with us when we deliver it? Maybe he'll even drive us," she added mischievously. What with all the work he and Gideon had done around their homeplace, it seemed only fair to feed those brothers Christmas dinner after Bessie and Mervin Mast had let them bunk with them these past few weeks. And Zanna would have another opportunity to be with Jonny—and his family, of course.

Zanna's eyes clouded over. "I'm not sure what he's been doing with himself lately," she murmured as she rose to scrape their plates. "Must be too busy at the house."

"The crew's not working today," Sam pointed out. "If you tell him you've got dinner for him and Gideon as part of the bargain, surely he'll consider that."

"Oh, all right." Zanna's sigh sounded forlorn. She dropped the silverware onto the pile of food-smeared plates and hurried over to put on her coat. "But don't say I didn't tell you so, if he's nowhere to be found."

The slam of the kitchen door behind her made them all exchange a look. "I wondered why Zanna seemed kind of quiet this morning," Barbara remarked as she took up the task of scraping plates.

"Jonny was sure looking like a fella head over heels in love that day we took lunch to the new house," Phoebe remarked with a puzzled frown. She ran hot water in the sink.

"She hasn't heard from him since then, though." Gail began putting food into plastic containers to take to the hospital. "Maybe the truth about the baby is sinking in and Jonny's back to his old ways. Or maybe he already went to see his dat, like the bishop suggested, and he never came back."

"Well, going for that visit is a gut idea, no matter how Zanna feels about it," Sam said. He went into the front room, and soon returned with a foxlike grin. The box he handed Abby was crammed with red and green envelopes— four or five dozen of them. "Some of these cards came to me at the store," he said, "and Vernon brought over the ones the postman's been holding, knowing the Ropps aren't home. After I opened a few, with letters asking me to pass the enclosed card along to Rudy and Adah, I stuck them away. Seems Plain folks from all over have been sending them money, Abby, on account of that report you wrote for the *Budget*."

Abby stared at the boxful of letters, dumbfounded. "But I didn't ask for donations or a card shower or—"

"Which makes folks more willing to send them," their mother pointed out. Her face lit up like the star of Bethlehem as she riffled through the stack of cards. "Some of these have come from New York and Georgia . . . Here's a couple from Jamesport, and some from Minnesota and Tennessee, as well. I have no idea how much money the Ropps lost in the fire, but this will certainly go a ways toward replacing it."

Abby felt downright giddy. Who would have believed this outpouring of generosity was possible? "I'm glad the bishop said we should tell the Ropps about the new house today. And about the buggies and wagons James made."

"Christmas is the perfect day for that," Barbara agreed as she tucked a big piece of ham into a covered casserole dish. "Adah's been worrying about where they'll go when Rudy's released from the hospital. They don't want to be a burden on anyone."

"Well, if this isn't a Christmas miracle, I don't know what is." Abby couldn't stop beaming in anticipation of the surprise—the joy—on Adah Ropp's face when she saw these cards.

"And it's *you* who should tell them about all this, Abby," Mamm added with a decisive nod. "Not only was it your piece in the paper that brought in the money, it was your doing that we made Adah a whole houseful of new curtains, plus four quilts. And you convinced Zanna to donate those pretty rugs, and you got folks to give food and clothes right off, too."

Mamm stood up at her place, quickly swiping at her eyes. "I can't say as I've ever been more pleased with my family, for the part you've all played in restoring the Ropps' home. Your dat's smiling down on you from Glory right now, kids."

Abby blinked back tears. This first Christmas without their father had made them all more emotional, and hearing these compliments reminded her of how Mamm, especially, had seemed more cheerful of late because she'd been involved in the Ropps' recovery. "Denki, Mamm. It's been gut for all of us, forgiving Rudy and Adah by providing things they need," she murmured. "Even if they don't accept our gifts with as much appreciation

381

as we'd like, we'll know we did right by them."

"Amen to that," Sam chimed in. His grin twitched. "Knowing Rudy as we do, he'll not enjoy being on the receiving end of Cedar Creek's generosity, which will put a damper on it for Adah, too. But I know you'll handle that just fine, Abby. Give them my best when you see them."

The kitchen door swung open, admitting a little puff of snow as Zanna stuck her head inside. She was grinning, short of breath from hurrying back from the phone shanty—and from excitement, too, Abby realized.

"Jonny's coming by for me in a few, and—well, Abby, I hope it's all right that he and I go to the hospital, just the two of us, so we can talk about, well . . . *you* know."

Abby hurried to the door to hug her sister. "You *know* I know. I'll find another driver, Zanna."

"Ferris North will be here in about fifteen minutes." Zanna's smile said she was tickled at setting up this surprise so quickly. "Far as it is to Kirksville, I didn't want you driving a carriage on such a cold day. He said he wanted to look in on the Ropps for a minute, and that driving you would get him out of a house crowded with his in-laws and hyper little kids."

"That'll be fine, Zanna, and denki for calling him."

"Merry Christmas, big sister," Zanna said, her eyes a-sparkle. "I'll see you there."

● ● ●

As Jonny's red van came up the county road, Zanna stood at the end of the lane waiting, and wondering. She'd felt so excited when he agreed to go to the hospital . . . but what if he was only stopping by to let his mamm know he was returning to his driving business? The new house was finished, so what would keep him here in Cedar Creek? The van stopped in front of her and Jonny jumped out to open her door. His grin flickered with the same uncertainty that filled her thoughts. "Hope it's okay that Gideon came along. I couldn't very well leave him at the Masts'," he said in a low voice.

Zanna's face fell. She'd been so happy about seeing Jonny that she'd forgotten about his brother. She tried to set aside her disappointment. "Your folks will be glad to see both of you."

"But you and I *will* talk, Zanna," Jonny murmured as he lightly kissed her cheek. When he swung open the van's front passenger door, warm air drifted around them. "I hope you know that this visit with Dat might either set a lot of things right, or it could go south in a hurry. If that happens, we'll be leaving sooner rather than later."

It struck Zanna then, how lucky she was that even when she'd had to tell Abby and Sam and Mamm about the baby, she'd never really believed they would banish her from their lives. The Lambrights had endured some difficult days

383

after she'd canceled the wedding, but because they believed *family* was everything, they had found the faith to work out a solution they could all live with.

And if you'll be living with them after Jonny leaves town, well . . . you'll still have a home. You'll still have a family who loves you and the baby.

Zanna nodded and climbed into the car. "Hey there, Gideon. Merry Christmas."

"Jah, we're hoping it will be." He sat by the door on the driver's side of the middle seat, wearing a down jacket and a tentative smile that looked very much like Jonny's. Gideon was taller and blockier, built more like Rudy, while Jonny resembled their mamm. "After three weeks of Bessie Mast's burnt biscuits and thin soup, it's gut of you to offer us dinner."

"We decided a few days ago to take a meal for your family," Zanna replied, "but it was Abby's idea to include you two, as well."

How would Abby deal with this dark cloud the Ropp brothers were under? Her older sister was so good at dispelling doom and gloom and the apprehension that lurked behind the boys' remarks. As Jonny pulled onto the road, Zanna smiled slyly. Maybe she could tease them into a better mood.

"Abby's bringing ham with pineapple slices, and corn casserole and candied yams," she said, watching Gideon's face. "And there's cinnamon red-hot applesauce and Barbara's gingerbread with lemon sauce. But you'll have to be in the room long enough to give your dat the benefit of the doubt before you get a plate."

Gideon pressed his lips into a thin line. He looked out the window as though he saw no humor in her remark.

Jonny, too, was awfully quiet. He watched the winding road, lost in his own thoughts—or maybe he didn't want to talk about the baby and his plans in front of his brother. Zanna sighed. This wasn't the happy atmosphere she'd hoped for when Jonny had agreed to pick her up, but she didn't feel like being the only one to make pleasant conversation.

Once they turned onto Highway 63, the main route to Kirksville, Jonny went a ways past Queen City and then turned onto a road Zanna wasn't familiar with. She wasn't concerned—Jonny drove folks to this hospital all the time—but she wondered if Abby might already be in Rudy's room, wondering where on earth they were.

"You're stallin', little brother," Gideon remarked.

Jonny smiled ruefully at Zanna. "Sorry. Hospitals aren't my thing. All the bad smells and the moaning you hear—"

"But Dat's out of bed now. Mamm and the girls will be there, too," Gideon said, sounding more positive now. "And with Abby bringing in dinner, the folks will have other things to talk about besides what you and I are doing here, little brother . . . and how long we intend to stick around."

As Jonny followed the narrow country road around modest farms blanketed in snow, Zanna realized that Rudy and Adah had no idea their two sons had been in Cedar Creek helping to build their new home. No one from around town would have thought it was their place to tell them, and they obviously hadn't spoken to one another. It was a sad reflection on the emotional state of the Ropp family. But maybe this surprise visit would patch up some damaged relationships. *Lord, help me shine with Your light,* Zanna prayed as she took in the pastures and snow-laced evergreens they passed.

In another few miles they spotted the hospital. Jonny pulled into the visitors' parking lot and circled the first row of parking spaces even though there were plenty of empty ones to choose from on this Christmas afternoon. He finally pulled in and shut off the engine.

"Not trying to be a wet blanket," he said, "but if Dat starts up with his name-calling and finger-pointing, I'm hitting the road." He looked at Gideon in the rearview mirror, and then focused on Zanna. "That's not how I want this visit to go, understand. But if it comes to us leaving that way, you can either ride with us or hitch in with

Abby and I'll catch up to you later. All right?"

What could she do except nod? Maybe she should have come with Abby . . .

Gideon threw open his door. "Okay, we're going in now," he said, forcing good cheer into his voice. "We're doing this for Mamm, remember. The sooner we get in there, the sooner we get out."

Once they stepped through the hospital door and told the volunteer at the information desk who they'd come to see, her face brightened. "Oh, you'll be pleased to see how your father's improved! Such a sweet man, too." She directed them to the skilled nursing ward.

Sweet? Zanna bit back a smile. No one had ever said that about Rudy Ropp! As they approached the room, the door was open and familiar voices drifted out. They heard silverware scraping against plates. "Awful nice of you to bring Christmas dinner," Adah said. "Be sure to pass along our compliments to Barbara and your mother until I can thank them myself."

"Jah, best ham I've had in a long while," Rudy chimed in. "And with the candied yams and the pink applesauce, why—it's a feast! Can't thank you enough for comin' today, Abby."

Zanna made out Becky and Maggie's softer voices talking in the background, but she couldn't distinguish what they said. It seemed they were all having a cozy Christmas Day visit, but when she started for the door Jonny grabbed her hand.

"Let's listen a bit. Get the lay of the land," he whispered. Gideon nodded beside him.

Zanna's brows rose. Were the boys thinking they would slip on out if the conversation didn't sound promising?

"If I could see that my cows are all right, knew where we'd be livin' when I get dismissed tomorrow, I'd be a happy man." Rudy let out a short laugh. "The bishop and Preacher Abe have been tellin' me not to worry about that—that it's been in God's hands and everything's taken care of. But that's easier said than done," he said matter-of-factly. "I . . . I can't recall much about the fire, or collapsing in the barn. And maybe that part's a blessing."

Was that Rudy Ropp talking? Zanna wondered. Since when had he spoken about being happy, or mentioned blessings? When Gideon stepped closer to the door, Jonny stuck his arm in front of his brother to keep him from peering into the room.

"This being Christmas, we brought along a surprise," Abby said in a lilting voice. "It seems my write-up about the fire for the *Budget* inspired folks to send you some Christmas cards and notes. Sam opened a couple, not realizing what they were, because they've been coming to the mercantile while you weren't home."

Gideon raised his eyebrows in a question. Zanna shrugged, itching to get into the room to see what was going on. She'd apparently missed something while she was out in the phone shanty.

"Oh, my stars! Rudy, would you look at these!" Adah exclaimed. "There must be three or four dozen envelopes—"

"Now, why'd they go and send money?" Rudy demanded, sounding more like himself. "Don't *tell* me you asked for donations, Abby. You know I'm not acceptin' anybody's charity."

"I never said a word about money." Abby's voice carried out into the hall on a wave of pleasure that made Zanna inch toward the door. "Plain folks all over the country knew you'd be hurting after losing your home and all your belongings. It's Christmas, and they wanted to send some peace and goodwill your way, Rudy. Sharing their blessings, they are, and thankful their own homes are still standing."

Jonny leaned toward his brother. "If folks from all over sent Mamm and Dat money, that will help replace the savings they lost."

"Dat will be able to hire help for the dairy," Gideon whispered.

"And Mamm can return to the cheese factory. Life can go back to the way it was before the fire."

With an exasperated sigh, Zanna slipped her hand from Jonny's. She was tired of the Ropp brothers' doubting attitude, and she wanted to watch this amazing surprise unfold—wanted to see all those cards and be a part of the Ropps' celebration. Every issue of the *Budget* had a column for card showers and donations, but she had never known anyone who'd received such a big stack of mail from total strangers.

"Merry Christmas!" Zanna said as she entered the room. Rudy sat in a recliner beside his made-up bed, while Becky and Maggie used the opposite edge of the mattress as a table. The girls jumped up to hug her from both sides at once.

"That was the best corn casserole, Zanna," Becky exclaimed.

"Jah, and the candied yams hit the spot, too," Maggie added. "Better than anything on the hospital's menu."

Abby's smile told Zanna her big sister had been waiting and wondering where she and Jonny had gone. And then Adah stood up beside Rudy to wave handfuls of green and red envelopes at her.

"Merry Christmas to you, Zanna! And would you look at these cards?" she crowed. Adah seemed a little older, but in a new pine green dress the girls had made her, she looked downright festive. "Who could believe such generosity? And this dinner Abby's brought. You Lambrights have turned a quiet day into a Christmas we'll never forget."

"It's a real Christmas miracle," Zanna remarked. She peeled off her heavy black coat and removed her bonnet, raising her eyebrows at her sister. "Shall I tell them the rest of the gut news?"

Abby grinned at her and then beamed at all the Ropps in the room. "We can never hear too much gut news, ain't so? And Christmas is a fine day for surprises."

Zanna nodded, feeling warm all over. Being in a room that smelled like ham and warm gingerbread, where these family members looked happier than she could recall, felt so much better than hovering out in the hall. Maybe Jonny and Gideon would catch the hint . . . or maybe she would simply have to call their bluff.

Zanna smiled at Rudy then, as the man who most needed to hear how God had supplied for his family's needs. "Since the day Jonny brought you to the hospital, Rudy, Amos Coblentz, the bishop, and some of the others have built you a whole new house and shed."

Adah let out a heartrending cry. Her hand flew to her mouth as tears sprang to her eyes. Becky's and Maggie's mouths dropped open.

"And Abby has organized sewing frolics to make new curtains and quilts," Zanna went on more boldly, "while James Graber has replaced your carriage and buggy, plus a couple of the wagons you lost."

"Now, why would they do such a thing?" Rudy protested. He sat forward in his recliner, scowling. "They know full well we can't afford to—"

"Nobody did it expecting pay." Abby stood up, opening her arms as she continued in her low, melodious voice. "You're one of us, Rudy Ropp. You and Adah and your kids are part of our larger family in Cedar Creek—and nobody would dream of letting *family* go homeless. Or go hungry, or without clothes."

Zanna was nodding, thankful that Abby had such a way with words. "And the *best* part," she added as she glanced toward the door, "is that Jonny's been one of the building crew, putting together Adah's new cookstove and repairing your farm equipment. And Gideon has come home to milk for you. And they're right outside this door, waiting to see you."

She heard Gideon's surprised cough out in the hall, and a few moments later he poked his blond head in the doorway. Adah rushed over to throw her arms around him as though welcoming the prodigal home. After a moment, Zanna stepped out into the hallway to see what was keeping Jonny.

He looked deeply moved by what he'd overheard, yet still uncertain about going in.

"We've got your dat buttered up now," Zanna said in conspiratorial whisper. "Abby's fed him Christmas dinner and kept him talking positive— and now that they know about the money in those cards, and the house you helped build, having you and Gideon here is one more big surprise. Like we saved the best for last."

Zanna stepped closer to him and took hold of

his hands. While nothing could erase the troubled relationship he'd had with his dat, she so hoped this crisis would lead toward something better between them.

"How can your dat not be pleased to see you, Jonny?" she said earnestly. "And how can he welcome you back—shake your hand and ask you to stay—if you don't give him that chance? He's not hooked up to any tubes or machines. There's nothing to be scared of in there—except your own face, if you look in his bathroom mirror." She squeezed his hands and then let them go.

Jonny's lips twitched at her attempted humor. "Don't get me wrong," he murmured, glancing toward the door. "I'm glad Dat's on the mend. But to forgive and forget all the times he said Gideon and I were thankless, and that he couldn't call us his sons anymore . . ."

Zanna smiled at his choice of words. Hadn't there been a time when she'd been less than grateful for all she had? "How can you forgive your dat, or see if he's truly a changed man, unless you stick around?" she went on before he could protest. "The doctors gave him a whole new life. A clean slate. Can *you* do that for him, too?"

He looked at her as if seeing her for the first time. "When did you get so good at asking the questions I've been trying to wiggle out of?" he murmured. "And when did you come to care so much about what happens to my family—

especially after the times Mamm and Dat railed at you about carrying a baby and calling it off with James Graber?"

Zanna paused. He'd asked a question that begged for exactly the right answer. "Remember in church when we were kids . . . when Vernon preached about how we love God because He first loved us?" she ventured cautiously. "Well, I'm trying to do that. Trying to show I care for your parents so they'll accept me, too, Jonny. I'd like them to be my family someday."

Had she said too much, too boldly? Had she gotten too heavy-handed, talking of religious principles? Zanna let out her breath, reaching for his hand again with a lighter smile. "Don't forget —Abby brought your Christmas dinner. And who better to eat it with than your own family? They'll probably take second plates just because you're here, Jonny."

He gazed at her as though she'd become a woman to be reckoned with in the best of ways. His gaze fell to her swelling middle, and the sight seemed to settle him. He took a breath and then stepped toward his father's hospital room—just as Adah came out into the hallway.

His mother grabbed him. "Jonny, you *did* come! I was so hoping you would, son!" Her voice cracked a little. She rocked him from side to side, then backed away to look up into his eyes. "Jonny, Abby and Zanna have been saying the fellas around town have built us a new place."

"Jah, and it's real nice, too," he replied. "It's the kind of house I always wanted for you, thinking Dat could have done better at taking care of you."

Adah's eyes took on that long-suffering look they all knew so well, but then she smiled. "You kids and I have turned the other cheek a lot of times," she admitted. "But I'm telling you, Jonny, that pacemaker they planted in your dat's chest—well, it's worked a miracle," she declared softly. "And now a house! And money to replace what we lost in the fire, and—well, I can't believe all this wonderful-gut fortune that's come our way."

She drew in a deep breath and leaned her head against his chest. "But the best miracle of all is having you back home, Jonny. You and Gideon are the answer to all of my prayers."

As Zanna smiled through a haze of tears, she wrapped her arm around her baby. A mother's love went beyond what words could say, and she vowed that on difficult days she would remember that her child, too, was an answer to her prayers . . . a way for God to enter her life and show her what love was really about.

"Come see your dat, son," Jonny's mamm murmured, leading him by the hand. "Don't let the past hold you back. And don't be letting Gideon get all the glory."

Jonny stepped into the room behind his mother—and then he extended his other hand back to Zanna, entreating her with his earnest blue eyes. There was no describing the feelings that raced through Zanna's soul: the love and joy, the sense that if everyone in this room was for Jonny, no one could be against him. Becky and Maggie rushed toward them, excited to see their brother. Gideon sat on the edge of the bed next to his dat's recliner, seeming a little astounded, yet pleased, by this turn of events.

No, he's downright amazed. Aren't we all? Zanna thought as Jonny's hand tightened around hers.

Rudy was watching Jonny closely. "Did I hear right that it was you who found me in the barn and you got the ambulance there with your cell phone?" his father asked. He looked rested and well, yet a familiar edge had crept back into his voice.

Jonny cleared his throat. "Jah. Zanna and I got there just in time, the way I understand it. You— you scared us, Dat."

His father sighed, shifting in his recliner. "Guess I've had a few things scared out of me, too," he remarked. "I had no idea of the damage I was doin' by ignorin' my sleep problem. Told myself I was draggin' from one day into the next because I was gettin' old. Had no idea my heart was so bad. The doctor—and the preachers—tell me I was eatin' away at myself by bein' mad all the time, too."

Zanna felt Jonny stiffen, maybe bracing for his dat's usual lecture about him and Gideon not joining the church. But she held Jonny's hand—right there where everyone could see it—and prayed for the rest of this conversation to go well.

Rudy's face sobered and he looked down at his own clasped hands. "It took some tall talkin', those times when Vernon and Preacher Abe and Preacher Paul came to visit, but they made me see how I'd created my own problems, mostly. I did some confessin' to them these past couple weeks. In case I didn't make it out of here," he added with a nervous laugh.

Jonny gripped Zanna's hand harder. He looked at his brother as though gauging Gideon's reaction to what they were hearing, maybe assessing whether they should believe it; whether they should go or stay.

"Your dat and I have had a lot of time to talk," Adah joined in. "The girls and I have forgiven him for all the hurt that came between us over the years. And now that you boys have rebuilt our home and kept the farm going in spite of the way your dat sent you away," she went on, looking pointedly at Rudy, "I'm hopin' that on this Christmas Day your dat will ask your forgiveness for his harsh words. We all love you, Jonny and Gideon. And I hope you'll find it in your hearts to come back to us."

Rudy sat straighter, his eyes narrowing, and

Zanna fully expected him to tell Adah she'd stepped over the line. To her credit, Adah stood tall and unflinching on the other side of Jonny. She probably knew Rudy and their sons might dance around the issue of forgiveness, and that once the boys left today, they might not return unless she gave them a reason to.

The room got quiet. Maggie, Beth, and Abby had been nodding as they watched with expectant faces. Zanna's palm pulsed steadily against Jonny's, sending a clear message: *I love you, too. And I hope you'll stay.*

After a long pause, Rudy cleared his throat. "We can't expect you boys to answer right out, seein' as how you've both set yourselves up in other businesses," he remarked. "And truth is, I'm glad you found other ways to support yourselves, knowin' how our little dairy farm won't provide a livin' for three families."

When he seemed unlikely to continue, Adah picked up the thread. "Your dat's not one to admit his fears and weaknesses," she said quietly, "but I can tell you he was mighty worried, while he was so sick, thinking he might never see you boys again. He regretted the way he'd fussed and fumed at you for not wanting to make the farm your life's work. But it's hard for him to say that."

Rudy's eyes widened and his face flushed. "Don't go puttin' words in my mouth, Adah," he warned, but then he caught himself. He squeezed the arms of the recliner with his strong, muscled hands. He looked at Gideon and then at Jonny, his lips twitching. "What I meant to say, if your mamm would let me get a word in edgewise, is that I . . . I can see why my shuttin' you out and railin' at you all those years would hardly be reason for you to come home . . . or to join the church."

Rudy exhaled as though such words were costing him. "You'd make your mamm awful happy if you came back, but I—I'll leave that for you and God to decide."

While Zanna wasn't surprised that Jonny's dat couldn't come right out and ask for his sons' forgiveness, and had made Adah out as the one who'd missed them, the change in Rudy was still something to behold. Everyone was looking to Gideon and Jonny for their answer, and the silence made a lot of questions swirl in her mind.

What about Jonny's driving business—the van and the stretch limo, not to mention the motorcycle he loved? Could he give them up, along with his cell phone, to live the Plain life again? More important, could he move back to Cedar Creek and become a member of his family?

Can he make a life with me and our child . . . join the church and make it all fit together like everyone here wants him to?

— Chapter 25 —

Never in her life could Abby have predicted the scene she was witnessing, nor could she look away from her sister's face. How many emotions had Zanna expressed in these past months? Bitter defiance . . . terror . . . soul-shaking loneliness . . . doubt . . . heart-wrenching rejection . . . unconditional love for the child growing inside her.

Right now, Zanna's quiet joy filled the crowded hospital room.

Jonny stood, focused on his father, so he didn't notice the radiant young woman on his left—nor could he realize how this picture resembled a wedding ceremony.

Abby set aside that romantic thought. But it seemed yet another blessing, to sense such a turnaround in Jonny and to feel Zanna's unflinching faith in how things would work out. With him or without him, she would make a devoted mother. Somehow Abby knew which way it would be as she waited for someone to break the spell by responding to Rudy's plea.

Maggie and Becky had stopped chatting about the new house. The Christmas cards and cash were strewn on the bed, forgotten. Gideon, too, was caught up in the anticipation: his strawberry blond hair framed his handsome face in a sleek English cut similar to his brother's, but his expression bespoke the tug-of-war in his mind. He was a couple of years older than Jonny, yet he waited for his little brother to make or break this moment.

Just when Abby felt compelled to end the silence, Zanna giggled. Her hand went to her midsection, her laughter filled the room—and then she placed Jonny's palm against her belly where hers had been. "This is *so* your child, Jonny Ropp," she said in a giddy whisper. "He's kicking me to get things moving again. Can't sit still for a minute, this one, and has to be the center of attention. Can you feel that?"

Jonny's anxious expression turned to one of utter amazement. "Is that his foot or his hand? Hey!" he cried, looking from Zanna's grin to her belly. "He's punching me on purpose. But he can't possibly know who I am."

"And why not?"

Zanna's arched eyebrow made Abby snicker. Jonny Ropp might own two cars and a motor-cycle, but her sister sat in the driver's seat now . . . and she was steering this situation exactly where she wanted it to go.

Adah elbowed Jonny, laughing. "You were the same way. Moving around inside me at all hours of the day and night," she said. "It's a wonder I didn't have sleep deprivation worse than your dat by the time you were born. Gideon was much better behaved, even then."

"Jah, but who do you love best?" Jonny teased without missing a beat. It felt like one of those questions he'd asked as a little boy, and after getting his mamm's reaction the first time, he said it whenever he wanted things to go his way.

Zanna knew that trick! They really were birds of a feather and they deserved each other.

Abby exchanged a knowing glance with the Ropp girls before winking at Gideon. It didn't really matter how Adah answered Jonny's question, did it? Zanna had found a surefire way to draw him into her life again, and he'd harked back to his childhood—a happier time with his family.

When Jonny realized everyone was watching him, he drew his hand back. He still looked bewildered, but in the best way possible. "All right, then, Dat—and Mamm. If you're wanting Gideon and me to come back to Cedar Creek, how do you propose we make our livings?" His voice sounded high and tight, but he went on. "I can't see Vernon letting me drive folks. And while it was fine to fix up your machinery and milk your cows while you were laid up, neither of us wants to be a dairy farmer."

A wry smile warmed Rudy's face. "Gut!" he

said with a chuckle. "You won't be cuttin' into *my* livin' that way, ain't so? I imagine my cows will be real glad to see me, after dealin' with the likes of you two and Mervin. But I thank you for keepin' it all goin'," he added in a more serious tone.

"What if Gideon started up a big poultry business like he's been managing for those Mennon-ites, only in Cedar Creek?" Adah suggested. "We've got that patch of land across the road that got cut off when the highway went through plenty big enough for a building or two. And you could go in with him, Jonny."

"*Me,* raising chickens?" Jonny screwed up his face. "The only thing worse than dealing with cows and their manure is tending to chickens and theirs."

"But you'd be right gut at setting up the buildings and adapting the machinery so's Amish could raise birds . . . probably on a smaller scale." Gideon's face lit up as the idea took root. "Cedar Creek's no place for a huge facility like I run for the Stauffers over in Bloomingdale, where we feed thousands of birds at once, but . . . maybe a better idea would be for families to raise cage-free birds and grow their organic feed. Restaurants and specialty markets pay big money for brown eggs and free-range chickens—and nobody around here's doin' that," he added in a rising voice. "It would be a gut way for farmers to diversify without needing a lot of land. I *like* it!"

Rudy sat taller in his recliner, his face brightening. "You boys got any money laid by for start-up? Probably wouldn't take all that much, because when you set up other fellas for this business, you'd be using their money rather than yours."

"Or," Zanna chimed in, grabbing Jonny's hand again, "Sam's always wanted to carry fancy stoves like you built for the house, but he's got no patience or time for putting them together. You could do that."

"You tinkered with the cheese factory equipment long before you were out of school," Adah recalled. "Can't you just see it, Jonny? An enclosed wagon with ROPP REPAIRS AND APPLIANCES in big letters on the sides! You'd be driving from place to place instead of being stuck on a farm with livestock."

"And nobody local does that, either," Abby remarked. It was hard to keep a huge grin off her face, the way this plan was shaping up. But it had to be Jonny's decision—his ideas for a business—or it would never work. Jonny wasn't the type to do what other folks thought he should.

Jonny raked his hand through his blond hair, looking out the window while he tried on these ideas for size. Then he smiled. He kissed his mamm noisily on the cheek before stepping toward his father, his hand extended. "Mighty gut to have you back with us, healthy again, Dat," he murmured hoarsely. "You've given me plenty to think about."

With some effort, Rudy rose from his chair to pull his son into an awkward hug. Neither man had ever been showy with his affection, but Abby believed that hug made the world spin in a whole new direction.

She held her breath. Jonny was good at going along with a tide of ideas until he got out on the road again. Was he only pretending he might make his living—make his home—in Cedar Creek, with Zanna?

"Don't you dare leave now," Maggie piped up. "We were ready to cut into that gingerbread Abby brought. Stay and eat with us."

But Jonny was having none of it. He swatted Gideon playfully, saying, "Eat my share, will you? We'll *talk,* brother." After nodding happily at his sisters and Abby, he hugged his mother. "Hope it all goes well when you get Dat out of here and into that new house, Mamm," he murmured. "Merry Christmas! Merry Christmas to all!"

Abby nodded, but she was ready to spring to her feet if this handsome young man sashayed out of the room—and out of Zanna's life again.

But Jonny pivoted to look at her sister, and then grabbed Zanna's hands. "Are you coming with me, girl?" he pleaded as he gazed into her wide eyes. "I'm thinking you and I, and Junior here, have a lot of plans to make."

405

— *Epilogue* —

Four months later

Jonny inhaled the fresh April air and grinned up at the rising sun: his wedding day! All his life he'd dreamed of doing something big—something beyond what he thought he'd find in Cedar Creek—and in about an hour, Zanna Lambright, the mother of his three-week-old son, would become his wife. It might not be happening in the order the Ordnung declared proper, but these days his life was running as smoothly as the machinery he tinkered with, every gear and cog meshing as they were meant to.

Because Zanna believed in him, he could do all things in God who strengthened him—just as he'd affirmed while preparing to join the church last week, on Easter Sunday. It had been a day of new beginnings. He felt like a new man, ready to take on the challenges of fatherhood and running his new machinery business. Folks had welcomed him back like the father who'd celebrated the return of his prodigal son . . . and it felt good to be home.

As Jonny gazed along the road, where the

carriages approached in a steady stream, the *clip-clop! clip-clop!* of the horses' hooves made his heart sing. What kind of craziness was this, that had him babbling nonsense to a newborn and hearing happy secrets in hoofbeats and the songs of birds as they feathered their nests?

A baby changes everything! Who knew a little child would lead you back to the family you once detested?

But then, Harley Leroy Ropp wasn't just any baby, was he? While it was true Zanna had chosen the names of a favorite uncle and her dat, she'd confessed to him that a certain motorcycle on a certain summer day had also inspired her choice.

"Gut morning to you! Gut to see you!" Jonny laughed, waving at the Detweilers, the Masts, and the Nissleys as they pulled in to witness his marriage—the black sheep of the Ropps hitching up with the wild-child Lambright who'd abandoned her previous groom at the altar. He and his Zanna had caused plenty of talk, each of them by running away from the faith and family values that had once felt so confining.

Yet now, Zanna's love—her unfaltering faith in him—had set Jonny free to be a successful man whose future looked as bright as the springtime sky. He'd sold his diamond earring, the van, the limo, and the motorcycle to pay extra for a rush order: a customized, horse-drawn wagon that carried his mechanical tools and supplies, which had been completed ahead of the vehicles other folks had ordered from Graber Custom Carriages. It was just another example of how far forgiveness went here in Cedar Creek: James Graber had every reason to hate Jonny for overturning the plans he'd made with Zanna, yet the carriage maker seemed sincerely happy about the way things had worked out.

James and Emma waved from the end of the lane, where each of them escorted a parent . . . the same Merle and Eunice who'd made Zanna hesitate to marry into the Graber family. Jonny saw them with new eyes: Merle's mental abilities were slipping, which drove Eunice to hover and cluck more often—and louder—as she peered through her outdated glasses. What a blessing that his own mamm and dat were healthy and happy in their new home. Some of their Christmas cash from well-wishers had gone toward a new house with a machine shop, which awaited him and Zanna on that parcel of land across the road from the homeplace . . . close enough that he could help his folks and Gideon, yet a private place where he and Zanna could make lots of babies. Dat had declared it a wedding present, and an offering of thanks to God for bringing the Ropp boys home again.

"Jonny Ropp! Are you gonna help with these tables?" Matt called from the barn. "Or are you feeling too pretty, all decked out in those fancy new duds?"

Jonny laughed and hurried toward the barn. Abby had made his black broadfall trousers and vest, and a shirt so white it glowed in the morning sun. He felt happy to be wearing Plain clothes again . . . happier still to be welcomed into this family he'd once humiliated with his careless behavior. Sam Lambright had spared no expense on preparations for this event—yet another miracle, considering this was his little sister's *second* wedding in six months.

"This time it will work," Sam had assured him not long ago. "Unless something—or somebody —makes Zanna's eyes twinkle, she won't stay with them long. And you, Ropp, have made the stars come out to play. I guess you're stuck with her, ain't so?"

Stuck *on* her was more like it. Jonny couldn't imagine loving anyone the way he'd come to treasure Zanna Lambright. While he'd always enjoyed her sense of humor and her refusal to submit to Leroy and Sam's rules, it was her faith —and her unwavering commitment to being a good mother—that had made him realize he had some growing up to do. She had a sense of purpose about her that had taken him by surprise . . . had made him *want* to join the church and give up his English ways, to become the husband and father she deserved to have by her side.

Had he seen that coming? Never in a million years!

"Jonny Ropp! We need a word with you—if you can pull yourself out of daydreaming about that bride of yours." Abe Nissley waved him over to where the bishop stood with Paul Bontrager, discussing the service.

Jonny excused himself from setting up tables to join the preachers. Women were entering the Lambright kitchen, and the aroma of baked chicken and creamed celery floated out to tantalize him. The celery had been an additional expense because it was too early for fresh garden vegetables, but Zanna's mamm had insisted on observing the tradition for their wedding feast. In so many ways the Lambright family—the entire community—had made allowances for this out-of-season wedding.

"Because everything's in its proper season now. The bride and groom are right for each other this time," Treva Lambright had insisted. Everyone wanted him and Zanna and little Harley to have the best possible start as a family.

Vernon Gingerich looked him in the eye, smiling yet solemn. "Are you ready—for this day, and for all you're about to take on, Jonny?"

"Jah," he replied in a husky whisper.

"I'm teasing, mostly, but what'll you do if Zanna doesn't show?"

"She'll be here."

Paul smiled, glancing toward the house. "Bet the women are flocking around that new son of yours. Mother and child are doing well, I hope?"

Jonny nodded, grinning as he did at every mention of Harley. "First thing out of Mamm's mouth was about how he's the spitting image of his dat at that age. I'm not sure if that's a compliment or a threat, but it's my story and I'm sticking to it!"

Abe and the other two laughed, but Bishop Gingerich continued to gaze purposefully at him. "If you have doubts about that baby's paternity, now's the time to lock them away forever, son. There was talk about Zanna's —"

"There was talk about a lot of things," Jonny cut in firmly. "Harley's my son, same as Zanna's my woman. You'll never convince me different, so don't even try."

The door opened and Abby stepped outside, cradling his son in her arms. Was it his imagination, or did the sun beam more brightly every time the baby came into view? For sure and for certain the Lord had blessed him—and the whole town—with Abigail Lambright's steadfast love. He couldn't begin to repay what he owed her. Jonny grinned at such a thought: not so long ago he had no idea at all about real love, yet this patient maidel had stood by her sister—and him —to allow this present, perfect wedding day to come about.

Vernon's eyes sparkled when he smiled. "Aunt Abby looks mighty happy right now."

411

"Jah," Jonny replied as he approached her to gaze at his son. "Abby knows a thing or two about what it takes to be happy—and about how to make other folks feel that way, too."

" 'Charity suffereth long, and is kind,' " Bishop Gingerich recited in his sonorous voice. " 'Charity envieth not . . .' "

Abby sighed contentedly. Had there ever been a brighter day, or a pair so perfect as Zanna and Jonny? Many a wedding she'd attended, but this one put a special glow in her heart. Sam's house was filled with the people they loved, some who silently mouthed the familiar passage as they gazed at Zanna and Jonny.

" ' . . . rejoiceth not in iniquity but rejoiceth in the truth. Beareth all things, believeth all things, hopeth all things, endureth all things.' "

The bishop's wedding sermon had never seemed more appropriate, and the couple in front of him bore out every detail of that favorite chapter of Corinthians—and would face its challenges in the years ahead. What a wonder it was that many of these folks had expressed their indignation when Zanna had confessed her pregnancy six months ago, but now believed things were working out for the very best, just the way they were meant to be.

Beside her, Adah nuzzled little Harley's nose as Mamm smiled at him from her other side. Had two grandmothers ever been more delighted by a baby? Mamm had come out of her grief to greet this new life—this new spring—with energy she hadn't shown in years, while Adah had become one of Cedar Creek's most cheerful women. With her husband fully recovered and her two sons home again, Adah bloomed with a renewed love as sturdy and bright as the rugs Zanna had made her.

And Zanna, the headstrong blonde who'd run away from her first wedding, sat attentively up front, drinking in every word of Vernon's sermon and wisdom. She'd chosen a deep shade of periwinkle for today's dress, and Abby had been so happy to make it for her—along with several sets of clothes for Harley, and the vest and trousers that made Jonny look so handsome, yet so Plain.

Their newehockers, Martha Coblentz and Gideon, Mary Coblentz and Matt, looked on happily from the bench behind the preachers. Because of the circumstances and the season, the congregation was smaller. Several of their relatives out East were preparing their fields for planting and not able to join them. What mattered, however, was that this home was filled to its rafters with love and a peace that passed all understanding.

Again Abby sighed. Across the room, James Graber sat with his dat, appearing every bit as pleased about this marriage as the rest of them. What must be going through his mind as he watched the young woman of his previous dreams marry the man who'd snatched those dreams away?

After the service, as the guests congratulated the newlyweds, Abby saw a chance to speak with him. Merle had joined a conversation with some other fellows, so she approached James with a smile—and baby Harley resting on her shoulder. "How are you today, James?" she asked. "I was just thinking this might be a . . . tricky service for you to sit through."

His deep brown eyes flickered, but the uncertainty passed. "I'm okay with it," he assured her. He looked around to find Zanna surrounded by well-wishers. "It's easy to see your sister's happy, and Jonny's made an astonishing turn-around. So all's well that ends well, ain't so?"

Abby smiled. "Jah, they've both done some growing up. Off to a gut start with Jonny's new mechanical service, and Zanna making her custom rugs at home while she tends this baby." She chuckled. "I never thought we'd be painting such a domestic picture of *that* girl!"

"Amazing, what the right man can do."

So true, she thought wistfully as she looked into James's deep brown eyes. "I didn't mean to be nosy or make you feel bad, James. I just—"

He clasped her arm and leaned closer. "Abby Lambright, you wouldn't know how to make anyone feel bad. You must be made of love and sunshine—just like this fine boy you're holding."

Love and sunshine. And wasn't that just about the nicest thing anyone had ever said to her? "Denki, James," she murmured. "You—you're a mighty fine man, you know it?"

James clapped his hands over his face.

Abby blinked. Had her compliment embarrassed him so badly that he had to hide?

"Peekaboo! I see you!" he teased the baby in a singsong voice. When James uncovered his eyes, he wore one of the silliest grins Abby had ever seen. And he looked good in it.

Harley's eyes widened. He burped so loudly that James's laughter made other folks turn to see what was going on—so Abby's wonderful moment with James became yet another conversation that centered around Cedar Creek's newest resident and ray of sunshine. Mary and Martha Coblentz both reached eagerly for Harley, which allowed Abby to help Barbara and the girls serve the meal. The way her heart skipped in her chest, she had to hold the steaming chicken casseroles tightly so she wouldn't drop them.

Love and sunshine. *Love and sunshine!* Even though James would never know how his remark had thrilled her, Abby's heart sang those words throughout the afternoon.

As the wedding festivities stretched into the evening, it seemed clear that love might also be shining on other couples besides Zanna and

Jonny. It was no surprise that Phoebe and Owen Coblentz were caught up in quiet conversation and flirta-tious looks, but her nephew Matt wore an intense smile such as she'd never seen as he escorted a pretty young woman and her little girl toward the sheep pastures.

"And who might *that* be, walking alongside Matt?" Emma demanded as she and Abby sliced pies for the light supper soon to be served. "Must be a couple hundred folks here, and I've met most of them—even your kin from Ohio and Kentucky. I'd remember a face like hers."

Abby fought a smile. Even though Matt was a few years younger than Emma, she had tried brownies and special smiles and every way she knew to win his attention lately, so her question deserved a . . . compassionate answer. It was ironic that her best friend was going through the same thing she was, with a fellow who lived across the road.

"That's Rosemary Yutzy," Abby replied as she cut a rhubarb pie. "She's Lois and Ezra's niece by marriage, come from over east of Bloomingdale with her father-in-law, Titus Yutzy. Titus raises sheep, too, I hear, and is looking to start some new bloodlines in his flock."

"So if that's Rosemary's little girl clinging to her skirts . . ."

"Jah, Katie's about three."

"Where's her husband?" Emma demanded sharply.

Abby winced. Even in this crowd, her best friend's voice carried so shrilly that folks at the nearest tables turned to look at them. "Her husband, Joe, got killed in a hunting accident last fall," Abby explained. "Not long before that, Titus's wife lost her battle with cancer, the way Lois tells it. They've had their share of sadness lately."

Emma's eyebrows rose, but she kept the rest of her thoughts to herself. She was watching every step Matt and Rosemary took, however.

Abby quickly put more slices of pie on plates. "I guess we'd better get this pie put out on the tables, Emma. Here it is nearly six o'clock. Where has this day gone?"

As folks sat down to enjoy the simple meal of sandwiches, salads, and pie, Abby sighed with a deep sense of satisfaction. While today's spring wedding went against tradition in many ways, it was nice that their family and friends could come for this celebration without having to decide which wedding invitations to accept, as they often did in the late fall season out East. Even better, the distant relations who'd been able to make the trip got to see Zanna redeem herself for running out on the wedding they'd come here for last October . . . and to share the joy of Jonny's return to his Plain roots—and to meet little Harley, of course.

The baby's escalating cry made Abby turn,

ready to help. Zanna rose from her chair with her wailing son on her shoulder, cooing and singing to him as she headed away from the crowd.

"Come on along," Zanna murmured. "Harley settles right down to eating when his Aunt Abby's with us. Besides—there's something I've got to say."

What could that be? Abby walked alongside her younger sister, down the lane to the little white house. "You'll be just fine, little man," Abby assured him in a low voice. "Your mamm's going to feed you, and then you'll be napping while the rest of us wish we could."

The sunset glowed on the pale yellow walls as they stepped inside Abby's house. Zanna looked so pretty in that shade of periwinkle, so grown-up and sure of herself as she settled into the spare room's rocking chair to nurse her son. He quieted immediately. The sounds of his sucking made his mother smile as though she already loved him more than life itself. Zanna looked at Abby then, her blue eyes alight.

"I guess you know this wedding wouldn't have happened, except that you stood by me, sister," she said softly. "When everyone else wanted to send me away, you took me in. You found me the work that's turned into a gut source of income. You put up with my pouting and fits even when Sam and Mamm were ready to toss me out."

"They'd never have done that, you know,"

Abby replied with a quiet laugh. It felt a little awkward to accept Zanna's gratitude, yet what a wonderful thing, that this girl who'd once been so reckless and immature was expressing her appreciation so sincerely. "If you'd left us like you threatened to back then, Sam would have been out hunting you the next day."

"Mostly because Barbara and Mamm would have made him."

Abby chuckled. "Jah, there's that. But he learned a few things about love and forgiveness, like the rest of us. Men might rule the roost and have the final say," she offered softly, "but if there's no love in their hearts, they make life awfully miserable for everyone else. And for themselves, if they'd only see it."

Zanna's smile warmed her. "Jonny won't be that way, I'm thinking. Oh, he's got a stubborn streak every bit as strong as mine, but . . . but he's a changed fella. And I've got to thank you, Abby, for allowing him to be his own man and choose the way he wanted to take."

"It wasn't easy for him to give up his English ways, I don't imagine. Or his cars."

"But he did it—for me. And for his boy here." Zanna smiled at her again, through tears this time. "Life's going to be so wonderful-gut for us, Abby! And I didn't want to let our big day go by without telling you how much I love you for it."

"Oh, Zanna." Abby rose to wrap her arms

around mother and child as they sat in her rocking chair. "Sister, sister . . . how could I have done any different? I love you, too, and I always will. No matter what, you can come to me and I'll be here for you." Abby looked into Zanna's face, fuller now and even lovelier because of it. "Nobody's happier than I am to see you standing before the world with the man you truly love. Things would've soured in a hurry if you'd gone through with marrying James, and we can all see that now."

Zanna swiped at her eyes and then blotted Harley's rosebud mouth. He was nearly asleep. "It's a gut thing God knew what was going on, and how it was all supposed to turn out."

"And a gut thing you listened to Him, and to your heart. Think what we'd all be missing if we didn't have our boy here."

Zanna sighed happily. "You say the nicest things, Abby." She looked up with shining blue eyes, as though she might laugh and cry at the same time. "You see the world as a wonderful place—and where it's not, you help make it that way. I—I hope I can be like you someday."

Abby paused over her notebook that night, thinking out her next report for the *Budget* as she sat against her headboard, ready for bed. Her little house felt very quiet without Zanna and Harley in the spare room. What a blessing, that she'd been able to offer Zanna a sanctuary where she could find her place, her purpose in the world. Abby had found her own calling along the way: restoring peace and mending torn relationships just as she repaired people's clothes in her Stitch in Time shop. Who could have believed, back in October, that a runaway bride would bring so many positive changes into all their lives?

How is it we meet our mates? Abby pondered the first line she'd written and decided to let God guide her pencil.

Why do some folks feel an instant attraction to each other—or love at first sight—while others search all their lives, yet remain alone? The wedding of Jonny Ropp to Zanna Lambright in Cedar Creek today pointed up a possible answer to that, while it also joined a young couple in a marriage we once denied would ever happen.

Three weeks ago Zanna gave birth to a fine baby boy, Harley Leroy, and in the meantime Jonny rose to her level of faith, believing that everything would work out if they trusted in God's plan for their lives. What a wonderful thing it is when two people tame each other's wilder ways and train themselves like morning glory vines that wind higher around a trellis to catch the sun!

Just as marvelous is Rudy Ropp's return to full strength, and his wife Adah's happiness in the home rebuilt for them after a fire destroyed the previous one. Now that Jonny and his brother, Gideon, have rejoined their family, they've launched their new machinery repair and cage-free poultry businesses, which are off to promising starts. All of us have learned a lot about loving folks whose opinions and needs don't always go along with our own—and don't always follow the Old Ways.

Forgiveness is such a gift. Forgiveness—for Zanna's going astray, and for the strained relationships within the Ropp family, and for strong words that caused a rift in Cedar Creek six months ago—has made her marriage to Jonny Ropp possible. Had so many folks not rethought their beliefs and allowed Zanna to follow hers, we wouldn't have witnessed this wedding today. We might have lost a young woman whose faith has inspired us all, and we wouldn't have rejoiced in the reunion of Jonny and Gideon Ropp with their parents. Better yet, we celebrated Jonny's joining the church last week as he dedicated himself to Christ and Plain living. And best of all, we have little Harley Leroy now! He's surely made of love and sunshine, and he spreads delight wherever he goes.

I've taken that as my purpose, too: to spread love and sunshine—or, as Isaiah said it, to preach good tidings to the meek and bind up the brokenhearted—and to give my best to the work God brings me every day. May April bring you many blessings, dear friends—along with opportunities to share yourselves and your love. ~Abigail Lambright

Abby extinguished her bedside lamp, smiling in the darkness. *Love and sunshine!* The words still rang in her heart. She looked out the window, past the mercantile and across the road toward the Graber house. The lamp still flickered in James's upstairs window. She settled into bed. Abby didn't know what tomorrow might bring, but she believed it would be wonderful.

About the Author

Drawing upon her experiences in Jamesport, Missouri, the largest Old Order Amish community west of the Mississippi, longtime Missourian **Naomi King** writes of simpler times in her new Home at Cedar Creek series. When she's not writing, she loves to travel, try new recipes, crochet, and sew. Naomi now lives in Minnesota with her husband and their border collie, Ramona. Write to her at: P.O. Box 18731, West St. Paul, MN 55150.

Connect Online
www.naomikingauthor.com
facebook.com/naomic.king

Center Point Large Print
600 Brooks Road / PO Box 1
Thorndike ME 04986-0001 USA

(207) 568-3717

US & Canada:
1 800 929-9108
www.centerpointlargeprint.com